BOOKS BY DANIEL QUINN

THE HOLY

THE HOLY

Daniel Quinn

ZOLAND BOOKS

an imprint of

STEERFORTH PRESS

Hanover, New Hampshire

10.31
3/06

Published in hardcover by Context Books in 2002

For information about permission to reproduce
selections from this book, write to:
Steerforth Press L.C., 25 Lebanon Street,
Hanover, New Hampshire 03755

The Library of Congress has cataloged the
Context Books edition as follows:

Quinn, Daniel.
The holy / Daniel Quinn.
p. cm.
ISBN 1-893956-30-X (alk. paper)
1. Fate and fatalism—Fiction. 2. Middle aged men—Fiction.
3. Midlife crisis—Fiction. 4. Temptation—Fiction. I. Title.
PS3567.U338 H65 2002
813'.54—dc21
2002010109

ISBN (paperback) 1-58195-214-7
ISBN 13 978-1-58195-214-8

FIRST ZOLAND BOOKS EDITION

For Bill Hearst,
whose faith in this book kept me at it for a decade.

Having conquered these nations, you must utterly destroy all the sanctuaries where they honored their gods—on the mountain heights, on the hills, and under every leafy tree. Topple their altars, smash their pillars, burn their sacred groves, and hew down their idols, and thus blot out all memory of them from these places.

Deuteronomy 12.2-3

PROLOGUE

One day the hand
of a god . . .

Tim sat cross-legged on the floor of his room, staring fascinated at the life that teemed within a column of early morning sunlight. It was a special world, that sunbeam—a world you could enter and disrupt but never belong to. The boy passed his hand through it and watched a swarm of golden sparks hurry out of its way, and he imagined them thinking, *"What was that, what was that?"* But after a moment the excitement subsided, and they resumed their dreamy wandering. Had this astounding event already been forgotten in their world, or would tales of it be told for generations? *One day, the hand of a god crashed through the world, sweeping us all into turmoil and panic. . . .*

In two months—an infinitude of time to him—the boy would enter kindergarten. He understood the significance of this event with great clarity. No one had explained it; he'd worked it out for himself, over the winter. He'd had to, in order to understand the great crime he'd committed just before Christmas. He had told JoJo, the three-year-old next door, that there is no Santa Claus. She had been shattered, heart-broken, and her parents had reacted as if he'd plunged a knife into her body. He was in disgrace for weeks—plenty of time to work it all out.

It's important (or perhaps even necessary) to keep small children in the dark about things—big things, little things: all things. It's important to deceive, to confuse, to pretend ignorance, to avoid a plain answer to a direct question. It's even important to promote lies where no questions are asked, as in the case of Santa Claus. By divulging the truth to JoJo, the boy had disrupted the plan, had committed a crime of cosmic proportions.

Everyone collaborated in the deception—even older children. And the boy would soon understand why. As a kindergartener, he would become one of the older children, and the age of secrecy and lies would be behind him forever. This, he was sure, was the threshold he'd be crossing in two months. He would be entering a world where one is shaped by the unfolding of mysteries hidden from the eyes of the very young. Older kids naturally pretended it was nothing—a bore and a drag. This was only to be expected; it was part of the plan. He wondered if he would agree to collaborate with them in the pretense. It would depend on the explanation he was given for it.

The boy's hand swam again through the living beam of light, and he thought contemptuously: Dust. His father had told him the sparks that live in the light are particles of dust. An obvious lie. Another obvious lie among multitudes he'd been told.

For him, the two months ahead seemed like two years.

He closed his hand gently around a cluster of glowing motes, knowing they couldn't be captured and taken out of their beam of light. He wondered if they passed through the flesh of his hand to escape or simply flowed around his fingers.

He opened his hand, his fingers together, and instantly a whole colony of sparkles was snuffed out in a column of shadow within the sunbeam. He turned his hand sideways, and a new generation was born to cavort in the light. But this generation only lived a moment, as some larger shadow outside swept them into nothingness.

The boy looked up from the floor and was startled to see a man standing at the window. Not exactly a man, maybe, since his massive, heavy-browed head sported snake-like horns, and his skin was strangely mottled. The boy stood up to have a closer look, and the creature outside watched him solemnly, with the eyes of a large, intelligent animal. They stared at each other in stillness and silence, and the boy felt he'd never been looked at with such intensity and penetration.

The bones of the man's face molded it into an expression of complete ambiguity—half a thunderous scowl and half an animal's grin, so that the boy didn't know whether to be frightened or delighted. The man seemed enormously proud of his colorful, strangely twisted horns, but the oddest thing about the creature—or man, if he was a man—was his clothing. A man with horns somehow shouldn't be dressed in an ordinary tan shirt and jeans.

Wanting his mother to come see him, Tim ran to the kitchen and said, "There's a man outside."

"A man?" his mother asked, drying her hands on a dish towel.

"He's got a face sort of like an animal and he has horns."

Ellen Kennesey smiled indulgently. "There's no man outside."

"There is! He's standing right outside my window!"

"You imagined it."

For a moment the boy stared at her, thunderstruck. He'd *imagined* it? She had never accused him of imagining things when he'd seen a praying mantis or a bull snake or a falling star. But now, for some reason, he was *imagining* things?

Then he understood, and his indignation was transformed into a bitter resignation. The creature he'd seen at the window belonged to that infinitely large world of things to be lied about to children. She knew perfectly well what the thing was, but she wasn't allowed to tell him. She wouldn't come to his room to look at it, because then she'd be forced to invent still more lies to answer his questions. It was easiest to put him off with a single, unanswerable lie: he'd imagined it.

At the age of four and a half, he'd learned a profound and unforgettable truth:

There is a lie to be told about everything.

PART I

Look into the smoke . . .

CHAPTER I

Although only visitors and new members notice it any more, there is a brass plaque on the door of the Herman Litvak Chess Club on North Sheridan Road in Chicago. It reads:

> Rascals are always sociable, and the chief sign that a man has any nobility in his character is the little pleasure he takes in others' company.
>
> —Arthur Schopenhauer

It may be that the club's founder imperfectly understood the quotation when he chose it. Considering the almost unwavering atmosphere of gloom inside, it appears more likely that he fully intended it to confound and dispirit those who enter there. A sorrowful presence seems to haunt the dark, heavily furnished rooms, and the older members know that this is the presence of Herman Litvak himself, who put a bullet through his brain in an upstairs room one evening in 1940.

In 1954, in the club's only political crisis ever, the members voted to apply for a private-club liquor license. The losers predicted with absolute confidence that the place would turn into a hangout for bookies and pimps, but of course they were wrong. The worst that happened was that a few chess tables were replaced by massive club chairs and cocktail tables. Even when it seems that only the drinkers are on hand, a few games of chess are played, if only out of an obscure sense of obligation.

In effect, it's a social club for Jewish men of a certain temperament, and those who don't have it soon find somewhere else to spend their evenings.

Howard Scheim was an exception. He'd joined in 1991 at the age of sixty-one, a year after his wife's death, with the idea of renewing a boyhood fascination with the game. After a few nights' play, he saw it would make as much sense to buy a tennis racket and go out after Boris Becker. It was a different game from the one he remembered, and even the most casual players could crush him in a dozen moves, laughing with embarrassment, as if they couldn't quite figure out how to throttle down their own power. There was no hope at all of learning from his mistakes; he was just too far outmatched.

This didn't drive him away—far from it. To be humbled by so frivolous a mystery delighted him. He gave up playing and became a watcher, and never failed to be joyously astounded when the masters' moves were completely outside his expectations.

He knew without thinking about it that some members found him an intimidating figure: *Howard the Hulk*. There was nothing he could do about that. In his mid-teens, already a giant, he'd gone into the ring with the notion of becoming the next Max Schmeling. The draft board had saved him from getting his brains beaten out, but they were too late to save his face. In repose, it was the face of a thug, an assassin. A hump of scars over his left eye forced it into a sullen wink, and the casual locker-room setting and resetting of his once-delicate nose had given it the look of an outcropping of shattered rock and made him a lifelong mouth-breather.

In his line of work, there had been times enough when his menacing appearance had come in handy, and he knew well how to enhance it. When he dimmed the intelligent glitter in his eyes, rolled his lower lip out to expose his teeth, and spoke in his throat like a dog, there were few men who wouldn't take a step back from him, even now. Smiling came more naturally, and anyone who knew him at all knew he was as mild as butter, the sort of man who, born a century earlier, would have buried himself in a study house to pore over the endless mysteries of the Torah.

What made Howard acceptable—even popular—was the fact that he was a listener. Before his arrival, such a thing as conversation at the Herman Litvak Chess Club was practically unknown. This is because it's part of the temperament of those who belong there that they yearn to be heard but have no patience for listening. And so they talk—and fall silent as others talk—but there's rarely any authentic interchange of ideas among them.

At first they hardly knew what to make of a man like Howard, who not only had things to say but seemed genuinely interested in hearing what *they* had to say. It was freakish, almost unnatural, like levitating or walking through walls. But it was also refreshing, and the members soon found themselves slyly competing for his attention. A strange subspecies of social interaction blossomed; men gathered in the lounge and sat around talking insurance, football, and the stock market like commuters on a train while waiting their turn at the club's one listener. None of them would have admitted he was there to talk to Howard the Hulk, but they became edgy if one member seemed to be monopolizing his time. "Hey," someone would shout, "give the man a break!" Meaning: Give one of *us* a break.

It was a rare thing for Howard to buy a drink for himself (which, on his budget, was just as well), and he thought it was very funny to become a social success at his age.

Aaron Fischer was the only one who wouldn't compete for Howard's attention. He didn't like starting a conversation with the feeling that others would soon be breathing down his neck. So he outwaited them all—a narrow, dainty man with a humorous face, and always impeccably, expensively dressed—savoring his long, expensive cigars and sipping the very special old brandy that was stocked at the bar just for him.

Aaron was as proud of his patience as other men were of their sexual prowess or business deals. While others hustled, Aaron took his time, and he credited everything to this sublime practice: his long life (he was seventy-three), his good health, and his fortune. He was one of the club's top players, but drove everyone mad with his interminable pondering of perfectly obvious moves. Legend had it that he'd once spent two minutes and forty seconds considering his response to an opening move of pawn to king four.

His approach to Howard had been no less cautious.

"Howard, tell me: Are you a religious man?"

"Howard, what do you think? Is a Jew who denies God truly a Jew?"

"Howard, do you think there is meaning to Jewish history—a sort of meaning that the rest of history lacks?"

"Howard, here is something I wonder about. As Jews, we're taught that the whole of man's interaction with God is somehow encompassed by Judaism. But Judaism is only five thousand years old, while mankind is millions of years old. What do you make of that?"

All these questions and many more like them, Aaron posed over a period of two years, and Howard began to feel he was being covertly interviewed for a job. He even wondered if Aaron was considering him as a match for some widowed or spinster relative. Although he couldn't grasp the tendency behind the questions (and had never contemplated such things himself), Howard admired the old man for asking them. It seemed like pretty deep delving for someone who, at the age of fifteen, had been an apprentice glove maker.

Characteristically, Howard would answer these questions with something like, "To be honest, Aaron, I've never thought much about that, but I'd be interested to hear what *you* think." The old man was well read, a rigorous thinker, and not at all inclined toward simplistic answers. In fact, though he talked for countless hours, Aaron never really answered the questions he asked. He left them hanging in the air, unresolved, and in the end Howard wasn't sure what Aaron thought about anything.

Finally, one winter night near midnight, Aaron portentously advanced a pawn in the game he'd made of their relationship. He took a sip of brandy, replaced the glass on the table between them, looked up, and said, "Howard, I'd like you to come to dinner at my house tomorrow night."

Howard the Hulk, his mouth drooping a little more than usual, stared at him in astonishment as he tried to analyze his reaction to this strange invitation.

Members rarely socialized outside the club. That's what the club was for, after all. But it wasn't just that. Within the club, social and economic lines were recognized but democratically ignored; if Aaron wielded more influence than Howard in club affairs, it wasn't because he was a millionaire but because he'd been a member for decades and Howard was a newcomer. Aaron's vote counted for no more than Howard's, but at the end of an evening, a chauffeured Cadillac whisked Aaron off to his house (or perhaps it was a mansion) in Evanston, while Howard caught a bus south to Ainslee and walked to his second-floor bedroom and bath.

It wasn't that wealth daunted him. Howard had seen too much of the world to be impressed by it or by the people who have it. Nevertheless he wondered if his comfortable relationship with Aaron could survive an encounter with his wealth.

Meanwhile, misunderstanding his hesitation, Aaron was nervously assuring him that his kitchen was strictly kosher and that his cook was a phenomenon of nature.

"I wasn't worried about that," Howard said, amused. "I'll be happy to come."

"I'm afraid I eat at an unfashionable hour, six o'clock," Aaron said. "Otherwise sometimes I don't sleep so good. Is that too early for you?"

Howard decided that, since it was Aaron's idea, Aaron should do the accommodating. "It is a bit early, for a weekday, Aaron. I keep my office open till five." For no very good reason, he added to himself.

"I don't want you to suffer a hardship for this, Howard. Just the opposite. Is seven okay?"

"That'll be fine," Howard said, understanding now that it was a business deal.

CHAPTER 2

Aaron's house was indeed what Howard considered a mansion, although it stood at no great distance from either the street or its stately neighbors. It pretended to no particular architectural style he could recognize; it was just a handsome and substantial dwelling built for some rich merchant of the 1920s.

The door was opened by a woman of striking presence, reminding him of a young Olivia de Havilland. When he gave her his name, she said, "Mr. Fischer is expecting you. Will you come this way, please?" with the cool competence of an executive secretary. As they walked, he asked her if she was Mr. Fischer's personal assistant. With a faint smile, she replied that she was his personal assistant, housekeeper, and everything else, short of cook and maid-of-all-work.

"Would you mind telling me your name?"

"Not at all," she replied. "It's Ella."

The room she led him to was huge, bright, and exquisitely furnished, and he wondered if it was known in the household simply as the living room. It certainly wasn't a room where you kicked off your shoes and settled down in front of the TV with a six-pack of beer. The furniture had the glow of great antiquity and value, and a picture sprang to his mind of its being burnished daily with wads of old, velvet-soft money. The pettiness of this reaction dismayed him, and, as Aaron approached to greet him across a vast Chinese rug in luscious reds and blues, he wondered what he was going to do about it. Then, almost without the aid of his brain, his tongue handled it for him.

"You got one hell of a sexy place here, Aaron," he said, nodding appreciatively.

The old man's head jerked back as though he'd been slapped. He stopped, appraised Howard's smile, and then looked around slowly, trying to see the room through Howard's eyes. Finally he chuckled and said, "Yeah. Real sexy."

He took Howard's arm affectionately.

Howard was relieved when, after a cocktail in the living room, Aaron led him to a small, octagonal dining room built out into the backyard—practically open to the backyard by virtue of its French windows. He'd had a chilling vision of their dining in a baronial hall, at opposite ends of a furlong-wide banquet table.

"This is the breakfast room, actually," Aaron pointed out. "Entertaining in the dining room makes me feel like Count Dracula in his castle."

The meal itself, served with watchful courtesy by Ella, was unquestionably the finest Howard had ever tasted—and one of the strangest, since each dish seemed to have been chosen as much for its distinguished provenance as for its flavor. The salmon marinated in sour cream, he was told, had been created in the kitchen of a Jewish banker in Imperial Russia, one Baron Günsburg. The black bean soup with plum brandy, it seemed, had been the Baal Shem Tov's favorite.

"Rothschild's chef created this," Aaron said of the grouse stewed in red wine. When Howard raised his brows, the old man went on: "It's true. Most of the dishes named after Rothschild are fakes, but this one is for real."

When Howard cut into the fork-tender chateaubriand sautéed in dry burgundy, Aaron said, "Disraeli invented this as a young man— himself, personally. It should be topped with breast of guinea hen," he added almost guiltily, "but I thought it would be a bit much after the grouse."

"My God, Aaron," Howard protested.

The old man seemed to have nothing to say about the dessert, a concoction of strawberries in port and Cointreau, and Howard asked about it with just a touch of irony.

"I don't know exactly who invented it," Aaron said without looking up. "Sarah Bernhardt got the recipe from a Jewish family in St. Louis."

Howard grinned into his crystal goblet, knowing he'd been sandbagged.

The room in which they were served coffee and brandy glowed with rich paneling and soft lights and smelled of new leather and, of course, cigars. In Howard's imagination, it was the epitome of the room to which gentlemen retire after dinner in English novels— except that he'd never managed to imagine it so large or so elegantly appointed. He smiled at this, thinking that it takes money even to furnish a room in your imagination.

Most of three walls were solidly books: serious books—read books, though many were bound for show. Taking a tour of them, Howard saw they were all history, philosophy, and religion, with a little anthropology thrown in for light reading. It was an intimidating collection, and he was beginning to feel vaguely snubbed by it when Aaron murmured, "Come and sit down, Howard."

Perversely, he continued his survey through the T's, just to satisfy himself that there was nothing so frivolous on these shelves as a copy of *War and Peace*. Then he went and sat down in a gray leather chair that welcomed him like a plump, affectionate mother.

"So," he said gravely, wondering what he meant by it.

"So," the old man echoed, carefully lighting one of his long cigars. He squinted up through the smoke and said, "I'm told you're an investigator."

This was the last thing Howard expected to hear, and he tried to cover his confusion with a smile. "Yeah, Aaron. Sure. Everyone at the club knows that."

"Tell me something about it."

Howard suddenly found himself unable to speak, his throat constricted with anger. He crossed his legs and looked away in an intense examination of the bookshelves, hoping without much hope that Aaron would skip it—pretend he'd never mentioned the subject, talk about something else, ask one of his absurd questions about the nature of Jewishness or the future of the world. He didn't want to have to come to grips with his feeling of betrayal.

"What's wrong, Howard?" the old man asked after a full minute had passed.

"You want me to tell you something about what? Being an investigator?"

"That's right."

"What is it, Aaron? A daughter-in-law you think is cheating on your son? A servant you think is stealing the silver?"

Aaron frowned. "I don't understand, Howard. What are you talking about?"

"What I'm talking about is . . ." Howard glared at him, too furious to know what he was talking about.

The old man shrank back in his chair, his eyes full of alarm, and Howard realized he was nearly snarling. He forced his face into the rough contours of a smile and said, "Just tell me what the problem is, Aaron, and I'll get on it in the morning."

Aaron looked at him with incomprehension for a moment, then groaned. "Oh my friend, forgive me. Living alone with my thoughts so much of the time . . ." He waved his hands vaguely in the air. "One begins to forget what words are for. I took it for granted that you'd understand what was in my mind without my saying anything, so you got the wrong idea entirely. I apologize most humbly."

"And what was I supposed to understand, Aaron?"

"That I didn't invite you here because you're an investigator, but because you're a friend. Do you see?"

"No, Aaron, I don't."

"Howard, my God! For investigators, I got the Yellow Pages— thousands of investigators! For people I can talk to and be understood, I got you."

"Okay. So go on."

The old man puffed on his cigar and peered at him through the smoke. "Not till you're through being insulted. Is it an insult for one friend to ask another about his work?"

Howard sighed and tried to relax into the sensuous embrace of his chair. "No, Aaron, I guess not. I'm sorry. I guess I just got defensive. . . . Being a private detective is no big deal. You've got to know that."

"I *don't* know, Howard. What I know is what I saw in the movies my kids dragged me to forty years ago. Humphrey Bogart with a cigarette in his kisser and a pistol stuck in his belt. Is that what it is?"

Howard smiled. "No, Aaron, it's not. I apologize again. I think of you as a man of the world, so I figured you knew. Being a private investigator is nothing. It's doing things for people they could do for themselves if they wanted to take the trouble or the time. Ninety-nine times out of a hundred, it's just running around asking obvious questions or looking things up in public records or making phone calls." He shrugged. "It's like taking the garbage to the dump, Aaron. People don't like doing it themselves, so they hire someone else to do it for them."

Scowling, the old man stubbed out his cigar. "Now that I don't believe, Howard. I don't believe Humphrey Bogart, but I don't believe what you're telling me either. I think there's got to be more to it than that. You're not a garbage man."

Howard laughed. Then, thinking about how it had all begun, in his sister's kitchen in Rogers Park, two months after the end of the Korean War, he laughed again.

Leaning earnestly across the kitchen table, his shrimp of a brother-in-law—all nose, eyes, nerves, and brain—said, "Look, Howard, it's a natural. It's logical, it makes sense. You've got police experience—"

"*Military* police, Simon. Not the same thing at all."

His brother-in-law dismissed this with a wave of his hand. "With your background and my background, it's a natural. We can sell it, Howard, believe me."

It was a family rumor, one that Simon wouldn't exactly confirm or deny, that he'd spent the war "in intelligence." Howard thought he'd probably been just far enough in to come away with some exciting delusions.

"So who's going to sell it, Simon? Not me. One look at me, and the customers go down the hall."

"You're wrong, Howard. One look at either of us *alone*, and maybe the customers go down the hall. But *together* we're gangbusters!"

Howard made a face. "What you're saying is that together we look like Brains and Brawn."

"You got it, brother. You'll be the brains and I'll be the brawn." He held up a fist the size of a walnut.

Howard smiled and shook his head.

"Seriously. From you, people get confidence, Howard. I kid you not. It'd be different if you were a dummy, but one word out of your mouth and people know you're a real heavyweight. I need you. The whole *operation* needs you."

"Come on, Si, what operation? It's crazy, it's kid stuff—Sam Spade, Philip Marlowe."

"You know I'm not talking about crap like that. It's the industrial side of the business that pays. Security, surveillance, counterespionage —that's all gonna be big business in the postwar world, kiddo, and we'll be getting in on the ground floor."

Still Howard shook his head. "I'd be out of my depth."

"Goddammit, Howard, what do you want to do? You want to go back in the ring and get your face rearranged some more?"

Howard shrugged. It was true he had no plans for himself at all.

And so, half reluctantly, the firm of Scheim and Hartz was born. With their savings and mustering-out pay, they invested in a first-class wardrobe for each of them, ordered a quarter-page ad in the Yellow Pages, and furnished a State Street office in a style designed to impress. Then Simon went out and started hustling while Howard sat at an empty desk beside a silent telephone, feeling extremely foolish.

After three months of indefatigable hustling, Simon was forced to admit that the kinds of accounts he wanted were out of reach of a company in its infancy. He reformulated his angle of attack on the market and went hustling again.

Meanwhile, with the Yellow Pages out, a few calls had begun to come in, mainly from the Jewish community, on the strength of their names alone. By default, Howard handled these. He dug out a little background information on a few prospective sons- and daughters-in-law. He put a few people in touch with mislaid relatives. He got his first taste of divorce work and hated it. He found a runaway girl for a couple in Gary, Indiana; big deal—an aunt in Skokie was hiding her.

Simon's hustling paid off now and then. An office supplies wholesaler he brought in was having problems with a writer of scurrilous, unsigned inter-office memos. Howard looked into it; he didn't find the culprit, but the memos stopped, and the client grudgingly paid their single largest bill to date: $157.16.

Although the business was paying for itself, they were still taking money from their savings accounts to live on, and Simon was getting burned out with hustling. "I think we could get a lot of business if you had some background in accountancy," he told Howard.

"Well, I don't," Howard replied.

"You could get it."

"I could reenlist in the army, too."

Simon knew he meant it, so he left it alone. But another idea was stirring in his brain, and he unveiled it a few weeks later.

"If I had a law degree," he said, "we'd be made. People take their problems to lawyers, not private eyes."

Howard saw the sense in this.

The next three years were nightmarish. Simon lost twenty pounds trying to keep up his end of the business while going to law school at DePaul, and Howard's sister was barely on speaking terms with him, having somehow decided it was his fault that Simon was working toward a nervous breakdown.

Although Howard continued to toy with the idea of reenlisting, his end of the business grew steadily, if not spectacularly, with old clients recommending him to new ones. He liked the work well enough, but he still considered it a temporary thing. An acquaintance from his boxing days offered him a partnership in a gym he was opening on Wilson Avenue, and he would have taken it like a shot if he'd had the capital.

Simon took a two-week vacation after passing his bar exam, and when he returned he told Howard he was bowing out of the detective business to open a law office with a fellow graduate. Howard found he wasn't much surprised, but Simon was obviously racked by guilt over it.

"The whole thing is yours, Howard," he said. "I don't expect anything for my end of it. The truth is," he confessed, "I'm no good at business at all. If I'd known that, I wouldn't have got you involved in all this."

Howard told him it was all right.

"Naturally, we'll throw all our investigative business your way, so, the way I figure it, you'll actually be better off with me out of it."

Howard told him this would be terrific. He'd been around enough to know that, Perry Mason notwithstanding, lawyers have little use for detectives, except for the divorce work he detested. He didn't mention this—or the fact that he was thinking of bowing out of the business himself. To ease his conscience, Simon insisted on closing up the office and buying him a drink. Howard went along with it and listened for an hour, stupefied, as Simon—the guy who was no good at business—lectured him on business and outlined all the improbable ways they could work together in the future. Then at last, with an awkward handshake and an exchange of promises to keep in touch, it was over, and Howard was on his own.

Standing outside the bar on State Street, Howard decided he felt pretty good about it, relieved. He bought a paper and spent the evening poring over the help-wanted ads. There was nothing of any interest, but this didn't discourage him. There wasn't any great hurry, after all; the detective agency would support him after a fashion till he found something else to do.

He never heard from Simon or his sister again. A few years later, when he was getting married, he tried to locate them and was told they'd moved to Los Angeles, where Simon was on the legal staff of a TV production company.

When the office lease ran out, he found a place he could rent month-to-month on Lawrence Avenue for about half what he was paying on State. Since he wanted to be able to close the office quickly when the time came, he left most of the boxes unpacked when he moved. They were still unpacked six years later, in 1964, when for the first time his income topped ten thousand and he realized he'd finally been snared by his own meager success: the jobs he was circling in the paper were only offering eight or nine thousand to start—and he wasn't even qualified for them.

In the first week of the new year, he stopped reading the help-wanted ads, told his landlord he wanted a two-year lease, bought three new suits, and sent an engagement ring to a woman who'd given up on him the previous fall. The day after they were married by a judge at the court house, Ada told him she wanted to open a savings account, held out a hand, and said, "Gimme."

Howard took out his billfold and laid a twenty across her palm.

"More," she said.

Under Ada's ruthless management, they saved nearly $75,000 before inflation cut the ground out from under them. People will pay what they have to pay for a loaf of bread or a shirt or a house, but there seemed to be a psychological limit to what they'd pay for the kind of services Howard offered. He was forced to choose between losing income by holding his rates down or losing customers by raising them. He chose to hold his rates down, and soon even Ada couldn't squeeze out anything extra to put in the bank.

By 1980, when her health began to fail, their savings were down to $60,000. By the time Howard joined the chess club, they were down to $35,000, and he was routinely withdrawing a couple hundred a month to make ends meet.

When he allowed himself to think about it, he knew he was facing a bleak old age.

"Okay, Aaron," Howard said. "I guess what you were hearing was a little bitterness. There's more to it than taking people's garbage to the dump. A little more."

"So tell me, Howard. I'm interested."

"Suppose I do this, Aaron. I'll tell you the story of what my wife called 'Howard Scheim's Most Baffling Case.' He paused, smiling at the recollection. "One day a young guy from our building snuck into my office looking like he was about to choke to death from embarrassment. He asked if he could talk to me for a minute, and I told him sure, sit down.

"He said, 'This is the silliest damn thing, and I feel like a complete fool bringing it here, but it's got us worried.' By *us* he meant him and his wife, who'd just had their first baby a few months before.

"I told him to go on, and he took a ring of keys from his pocket and shoved them across the desk. He said, 'Last night I went over to the bookcase for something and found these sitting on one of the shelves. They aren't ours. We've never seen them before.'

"I picked up the keys and looked them over. 'So you're thinking what?' I said.

"'Obviously someone's been in our apartment when we weren't there.' I asked him if they'd checked with their friends, somebody who might have left the keys behind. 'We haven't had anybody over for weeks,' he told me.

"I asked him if anything was missing from the apartment, and he said not that they knew. 'That's what makes it so spooky,' he said. 'It looks like someone just came in, put the keys in the bookcase, and left.'

"Well, I looked at the keys some more. There was nothing unusual about them. They looked like dime-store duplicates on a dime-store key ring, chained to a clear plastic medallion with a violet embedded in it. I told him I thought they belonged to a young girl.

"'A young girl? Why a young girl?'

"'I don't know,' I said. 'The key ring looks like something a young girl would buy.'

"He didn't think much of this bit of deduction. He wanted to know if I thought he should talk to the police about it, and I told him I didn't think they'd be too interested. He wanted to know if I thought he should change the locks on the doors, and I said sure, it'd probably help them sleep better.

"He left looking pretty disillusioned, but he called back the next morning.

"'It was the baby-sitter,' he said. 'She left them here when she was sitting for us last week.'

"'I see. Didn't she miss them?'

"'Yeah, well, not right away. She met her sister going home, and she let them in, so she didn't notice they were gone till she got home from school the next day, and she figured they'd fallen out of her purse or something.'

"So I asked him how he found out about it, and he said his wife had thought of the baby-sitter as soon as she heard what I'd said about the keys belonging to a young girl.

"And that," Howard concluded, "was Howard Scheim's Most Baffling Case."

Aaron nodded solemnly. "And what's the lesson of this story, Howard?"

"It shows the difference between the ordinary citizen and an experienced investigator. The young man who came to me was obsessed—overwhelmed—by what he *didn't* know about those keys. Looking at them, all he could think was: why would someone break into our apartment and put those keys in a bookcase? But an experienced investigator doesn't start with what he doesn't know. He doesn't get panicked by all the data that's missing, so he's free to look at the data that's actually there. And that's all I did."

"Ah!" Aaron whispered ecstatically. "Ah, yes."

Howard chuckled. "That's good, is it?"

"Very good indeed," the old man said. "As you'll see."

CHAPTER 3

"I've got a thing I want looked into, Howard," the old man said, "and it's no small thing—nothing like missing silverware, believe me. It's big, and it'll take someone like you, someone who's not overwhelmed by all the data that's missing."

Howard waited, but, having made this announcement, Aaron seemed to lose all interest in it. He sat swirling brandy in the glass poised between his fingertips and smiled gently at his own thoughts. After several minutes he looked up and asked which feast Howard considered the most central to Jewish life.

The question disoriented him and it took him a few moments to shift gears. "I'd have to say Passover."

"Of course. The commemoration of our liberation from Egypt. This occurred in about 1210 B.C. And when do you suppose the first Passover was celebrated in the Holy Land?"

Howard thought for a moment. "I'd assume it was forty years later, when they *entered* the Holy Land."

"It was six hundred years later, Howard. Not a single Passover was held under all the judges and kings of Israel until the eighteenth year of the reign of Josiah, just a few years before the Babylonian exile began."

"I didn't know that," Howard admitted.

"And why do you suppose that was, Howard?"

"Tell me, Aaron."

"It was because during those six hundred years the Israelites worshiped the gods and goddesses of the Sidonians and the Amorites and the Moabites and the Philistines and the Babylonians. During most of this time, if you'd asked them about the God of Israel, they wouldn't even have known what God you were talking about. I'm not kidding. Their gods were Baal and Ashtaroth and Dagon and Azazel and Milcom and Asima and Succoth Benoth and Anamelech and Nergal and Kemosh and Moloch. And if you'd asked them to point out a priest, it would have been one who burnt offerings to Baal or who tended one of the hill shrines."

"But I thought. . . . Wasn't the temple set up in Jerusalem?"

"Certainly. And inside you'd have found altars dedicated to all these gods and goddesses—except for Moloch; he was set up in the valley of the sons of Hinnom. And attached to the temple you'd have found quarters for the temple prostitutes—male prostitutes. The Mosaic teachings had been abandoned from the outset, Howard—abandoned and then lost. It was Josiah who rediscovered them around 610 B.C., and Judaism as we know it began with this event—not with Abraham, not with the Exodus, not with the Israelites' entry into the land of Canaan."

"I see," Howard said, feeling like a schoolboy.

"But this happened too late to save us, Howard. God had already washed his hands of the people he'd chosen to be his own. He'd asked us only to trust him and to be faithful to him, and after six centuries of rejection, he said, 'No more. You've broken the covenant I made with your fathers. I now bring on you the catastrophe I promised—a catastrophe you can't escape. You'll cry to me for help, but I won't listen. Cry for help to the gods you've worshiped during all these generations. You have as many of those as towns, as many altars to Baal as streets in Jerusalem. So don't call to me, because I'll listen no more. I have forsaken the house of Israel. I've cast off my own people.'

"And so he did, Howard. For two and a half millennia we've cried out to no avail. We've been scattered, despised, tortured, murdered, oppressed, and in all these centuries God has been silent."

Aaron paused to begin the lengthy ritual of lighting a cigar.

Howard asked: "What about Israel today, Aaron? Where does that stand in your thinking?"

The old man shook his head disdainfully. "Do the Israelis rely on God to take care of them? I think not, Howard. Their gods are tanks and machine guns and rockets and jet fighters. As in ancient times, they put their trust in the gods their neighbors trust. The gods they worship now are the gods of Russia and the United States."

"True, I suppose."

Aaron sent a puff of smoke up toward the ceiling. "Now here is a thing I wonder about, Howard. What is it that made Baal and Ashtaroth and Moloch and all the rest so attractive to the Israelites—so much more attractive than the God who delivered them from slavery in Egypt and gave them victory over all the kings in the land of Canaan?"

"Well . . . these were idols, weren't they?"

"So it was said."

"Then I suppose the attraction was that these were gods they could see."

Aaron wrinkled his nose in distaste. "That's a schoolboy's answer, Howard. The fashion is to imagine that these people were simpletons, just because they lived long ago, but they were no more simpletons than we are. The Israelis don't worship tanks and machine guns and rockets because they can see them but because they trust them: these things can be relied on to *do* something for them. The Israelites were just the same, Howard. They were Jews—just like us, hardheads, pragmatists."

"So? What are you getting at?"

"Howard, nowhere in the scriptures does it say that Baal and Ashtaroth and Moloch and all the rest weren't real gods. Nowhere does it say they don't exist. What it says is they're *false* gods—gods who will play you false, gods not to be trusted."

"Okay."

"But the Sidonians and the Amorites and the Moabites and the Philistines and the Babylonians—and the Israelites—trusted them.

The Israelites trusted these gods even more than they trusted the one who parted the Red Sea for them."

Howard shrugged. "I still don't see what you're getting at, Aaron."

"Howard, what would a prophet say to the Israelis today?"

"Tell me."

"He would say, 'Don't put your trust in tanks and rockets and machine guns and jet fighters. Throw these idols into the fire, because they're false gods, gods not to be trusted—gods who will ultimately let you down. Put your trust in the God of Israel, not the gods of the Russians and Americans. The God of Israel—the same God who promised you this land and delivered it to your forefathers—will never let you down.'"

"Okay. I guess I see what you mean."

"But the Israelis would pay no attention to such a prophet, would they?"

"No, I wouldn't think so."

"Because they know for sure what a tank and a machine gun and a rocket and a jet fighter will do for them. They're not about to trade in these things for a spook in the sky."

"I think you're right."

"So we come again to my question, Howard. What did Baal and Ashtaroth and Moloch and all the rest do for the Israelites? It couldn't have been nothing, because the Israelites weren't fools any more than the Israelis are fools. Therefore it had to be something."

Howard nodded grudgingly. "Okay. I can't argue with your logic on this, Aaron. Maybe somebody else could, but I can't."

"You see what I'm after here then?"

"Yes, I guess I do."

"Good," the old man said. His cigar had gone out, and he spent a few moments relighting it. Then, squinting through the smoke, he said: "So, Howard. Will you take it on?"

Howard blinked at him dully, feeling he'd lost track of the conversation. "Will I take what on, Aaron?"

"This investigation." He waved his hand through the smoke. "All this."

"Aaron," Howard said, staring at him in disbelief. "You're not talk-ing about Baal and Ashtaroth and . . ."

"I am, Howard."

"Aaron, for God's sake. Tell me you're kidding."

"You know I'm not a kidder."

Howard thought about his bed—unmade, sagging in the middle, and with a book lying open beside it—and about the quickest way to get to it. He said: "Tell me again what you're looking for."

"Listen, Howard: for the sake of these gods, our people forfeited Israel. I want to know something about them. I want to know what made these gods so fantastically attractive."

"That's a scholar's job, Aaron. You've got to know that."

"No, it's nothing like a scholar's job. The answer isn't in any of the places where scholars look for answers. That much I know for a certainty."

"Then where is it?"

Aaron jabbed his cigar over his shoulder. "Out there, Howard. If the answer's to be found anywhere, it's to be found out there."

"Aaron, are you telling me you want someone to go to Israel and dig in the hills or something?"

"Not at all. Definitely not."

"Then I don't know what the hell you're talking about."

Aaron gazed at him sorrowfully, reproachfully. "I've never seen you like this, my friend. It's like you got your hands over your ears. It's like you're sitting there shaking your head and saying no, no, no, no, no. This isn't like you, Howard."

Howard laughed and shook his head. "Okay, Aaron, I'll give it an-other try. You say the answer's out there. The only place I know of to look out there is the public library."

"Not the public library, Howard. I'm not talking about things in books."

"Then, Goddammit, what are you talking about?"

His eyes wide, the old man quickly put his hands over his ears. Howard sighed and sank back in his chair.

"Explain it to me, Aaron. I don't understand."

"Howard, I told you: in the scriptures, it says these were false gods, gods not to be trusted. It doesn't say they were figments."

"So? "

"So, if they weren't figments. . . . Howard, tell me. Do gods die?"

"What?"

Aaron shrugged. "Okay, maybe they died. Maybe that's what you'll tell me after you've looked into it: 'Aaron, those gods must have died back in the sixth century before Christ, because there's no trace of them now.'"

Howard stared at him open-mouthed.

"Or maybe you'll tell me the opposite. You'll say, 'Aaron, maybe I got something. Maybe they didn't die. Maybe they just aren't called the same names any more.'" The old man frowned into Howard's incredulous look. "Damn it, haven't you ever looked for somebody who might be dead? Who might not even be there to be found?"

"Aaron, you've got to be kidding."

The old man sighed, pulled himself out of his chair, and went to a desk at the other end of the room. When he returned, he handed Howard two checks, one marked "Advance against expenses," the other marked "Advance against fee (Retainer)."

Both were for ten thousand dollars.

Aaron sat down and picked up his brandy glass. "My children think I'm cheap, Howard, because I get no kick out of spending money on worthless things. When it comes to something important, believe me, I'm never cheap. If you need more than that for expenses, you'll get it. There's no rush about this thing. Take a year. Take two years. Get me an answer to my question—satisfy me either way—and your fee will be fifty thousand."

Howard was gazing at the checks as if they were photographs of his unborn children. Finally he tore his eyes away and looked up.

"Aaron, I can't."

"You can't?" He grinned at him slyly. "You got more business than you can handle?"

"I mean it wouldn't be right. I can't take money for a job that can't be done. For a job that's impossible."

"I tell you what, Howard. Do a little looking for a month. Poke around—whatever you ordinarily do when you're starting a job. Then if you still think it's impossible, we'll call it quits. You can give me whatever's left for expenses and keep the retainer. Or if your conscience won't let you do that, just keep half the retainer. Whatever you say."

"Aaron. . ."

"Yes?"

"It's crazy. It's like. . . I don't know what it's like. It's all just shadows, just smoke. There's nowhere to start."

Aaron raised his brows in mock astonishment. "Howard, it almost sounds like you're telling me you're panicked by what you don't know here, that you're overwhelmed by the data that's missing."

"It isn't that there's data *missing*, Aaron. There's no data at all. Words in a book written two thousand years ago aren't data."

The old man sat blinking for a moment, then he got up and went to the bookshelves for a thick, black-bound volume. He stood paging through it for a few minutes, then handed it to Howard open near the middle. "Baal," he said, "and Ashtaroth. It's a popular work, but it brings together the best collection of portraits in print."

Scowling, Howard studied the two pictures. "I can't believe these are ancient."

"Ancient? A minute ago you were bitching because all I had was words two thousand years old. These two portraits are something like a hundred years old."

"Aaron. . ."

"You want ancient?" He snatched the book back and started paging through it again. "There," he said. "Not exactly ancient, but that's Ashtaroth in the sixteenth century."

Howard glanced at the portrait and shook his head.

"Aaron, these things are worthless."

The old man nodded thoughtfully and sat down. "I understand,

Howard. You mean they're worthless like the key ring in the book-case."

Howard sighed and closed his eyes for a long moment. "Okay, let me look again."

He spent a few minutes examining the portraits of Baal, Ashtaroth, Moloch, and others Aaron had talked about, then turned the book around to look at the title on the spine: *The History of Magic.*

"Okay," he said. "You're right. I was being panicked by what I didn't know. There's a place to start."

"Good."

"But *why*, Aaron? Why do you want to pursue this thing?"

Aaron sank back in his chair and stared at the ceiling. "Howard, I understand that, for you, this is all just plain foolishness. A lot of people would agree—maybe even most people. Who cares about the past any more? It's all dead and gone, so we should just throw it in the trash. Who cares that we were once God's chosen people? Who cares why we blew it? That's all just crap, isn't it, Howard?"

"I didn't say that, Aaron."

"No, not in those words. But that's what you meant. You meant: Why do you want to pursue this crap nobody cares about?"

Howard stared guiltily at his hands.

"You want to know why I want to pursue this. Here's a better question for you, Howard: Why am I alone in this? Why am I the only one who's ever *wanted* to pursue this question? In the past two thousand years, a billion questions have been asked. But no one has ever asked this one but me."

CHAPTER 4

The next morning Howard spent in a moral turmoil, alternately cracking his knuckles at his desk and staring broodily down at the traffic on Lawrence Avenue.

Though never a ditherer under ordinary circumstances, he had an almost superstitious dread of meddling with fate: of making decisions that would alter the course of his own life. He preferred to see himself as being swept along in an irresistible tide of events, as when the army took him in 1950, as when he opened the agency with Simon, as when he kept the agency going, year after year, following Simon's defection.

Now he was in a stew, because a cross-current had appeared in the tide to baffle his footsteps. Fate had set in his way a job that would give him a finger-hold on the future (and that was all to the good), but it was a job he could only accept at the expense of his self-respect. In spite of his glib talk about having a place to start, Howard knew he could only earn Aaron's fifty thousand by fraud.

Find out whether the ancient gods of the Middle East are still around? Aaron might as well have asked him to find out whether cheaters ever prosper or whether love makes the world go round. It wasn't even laughable. If he took on the job, he wouldn't be looking for an answer to Aaron's question. He'd be looking for something that could be tricked-up to look like an answer—something so much like an answer that the old man would cheerfully cough up that fee.

And was that how he wanted to end his career—as an outright con man?

Strangely enough, when he got around to asking himself this melodramatic question, Howard smiled, and his turmoil subsided, because he realized he was doing something he'd often yelled at Ada for. He was creating a crisis by *preparing* for a crisis. He was pressing for a decision before a decision was needed.

Aaron himself had suggested he spend a month looking the problem over. Well, why not? He was ninety-nine percent sure that a month's work wouldn't change the situation, but he could undertake it with complete honesty—and pocket Aaron's retainer without a qualm. And who knows? Maybe after a month in the water he'd have a better sense of which way the tide was flowing.

All hesitancy gone now, he pulled over a card file, looked up an old friend's number, and called to invite him to an expense account lunch at the Sheraton.

"Are you getting or giving?" his friend wanted to know.

"Getting, of course. Do people buy you lunch to give?"

"Every day, son. Sometimes twice a day."

Hayes Peterson was a leg man for a columnist at the Chicago *Tribune*, and he had almost as many names in his head as the telephone directory.

"God, you're ugly," he said as Howard slid into the booth across from him. "I keep forgetting. Between times, the gray cells iron out all those crags and gullies and scars."

"I know," Howard said. "I do it myself. Until I actually look at myself in the mirror, I get to thinking I'm a pretty good-looking guy, from when I was a kid. Club soda with lime," he told a waitress who paused at their table.

Hayes Peterson held up a finger for another martini. He was in his mid-fifties, a perfectly round little man who carried his extra weight with complete aplomb—helped by a tailor who knew his craft. He had a cherub's pink face, a rosebud smile, and a tongue that could tear the flesh off living bones.

"So what are you after?" he asked after they'd gossiped for a few minutes.

"A name. Maybe."

"Maybe?"

"Maybe you don't have such a name."

The little man sneered at this improbability. "Go on."

"A few years ago your man did a story about a psychic fair held at that shopping center at Broadway and Diversey. I'd like an in to that scene."

Hayes looked at him with distaste. "You want an in to the *psychic* scene?"

"I think I do. It's just a place to start."

"So what name do you want?"

"The name of someone I can talk to, someone who'll level with me, someone who can maybe give me a useful steer."

"Christ, you don't want much, do you. These are all kooks and con-artists, you know."

Howard shrugged. "That's why I said maybe you don't have such a name."

"Don't pull those bullshit *schnorrer* tricks on me, Howard. I can give you a name okay. She's not a con-artist and I don't think she's a kook, but she's also not that far into the scene."

"Anything's better than what I've got right now."

"And, besides lunch, what am *I* supposed to get out of this deal?"

"What do you need, Hayes? I'm on call. You got my number. You want something looked into in Uptown?"

"Yuck. Is there human life in Uptown?"

"Traces of it."

"Fuck it, Howard. Shove it up your ass. Her name is Denise Purcell."

Smiling, Howard jotted it in his notebook. "And what does she do? Does she claim to be a psychic?"

"No, that's the thing. She doesn't pretend to be Madame Carlotti. She does Tarot readings—very straight, very matter of fact. I watched her work, talked to her for a while, and she impressed me. No big come-on, no mystical vomit."

"Sounds good. . . . Do you think I should I offer to pay for her time?"

"I'd say no, offhand, but that's not guaranteed. Who knows what evil lurks in the hearts of Tarot-card readers?" He glanced at his wrist. "Come on, let's order. I gotta meet a guy at Ricardo's in forty-five minutes."

The doorman at the south side condominium was obviously reluctant to pass Howard in, but there wasn't much he could do about it after he'd confirmed that he was expected. Howard wondered if this was just a reaction to his appearance or a special protectiveness Ms. Purcell inspired. Ascending to the eighteenth floor, he decided it was the latter; he'd already formed an image of her: a wispy creature full of hesitant, mousey gestures. And because of this, he would have walked right past the woman standing outside the elevator if she hadn't stopped him with: "Mr. Scheim?"

He paused and looked down at a slender, self-possessed woman of about forty, handsome rather than pretty, in a smart tweed suit he felt sure she hadn't put on for his benefit. She was examining him with a grave, competent look, as if he were a statue she was thinking of buying.

He understood immediately why Hayes Peterson had been impressed.

"I wasn't born with this wreck of a face," he said.

She smiled politely. "Carl—the doorman—thought I should have a look before letting you in."

"Always a good policy."

"Come this way."

She led him to an apartment that reminded him of an impressionist painting—full of light, color, plants, blossoms. It was cheerful and feminine, but not oppressively so. They sat down across from each other, and he felt a twinge of disappointment when he realized she wasn't going to make the usual social gesture of offering coffee.

"And now, how can I help you, Mr. Scheim?"

"Ah," he said vaguely. He wished there was an opening more graceful than the simple, inelegant plunge, but, after nearly forty years as an investigator, he had yet to find it. "This is my situation, Ms. Purcell. A client has asked me to look into something for him, to find an answer to a question he has. I won't try to judge the usefulness of the question, but it's one that, for an investigator, is a little hard to come to grips with. To say the least."

She nodded just as if he'd said something that made sense.

"At this point, to be completely honest, I'm not even looking for an answer to the question. I'm just looking for a place to look."

"On the phone you mentioned a psychic fair I did in 1989. Does that have some connection to this?"

"Well, it does or it doesn't. At this point I can't be sure." Howard felt like a burglar trying to pick a lock with a feather. "What I'm trying to tell you is that I'm right at the beginning, just poking around, and my first thought was to have a look inside the world that psychic fair represents."

"I think you have a misapprehension about that, Mr. Scheim. There is no world there. It's just a bunch of people shooting off in all directions, pursuing their own individual interests. It has no more coherence than a flea market, really."

"Go on."

"Well . . . at one table you have a phrenologist or a palm reader. At the others, you have people painting mandalas, passing out Rosicrucian literature, casting horoscopes, doing Kirlean photography, selling stuff—body oils, incense, occult books, biofeedback gadgets. What does that all add up to, Mr. Scheim?"

"Yeah, I see what you mean." Howard sat blinking at her for a few moments. "Maybe I'd better just tell you what it is my client is after."

"All right."

"I make no apologies for it. I don't say it makes good sense. It's just what it is, okay?"

"Okay."

"Do you know the Old Testament, Ms. Purcell?"

Her eyes widened impressively. "I suppose I've read it half a dozen times over the years."

"Then you know it a lot better than I do. In outline: the Jews, the Israelites, were ultimately rejected by God because they were unfaithful, because they preferred to worship the gods their neighbors worshiped—Baal and Ashtaroth and Moloch and that lot."

She nodded.

"Okay. My client wants to know something about these gods. He wants to know what made them so much more attractive than the God of Israel."

She studied him with disapproval for a moment. "You're joking."

"Frankly, that's what I said to him myself. Maybe if you heard him explain it, it would sound more reasonable."

"It isn't that the question itself is ridiculous, it's that. . . . A private detective?"

Howard nodded. "Again, I said the very same thing to him, Ms. Purcell. What you have to understand is that he's not looking for theories. He's not looking for what a theologian or historian might say. He's looking for what can be found out by an experienced investigator. He wants me to approach this the same way I'd approach any other case."

"Good heavens. . . . And you've taken it on?"

"I haven't exactly taken it on yet. I'm trying to find out whether there's anything there to take on."

"I see." Her brows came together in a frown. "But why on earth are you talking to me?"

Howard sighed, and he wasn't sure whether it was from relief or exasperation. What he needed was a nerve to grope for. "Ms. Purcell, it's been said that, with the right three introductions, you can reach anyone in the world—a president, a king, anyone. I've reached you with one introduction. You may not be able to help me directly, but you may be able to give me another introduction—an introduction to someone you think might be able to help me. And if this person can't help me, maybe he can give me an introduction to someone else. Since I don't know exactly who I'm looking for, it may take five introductions—or a dozen."

"To reach whom, Mr. Scheim? Who is this ultimate person you want to find?"

"As I say, I don't know. There may not even be such a person."

"But what would he do for you if you found him?"

"Again, I honestly don't know, Ms. Purcell. Sometimes this is the only way an investigator can operate. Sometimes you don't know what you're looking for, all you know is how to go about finding it. Do you see what I mean?"

Denise Purcell had stopped listening some time back, and Howard waited for her to catch up. When she did, she went very still and the blood drained from her face. "I've been very naive, haven't I?"

"What do you mean?"

Her eyes glinted with an icy fury. "You came here thinking I would hook you up with some miserable coven of devil-worshipers, didn't you?"

"Believe me, I didn't," Howard said earnestly.

"What else would it be? You're not stupid, Mr. Scheim. I'm sure you know perfectly well who these old gods were—or are. In ancient times people called them gods. In modern times they call them demons. Baal is still Baal, Ashtaroth is still Ashtaroth, and Moloch is still Moloch, and the only difference is that people worship them as devils instead of gods."

"Yes, that's true, Ms. Purcell. I knew that. But, believe me, if you handed me the names and addresses of a group of devil-worshipers, I'd throw it in the trash."

"Why?"

"Why?" He looked around helplessly. "Because I'd assume they were a bunch of screwballs, that's why. What am I going to find out from screwballs? That's in the first place."

"Go on."

"In the second place. . . . Sure, I know there are devil worshipers in Chicago. I read the newspapers, Ms. Purcell. I watch the talk-shows. So what do these folks do at their meetings? Hold Black Masses? Mutilate hosts they've snitched at the communion rail? Spit on the crucifix? This has nothing at all to do with what was going on in Israel twenty-five hundred years ago. Does it?"

"No."

"Then why would I want to get hooked up with them, for God's sake?"

Denise Purcell closed her eyes and looked as if she was resisting the temptation to gnaw at her lower lip. Finally she nodded contritely. "I apologize, Mr. Scheim. I really do. I jumped to a conclusion there."

"It's understandable," Howard conceded gravely.

"I also underestimated you."

"That too," he said and astonished himself by adding, "So how about a cup of coffee?"

She laughed, relieved, and headed for the kitchen.

It was one of those moments when he missed Ada badly. Leading Denise Purcell up to that little 'misunderstanding' had been as tricky a move as he'd ever made, and he had no one to share it with.

When there's ice to be broken, make the ice-maker break it.

It was broken now.

CHAPTER 5

"Once upon a time," Denise said a few minutes later, "there was a young woman of twenty-five living in Marina City; this is before it went condo. She was lonely and bored and at loose ends, because she'd just ended a very bad marriage she'd gotten into when she was a sophomore in college. She didn't have to work, because her ex-husband was well-heeled and paid her a generous alimony. Nevertheless, she was a little afraid there in her tower, because it stood in the middle of a world she really didn't know very much about—a world where people worked for a living and did all sorts of very ordinary things she could only guess at.

"In order to disguise her fear a little bit, she became an exotic and made friends of a few other exotics, who were, among other things, into contacting the spirit world through the Ouija board, automatic writing, and seances. The young woman thought this was very nifty, very exciting. She especially enjoyed the Ouija board, because of Roger. Her friends were also very impressed with her performance at the Ouija board, because of Roger. He made an appearance the very first time she tried it. When her turn came, she asked, 'Is anyone there?' and Roger answered immediately: The planchette spelled out 'Hello.'

"Unlike most of the spirits you meet through the Ouija board, who tend to be lazy, stubborn, and flighty, Roger was a dream. He was almost always available and would talk to them and answer their idiotic questions for hours. One skeptic suspected the woman of controlling the planchette herself and challenged Roger to supply her mother's maiden name, and he did. He did all sorts of things like that.

"One night the woman was lying in bed reading when a globe of green light about the size of a billiard ball appeared in the corner of the room just above the floor. It slowly crossed the floor, climbed the foot of her bed, rolled across the sheets, and ran up her left arm. It wasn't a frightening experience at all. In fact, it was rather nice, and she told her friends about it the next time they got together. They thought it sounded very neat and was a sure sign that she was specially favored in the spirit world.

"One night a few days later, the woman woke up near dawn with the terrible feeling there was someone lying beside her in the bed. You know: she could feel it sagging at her side. For a long time she lay there absolutely petrified, but finally she couldn't stand it anymore, and she rolled out of bed, ran into the bathroom, and locked herself in. She didn't come out until she saw daylight under the door. And of course there was no one in her bed. In the daylight she was able to convince herself that it had all been her imagination.

"But the next night she woke up again—and this time she woke up fighting to breathe. She couldn't breathe because a heavy weight—a crushing weight—was pressing down on her, as though someone were kneeling on her chest. Fortunately, she passed out from sheer terror. The next day she moved into a hotel and started looking for another apartment. She never again touched a Ouija board or made any other attempt to fool with the spirit world, and she was never again bothered in her sleep."

Howard nodded thoughtfully. "I assume the young woman was you."

"That's right."

"And I assume there's a moral to the story."

"Yes. Open no doors."

"Meaning?"

Denise was leaning forward in her chair studying her folded hands. "Ouija boards are toys. I'm sure you know that. They're manufactured by the thousands and they have no power at all. In themselves. I suppose millions of people have played with them, gotten nothing, and thrown them in the trash. But every once in a while someone comes along who opens a door, just a tiny crack no wider than a hair, the way I did, and then—look out."

"And you evidently intend this as a warning to me. You think I mean to open a door."

"Mr. Scheim, it sounds to me like you mean to knock down a whole wall. If you can."

Howard sighed. "I accept your warning and I take it seriously. Now here's something I hope you'll take seriously. I don't always know what I'm doing, but I always know what I'm not doing. And one thing I'm not doing and will never do is waste my time investigating the spirit world. It's been tried, Ms. Purcell—I'm sure you know that better than I do. After a hundred years of very determined work, the investigation is right where it started: nowhere. I'm not about to contribute to that futility. If I ever found this investigation heading in that direction, I'd walk away from it. Not because of your warning, frankly, but because there just wouldn't be anything there for me. That's definite."

"The thing is, you may think you're not heading in that direction, but . . ."

"Ms. Purcell, I was told you do Tarot card readings."

"That's true. And so?"

"And so how do you square that with this advice you're giving me?"

"Oh," she said with a dismissive toss of her head. "That's entirely different."

"I believe you. I give you credit for knowing what you're doing. Please give me a little credit too."

She nodded, not in agreement but in resignation. "So you want a name."

"A name would be deeply appreciated."

She leaned back in her chair and gave him a long, speculative look. "Would you let me do a reading first?"

Howard shrugged. "You know, Ms. Purcell, I forgot to bring a gun to point at you, so what can I say? I'm in your hands."

They went to a table by the window, and Denise refilled their coffee cups and produced a thick deck of outsize cards. She ran through them quickly, selecting one and laying it face up between them.

"This is you: the King of Pentacles. It's called the significator. The King of Pentacles seems appropriate because you're a dark man, as he is, and you came to me over a matter of business, and the suit of pentacles is generally about work, craftsmanship, and fortune."

She shuffled the cards three times and asked him to do the same.

"I should have done a reading before we talked," she said.

"Why is that?"

She smiled. "Because you'll undoubtedly think the reading I'm giving you now is being slanted by what you've told me."

"And it won't be?"

"No, but I'm sure you'll think it is."

He handed her the deck. "You're that sure of the cards?"

"Yes. Once I did a reading for a friend of a friend—a woman I didn't know. All I knew about her was that she was immensely wealthy. The first card I turned over to cover the significator almost made me swallow my teeth. This first card is the key card in the reading, the card that indicates the predominant influence in the subject's life. In this case, it was the Five of Pentacles, and it was so incredibly wrong I just sat there gawking at it and wishing I could sink into the ground. Finally the woman asked what was wrong, and I began to stutter out an apology: I must have done something wrong, I must have made a mistake, this couldn't be right. And she asked me what the card indicated. I told her it was one of the most explicit cards in the deck. It indicated plainly that the ruling influence in her life was poverty—absolute destitution. She threw back her head and roared with laughter, and then she said, 'My dear, I doubt if you could find anywhere in that deck a better card than that for me. The fear of poverty has ruled my life from the age of fifteen, and every important decision I've ever made was driven by it.' After that I never again worried about what the cards would turn up.

"And this is what covers you," she said, turning up a card over the King of Pentacles. "This is what's presently setting the tone of your life, what's influencing you and will continue to influence you in the near future. It's the Seven of Swords."

She picked it up and handed it to him. "See if you can tell me what it's about."

Howard glanced uneasily at the card. "Do you usually work this way?"

"No. It's as I said. If I proceed normally, you'll think I'm slanting it. See what you can figure out for yourself."

"I wouldn't know where to begin."

"Don't be silly. Look at the picture."

He studied it with bared teeth. "It shows a man sneaking away from a camp with some swords."

"He's stealing the swords?"

"That's what it looks like."

"Why is he stealing these swords? Look at him and see if you can tell me what's going through his mind."

"Well . . . he's grinning. He thinks he's pulled off a real coup."

"What does he think he's achieved with this coup?"

"I'd have to guess he's stealing these swords for *his* side."

"So what's in the offing here, between his side and the other side?"

"A battle, I'd assume."

"Of course. Now have another look at what's going on. The thief seems to have overlooked something."

"Well . . . He's left two swords behind. He's taken five and left two."

"Does that worry him?"

"It doesn't seem to."

"How is he holding the swords?"

"By the blades."

"It doesn't seem to occur to him that he could get cut."

"Apparently not."

"Now what would you have thought if I'd said to you, 'Here is what's going on in your life at the moment: You're getting ready for a battle and you're overestimating your own cleverness and underestimating the strength of your enemy. You're overconfident and you think you can't be hurt in the enterprise you've planned.'"

Howard nodded, smiling. "I would've thought you were slanting it."

"Put the card back."

He put it back.

"If it had been another sort of card covering the significator—any of the major arcana, for example—a more general reading would have been indicated. But the Seven of Swords, with its very explicit story, indicates the reading will center on the conflict you're preparing for."

She laid a card sideways across the Seven of Swords.

"This crosses you: this is the obstacle you face in your endeavor." She smiled gently. "The Two of Pentacles. It depicts a young man with a pentacle in each hand, and the pentacles are bound together in a figure eight on its side—the symbol for infinity. The pentacles therefore represent grave extremes: the beginning and the end, life and death, the infinite past and the infinite future, good and evil. Nevertheless, as you see, the young man is dancing. The weighing of these matters isn't something he takes very seriously. In the background, two ships on a storm-tossed sea are trying to reach shore, but the dancing man is unaware of them. Given the context, it seems likely that these two ships are carrying the two swords the thief left behind in the first card.

"In this position, the card indicates it's your own attitude that threatens you. You underestimate the magnitude of your undertaking and take it lightly."

She placed a card above the Two of Pentacles.

"This crowns you; this is the best outcome you can hope for: the Eight of Cups. A man walks into the distance along a desolate, moon-lit shore, away from an array of eight cups, which represent the good life—normalcy, security, comfort. In other words, at the best, you can hope for a strange journey, an adventure into the darkness.

"This is beneath you," she said, laying a card below the Two of Pentacles. "This is what you bring to the enterprise, what you build on: the Three of Wands. A stately man stands looking calmly out to sea, where several ships are sailing into the distance. Three staves are planted in the ground, and his hand rests lightly on one of them. All three belong to him, but he needs only one for support; he is a man with strength in reserve. The ships, too, belong to him, and the car-goes they carry are his; he has much to give the world. What his wis-dom has garnered he shares with others.

"This lies behind you." She put a card to the left of the Two of Pentacles. "This is the past, the tide that brings you to the matter at hand: the Five of Wands reversed. Five young men are engaged in mock battle with staves. In this position, and in context with the other cards, this suggests that you've had practice in the sort of battle you're getting ready for—which of course we know to be true. But note that the five staves in this card correspond exactly to the five swords stolen in the first card. This makes it plain that the battles you've fought in the past have only been play-acting in comparison to the one that lies ahead. The fact that the card is reversed suggests that you should be on guard against trickery.

"This lies before you." She laid a card to the right of the Two of Pentacles. "This is the current you're entering; this is what will influ-ence the matter at hand: the Page of Swords. A young man strides through the countryside with his sword aloft, but he gazes back over his shoulder rather wistfully, as if he regrets having left home. As you see, he's not in armor; this suggests either that he's not prepared for the battle ahead or that he's a spy rather than a warrior."

Denise pondered the card in silence.

"Three different readings offer themselves. The first, most obvious reading is that you yourself are unprepared for the battle you face. But this doesn't feel right to me; the point has already been made. The second reading is that the person whose name I'm thinking of giving you will become your ally. This troubles me, because I will explicitly forbid him to ally himself with you, and I believe he'll obey me in this. The third reading is that another young man or boy will become involved in the affair. He may be a runaway or an orphan. He'll need your protection, but it's his sword you'll follow."

She shook her head, dissatisfied, and turned up a card to the right of the layout. "This is yourself, your relation to the matter: the Tower. A bolt of lightning shatters a tower, and the king and queen are hurled to their deaths. A very telling card, in this position. What you bring to the matter is your vast strength, but being a tower of strength has its own special hazard—it attracts the lightning of destruction. By rearing up above your fellows, you make yourself a target—and put those close to you in danger as well."

She laid a card above the Tower and smiled.

"This is your house, the environment in which your endeavor will take place: the Seven of Cups. A man is disconcerted by an array of tantalizing apparitions of love, mystery, danger, riches, fame, and evil. Illusions will bedevil you. You'll be pulled in many directions, and your choices will be confused.

"These are your hopes and fears," she said, placing a card above the last. "The Two of Swords reversed. A blindfolded woman sits by a moonlit shore. Her arms are crossed, and she holds a sword in each hand. The two swords exactly balance each other; a concord has been reached between opposing forces—peace prevails though neither has conquered. However, because the card is reversed, the concord is a false one, and will be broken by treachery. These two swords, of course, are the swords the thief neglected to carry away in the first card. This is what's become of them."

She turned up the tenth and last card and said, "Ah. This is what's become of the five swords that were stolen. This is the outcome of the matter: the Five of Swords. A man grins disdainfully as his opponents trudge away empty-handed, leaving him in possession of their swords. Is this the same grinning man who stole the five swords in first place? Perhaps. The card is irreducibly ambiguous—this is its point. The victor's triumph seems hollow, not a cause for rejoicing. He's won the field, but he hasn't slain or even wounded his enemies, who are free to reassemble and avenge their defeat. The card is oddly placed here, since it suggests the middle of a story, not the end of one. What it indicates is that you'll take the first round of the conflict and imagine you've won it all."

"Not too good, huh?" Howard observed.

Ignoring the interruption, she continued to study the cards.

"There are only seven cards in the deck that show the principal character with his or her back turned to us. Three of them are in this layout, indicating that you've already firmly made up your mind to pursue the matter. You've already turned to it; you're resolved to see it through.

"The preponderance of swords makes it clear that it's going to be a battle. It's unlike anything you've ever undertaken—more serious, more dangerous—but this doesn't worry you at all. You set out on the adventure with a light heart. What you've failed to take into account is the power in the two swords left behind—the power of your opponent. In fact, you don't see him as an opponent at all. You're sure there is peace between you, that you can do as you please and he won't move against you, but in this you're deceived. At the very end, he'll take your weapons away as if they were toys, and you'll be helpless in his hands."

Howard leaned back in his chair. "Not too good, huh?" he said again.

"Not too good, indeed," she agreed and gave him an ironic smile. "But it doesn't worry you, does it?"

"I'd be lying if I said it did, Ms. Purcell. I've just never been much of a worrier."

She gathered the cards together and stood up. "I'll get you that name now. And something else. It'll just be a few minutes."

She disappeared into a bedroom and Howard got up to look out toward Jackson Park and the lake, which was disappearing under a mounting snowfall. By evening, he suspected, it would be a full-scale blizzard—maybe, with luck, the last of the season. Every year around the first of March, despite sixty years of experience to the contrary, Howard began to tell himself that the dragon of winter was surely in its death throes, that at worst there was only one more lash of the tail before the end. Thereafter he managed to view sub-zero weather and six-inch snowfalls as unseasonable encroachments on spring.

When Denise returned, she handed him a three-by-five card and an envelope. He turned the envelope over, noted it was sealed, and asked what was in it.

"Something for later."

He looked at the card. "Richard Holloway."

"Yes."

"Who is Richard Holloway?"

"A young man. A boy, really. Just in his last year of high school."

Howard continued to study the card, wondering whether it would do any good to voice his disappointment.

"What is it that he . . . does?"

"He's a clairvoyant."

"A clairvoyant," Howard repeated dully.

"Don't ask me if he can help you, Mr. Scheim. I don't know."

"May I ask what your relationship with him is?"

She shrugged. "Living with an infant clairvoyant—when you don't know what's going on—can be a pretty unnerving experience. His parents went looking for guidance, and they ended up with me. I've become a sort of special aunt to Richard. He talks to me about things his parents can't handle."

"I see." He put the card and envelope in the breast pocket of his jacket and picked up his overcoat. "You're going to talk to him about this?"

"Yes. I'll tell him to help you if he can but not to become personally involved in your project."

"He must have a lot of confidence in you."

She smiled affectionately. "He's a rare one. He has the outrageous idea that, at the age of eighteen, there may be one or two things he still doesn't know."

He opened the envelope on the northbound IC train. A note in Denise Purcell's crisp handwriting was folded around "the outcome of the matter"—the Five of Swords:

Mr. Scheim, though I don't suppose you'll take this seriously, I feel I should say it anyway. The "gods"—she, he, it, they—the creatures —you're looking for are not (as movies like *The Exorcist* would lead you to believe) vile. How could they ever have gained power over human lives if they'd been merely vile? They're dangerous because they're *attractive*. This, I think, is why the author of Proverbs thought it necessary to write his warning this way: "But now, my son, listen to me, attend to what I say. Don't let your heart entice you into her ways, don't stray down her paths; many has she pierced and laid low, and her victims are without number. Her house is the entrance to Sheol, which leads down to the halls of death."

CHAPTER 6

Howard's presentiment about the weather proved correct. By morning the streets were choked with six inches of snow—enough to make traffic a nightmare but not enough to give the city a giddy snowbound holiday. Nevertheless he decided the detective business could do without him for a day and stayed in bed reading till almost noon, when he dressed and went out for a paper.

The big news was the blizzard, which had mercifully left most of its bounty behind in Nebraska and Iowa. More snow was predicted for the afternoon, and a general school-closing had been announced before it was learned that this second wave of the storm would bypass Chicago to the south. Howard registered this fact a bit ruefully; with the schools closed, he could hardly ask for a better opportunity to find Richard Holloway at home and available.

He dug out the card Denise Purcell had given him, cross-checked the telephone number with the directory, and found that it belonged to an address on Astor, just off Lake Shore Drive and not an arduous journey, even on a day like this.

He thought about the ten thousand dollars he was trying to pretend he was earning and then reluctantly dialed the number. The phone was answered in the middle of the second ring by someone who sounded out of breath:

"Yes? Who is it?"

"Uh, I'm looking for Richard Holloway."

"Junior or senior?" A sort of hoarse shriek.

"Junior, I suppose. Whichever one is eighteen years old." This amazing witticism was greeted with a braying laugh.

"This is Richard Holloway, Junior. Who is this?"

"My name is Howard Scheim. I'm a private detective, and Denise Pur—"

"Yeah, I know, she told me."

"Ah. Well, I thought maybe, since you don't have school today, we could get together."

"You mean *today?*"

"It doesn't have to be today, but—"

"God. I'm real busy."

"As I say, it doesn't have to be today. Whenever it's convenient."

"Oh *God!*" The boy sounded as if he was being confronted by a major life crisis.

"Look," Howard began.

"What's your address? Where are you?"

"I can come there. That's no problem."

"No, you *can't* come here. There'd be no *point* in coming here. *God!*"

"Look, let's not make this into a Greek tragedy. We'll get together when you have the time."

"I *never* have the time. Not till after graduation anyway. What kind of computer do you have?"

"What?"

"What kind of computer?"

"I don't have a computer."

"Really? Well, look, I could give you a real good deal on a little XT, hard disk drive, a ton of software. It's only 4.77 megahertz, of course, but it's not a bad little machine, especially for a beginner. Five hundred dollars? The software alone has got to be worth close to two thousand."

"I don't know what you're talking about. I don't need a computer."

"See, I've got a 486 that I'll be upgrading to a Pentium OverDrive Processor chip and adding 128K of motherboard cache RAM. I may go up to 256, but that'd probably be pointless unless I switched to UNIX, which they say is better optimized for using cache RAM than DOS or Windows. A monster, y'know? I mean, compared to the XT, for god's sake."

"I don't need a computer," Howard told him firmly.

"Well, okay. What time is it?"

Howard shook his head, dazed. "Just after one."

"Where are you? What's your address?"

"Well, I'm home right now, but you could meet me at my office, which is a little easier to—"

"No, your home, *your home!*"

Howard told him.

"Ainslee. Where's Ainslee?"

"Two blocks north of Lawrence."

"*God!*" the boy said. "I don't know when I can get there. Three o'clock, four o'clock, something like that."

"Whenever you get here will be fine," Howard said, but the last half of the sentence was spoken into the dial tone.

When he saw the boy standing in the doorway in his Abercrombie & Fitch arctic explorer's outfit, he expected him to look around the apartment and say, "*God!*" But he just looked around, his eyes wide with horror. Howard had spent the interval neatening the place up and airing it out, but he knew how shabby it must look to this spoiled child from Astor Street.

Finally he blinked and stepped inside. He was nearly as tall as Howard, scrawny, and had a long, astonished face that would probably be handsome someday, when he calmed down and grew up. He tore off a quilted helmet and made no attempt to reorder the spiky black hair that sprang out as if released from a trap. Howard helped him out of his parka and hung it in the closet.

"Can I get you something to drink? A Coke? Seven-Up?"

"Yuck," the boy said.

Howard had made a special trip out through the snow for a selection of junk food and now felt a dark wrath well up from his stomach.

"Has anyone ever told you you've got the manners of a camel?"

This seemed to interest him. "A camel? No. Really?"

"Really."

"You mean because I said yuck? I'm sorry. I'm just a very spontaneous person."

"Yeah. Well, camels are very spontaneous too. You can hold it in a little. It won't kill you. That's what manners are for."

"I never thought of it that way."

Howard sighed. "Would you like to sit down?"

"Not really. I'd like to look around a little."

"Go ahead."

The young man did so, starting at one corner and sweeping his gaze up and down the walls until he'd made a complete circuit of the room. Then he walked over to a walnut sideboard that stood against the south wall. Howard winced as he opened the glass-paneled doors; he felt a special protectiveness for the old monstrosity, because Ada had had it from her grandmother and considered it a family heirloom. In their old apartment, it had contained a set of Haviland china. When Howard moved to the smaller apartment after Ada's death, he sold the china, knowing he'd have no use for it. Now the sideboard held Howard's collection of limp, dog-eared paperbacks.

Richard scanned the titles blank-faced and closed the doors. When he went on to open the drawer below, Howard asked him what the hell he was doing.

The boy looked up, puzzled. "I'm looking around. You said I could."

It was the junk drawer, containing whatever didn't belong somewhere else: household tools, a flashlight, old address books, calendars, receipts, and bank statements, lapsed insurance policies, a worn-out wallet, a Hamilton watch broken for two decades, a Smith &

Wesson revolver (never fired or even loaded) that his brother-in-law
had given him on his twenty-fifth birthday.

Howard breathed a furious sigh as the boy began paging his way
through an old photo album to which no pictures had been added
since 1967, when Ada learned she would never have children.

After putting the album back and closing the drawer, he crossed
the room to survey the library books Howard kept on a chest of
drawers beside his bed.

"Don't you read anything but trash?"

"No," Howard snapped.

He opened the top drawer and Howard said, "That's just clothes."

Richard nodded and went on to grope his way through each
drawer while Howard watched, grinding his teeth.

"Nothing," he said finally, straightening up from the bottom
drawer.

"What were you expecting?"

"A ping or two."

"A ping?"

The boy shrugged as if anyone with half a brain should know
what a ping is.

"Would you like to sit down now?"

He looked around uneasily, as if the furniture might be infected
with typhus, then sat in an upholstered chair Ada had bought at Mar-
shall Field's twenty years before.

"Did Ms. Purcell tell you what I'm looking for?" Howard asked,
sitting down across from him.

"Yes."

"Well, what do you think?"

"What do I *think*?"

Howard stifled a groan. "Do you have any *suggestions* for me?"

"Not at the moment. I've sort of lost track of what's going on."

"I don't understand."

"I mean, this is *really* a bad time. My folks are trying to railroad
me into the University of Chicago, and I'm—"

"Excuse me, Richard. Is it all right if I call you Richard?"

"Sure, why not? If I can call you Harold."

"Howard."

"Howard. Sorry."

"Richard, a minute ago you said you'd lost track of what was going on. Going on where?"

"Well, with the people you're interested in."

"And which people are those?"

Richard gave him a baffled look. "Now *I* don't understand."

Howard paused, sensing that this was one of those moments when everything could go to hell if he put a foot wrong. "When you know what's going on—when you're keeping track—what is it you know?"

"Oh." The boy waved his hands in the air. "Movements. Where the nexus is going to be. Where the heat is. You know."

"No, Richard, to be truthful, I don't."

Bewildered, Richard sent his gaze around the room as if he were following the flight of a bat. "You really are confusing me, Howard. You talked to Denise, didn't you?"

"Yes."

"Then I don't get it. She said you were looking to get in with the yoo-hoos."

"The *what?*"

Richard sprang up out of his chair quivering. "Look, don't do this to me. You're freaking me out. Really."

"I'm sorry, Richard. But who the hell are the yoo-hoos?"

The boy groaned, grabbed two handfuls of hair, and tried to twist his head off. "Ohhh, that Denise! I'm going to kill her. I'm absolutely going to kill her!"

"Take it easy, son."

"Where's your phone? I'm going to give her such a *blast!*"

"Not right now, Richard, please. Sit down and tell me what this is all about."

"It's about a goddamned *betrayal*, that's what it's about." But he sat down calmly enough.

"So who are the yoo-hoos?"

"I see what she's trying to do, all right. She told me you were a stone, of course, but I took it for granted that she would have explained all this. This is her idea of a test."

"She told you I was a stone?"

"That's just our slang. A stone is someone who's only aware in the usual way."

"You mean not a clairvoyant."

"I consider that a bullshit word, personally."

"Okay. And where does that leave us?"

He sighed. "I guess it leaves us here, Howard: I spend ten minutes telling you about the yoo-hoos, then you tell me I'm a fruitcake, then I go home."

"I won't do that, Richard, I promise you."

"I'm leaving."

"Hold on. Think about this for a second. I went to your friend Denise to—"

"Ex-friend."

"To learn something. That's straight. I went to her to learn something and I went with an open mind. And she said you could help me. Give me the benefit of a doubt, okay? I didn't ask her about yoo-hoos, because I've never even heard of a yoo-hoo. If she told you to tell me about yoo-hoos—"

"She didn't say to tell you about them. She said you wanted to get *in* with them. In which case you're a lunatic."

Howard spread his hands in a pathetic gesture. "There, you see? You're afraid I might call you a bad name, and then you call *me* a bad name. But look: Am I bleeding? I can take it, Richard. I'm not made of sugar and neither are you. So relax."

The boy frowned, obviously muddled by this weird appeal.

"Look," Howard went on, "according to Denise, I want to get in with these yoo-hoos. Should I argue with that? I don't even know what it means, for God's sake. At least tell me what it means!"

"I just *call* them yoo-hoos," Richard replied sullenly. "That's just my name for them."

"Go on."

"I'll *get* her for this."

"Go on, Richard. Please."

"Okay. Goddammit. Here's the way it is: Not all the people on the bus are *human* people."

Howard blinked. "What are they then?"

"Yoo-hoos."

"And what is a yoo-hoo?"

"One of the people on the bus who isn't human."

"That isn't much help, Richard."

"I don't know what else to tell you."

"Well . . . where do they come from?"

"From the same place the rest of us come from."

"What do you mean?"

"I mean they're natives. They belong here just the way we do."

"How can you tell that?"

"From the way they act."

"How do they act?"

"Just like everybody else."

"What do they look like?"

Richard eyed him with disgust. "What do you think I'm going to say? That they're pink with little green antennae growing out of their heads?"

"No, I'm just trying to find out how to recognize them."

"*You* can't recognize them. *I* can. They look just like everybody else. Sometimes they dress a little different, but you wouldn't notice that unless you know who they are."

"Okay. And how do *you* recognize them?"

"Different ping. Different resonance entirely. It's very obvious, really, like the difference between crystal and mud."

"They have a resonance like mud?"

"It's like mud to *me*—thick, heavy. Impenetrable."

"How many of them are there?"

"I have no idea."

"Well, how many have you seen?"

"You mean in my whole life? I don't know. Maybe a thousand. I've never kept track."

Howard thought for a moment. "You said you see them on buses. *Only* on buses?"

"On buses, on the street, in cars. You never see them in museums or book shops or movie theaters. You never see them at football games or concerts or plays. At least *I* haven't. I've seen them at restaurants a few times. They're usually on the move."

"Where are they going?"

"Where they go. To the next nexus. To the next hot spot."

"I don't understand."

"Well, look. A year ago people from all over the world—I mean *human* people—were converging on Barcelona. Maybe the yoo-hoos wondered why."

"Why were people converging on Barcelona?"

"For the 1992 summer Olympics, of course."

"Ah." Howard nodded sluggishly, feeling lost. "And what are you saying about the yoo-hoos?"

"That they converge too. When something's going on in their circle."

"Something such as what?"

"Such as I don't know what. Something as relevant to them as the Olympics are to us."

"I see. And you know where they're converging?"

"I usually have a pretty good idea. If I'm paying attention."

"How can you tell?"

"It's hard to explain. Have you ever had the experience of learning a new word and then seeing it in the next thing you read?"

"I don't recall."

"It's called synchronicity. Once when I was little I went to a movie with my folks and someone in it used the word *pedantic*. I asked what it meant and they told me. And the next day I read it in a book. I'm sure I'd never seen it before. That's happened to me lots of times. Denise says it's a common experience."

"So? "

"So this is a little like that. It isn't really, but it's a *little* like it. I'll be sitting there doing my homework or something and I'll think, 'Oh, it's southern Missouri this time. Something's happening in southern Missouri.' Then when I look back, I see there were a lot of little signs. Somebody talking in an accent I'd never heard before. A story in the newspaper. Something written on a wall in the subway. A matchbook cover left on a lunch counter. A song on the radio."

"And you mean these things are about southern Missouri? The matchbook cover? The song on the radio?"

Richard squirmed uncomfortably in his chair. "No, not really. None of them may have anything to *do* with southern Missouri. But they *add up* to southern Missouri." He shrugged. "It's hard to explain."

"I believe it. Why do you call them yoo-hoos, by the way?"

"Oh." He looked away, embarrassed. "I don't remember why I started calling them that. Denise says it's reverse magic: they're the people you *don't* say 'yoo-hoo' to."

"You've never talked to them?"

"God, no."

"Why not?"

"I just wouldn't care to."

"Do they seem dangerous?"

"Not exactly. The ping says, 'Keep off.'"

"I see. And what do other people do—the stones? Do the stones keep off?"

"Generally, but not always. The yoo-hoos seem to like talking to the stones. Sometimes. When *they* want to."

"But they don't talk to you."

"No, we ignore each other completely."

"I see. . . . And what does Denise call the yoo-hoos?"

"She calls them yoo-hoos."

"She sees them herself?"

"Everyone *sees* them, Howard. They're not invisible."

"I mean, can she pick them out?"

"No."

"What does she think they are?"

The question seemed to bewilder him. "I don't know."

"What do *you* think they are?"

Richard stared at him as if the question were in a foreign language. "What do you think water buffalo are, Howard? What do you think palm trees are?"

"I don't understand your question."

"I don't understand yours either."

"Let me ask it another way. Do you think the yoo-hoos are demons?"

Richard's eyebrows shot up toward his hairline. "Good God. And what are demons, exactly?"

"Well, I don't know."

"Neither do I."

Howard sank back in his chair, suddenly overwhelmed by an illumination so powerful that it had come to him almost as a physical blow. He looked at the boy and groaned, though he didn't hear himself doing it. His eyes closed and he listened, appalled, to the questions he'd been asking for the past half hour. He knew then that the revelation was no deception: *money is a mind-killing drug as surely as alcohol or heroin.* Like those drugs, it does worse: it rots character, it undermines all integrity. For half an hour Howard Scheim had been gravely—even aggressively—interrogating someone about *yoo-hoos.* Because, in order to fulfill a senile fantasy, an old fool in Evanston was drooling *money.*

He had never before tasted the nauseating bile of self-loathing, and he wondered now if he'd ever be able to get it out of his mouth.

He gradually became aware that Richard was squeaking and hopping around in front of him like a puppet on strings. He looked up and asked him what was wrong.

"My God! You scared me to death! Are you all right? I thought you were having a heart attack. You went completely *white!*"

"I'm all right," Howard said wearily. "It wasn't a heart attack, it was an integrity attack. It's okay."

"Look, I'm sorry if I came on like a smart-ass. Honest to God, I don't know how to answer the questions you're asking me."

"Be at peace, Richard. It's not your fault, not at all your fault. The questions were stupid questions."

"Well, I don't know about that," the boy protested gallantly and added, "Can I get you something?"

"No, I'm really all right."

"I was ready to start giving you CPR."

Howard smiled weakly.

"Look, I'll keep my eyes open, okay? You want me to do that?"

"You mean to find the yoo-hoos' next nexus?" He had the feeling that, at this point, it would take more energy to call the boy off than to let him go ahead. "Sure," he said. "That'll be fine, Richard."

CHAPTER 7

Dear Aaron:

I'm enclosing a check for $19,648, which represents the balance of the $20,000 you advanced to me a few days ago, after expenses (see receipts attached) and a fee based on two days of work on the matter we discussed (see invoice attached).

Ordinarily I would include a detailed account of my activities on your behalf (and I will provide one if you wish), but I'm hoping you'll take my word for it that these activities simply demonstrated the complete futility of pursuing this investigation.

I know you must be asking yourself how two days of work could possibly be adequate to

Howard ripped the letter in two, wadded the pieces into a ball, and threw it across the room.

It was grotesque. Having gotten into the goddamned investigation, he couldn't honestly get out of it—not after spending less than four hours on it. To bow out after two brief conversations would be patently unprofessional, and he had no doubt that Aaron would emphatically agree. And he'd do more than agree. He'd see it as an insult, as a mark of contempt for him, his friendship, and his big idea. And Aaron was not the sort of man to overlook an insult—far from it. He'd quietly let it be known at the club that, fine fellow though he may be, Howard was not a man to be trusted in a matter of business. By quitting the job at this point, Howard would be throwing away not only the largest fee of his career but a part of his life that had become very valuable to him.

There was only one way to come out of the fiasco in one piece. He had to turn the whole thing around and look at it a different way. The task was obviously impossible as Aaron had defined it. Howard would therefore redefine it. He would take it as his goal to prove that Aaron's question was *beyond investigation*. This was a task he could undertake with complete conviction and without sacrificing his self-respect. Aaron wouldn't be overjoyed by the results, but, if Howard did the job properly, how could he reasonably quarrel with them?

After a month's work, Howard would present him with a tome. A ten-thousand-dollar bundle of nonsense assembled in a thoroughly professional way, complete with warnings from the Tarot cards, admonitions from the Bible, and the muddy ping of yoo-hoos.

Sunday Howard spent writing summaries of his conversations with Denise Purcell and Richard Holloway. These established a pattern for his report.

On Monday he made a few phone calls, one of which led to an appointment for Tuesday, and then went downtown to purchase a high-quality miniaturized tape recorder. He debated whether to consider this an expense and decided he would; after all, he'd managed for forty years without such a device and wouldn't have bought it except for Aaron's job.

That night around midnight, in a small city eighty miles southeast of Chicago, twelve-year-old Tim Kennesey got out of bed and stood for a moment with his head cocked, as if tracking a distant sound. Then he left the bedroom and walked down the hall past the bathroom, kitchen, and dining room.

As he passed the living room headed for the front door, his mother looked up from her book and said, "Hey, kiddo, where do you think *you're* going?"

The boy didn't seem to hear her. He was unlocking the door when she caught up with him. Holding the door closed, she asked him what he was doing.

He looked up at her vaguely as if unable to place her face. "Some-one outside," he mumbled. "Wants me."

"You're sleep-walking, Tim," the woman said gently. He went on gazing at her without expression. "There's no one outside. Go back to bed."

He blinked at her dully for a moment, then turned and obediently marched back to his bedroom.

When she told him about it in the morning over breakfast, he was astonished and more than a little delighted.

"I wonder where I was going?" he said.

"Nowhere," his father snapped, immediately regretting his tone. The boy's somnambulistic adventure had stirred some dim memory in him—all he knew was that it was something he didn't want to think about—and he felt he was beginning the day on the wrong foot.

His son and his wife looked at him with a mixture of wariness and pity.

He'd been in an odd mood all winter, suffering some obscure distress he could neither hide nor explain.

CHAPTER 8

Tuesday, March 23

INTERVIEW: Rabbi Charles Weigand (Temple Shomrei Torah); very serious young man, mid-thirties. Listened attentively to the end, though obviously upset by what he was hearing. Relevant remarks (from tape):

"Really, I have to say that this is the most frivolous conversation I've ever been drawn into. I frankly have to question your good faith in asking for an appointment. . . . Frivolity in such a matter and to this degree approaches blasphemy. I cannot condone or encourage an inquiry of the sort you're engaged in, and I seriously question the mental health of your client. To seek out these gods—to actively try to put yourself in their way—is to acknowledge them, is in fact to worship them. . . . I certainly don't consider myself an old-fashioned or prudish man, but what you're proposing to do strikes me as irreligious, to say the least. . . . I certainly do not know of anyone who could be helpful to you, and if I did I couldn't in good conscience give you their names. . . . I'm sorry to have to say that I wish you no luck at all in this enterprise."

Wednesday & Thursday, March 24 & 25

INTERVIEWS: Various personnel, Archdiocese of Chicago; my presence at the archdiocesan offices—and particularly my persistence in trying to find someone who would talk to me—obviously created a lot of dismay. Finally, when I made it clear I wasn't leaving without some kind of answer to my questions, I was presented with a Fr. McClane, position not specified, who told me:

> "Mr. Scheim, as I understand it, you're not claiming to have any official standing or any official business here. Is that right? You're not here, for example, as a representative of the government, not an officer of the court, not delegated to speak to us from some educational institution we've agreed to cooperate with."

I told him I wasn't.

> "Then obviously what you're looking for is someone to sit down and chat unofficially with you about the matters you're interested in. Believe me, Mr. Scheim, that's simply not going to happen. Even if you hang around here for the next six months, it's not going to happen. If what you're interested in is the Church's official position on these matters, I can have someone in my office prepare a reading list for you, and, believe me, it'll be a good one. That's the very best I can do for you. [In answer to a request for a referral to someone who would talk to me unofficially:] I'm sorry, I couldn't give you such a referral. Officially I can't and unofficially I won't."

Monday, March 29

INTERVIEW: Fr. Ralph Whitte, editor-in-chief, *Greystone*, a scholarly journal founded to serve as a forum for liberal-conservative debate within the Church. Fr. Whitte was recommended to me as a very open-minded and knowledgeable person with a broad background in Church and religious matters, and he impressed me as such. Relevant remarks (from tape):

"I'm not surprised you got that reaction [at the archdiocesan offices]. I'd've been astonished if you'd gotten any other. The point Fr. McClane was making is very relevant. This is a case in which the Church's official stance is something of an embarrassment. You see, officially, the Church endorses all sorts of folk-beliefs that the clergy and the educated laity either never took seriously or abandoned long ago. In some cases the endorsement is quite explicit, in others it's more or less by default—meaning it's something the church winces at a little bit but doesn't want to disavow outright. It can't officially rescind these endorsements without appearing foolish—but it doesn't like to be put in the position of officially endorsing the endorsements either, if you see what I mean.

"For example, I'd say that nowadays only the very naive believe—in a serious, literal way—that the world is infested with demons who lurk about putting naughty ideas into our heads. But this is still what many Catholics teach their children, having learned it as children themselves, and no one's leaping up to denounce it, simply because we have much more serious—vastly more serious—problems to solve in the modern church. Do you see what I mean?

"I guess what I'm saying in part is that your client's question isn't so much a foolish one as it is a severely unfashionable one. Did the old pagan gods become the demons of modern times? To a present-day theologian, this question wouldn't even be worth a sneer. But, since I'm a generalist and not a theologian, I've done some reading in this area and I don't mind sharing what little I know.

"Since the 1920s, it's been fashionable in occult circles to believe that the rites of modern witchcraft can be traced back in an unbroken line to the pagan rites of pre-Christian times. What this would mean, if it were so, is that the witches of the Middle Ages were cruelly misunderstood. They weren't worshiping the wicked horned god Satan, they were worshiping that benevolent old pagan horned god Pan. It's an appealing theory, but it bears almost no relation to historical reality.

"It's perfectly true, of course, that the worship of the old pagan gods survived long after Europe was presumably Christianized. Jupiter, Minerva, Venus, Diana, Pan, and the others were old, old friends, particularly to the peasants, who saw no conflict between them and Christ. After all, it was just as the priests said: the old gods were gods of this world, while Christ was the god of the other world. But the church had no intention of allowing this to go on. The old gods had to go. The psychologically smart move would have been to Christianize them as angels. Instead, in a terrible blunder, the church Christianized them as devils, hoping to blacken them in the peasants' imagination. But instead of blackening the old gods what they did was whiten devils. You see, the peasants had known these gods as benevolent protectors for thousands of years. These were gods who looked after the fertility of their fields and their herds—things that were obviously beneath the notice of the austere and remote Christ. So, if the old gods were devils, then devils really couldn't be all that bad, could they? In other words, instead of making pagan worship abhorrent, the church simply made devil worship an ordinary, almost respectable, part of life.

"Having failed to get the peasantry to recoil in horror from the old gods by calling them devils, the church went on to promulgate a new teaching that was sure to make them recoil in horror. These devils who were the pagan gods were servants of evil incarnate: of Satan. Note well: merely servants. Compared to Satan, the old gods were practically nothing. But Satan was very nearly as powerful as God himself—so powerful they didn't hesitate to name him Prince of the World. If you put yourself in

Satan's hands, they said, he would and could do almost anything for you. He could make you as wealthy as a baron or as powerful as a king. He could defend you against your enemies and wreak vengeance on your oppressors—and the peasants had plenty of those. All he expected in return was your immortal soul. Now note that these weren't heretical doctrines or backwoods superstitions. These were mainstream teachings of the Church, and the Church didn't just teach them, it insisted on them. Well, you can imagine the peasants' reaction to this news. Far from being horrified, they said, 'Just exactly how do we go about getting in touch with this paragon of gods?' Naturally enough, the old pagan gods were completely forgotten in the stampede to get next to Satan. Why deal with Jupiter and Minerva and Pan when you could deal with the boss himself?

"In order to kill off paganism, the church—in one of the greatest promotional campaigns of all time—succeeded in converting the peasantry of Europe to Satanism. Then, of course, they had to spend the next four or five centuries killing off Satanism. On the whole, it was a tragic and colossal fiasco, but it did achieve the original goal. By the end of the Middle Ages, the old pagan gods had been completely obliterated from popular memory. But this is the point you're really interested in: by the end of the Middle Ages, the god of the witches had been for literally centuries the monstrous and malevolent horned god Satan—nothing whatever to do with jolly old Pan, long forgotten, along with all his brothers and sisters.

"So where does that leave you, Mr. Scheim? You can certainly find modern witches who will tell you that their god is Pan or one of the others. But if they tell you the rituals they use to summon him have been received in an unbroken tradition from ancient times, they're either lying or deluded."

CHAPTER 9

One of his contacts told him "there was something about witchcraft in the paper last fall," and this was the strongest lead Howard got during the first two weeks of April. Three dozen calls had yielded the names of four "practicing witches" and one warlock, but that's all they were—names. Three of them were obviously assumed and the other two couldn't be attached to anyone who had a phone, owned property, or paid taxes.

Desperate to find a way into the circle, he consulted an advertised psychic, who offered to balance his aura but had no information about witches. He tracked down a woman on the south side who was said to cast spells for friends, but she claimed this was just "natural magic"; when it came to worship, she was a Baptist. He talked to an anthropologist at Northwestern who became indignant. Finally, with nothing left but "something about witchcraft in the paper last fall," he went to the library. It took him two days to dig it out. It was the November 2nd issue of the *Tribune* under the headline "Legislative brew brings witches to the boil." The U.S. Senate had passed an appropriations bill that included an amendment that would deny tax-exempt status to witchcraft groups and Satanic cults. The bill was currently in committee in the House. A witch in Albuquerque protested that witchcraft shouldn't be lumped in with Satanism. "Our witchcraft," she was quoted as saying, "is a pagan religion, which comes from the

Latin word *paganus,* meaning 'of the country.' It's an ancient religion, a folk religion."

Also quoted was a Chicago warlock, Joel Bailey, a somber, bearded man with dark, wavy hair and a short, blunt nose. "The effect of the bill would be to sort out religions into 'government approved' and 'government non-approved.' In other words, it would put the government in the position of saying which religions are established and which aren't. I always had the impression that this was precisely the sort of thing the founders of our country had in mind when they wrote in the first amendment that 'Congress shall make no law respecting an establishment of religion.'" The story went on: "Bailey makes no bones about being a Satanist, but adds 'probably fewer than a thousand people in the country know what that really means.'"

Joel Bailey was in the phone book, with an address on Commercial, just east of State Street. Since it was only a few minutes away from the library, Howard decided to have a look. The building was a warehouse converted into artists' studios and apartments. That they were probably very expensive apartments was demonstrated by the outer hall, with its spotless tile floor, grass-cloth covered walls, and brass and steel mailboxes. Bailey's was the only name listed on the sixth floor—the top floor—which meant either that he had an enormous space or no neighbors. He gave the button a push.

"Yes?"

"Is this Mr. Joel Bailey?"

"Yes."

"My name is Howard Scheim. I wonder if I could talk to you for a few minutes. I'm not selling anything or collecting for anything."

"Talk to me about what?"

Howard paused and decided that, if Bailey made no bones about it, why should he?

"Satanism."

"I see. . . . Are you a reporter?"

"No."

"If you are, you'll just be a wasting your time."

"I'm not, Mr. Bailey."

"All right. Wait there. It'll be a few minutes."

The bearded warlock sized up Howard carefully before coming through the inner door. He might well have been daunted by Howard's size, since he was only a few inches over five feet, but if so he didn't show it. He was wearing a suede windbreaker, jeans, and black patent-leather loafers.

"There's a place around the corner where we can get some coffee," he said, not offering his hand.

"That'll be fine."

"I know it must seem uncivil not to ask you up," Bailey said a few minutes later when they were sitting down, "but I've become wary of getting cornered in my own apartment by people I can't get rid of."

"I understand."

"So what's on your mind?" he asked in a tone that wasn't meant to be too encouraging.

Howard explained what he was doing, summarized his inquiries to date, and, since Bailey seemed interested, described his conversation with the editor of *Greystone* in detail. The warlock listened to the last with a crooked smile.

"I've met Whitte," he said when Howard finished. "A bright man, though his understanding of history is a bit constrained by his training."

"You don't agree with his analysis?"

He shrugged indifferently. "It misses the point. Besides, if you accept his analysis, why are you talking to me?"

"I'm groping, Mr. Bailey, and I don't necessarily swallow Whitte's theory whole. It makes sense, but I've heard a lot of things in my life that made sense but weren't so." Bailey smiled sourly as if this were something he himself was fond of saying and Howard had plagiarized it.

"So," Howard said after a few moments of silence, "what do you think?"

The other's smile brightened to a kind of cynical innocence. "What do I think?"

"Can you help me?"

Bailey slid a black enamel case from his jacket pocket and thoughtfully withdrew a cigarette, which he lit with a matching lighter. "I can only do what I do, Mr. Scheim. Whether it helps will be for you to decide."

"Go on, please."

"Mr. Scheim, I'm sure you must realize that you're not unique in coming to me. People come to me for all sorts of things. For a giggle, for a jolt, for a kick. Some come simply out of boredom. Some come out of idle curiosity. Some come out of desperation. Some, like you, come in a spirit of inquiry. To all I give exactly the same thing. Some are disappointed. Some get exactly what they expected. Some get vastly more than they expected. Some are deeply moved. Some are deeply shocked. Some leave exalted. Some leave defeated. But for all I do the same."

He tapped a bit of ash into an ashtray.

"There is a procedure," he said.

"Okay."

"For you to come to one of our initiates' rites would be too much for you. You would be overwhelmed and would misunderstand the things going on around you. You must first be guided through the ritual in slow motion, as it were, with each step fully explained. During this orientation phase, which we call the postulancy, it's all made very easy for you; we do virtually all the work and simply invite you to participate. Many find the postulancy is enough for them and remain at this level indefinitely. Others who feel capable of participating more fully enter the novitiate after a few weeks or months, if we feel they're ready for it. And again, usually after a period of a year or more, some who feel capable of participating at the profoundest level go on to become initiates. There are also levels within each level. For example, I wouldn't want you to begin with an experienced group of postulants but rather with someone exactly like yourself, someone going through it for the very first time."

Howard nodded.

"As it happens, a young woman has been waiting for several weeks for someone else to join her. I should be able to set something in train for the two of you within a week. Is there any night that is not convenient for you?"

"No. I'm free anytime."

He handed Howard a business card. "Dr. Holland examines all new candidates. I'm sure you understand the precaution. We have to be careful."

"I understand."

"Upon entering the postulancy, a donation of one thousand dollars is usual. Thereafter attendance at any rite is usually accompanied by a donation of two hundred dollars. You can mail a check to the address on Commercial. All donations—for the moment at least—are tax-deductible." He stabbed out his cigarette and favored Howard with a twisted smile, as if he didn't expect to be believed. "Many have told me they've spent more on psychotherapy with less satisfactory results."

"Uh huh," Howard said.

Later that afternoon Aaron called to ask if Howard had abandoned the club.

"No, not exactly. I guess I haven't been feeling very sociable."

"I hope that's not my fault," Aaron said.

It was, but Howard saw no point in saying so. "As a matter of fact, I was thinking of dropping in tonight."

"Good."

"But, Aaron . . . I don't want to talk about this thing yet, okay? I'm not ready to give you a progress report. I'm making progress, but it'll be a week or two."

"Howard, you should know me better. Did I tell you to hustle?"

"No."

"Don't worry about it then. We'll talk when you're ready."

Howard went to the club but found he couldn't really relax with Aaron there hovering in the background. He drank a little too much and decided that, when this was over, he'd never again accept a fellow member as a client.

Later, changing into his pajamas, he realized he was in a very bleak mood. It had nothing to do with Aaron, the club, or the job he was doing, and it took him a few minutes to figure out what it was: He didn't want to go to sleep.

On the verge of unconsciousness, he was nevertheless reluctant to commit his head to the pillow. A strange state of affairs, because, for Howard, sleeping wasn't just something he did when he was too tired to go on; he took an active pleasure in it—looked forward to it. But he wasn't looking forward to it tonight.

Because of that goddamned *dog*.

For the past three or four nights his sleeping hours had been haunted by an enormous black dog that padded endlessly through the dark streets of Chicago. Not exactly a dog: a dog with the face of a bull.

It was sniffing him out.

There was something obscene about the thing. Its inky sleekness wasn't that of fur but of slime. It was mindless, relentless, unstoppable. It didn't frighten him; it sickened him, exhausted him. He hoped it would leave him alone tonight.

But it didn't.

CHAPTER 10

The elevator doors opened at the sixth floor of the Commercial Street building, and Howard stepped out into a dimly lit, high-ceilinged room twice the size of his apartment.

"Good evening. Thanks so much for being prompt."

Howard scanned the ceiling but was unable to spot the speaker from which Joel Bailey's voice issued.

"Please proceed to the black door and go in."

Following these instructions, he entered a long corridor lined with doors on either side. This was even more dimly lit, though a single green light glowed some twenty yards down the hallway.

"Please proceed to the door indicated by the green light and go in."

The voice seemed to be directly overhead and stayed with him as he walked. "You may, by the way, speak at any time, Mr. Scheim. I will hear you."

Opening the door under the green light, Howard found himself in a dressing room about ten feet square. One wall was paneled in mirrors. Along the other ran a counter with four chairs facing large make-up mirrors. The counter was cluttered with powders, scents, "There's a coat rack beside the door. Sit down and let's talk for a moment.

"My name in these rooms is Verdelet. I shall address you as Howard unless there is some other name you'd prefer."

"That's fine," Howard muttered.

"Behind the mirrored wall you'll find a closet with a selection of costumes, most of them simply loose-fitting gowns and caftans. You'll be much more comfortable tonight without the constraints Western fashion imposes on us."

"I can't just wear my street clothes?"

"You can, of course, Howard. Every choice is yours. But I should point out that your partner for the evening has chosen a sumptuous gown of embroidered green silk. If you join her in ordinary street clothes, you will both feel awkward, and this would be distracting for you."

"True."

"In the bathroom you'll find a disposable razor and toothbrush, should you wish to use them. Shave, shower, make yourself feel your best—if you so choose. The makeup is there for your use, if that strikes your fancy. All the areas you'll be visiting are carpeted and warm. There are slippers and sandals, or you may prefer to go barefoot. There's no rush. I believe your partner is bathing now. You are, by the way, completely alone there, completely private. There are no hidden video cameras, no peepholes, no see-through mirrors. Be at ease. Prepare yourself for a sensually and spiritually fulfilling experience."

Three quarters of an hour later, Howard was dressed in sandals and a midnight-blue cashmere caftan that he thought suited him very well. Following Bailey's directions, he left the dressing room and followed a trail of orange ceiling lights that led him to a pair of red-lacquered doors. At a touch, these swung open onto a scene from the Arabian Nights. Gauzy drapes in opalescent pastels floated down from the ceiling through colored spotlights and the reflections from several mirrored revolving balls. The drapes served to divide the room into intimate areas carpeted with oriental rugs piled four or five deep and mounded with cushions around low, candle-lit tables. The air had an unidentifiable earthy scent, a cross between new-mown grass and burning leaves. It pulsed with a low beat of exotic music just at the threshold of hearing.

At the center of the room was a stone-lined pit five feet square, filled with kindling and sprinkled with what looked like alfalfa; the exhaust hood that hovered over it had been draped so that it resembled an oriental tent suspended in the air. Beside the pit, a ramp led up to a tall door at the left. At the far end of the room stood a small platform surmounted by a white-draped altar. A pair of doors behind it swung open and, at a distance of some forty feet, Howard watched a slender woman in a green gown step hesitantly into the room.

"Come in, Leslie," Bailey's voice purred overhead. "Your companion for the evening is waiting for you." She looked up at Howard and her eyes widened.

"Howard, go to her. She seems uneasy."

His mouth went dry as he moved forward.

"My children, let nothing trouble you. You're both safe. Nothing terrible is going to happen here, I assure you."

Howard and the woman paused, facing each other across the wood-filled stone pit.

"Come, Howard, summon up your gallantry. Go to her and take her hand. Leslie, my dear, don't look so thunderstruck. All is well. Lift up your hand and offer it to him. Good, good."

The look on her face as he approached was one of white terror, and her trembling fingers settled on his like a glitter of butterflies.

Howard lowered his head and whispered, "Don't worry."

"Come, come, children. Relax. Be at ease. Howard, take Leslie to one of the tables. Good. All is well. Please make yourselves comfortable."

They sank awkwardly into the cushions around a table, and he saw that she was barefoot. She drew her legs up under her, covering her feet. To Howard, she seemed very young, perhaps twenty-five. Her face, under loosely-waved auburn hair, was fragile rather than beautiful, with delicate nose and cheekbones, a tiny chin, and the kind of overbite he'd always found endearing. Her makeup was romantic and carefully applied to accentuate her huge dark eyes.

"Speak, Howard. Give tongue."

He swallowed doubtfully. "You look very lovely, Leslie."

"Excellent. Well done. Now, Leslie. Your turn."

She opened her mouth and her lower lip trembled.

"Speak!"

"You ... Ah ..."

"Look like an escapee from a horror movie," Howard suggested gently.

She pressed her lips together in a timid smile. "No. You look like . . . a kind man."

"I think of myself as a kind man."

"Splendid!" Bailey intoned. "Délices, you may enter now. These children are finally speaking to each other."

The doors through which Leslie had entered opened again, and a young woman in a light, almost transparent white gown flowed in carrying a brass tray suspended from three chains that came together in her hand. She served them two cups of tea and two snifters half filled with amber liquid, then straightened and bowed, loose honey-colored hair cascading over her shoulders.

She was easily the most beautiful woman Howard had ever seen in the flesh, her face classically perfect, her lips a velvety red-orange.

"This is Délices," Bailey said. "She is your servant, your mother, and the priestess of our rite. Please make our children welcome, Délices."

She knelt beside Leslie, kissed her hand, and then embraced her and delicately kissed her on the mouth.

"I bid you welcome," she said in a low, silky voice.

She turned to Howard, kissed his hand, and put her lips softly to his. Without moving away, she looked into his eyes with the grave innocence of a cat and murmured, "I bid you welcome."

His mouth filled with saliva and his member stirred.

She rose gracefully, bowed, and left.

"Do try to relax, my dears. You look like you're waiting for the hangman."

Howard and Leslie settled fractionally deeper into their cushions.

"That's better. Now, to the liquids before you. The cups contain an herbal tea, a mild hallucinogen. It isn't intended to befuddle you or excite you to visions or to put you into a delusional state but merely to loosen somewhat the censorious grip our culture tells us we must maintain on ourselves at all times. It is of course your choice to accept it or not. Its effects are of brief duration, and of all the hundreds who have sampled it, none has ever reported any disagreeable side effect. If you accept it, I recommend you drink it off all at once."

He paused. Howard and Leslie exchanged a shrug and picked up the cups.

"Good. We've found that the other drink, which is Benedictine, is an effective antidote to the bitterness of the tea. Now I want you to close your eyes and listen to me. Only to me: Don't listen to the doubts and anxieties that have been distressing you. Make them be still. Give yourselves up to my voice as if it were the voice of your own thoughts.

"Now let me tell you this. When I met with you in the guise of Joel Bailey, I was gruff, unwelcoming, and cold. I displayed no interest in you as persons, asked you nothing about your hopes or desires. This was deliberate. I didn't want to charm you into pursuing your interest here. I wanted you to wrestle all alone with your misgivings. I wanted you to find *entirely within yourselves* the courage to risk this step into the unknown, because courage is a thing that pleases our lord above all else.

"Ah, I see that this surprises you. I say that courage is a thing that pleases our lord above all else—and you wonder what lord I can possibly mean. Surely I don't mean . . . *Satan*? Oh, who can speak his name and call him lord? Satan is the embodiment of evil, of all that is vile and foul and detestable. He is the central malignancy of the universe. And above all, he *hates* us. His unquenchable passion is to deceive us, pervert us, degrade us, and ultimately to win us for an eternity of torment. His delight is in our weakness—surely not in our courage!

"My children, I tell you these are lies. Lies promulgated through the ages by those who would make us slaves. These slave-masters don't want us to follow a lord who delights in courage. They tremble at courage, because courage is the virtue of the free. They want us instead to follow a lord who delights in submissiveness, the virtue of slaves. I'm sure you all know what lord I'm talking about—the lord these slave-masters would have us call lord.

"Behold! *There he is now!*"

They opened their eyes and saw a giant, white-robed mannequin lurch through the door and roll unsteadily down the ramp, flailing its arms and waving a shepherd's crook.

"Blessed are the meek!" it shrieked. "Blessed are the meek! Slaves, obey your masters! Deny yourselves! Follow me! I am meek and humble of heart!"

Rocking at the bottom of the ramp, the figure thumped the floor with its crook and screeched, "I am the good shepherd, and ye are my sheep! Sheep! Be as sheep! Blessed are the meek! Blessed are the sheep! Blessed are the—"

It shuddered to a halt, its arm raised in mid-thump.

"Ah yes," Bailey murmured. "This is the lord beloved of the slave-masters. Can you believe that some liar put the words 'Be as little children' in this creature's mouth? How absurd! Children are never meek, unless someone has broken their spirits. They are forever saucy, forever daring, forever testing the limits of their world, forever casting themselves into reckless adventures.

"The Nazarene's followers have always known that he couldn't possibly have meant us to be as little children. He meant, 'Be as the elderly.' Be cautious, wary, judicious, decorous, grave. Oh yes, above all, be grave! Drain the sap of youth from your spirit. Chastise the flesh. Deny yourself. Stifle impulse. Censor your thoughts. Be on guard against feelings.

"Be as little children? Never! For behold, *this* is a child. . . ."

The doors at the end of the room flew open and Délices raced into the room, skipping with delight. She danced wildly around the

altar and around the stone pit, then, catching sight of the figure of
the Nazarene, stopped abruptly, her mouth falling open.

Gradually her look of astonishment was replaced by a roguish
grin. Lifting her feet high in a parody of caution, she began to sneak
forward. When she was directly in front of the mannequin, she
threw up her hands and shouted "Yah!"

The figure silently lifted an arm to cover its face.

She laughed and began a mad, cavorting dance.

"Délices!" Bailey commanded in a horrified voice. "Stop that this
instant!"

She stopped and looked up, stupefied.

"I've never seen anything so disgraceful in my life! What the *devil*
has gotten into you? Is that how a *lady* acts? Behave yourself!"

She rolled her eyes at Howard and Leslie, her lips turned down in
mocking contrition. With a shrug, she began trudging around in a
circle like a prisoner in an exercise yard. As she walked, she grabbed
the sides of her gown and began tugging them forward and backward in time with her strides. Gradually she quickened her pace and
narrowed the circle until she was whirling giddily in place, her arms
outstretched, her head back. At last she staggered and collapsed in a
giggling sprawl.

She lay for a minute gazing up into the air with a foolish smile,
then sighed. She hunched her shoulders, and a petulant look crossed
her face. Her gown had gotten twisted beneath her when she fell,
and she tried unsuccessfully to tug it back into place. She sat up and
gave it another tug, but it still wouldn't come free. Suddenly, with a
growl, she pulled it up and over her head and was free of it.

A terrible groan issued from the figure of the Nazarene.

The girl yawned, stretched, and lay down again, moving her
shoulders against the carpet as if she were scratching her back. For a
while she stared up at the ceiling. Then, as if of its own volition, her
right hand pulled free of the left. It performed its own little dance of
liberation in the air before coming back to rest on her stomach. Then
it stood up on its fingers and, with a little flourish, began walking. At

first it wandered aimlessly, then it paused thoughtfully and with an exaggerated air of stealth began to sneak down her belly.

The figure in white shuddered and moaned.

The hand straightened up, and Délices gave it the accompaniment of a little tuneless whistle as it sauntered, all innocence, down her leg. At mid-thigh it abruptly leaped into the air and seized her crotch.

"Gotcha!" Délices squealed.

"*For-bid-den!*" the Nazarene groaned.

"Délices!" Bailey gasped. "What are you *doing?*"

She leaped to her feet, hid the offending hand behind her, realized it was needed elsewhere for modesty's sake, but found that even two hands weren't enough for the job. She scrambled back into her gown.

"Wicked, wicked, *wicked* girl! Oh, truly you are a daughter of Eve!"

The figure of the Nazarene intoned: "If thy hand offends thee, cut it off!"

"Ah, my poor misguided child! Don't you realize that this touch—even the very *thought* of this touch—imperils your immortal soul, that it is death itself? Alas, idle hands! Idle hands that are the devil's playthings!"

Délices hung her head penitently but managed to sneak Howard and Leslie a rueful grin.

"My child, don't you know what you must do when vile temptation steals into your thoughts? You must say, 'Get behind me, Satan!' Come along now, let me hear you say it!"

Délices shrugged in disgust and mumbled some words.

"With *conviction!*" Bailey demanded.

"Get behind me, Satan!"

Just then a twisted, hairy tree trunk crashed to the floor behind Délices, setting her bounding off with a shriek and bringing Howard and Leslie up out of their cushions.

"Ah! There's the cursed monster himself! Behold his loathsome form! Behold the hideous visage of Satan!"

And hideous it was. It squatted, quivering and malevolent, its legs splayed to reveal a vast, deformed phallus. Leprous arms ending in claws of splintered wood reached out from a body shaggy with rotting moss. Its head, split in a vicious grin, was the head of a nightmare pig, with elongated snout, a mouth full of jagged teeth, and eyes ablaze with glee and rage.

"This, my children, is the lie," Bailey resumed in his normal tone. "Please sit down."

They returned to their places.

"Did you imagine that we worship a creature like this in our rite? Can you imagine that such a creature was ever worshiped? No, this is the lie—the lie told by a hundred generations of slave-masters. It is the lie in which the truth was *buried*."

The awful shape on the floor quivered and moaned and, with a crack like a pistol shot, split open.

"Look now, and see who it is our priestess brings forth!"

Délices stepped up to the crack in the tree trunk and drew out a hand covered in green leaves. A moment later a dark face peered out nervously. Catching sight of the figure in white, it quickly ducked back inside.

"Come forth, our Satanic lord, and reveal yourself in all your terror to these children!"

A young man with a dancer's body stepped out of the tree. It took a moment to realize he was naked; his body was everywhere painted with green leaves. He bowed to Howard and Leslie, then turned back to Délices and they embraced, their open mouths meeting tenderly.

The lights went out, and Leslie squeaked.

"Don't be alarmed, children. I've blinded you not to terrify but to enable you to listen better."

In the wavering candlelight Howard saw that Délices was kneeling beside them. In a clear, sober voice she said:

"Our worship of Satan isn't a worship of evil; it's a worship of affirmation. Our denial of Jesus isn't a denial of goodness; it's a denial of denial."

CHAPTER 11

When the lights came up again a few minutes later, Leslie and Howard saw that the figures of Jesus and Satan had been cleared away and that they were alone.

They exchanged a long, untroubled smile, and in a fit of sheer recklessness, he gave her an amiable nod, which she returned with an even broader smile. Of the awkwardness he would ordinarily feel lying beside a girl forty years his junior there was no trace, and he understood that this was the blessing of the drug. Looking into her eyes, he felt sure she realized that he was just like the grotesque figure of Satan that had crashed to the floor: inside his monstrous, aged hulk was hidden a vigorous and attractive young man capable of facing a ten-round bout without flinching, capable of running for hours without dropping in his tracks, capable of. . . .

He suddenly became aware of the music, which had risen by imperceptible degrees over the past few minutes. It had a smokey, exotic, Mideastern flavor, and he was listening with such concentration that it was a moment before he realized that Verdelet was speaking again.

". . . and for the sake of this, two elements of our rite are omitted tonight, one of them the traditional feast. You will participate in these when next you come. But, while we have omitted two, three remain, and these we would not omit on any account. Please join Robin and Délices at the altar."

As they got up, he continued. "You now approach the central mystery of our rite. And for tonight it is only an approach, simply the briefest of introductions."

Howard saw that Délices, once again naked, was lying on the altar. The young man who had emerged from the Satan tree, presumably Robin, now dressed in a leaf-patterned gown, was facing them from behind the altar.

"I've told you," Verdelet went on, "that Délices is the priestess of our rite. She is also the sacrificial offering and indeed the very altar upon which the sacrifice is offered. Please look at her."

They stood in front of the altar, Howard at her shoulder, Leslie at her waist. Délices, apparently unconscious of their presence, gazed upward, completely relaxed, hands at her sides.

"In the rite of the Nazarene, the offering is *Adam redeemed*: Adam redeemed by self-denial and mortification of the flesh. In our rite, the offering is *Eve redeemed*: Eve redeemed by self-acceptance and joyous gratification of the flesh."

Robin lifted his head and called out. "Eve! Where are you?"

"I am here, my lord."

He looked down at her, puzzled. "Why do I find you thus laid low?"

"I have been cast down from my place, my lord. My name has become a curse in the mouths of my children."

"And these wounds? What are these wounds I see upon your spirit?"

"My lord, I am burned by the brand of my sons' lust and pierced by the blade of my daughters' envy."

"Can this be so?"

"It is so, my lord."

The young man looked up and studied Howard and Leslie gravely.

"Howard, speak the truth. Have you burned this woman's spirit with the brand of your lust?"

Howard looked down at Délices and swallowed. "You mean . . . *this* woman?"

"Yes."

"Oh. Well. I thought . . . I'm not sure what you mean."

"Délices, has this man burned you?"

"Yes, my lord, he has burned me."

"Howard, Délices accuses you. Look into your heart and don't be afraid to tell me the truth. Is she mistaken? Have you burned her with the brand of your lust?"

"Yes, I guess I have."

"Howard, Verdelet has told you I value courage above all else. Be courageous now and answer me directly and without qualification. Have you burned this woman or not? If you haven't, don't say you have."

"God . . . I'm just not sure what you're talking about."

"Howard, embrace her."

"Embrace her?"

"Embrace her and we'll see if she's burned by your touch."

He turned helplessly to Leslie and asked her if she understood what they were saying.

"I think so," she said. "If you can't embrace her, then . . . yes."

"Leslie's right," Robin said. "You have indeed burned her with the brand of your lust. Can you withdraw the brand?"

Howard blinked at him. "I don't know. How?"

"Watch." Robin gently kissed Délices on the breast, throat, and lips.

Stroking her head, he asked, "Have I burned you, Délices?"

"No, Robin, never."

He looked up at Howard. "This is how."

Howard felt as if a steel band were being tightened across his chest. "I don't understand."

"Do it as Robin does," Robin said.

"I can't," he said in a strangled voice.

The young man nodded. "Délices will teach you." He turned to Leslie. "Leslie, speak the truth. Have you pierced this woman's spirit with the blade of your envy?"

"Yes."

"Why?"

Leslie looked at her thoughtfully. "Well, I suppose—" She shook her head. "I was going to say because of her beauty, but it isn't that. It's her . . . freedom."

Robin looked down at the girl on the altar. "My daughter, you are blameless, as you see. These stains are from your children, and only one water will wash them away." He looked up at Howard and Leslie. "This water, the water of compassion, must come from you. Will you wash her?"

They stared at him blankly.

He took two bowls of water from a table beside the altar and offered them across Délices's body.

"Oh God," Howard whispered and accepted his. He looked down, stricken, into the girl's eyes.

"Howard," she called to him softly. "It's your fear that burns me. I'm just a woman. I don't belong to an alien race. I'm like you. Accept me."

His arms began to tremble.

She took his hand and laid it on her chest.

"This is my chest, Howard. Just a chest, a lot like yours, but not so hairy."

She moved his hand down and to one side.

"Oh my," she said. "What's this?"

"Your breast."

"It's not so terrible, is it?"

"No."

"What is it, if it's not terrible?"

Howard swallowed. "It's beautiful."

"Yes, I think so myself. Not a bad breast at all. Do you like having your hand there?"

"Yes."

"It doesn't *feel* like you like having it there. Are you scared to show me you enjoy it?"

"Yes."

"It's your fear that burns me."

Trembling, he caressed her breast.

"Is that so terrible?"

"No."

"Wet your hand, Howard."

He straightened up

"Wait!" she said, raising her head to look between her breasts. "When you stood up, something fell on my chest. What was it?"

"Well . . . I'm afraid it was a tear."

"Afraid? Silly man." She touched it thoughtfully. "Do you know what this teardrop is, Howard? It's the water of compassion. You know at last that there is a real human person here inside this body just as there is inside your body. This is the water you must wash me in."

"I don't understand."

"Of course you do. Give me your lips."

He gave her his lips, and washed her in the water of his tears.

Half an hour later she was pummeling him on the chest with her fists and shouting, "You *will* dance with me!"

Robin and Leslie, dancing nearby, laughed.

"Honest to God," Howard said, "as far as I got was the foxtrot, and that was thirty years ago. I don't know these steps!"

"There *aren't* any steps! Just move!"

"I feel ridiculous."

"Go ahead, feel ridiculous! *Be* ridiculous! Come on, Howard. Pretend you've got a broken neck. Is your spine fused? Wriggle a little. Give us a little pelvis."

"I'm exhausted."

"You're exhausted because you're tense. Loosen up. Throw it around."

"Why are we *doing* this?"

"It's part of the rite, of course."

"It's not."

"Verdelet!" she called out. "Explain this part to Howard."

"Certainly," he responded promptly. "Most who come to the rite understand the dance of frenzy and need no explanation. It's a form of ecstatic release that our puritanical society—"

Panting, Howard held up his hand to stop him. "I don't think I can make it all the way to ecstasy, Délices. Honest to God."

Laughing, she gave him a hug and told him to go sit down. She returned a few minutes later with a bottle of Benedictine and two snifters.

"We'll have to get you in shape for this, Howard. Are you okay?"

"I'm okay. That was about the equivalent of three rounds in the ring."

She looked at him surprised. "You were a fighter?"

"Long, long ago."

"Wow. Aren't you hot in that caftan?"

"Yes."

"Well, take it off."

He shook his head. "I'm an old man with a big sagging belly, and I feel more comfortable dressed."

"It is your choice to make, of course," she intoned, mimicking Bailey's lofty accent.

"You mock him?"

"Certainly. Because I respect him with all my heart, I'm free to mock him. Besides, I wouldn't be Délices if I took things too seriously."

When they'd arranged cushions on either side of the stone pit and had settled into them, Verdelet joined them, wearing a plain black caftan. He spent some time lighting the fire and then sat down cross-legged at one end of the pit.

"You've done well tonight, my children," Verdelet said. "Particularly you, Howard. You had to make a long journey to find the path, and I hadn't expected you to make it in a single night."

He turned to Leslie. "Your fears and misgivings have vanished?"

"Yes. Completely."

"Good." He gave his attention to the fire.

After a few moments the lights went down and a spotlight within the hood shone down on the fire, which seemed to have been laid for smoke rather than flames. The smoke rose as if it were a solid column supporting the hood.

"This is how our rite ends, children. We gaze into the world to seek the shape of our god. Look into the smoke. . . . There's nothing special about this smoke or this fire. We could just as well look for him in the clouds, in the leaves of a tree, in the dust blowing over a prairie, in the waves of the sea. With alertness and insight, we may discover him anywhere. . . . Howard, what do you see in the smoke?"

"Well. . . . It's moving upward, swirling upward. But there's something in it that isn't moving, or that isn't moving upward. It looks like a shadow."

"It is a shadow. It's stationary?"

"No. It's turning, revolving."

"What does it look like?"

"I don't know. It keeps changing. Just then it looked like the torso of a man with an arm over his head. Now it looks like . . . I don't know. Like a television satellite dish."

"The shadow is cast by a piece of wood suspended under the light. I think you could watch it through a thousand nights and never see the same shape twice. Now look into the shadow and tell me what your eyes find there."

"You mean what shape?"

"No. What do you see within the shape?"

Frowning, Howard studied it through a full minute. "I personally don't see anything."

"Leslie? What do you see?"

"I see glimpses of Howard and Délices. Where the smoke is in shadow I can see through to them. Where it's lit up I can't, because it's opaque."

He turned to Howard and asked him what he saw now.

"I see Robin and Leslie."

"Why didn't you see them before?"

"Well, I did, of course, but. . ."

"But you told me you saw nothing, because you rejected what your eyes were presenting you with. Within the moving shadow you saw glimpses of Leslie and Robin, but your mind said, 'There is nothing within the shadow,' so you denied seeing what you were seeing."

"Yes."

"To discover the shape of our god in the world, you must learn to accept what your eyes see. You must learn to see as a child sees, without rationalizing or censoring. Our rite ends in the contemplation of light, smoke, and shadow because our god is a compound of light, smoke, and shadow, a confounding of the neatly-arranged universe of our adversaries, who long ago sorted the universe into light and shadow: into spirit and flesh, into good and evil. For them there is no smoke, nothing to confuse. But behold: In this confusion of light, smoke, and shadow before us, it is the shadow that enables us to see and the light that blinds us. In other words, we have learned a truth that is unknown to them: a very special, humanizing, and liberating illumination occurs when the shadows of our flesh meet and commingle in the rite. When our adversaries worship their god, they become haughty and righteous, because theirs is a god of pure light. When we worship ours, we are humbled and awed, because the mystery of the light, the smoke, and the shadow of which he is compounded is forever beyond us."

He sighed.

"As always, my words are feeble. What is strong is the rite, which restores to us a universe that is forever ambiguous and pregnant with mystery. That is its purpose."

After a few minutes the fire began to burn low and the column of smoke slowly faded. Verdelet told them to embrace one last time and to depart in silence.

An hour before dawn, in the darkened city of Howard's dream, the black dog with the face of a bull padded silently beside the elegant shops of Michigan Avenue. Its nose to the pavement, it loped on purposefully but without urgency: The night was endless.

It crossed Oak Street and continued northward alongside Lake Shore Drive, eerily devoid of traffic. The miles were paced off, one by one. At last it turned west a couple blocks beyond Lawrence. It paused in front of Howard's building, circled twice, snuffling at the sidewalk, and sat down. Then it looked up at the windows behind which Howard slept. The hunt was over.

Howard rolled over and sighed heavily. If he'd been awake he could have given a name to what he felt.

It was relief.

CHAPTER 12

Over his third cup of coffee the next morning, Howard decided he'd probably been very expertly had. Bailey's blend of sensitivity-training, feminism, and metaphysical gobbledygook was cunning as hell and smoothly put over, but his "rite" was a forgery. It had the right elements, of course—Howard had done enough research to recognize that—but it bore the unmistakable hallmark of the con-artist: it was just too good to be true.

But what did that mean? In some sense or other, aren't all religions too good to be true? Isn't that what makes them religions?

When Howard phoned him, Bailey said: "I very much dislike meeting members of the rite outside my role as Verdelet. It confuses them, and it's almost physically painful for me."

"Why is that, Mr. Bailey?"

"I doubt if you called to ask me that."

"True. I must say you seem . . . a little unfriendly."

"Did I seem friendly last night?"

"Well, yes, you did."

"That's because, as Howard in the rite, you are my child, a person to be cherished and enlightened. As Howard Scheim, private investigator, you're a bore and a bloody nuisance."

"I see. That's plain enough."

"Good."

"So you'd rather not meet with me."

"That's right."

"But look. You understand that I wasn't there last night on my own account. I was there on behalf of a client. I was doing a job."

"So?"

"So I'd like to try and finish that job. I'd like to ask you some questions."

"Go ahead and ask them."

Howard sighed. "Couldn't we just get together and talk for a while?"

"You mean sit down and shoot the breeze about Satanism."

"Well, yeah."

"No thanks."

"Why are you so hostile? I'm not your enemy."

"Believe me, Mr. Scheim, you don't know what the hell you're talking about. Outside the rite, everyone is my enemy."

"All I want to do is understand, for God's sake!"

"Come to the rite and you'll understand."

It took Howard almost half a minute to throttle the desire to growl into the phone. "You win, Mr. Bailey. Can I at least ask a couple of questions?"

"I already told you to go ahead," Bailey snapped.

"Okay. When did the worship of Satan begin, as you see it?"

"To me, your question means, when did the god we worship come to be called Satan."

"All right."

"You know the answer already: during the Middle Ages."

"What was he called before that?"

"The Romans called him Faunus, the Greeks called him Pan, and in the Near East he was called Baal. This is the earliest name known for him, dating back about three and a half millennia."

"Okay. This is the key question for me, and I hope it won't offend you. What makes you think the god named Baal is the god you worship as Satan?"

"It doesn't offend me, Mr. Scheim. I think Baal and Satan are the same, because they're hated by the same people. By the righteous and the sanctimonious. By those who believe that the spirit can only be liberated if the body is mummified."

"That's sort of negative evidence, isn't it?"

"Is it?"

"Yeah. . . . Well, again I don't want to seem contentious, but I have done a little looking around about this. As I understand it, the only thing that's definitely known about Baal—I mean on the positive side—is that he was a Syrian rain god. And even this was only recently discovered."

"I take it you're referring to the Ugaritic tablets discovered at Ras es-Shamrah in 1929."

"That's right."

"I'm aware of this discovery, Mr. Scheim. What's your question?"

"My question is: What's the connection between a Syrian rain god and the god you were talking about last night?"

Bailey sighed wearily. "Contemplate the mystery of the light, the shadow, and the smoke and you'll find the connection, Howard. Or Verdelet will show it to you when next you come to the rite. Since this is a matter that troubles you, he'll make a special point of it."

"I see," Howard said, since there didn't seem to be anything else to say.

By noon, it was obvious that he was coming down with a cold. Ada had always maintained that he got a cold when he needed a vacation or was working on a job he didn't like.

Colds didn't just annoy Howard, they felled him. Once he'd tried carrying on as usual through a cold and had ended up hospitalized with pneumonia. After that, he just went to bed and stayed there till it was completely over. Without Ada to look after him, this meant getting in a two-week supply of antihistamines, tissues, cough syrup, and food before the symptoms overwhelmed him. Books he didn't need to worry about, because he had all the Nero Wolfes in tattered paperback, and these were reserved for reading during colds.

He went to his office to collect his mail and change the message on his answering machine. Though it wasn't strictly necessary, he considered calling Aaron to let him know he'd be sidelined for a while. He decided he'd wait until his symptoms were fully and audibly established. By four o'clock he was in bed with *Fer-de-Lance* and a large piece of chocolate fudge cake, which from at least the age of ten had been his special sickbed treat.

He was up to *Plot It Yourself* when a breath of air from the Gulf of Mexico broke the city's persistent cold spell. Light coats and jackets were pulled from the backs of closets for the day, though no one was fooled into thinking that spring had come to stay.

That evening Howard was attacking a week's accumulation of dirty dishes when he got a telephone call from Richard Holloway.

The boy observed that he sounded terrible. Howard admitted he had a cold.

"Spring colds are the worst," Richard noted prosaically.

"Yeah."

"Well, look. I've been picking up some things. About our friends."

"Uh huh?"

"I think something's going on in Colorado."

"Colorado."

"Southern Colorado or northern New Mexico. In the Rockies somewhere along in there."

"Okay."

"I have the impression it's about a child, a boy."

"What is?"

"Whatever's going on."

"I see."

"Is this any help to you?"

"I don't know, Richard. I'll have to think about it."

"You want me to keep you posted if I get anything else?"

"Absolutely. I appreciate the call. Say hello to Denise for me."

"Will do, Howard. Take care of that cold."

Howard promised he would, and by the time he was back at the sink he'd put the conversation out of his mind. He was giving Aaron's problem a complete rest for the duration of his cold, and by now it was all but comatose.

He fixed his attention on washing the dishes, a chore he detested because it seemed to require so much attention. Unlike Ada, who could whip through a bushel of dishes in twenty minutes, he had no method, no rhythm; he washed each dish, each utensil as laboriously as if it were to take its place in a surgery.

He was so absorbed in the task that it was only by degrees that he became aware of the murmur of voices nearby. He cocked his head toward them, perplexed, because none of his neighbors were party-givers. After rinsing and racking the last plate, he draped the dish-cloth over the faucet, dried his hands, and went into the living room. There the puzzle deepened, because the voices seemed to be coming through the south wall—the outer wall of the building.

He went to the window and gazed into his neighbor's windows, a dozen feet away; they were dark. From this position, the voices seemed to be coming from his left. In fact, they seemed to be com-ing from Ada's sideboard. Feeling a bit foolish, Howard opened the cabinet.

The voices became noticeably more distinct, and he listened to them with a frown of bewilderment. There seemed to be half a dozen different speakers, most of them male. He couldn't make out what anyone was saying, partly because they were all talking at once and partly because there was a persistent background clatter of dishes and silverware. A sound engineer would have described it as "a restaurant presence."

Howard shoved the sideboard away from the wall and stood there blinking. He wondered briefly if he was dreaming but knew he wasn't; in dreams you never wonder if you're dreaming. There was a door in the wall—an old wooden door with cracked, peeling brown paint, and he stared at it with a woozy sense of *déjà vu*. Thinking about it, he seemed to remember now that the door had been there when he moved in, that he had deliberately used the sideboard to cover it up, since it led nowhere.

The dining room babble was coming from behind this door.

His head felt leaden on his shoulders. He shook it irritably, reached for the doorknob, and paused, wondering if he should knock. Knock on a door in your own apartment? He pulled the door open and found himself looking into a large, vaguely familiar kitchen. A short, blocky woman was standing at the sink washing dishes, her back to him. Without turning around, she said:

"Well, don't just stand there, you oaf. Come in."

Howard's heart rose up in his chest like a helium-filled balloon. "Ada!" he whispered ecstatically.

She turned off the water and faced him, drying her hands on her apron. "Well, look at you," she growled humorously. "I bet that bathrobe ain't been washed in four years."

Howard barely heard her words. He was taking in the all-but-forgotten features of her dark, square face, with its beaky nose and bright black eyes. Tears welled up in his eyes and he squawked: "But they said . . . the doctors said . . ."

"Doctors! What did they tell you? That I was gonna croak? Well, that shows what doctors know, don't it."

The tears spilled down his cheeks, and he felt a great laugh of joy swell up inside of him as he realized that her death and the lonely years that followed had been nothing but a bad dream after all. Ada was still alive—still *young!*

He looked around, trying to reorient himself to reality, and at last recognized the apartment they'd moved into in 1973 when Howard's income had been at its peak.

"I gotta finish these dishes, sweetie," Ada said. "You go on in and look after our guests."

"Guests?"

"In the living room, dummy."

Howard nodded, vaguely remembering the people he'd heard; they were silent now. They remained silent as he entered the living room and stood blinking down at them, feeling awkward in his pajamas and bathrobe. He shook his head, disoriented; they were all strangers—and a strange assortment at that.

A slight old man with a face like a sheep, an air of amused benevolence, and a tidy pot belly buttoned up in a shapeless old cardigan sweater.

A wiry, unpleasant-looking redhead in his thirties who sprawled and sneered. A heavier man of the same age whose dull eyes peered at Howard from a face that might have been kneaded from dough.

A shriveled Hispanic man of indeterminate age, his eyes haunted by centuries. Sitting beside him, a boy who might be his son or his grandson, with glossy skin but the same haunted eyes.

An ancient, scrawny crone with hair like cobwebs, dressed in a faded house dress and broken-backed slippers; her voice, if she spoke, would be like the scrape of chalk on a blackboard.

A solemn American Indian with a head like a chunk of dark rock and the body of a tree trunk.

It was impossible to think of these people as guests in his home. He didn't know what to make of them; no one spoke, no one nodded, no one offered any introductions. Under their silent, staring appraisal, he felt like a bull that had been led out into the selling ring for inspection. It was a curious moment—one that seemed to stretch on forever, outside of time. His eyes circled the room restlessly, meeting theirs again and again, searching in vain for a spark of human contact.

Then Ada appeared in the doorway behind him, and the spell was broken.

"Honey, go get the ice bucket from the basement, would you?"

Howard frowned, trying to make sense of this. Their apartment was on the third floor. Why would the ice bucket be in the basement?

"Go on," she said.

He wanted desperately to tell her to forget the goddamned ice bucket. He wanted to send these strangers away and spend the night talking to her, holding her, but he felt completely paralyzed. He couldn't even turn to her, couldn't even look into her face.

"Go on now, Howard," she repeated firmly.

He shuffled forward, opened a door, and found himself at the top of a flight of stairs lit by a naked bulb. He could see that they led down to the bare cement floor of a basement. "Ada . . . ," he pleaded.

But the silence behind him was total now.

Oppressed by a dreadful sense of impending loss, he descended. At the bottom of the stairs, he shivered and looked around bleakly at the emptiest basement in the world. It seemed like the basement of a house waiting for its first tenants—or a house that would never have tenants.

There was no ice bucket.

But, under another naked bulb, he found a suitcase with a raincoat draped over it. He recognized these things immediately as his own. They were infinitely tired objects; the suitcase had suffered too many journeys, the raincoat too many seasons. They seemed grubby and pathetic in this pristine room.

He couldn't remember exactly what his errand was supposed to be, but it was evident that Ada was preparing him for some horrendous unwanted journey. The very thought of it wearied him to death. Dragging himself like a vast, unwieldy burden, he mounted the stairs, groped his way through the apartment above (now dark and completely deserted), and stumbled into his own living room. Somehow he found the strength to push the sideboard back into place before crashing into his bed like a felled tree.

Sleep washed away all memory of his visit to the rooms that lay behind Ada's sideboard, and he woke the next morning merely amazed to find himself still in his bathrobe.

Nevertheless, as the day wore on, he began to feel burdened with a sense of desolation he couldn't trace to any source.

CHAPTER 13

By the time he finished *The Doorbell Rang,* which he always saved till last because it was his favorite of the Wolfe books, his symptoms had been gone for two days. He should have felt ready to get dressed and visit his office, but didn't.

Another mass of chill arctic air had settled over the city, and he tried to convince himself that it was only the cold that was holding him back. Staring out at the clear sky, he told himself it was a gorgeous day to get back to work. He was trying to suck some of that brilliance into himself, to dispel the shadow that had dimmed his spirit since the night Richard Holloway called. Finally he shrugged and began to get dressed. It was probably just one of those circular things: He was idle because he was depressed, and he was depressed because he was idle. Maybe just getting back into the routine would break the circle. When he got to his office, he scooped up the mail from the floor, went through it standing over the wastebasket, where most of it went, listened to the few messages on the answering machine, sat down, and swivelled to face the window.

It was time to consider what else he could do to justify keeping Aaron's money. He wondered what Nero Wolfe would've done if Aaron had shown up at his house on West 35th Street. That was no help. Wolfe would have wiggled a finger, told Archie to put him out, and returned to his crossword puzzle.

Howard could go back to Joel Bailey's rite and have the connection between Baal and Satan explained to him. But he knew in advance it would sound terrific and have as much substance as a soap bubble. With a little effort, he could probably track down Sybil Leek, Louise Huebner, or some of the other "public" witches. With a little more effort, he could look into voodoo in Haiti and obeah in Jamaica. And of course if he was really ambitious, he could do some nosing around in the Middle East. Two experts, one in Middle-Eastern studies and one in comparative religion, had assured him this would be a complete waste of time.

With a bleak little smile, he recalled that he could also check out the Rocky Mountains and see what the yoo-hoos were up to.

In the end, there was really no doubt about what he had to do next. It was time to waylay his client at the club for an informal consultation.

For two nights Aaron didn't show up, and this was just as well. During Howard's absence, the members had been bottling up things to tell him, and his services were in great demand. On the third night a giant, muscular warm front had moved into the area to vanquish the dragon of winter for good, and the atmosphere inside the club was as close to lighthearted as it ever got. This meant that ordinarily sober and respectable members allowed themselves to be talked into such giddy revels as bridge, cribbage, and even canasta. It also meant that Howard was free of listening duties when Aaron arrived at nine.

The two men exchanged health reports, and Howard began to summarize what he'd accomplished before the rhinovirus laid him low. Aaron interrupted to ask if he really felt ready to report at this point.

"Aaron, I feel like I've run out of obvious moves. Everything I can see to do at this point looks pretty tangential, but maybe you'll come up with something I've missed. That's what I'd like to explore after filling you in on what I've already tried."

The old man nodded and told him to go ahead.

It was well after midnight by the time Howard finished. "To me, frankly," he said, "it looks like I've gotten nowhere for you. Am I going about it the wrong way? I'd like to hear your honest opinion."

Aaron worked his way through a half-inch of cigar before answering. "To be honest, I'm a little puzzled by your attitude toward this man Bailey. He seems to be trying to give you at least part of the answer to my question, and you're pushing him away."

Howard scratched savagely at the side of his jaw. "Don't take this wrong, Aaron, but if you think he can answer your question, then you don't need me. You should go to him direct."

"God in Heaven!" Aaron exclaimed in alarm. "Now you're taking *me* wrong. If you tell me this man's a fraud, I believe you. What I'm saying is, maybe you're calling him a fraud just *because* he's saying he can give you an answer. I mean, maybe you started out with the idea that everyone who says there's *no* answer is automatically reliable and everyone who says there *is* an answer is automatically suspect. I'm not saying this is so, Howard, I'm just asking."

"You could be right, Aaron. I've got to be skeptical of what I hear, but I've also got to have an open mind. Maybe I'm kidding myself when I think I've got an open mind about this thing. If I am, then I should quit."

"I don't want you to quit, Howard. Definitely not. I think you've done a fine job so far. But do you want an opinion?"

"Yes."

"You're holding back on this. You act like you're tracking down a lost cat for some penniless widow. I gave you that ten thousand to *use*, Howard. Who says the answer can be found in Chicago? Chicago's not the world, God knows. You think you can find out something in the Middle East? I don't care what the experts say—go to the Middle East. You think you can find out something useful in Jamaica or Haiti? Go to Jamaica, go to Haiti."

Howard barely managed to stifle a groan. "Aaron, why the hell are you so *bent* on this thing?"

The old man's face split in a wicked grin. "I'll tell you, Howard. In my whole life, this is the only exciting thing I've ever done with my money. I kid you not. I've never spent a nickel on excitement. A lot of years my wife dragged me to Nassau to blow a few thousand at the gambling tables, and for her this was excitement. For me, I would have been happier to stay home and flush it down the toilet."

"But how does what I'm doing add up to excitement for you?"

"It does, believe me. Look, I'm almost entirely retired from the leather business. What am I supposed to do with my money? Blow it on chorus girls, at my age? Play the horses? Like I said, I'd just as soon flush it down the toilet. Give it away? There's no excitement in picking charities, I can tell you. Travel? I can't stand the aggravation.

"You go to the Middle East, Howard. For me, that's excitement. For me to be able to think, 'I got a man looking into something for me in Syria'—that's excitement. I know what I'm doing, so don't worry about it. Don't hold back. I've set this money aside, and it if takes more I'll set aside more."

Howard gave in with a defeated smile. "Okay, Aaron. I'll dye my hair orange and get a passport in the name of Clancy O'Brien."

As Howard stepped off the bus at Ainslee, a boy sitting on the waiting bench looked up hopefully, then dropped his gaze back to his hands, folded in his lap.

"Are you waiting for this bus?" Howard asked, still holding the door.

The boy looked up, puzzled. "No," he said, then added a polite thank you.

Howard let the door close and began walking up Ainslee. After half a block he turned back. The boy was completely out of place. It wasn't just that kids that age don't belong at bus stops at one in the morning. He was too clean, too polite, too well-dressed to belong in this neighborhood at all.

When the boy looked up from the bench, Howard asked him if he was lost. He considered this gravely through half a minute, then gave Howard a doubtful smile and said: "Tonight, everybody seems to be lost."

Half a block away, on the other side of the street, a man in a parked
Volvo sedan watched as Howard sat down beside the boy. For no very
good reason, since he ordinarily gave little thought to time, the man
checked his watch. After a few minutes Howard and the boy stood
up and strolled down Ainslee together. The man watched them
till they were out of sight, then started the car and headed for the
Holiday Inn at O'Hare. When a small crowd off a flight from Los
Angeles appeared in the lobby, he mingled with them to check in.
After he'd paid for the night and received his key, he asked the desk
clerk to reserve a room for him at the Inn in Omaha for the following
day. The young woman went to work at the computer, and he waited
placidly until she gave him an empty smile and told him it was all
taken care of.

She had long ago stopped noticing the people she served, otherwise she would have seen a trim man in his mid-thirties, with black
hair and a square face that was handsome in a dark, brooding way.
Richard Holloway would have recoiled from him with a shudder of
distaste, but to the desk clerk he was just another face in the crowd,
and she'd forgotten him before his back was turned.

After a brief visit to the room he'd just paid for, the man left. On
his way out of the lobby, he dropped the key into the lobby mailbox.

PART II

*Everybody seems
to be lost . . . .*

CHAPTER 14

Sometimes it's as though the gods permit an imp to lodge in a man's body and take root there like the embryo of an evil child. This is how it was for David Kennesey.

It had happened without any fuss, one Saturday during the previous fall. He didn't even notice it at the time. For no reason at all, he'd felt like getting out of the house by himself and went for a drive in the country. He parked at the side of a rural road and let the tangy smell of burning leaves fill him with nostalgia. A red Fiero whipped down the highway toward him, and, as it shot past, he had a glimpse of the driver—a woman. At seventy miles an hour she was little more than a white blur, but David's imagination made her a beauty.

It was as small a thing as that.

Within an hour he'd forgotten the country road, the tangy air, the Fiero, the woman at the wheel. He was back at his house going over a contract that had to be ready on Monday.

But in the months that followed he began to be a little worried about himself. He didn't mention it to his wife, Ellen, seeing no reason to worry her as well. He wasn't sick, wasn't in any kind of pain, after all. It was just that he'd gradually become aware of a mounting, unrelenting tension in the center of his body, of a perpetual tingle of anxiety in his genitals. By midwinter he'd become almost unbearably nervous. Things at the edge of his field of vision seemed to be in constant, furtive movement. When he was working—or trying to work—the softest greeting would startle him like a gunshot.

Without mentioning it to Ellen, he took his symptoms to their doctor, who told him all the things he expected to hear, and prescribed a tranquilizer; although he hated to think of himself as one of those people whose well-being comes out of a bottle, David stuck with the pills for a month and then didn't bother to renew the prescription, since they weren't doing any good anyway. He had his eyes checked, got new glasses with a minutely changed prescription, and developed a maddening tic below his left eye. His bowels seemed to turn food of any kind to gas. On his forty-second birthday in the first week in May, he wondered what the symptoms of a nervous breakdown are like.

Then the very next morning a sultry wind from the Gulf brought a false spring to northern Indiana, and the imp stirred and delivered itself of a kick that left David Kennesey in no doubt about what had been growing inside him. At that moment he was standing in an upstairs bedroom in front of a mirror, slowly busy with a necktie. A breeze was flowing in through a window that hadn't been opened since November, and it was as though enlightenment flowed in with it. The tic below his eye vanished as he understood—and instantly accepted—what he was going to do.

He was going to give the mold of his life a twist and shatter it completely.

He sighed so deeply it was as if all breath were leaving his body. *This*, he thought, *is how a patient must feel on being told it isn't cancer after all.*

Their task forgotten, his hands fell heavily to his side. He stared into the mirror, and his eyes met the eyes of a stranger. Was this actually the way he looked to others? The solemn square face—handsome perhaps—thick dark hair, and wide, full mouth were vaguely familiar. But when had his eyes acquired that black, empty look? Not exactly empty. Haunted? They were the eyes of a man he'd expect to meet on death row. Was it really possible that this had become his face?

Suddenly the outline of his life shimmered like a mirage and twisted itself into an entirely new shape in his mind, and he nearly laughed out loud.

"Of course," he whispered triumphantly. "Of course!" And he meant by this: *Of course I've betrayed myself. I was sure I wouldn't, but of course I have. For comforts, for pleasant companionship, for acceptance, for respectability, for security. For the sake of appearing to be a sensible, mature fellow. I thought I could get away with it, but of course I didn't. No one can.*

It didn't matter now. The betrayal was over. By nightfall he would be behind the wheel of his Volvo with all he would ever need from this life in a single suitcase. It was going to be a nightmarish day, an agonizing day. There were other lives to be shattered along with his own, because other lives had been molded against his. Three others would share in the common disaster, but he would defer all guilt until later. This was the way it had to be.

Because it was time to resume the abandoned search. The search for a road. A certain road.

He pulled on his suit jacket and went downstairs. Ellen was washing the breakfast dishes, lost in her own tranquility. She had long ago accepted her figure's tendency toward a matronly fullness; it suited her, really, and her upright posture confirmed it. Her dark hair had been prematurely graying when she was still in college; it didn't detract from her palely handsome oval face (which reminded many of Virginia Woolf's), so she had never tried to disguise it.

To save an explanation, David used the kitchen extension beside her to call the office to say he'd be a little late. She watched with an air of puzzlement. When he was finished, he led her into the living room, sat her down, and explained, as calmly and as gently as he could.

Ellen had never needed to develop a capacity for astonishment, so she listened in simple disbelief. She didn't react with grief or outrage, not at first. This was just a terribly wrongheaded idea that had to be dealt with, as if he were telling her he planned to buy a Jeep or to send their son Tim away to a military academy. It was simply a matter of finding out where he'd gone wrong in his thinking.

Obviously he was tired, she told him—as he had every right to be. He'd been working himself to death for years and needed and deserved a break. She could certainly understand it if he wanted to go off by himself for a while and do something completely different. But to talk about destroying their marriage for the sake of getting away was overreacting a bit, wasn't it? She actually smiled at this jokey attempt to put things into perspective for him.

"I'll be gone by tonight, Ellen," he said, his voice chillingly flat.

Then she realized that something was really wrong, and her stomach clenched with the first taste of fear she'd ever had.

No, she told him, he wouldn't be gone by tonight, because they were going to talk this thing through and get to the bottom of it. Whatever was troubling him could be handled, perhaps with help from others. A mature, responsible person didn't just walk away from a family, a home, a career. Not in a single day. Whatever was wrong, this couldn't possibly be the way to handle it. He had to see that, surely.

What was it exactly that was bothering him? When he didn't answer, she began to explore the alternatives for him. Certainly he was tired; that could be remedied. She wouldn't blame him even if he was bored; they both could use a change from Runnell, Indiana. Was it his job? Disillusionment with Bob Gaines and Educational Enterprises? Disillusionment with the whole field of educational publishing?

With a sigh, she admitted that their sex life had become routine and unadventurous. It was probably her fault, but this too could be changed. In fact, she was eager to change it. Quite honestly, now that it was out in the open, she confessed to suppressing certain inclinations, thinking they might shock him. They could begin to explore them now. Perhaps there were inclinations he himself wanted to explore. She was open—more than open—to anything.

It went on and on, becoming more and more pathetic.

After nearly two hours of talking, she finally saw the appalling, unmanageable truth. David didn't want to better his present life, he wanted to destroy it entirely. His resolve nearly caved in then, because, without reason and good sense to appeal to, she was reduced to begging, to groveling for his pity. Did he really mean to shatter both their son's and her future? Did he really mean to abandon them to poverty, despair, and humiliation? Did he really have no sense of compassion for them, no sense of responsibility toward them?

He explained wearily that he had those senses but was going to smother them for the sake of his survival as a person. What he was doing was an act of unalloyed selfishness that he couldn't excuse, rationalize, or expect forgiveness for.

But what was it he wanted? More freedom? Other women? She could tolerate that. If he wanted to have affairs with other women, so long as he didn't flaunt them, so long as she didn't know. . . .

It was all very squalid, and toward noon he left the house thoroughly ashamed of himself. He didn't head for his office. Ellen would quickly realize she needn't be alone in the effort to save David from himself. Her most powerful ally would be Bob Gaines, his boss, his friend, and his mentor in a career he'd poured his life's energies into for more than a decade. If anyone could bring him to his senses, it would be Bob Gaines. And so he dawdled, giving her time to call Bob and giving himself time to prepare for this next (and in its own way more deeply testing) encounter. A few minutes after twelve he stopped at a phone booth and called the office. Tillie, the receptionist, answered, and David asked if Bob was available.

As expected, the question puzzled her.

"Actually, he's on the phone with. . . . He's on the phone, David."

"I see," he said. "Do you know if he's free for lunch?"

"I think he is. There's nothing on his calendar, anyway."

"Good. Will you ask him to join me at Fredo's then? When he's free, of course."

"Sure. Uh. . ."

Tillie was burning to know what was going on, but David thanked her and hung up.

Poor Tillie. Poor Bob. Poor Ellen. Poor Tim. It was going to be an upsetting day for everyone.

———

David looked around Fredo's with the grateful thought: *I'll never have to see this place again.* It was the town's one Elegant Restaurant, where you took clients to lunch, where you celebrated birthdays and anniversaries, where you spent what passed as a romantic evening, but even its pretensions were second-rate. Until now he hadn't let himself realize how thoroughly tired of it he was.

He was toying with a Bloody Mary when Bob pulled out a chair across from him and sat down.

"Forgive me for staring," he said.

David shrugged. "I expect to be stared at."

Nearing sixty, Bob looked to be in his mid-forties, with a broad, humorous face, a haircut that hadn't changed since prep school, and the body of an athlete just a bit gone to seed. Right now, giving David a speculative, almost wounded, inspection, he looked like a football coach who'd been asked for a brief explanation of quantum theory.

"I suppose you know I've just been talking to Ellen," he said.

David nodded. "Did you really say what she says you said?"

"I expect so."

"She says you're going to pack up and leave."

"That's right."

Bob sagged in his chair. "Do I get an explanation?"

David took out a felt-tip pen, wrote ten words on the back of a cocktail napkin, and passed it across to him. Bob studied the words with a thoughtful frown. He knew them well, since they were his own; he'd spoken them a dozen years ago at a convention of the National Education Association, held that year in Dallas: WHAT YOU DO NOT KNOW YOURSELF, YOU CANNOT TEACH ANOTHER. They were the words that had brought them together in the first place.

David really had no business being at the convention at which they were spoken. In his first seven years in educational publishing, he'd moved around a lot—and up a lot—and had gained the reputation, in that small, muddy pond, of being someone who might turn out to be a fairly big frog in ten or fifteen years. By sending him to

Dallas, his current employer was tossing him a bone usually reserved for middle-management executives. David had no authors to talk to, no contracts to wave, no producers to prod. He was just there to meet people, to finger the competition's merchandise, and to attend a few lectures if he felt like it.

One of these was being given by a man he was curious about: Bob Gaines. Everywhere David had gone in the industry, Bob Gaines had been there ten years before and was spoken of in almost legendary terms: "That was the policy when Bob was here. . . . That was Bob's idea. . . . That was something Bob started. . . ." David had never met the man and had the vague impression he'd drifted out of the industry.

He was scheduled to speak on "Changing Roles in Education," typical convention fare, but evidently people thought that anything Bob Gaines might have to say would be worth listening to. By the time he stepped to the lectern, the room was filled to capacity both with school people and with David's colleagues from the publishing world. Within ten minutes it was obvious that something strange was going on, and the audience was restless, not from boredom but from disorientation. They'd come expecting the usual blather about how important they all were, how roles change in changing times (like these), and how vital it was (now more than ever) to pull together as a team—and they weren't getting it.

Bob Gaines wasn't talking about roles that were *altering*, he was talking about roles that had been *exchanged*. He seemed to be saying that the educational system of the twentieth century was the result of fundamental role-exchanges made in the nineteenth century, and people were giving one another bewildered looks. They were no less bewildered when he took them back in time to examine classical models of the teacher. From these he derived and offered to his listeners a postulate he felt no educational theory could ignore. There was a long, stunned silence as listeners played back in their heads the words he'd finally spoken—the Gaines postulate:

"What you do not know yourself, you cannot teach another."

People shifted in their seats uneasily as they tried to decide how to take this apparently harmless, apparently obvious, even vacuous statement. Then, getting it, David began to chuckle. Then, getting it some more, he began to roar with laughter. The people around him—some still puzzled, some beginning to be alarmed—played it back again and grew very still. Someone at the back of the room gave forth a low, almost embarrassed, *boo*. Others joined in. People began to stand up, gathering the courage to walk out in indignation. It seemed to settle the matter for them when David began, all by himself, to applaud. They scrambled to be gone, piercing him with icy glances they didn't have the nerve to direct to the speaker.

With those ten words, Bob Gaines had just thrown a big, ugly rock at a cluster of notions that form the foundation of modern education: the notion of professionalism in teaching, the notion that teaching is primarily a matter of technique, the notion that a well-trained teacher can teach anything—whether he knows it himself or not.

It had been an astounding, appalling, and delightful performance, and when the room was empty, David went up to the lectern and said he'd never met a dead man before. Gaines asked him what he meant.

"I believe you just committed professional suicide."

"Oh, I did that long ago," Gaines said airily. "I keep going all the same, making enemies where I can—and an occasional friend."

Over drinks he told David what keeping on going meant: He had his own publishing company, desperately undercapitalized and only marginally solvent, but one that supplied honest and challenging materials to a growing number of like-minded heretics in the world of education.

"I decided long ago," he said, "that I'd rather be a flea jumping an inch on my own than a flea on the back of a giant going nowhere."

A month later, after convincing Ellen that doing what seemed to be valuable work was worth taking a substantial cut in salary, they moved to Runnell, Indiana, home of Educational Enterprises, Inc. Bob Gaines and his wife had welcomed them by taking them to dinner at Fredo's.

"So?" Bob said, tossing the cocktail napkin aside.

"What is a teacher who knows nothing except how to teach?"

"A state-certified fraud," Bob answered after a moment's thought.

"It came to me this morning, after all these years of producing what we consider the most exciting and sophisticated educational materials in the world, that I'm the biggest fraud of all."

"Okay, I'll bite. Why are you a fraud?"

"Because all I know is what kids are supposed to learn in school. That's where I start. I know math and physics and chemistry and geology and meteorology and sociology and geography and history and literature. I'm a goddamned walking universal textbook, Bob. And that's all I am. That's not just where I start, that's where I end. At the age of forty-two I am the world's champion high-school graduate."

"Jesus," Bob said. "Okay, I guess I see that. But how does that make you a fraud?"

David spent a while studying his Bloody Mary. "You may not believe it, Bob, but I've always had the strange feeling I was missing something profoundly important in my education—something absolutely fundamental. I felt humanly inadequate on a very deep level. Does that make any sense to you?"

"No."

"It didn't to me either, so I ignored it, and I thought I was ignoring it very efficiently. But this morning I woke up to the fact that, more than anything else, this sense of inadequacy is what's shaped the whole of my adult life."

"How so?"

"Bob, you know there are a lot of young people out there who go into psychology or psychiatry because they need psychological help themselves. Consciously or unconsciously, they figure that making other people feel adequate and whole is bound to make them feel adequate and whole."

"True. So?"

"I'm telling you it was the same sort of motive that drew me to education. I figured if I could supply what was missing in other people's education, I was bound to supply what was missing in my own.

I became an educator not because I was convinced I had something to teach but because I was convinced I had something to learn."

He flicked a finger at the Bob Gaines postulate. "And that makes me a fraud."

"Well, I guess it would if . . ." He shook his head angrily, like a bull trying to throw off a fly. "What the hell is it you think you need to learn?"

"How could I know that, Bob? All I know is what it *isn't*. It isn't something you learn pretending to be an educator. It isn't something you learn in Runnell, Indiana, working at a nice respectable job, living in a nice respectable house, trying to be a nice respectable husband and father."

Bob looked at him, away, and back again—a little pantomime of amazement and disgust. "I can't believe I'm hearing this crap from you, David. You really believe there's something out there you've missed?"

"Yes."

"Missed how, for God's sake? By not being a drug addict? By not living in a slum? By not doing stoop labor in a tomato field? What the hell are you talking about? Don't just shake your head at me. I think I have a right to an answer."

"I don't have the answer. That's why I have to get out."

"This is intellectual garbage, David. It isn't worthy of you."

"I know, Bob."

"Shit. Look, take a month's leave of absence. Two months, at half salary. We can both survive that."

From that point on, David hardly bothered to listen. He was thinking about the next confrontation to be gotten through—by far the most painful.

CHAPTER 15

He was parked outside the schoolyard long before the last bell rang and kids began scrambling, shoving, slouching, and straggling out. Tim was one of the stragglers. For nearly ten minutes he stood with another boy just outside the doors, listening to some problem with the air of a thousand-dollar-a-day consultant: respectful, composed, alert, fully focused—all personal thoughts and concerns set aside for the sake of his client.

Tim had the sort of lithe and long-limbed figure Ellen had had as a girl—though there was nothing soft or feminine about it. He had her oval face as well, but the eyes that looked out of it were thoughtful and rather solemn, like David's. The calm, confident presence, however, was entirely his own.

Finally, after asking a few questions, Tim gazed off into the sky for a while and then delivered his opinion, which was received with an expression David had often seen on the faces of executives hearing things they didn't want to hear. As Tim went on, the other boy nodded in defeat and finally took his leave with a sour grin.

Tim was crossing the yard to the bus stop when David tapped on the horn. He paused, stared at the car with puzzled recognition, and strolled over to peer in through the open window on the passenger side.

"Mrs. MacGruder told us in the second grade never to accept rides from strangers," he said.

"That's only if they offer you candy," David countered.

Tim got in and asked, "What's up?" Instead of answering, David put the car in gear and pulled away.

He'd always felt an almost suffocating pride in Tim—not because he was his son but because he was in so many ways *not* his son. It was as though, in fathering Tim, David had exceeded himself, had participated in a miracle. It was as though Tim had been constituted to inhabit a different world from his. David's had always been a hostile, tight-fisted world that would yield up success only to bitter striving. Tim's world, by contrast, seemed welcoming and open-handed, and success came to him without effort. Even at his present age of twelve, tall for his age and a good-looking boy, Tim had a kind of assurance about himself and his place in the world that David envied. He'd always hoped it would survive the turmoil of adolescence. Now he hoped it would survive the blow he was about to deal him.

"What do you think of me, Tim?" he asked, turning into a street that would take them out of town.

Tim raised his brows comically. "What's this?"

"This is talk time. Serious talk time."

"You want to know what I think of you?"

"That's right."

"Wow." He slumped down in the seat and propped his knees up against the dashboard. "I don't know."

"You've met your friends' fathers, haven't you? Think about them and think about me."

"Compare and contrast, huh?" The educator's son. "Well, you're intelligent. That's obvious. You're very fair." And, as if this were what he'd been groping for: "You worry a lot."

David laughed. "What do I worry about?"

"About being fair."

"Oh. Go on."

"Well . . . you *try* real hard."

"What do you mean?"

"Hmm. Do you mind if I smoke a joint before answering that question?"

The year before, David and Ellen had asked Tim if drugs were being sold at his school, and this—after a few moments of thought—had been his answer. It had become a running joke that was repeated whenever he was asked a question he thought was inane or an invasion of privacy. David ignored it now.

"I don't know. Other kids' dads just seem to *be* there, you know what I mean?" David said he didn't. "I mean, some of them are creeps and some of them are nice guys. But sometimes . . . I don't know what I'm trying to say."

"Take your time."

"Frank Hawkins' dad seems like a nice guy most of the time, but every once in a while he gets juiced up and starts slugging everyone. You see what I mean?"

"Not yet."

"What I mean is, he's not *trying*. You would never do that."

David thought about this for a while, a little disconcerted by the portrait Tim was painting of him. "You're saying that other people just let themselves be what they are, and sometimes that's good and sometimes that's bad. But because I try very hard and worry a lot, I'm very fair, very consistent."

"Yeah, I guess so. That's the way it seems."

David nodded. "Let me give you some advice, Tim, and I hope you'll take it very seriously. Keep on going the way you are. Be like them, not like me. You don't need to try hard. You don't need to worry a lot. You really don't."

Tim gave him a doubtful look and said, "Okay."

By now they were out in the country, and Tim asked where they were going. David said they were just driving.

"Is Mom okay?" the boy asked tensely, and David knew he couldn't put it off any longer.

"Your mother's fine, Tim. We have to talk about you and me." He swallowed, and his face twitched with pain. "I have to do something that's going to hurt you worse than an occasional belting, and you'll probably never forgive me for it. I know I'll never forgive myself for it."

The boy looked at him with worried eyes.

"I'm leaving, Tim. And I don't expect to come back."

"Leaving?" David nodded. "You don't mean . . . leaving *here?*"

David nodded again.

"But why?"

"I'll try to explain, Tim, but no explanation will be good enough, believe me."

Tim took in a shocked breath that was half a sob.

"First of all, it's not because of you or your mother. I want you to know that for a certainty. I love you both very much and I always will."

"But then . . . can't we come with you?"

David's insides shriveled into a ball of self-loathing.

"No. I'm sorry, Tim."

"But where are you *going?*"

"I don't know."

He pulled off the road, killed the engine, and turned to face his son. "I told you I'd try to explain, and I will. It won't satisfy you and it won't make you feel any better, but it's all I can do. Okay?"

Tim nodded, and tears spilled down over his cheeks.

"I'm a man who tries hard, Tim. I'm a man who worries a lot. Remember?"

He nodded again.

"You nailed me there, Tim, right on the button. And that's got something to do with what I'm doing now. Your friends' fathers are the way they are because they're not acting a part. They're just being themselves, so they don't have to try hard, don't have to worry a lot. Do you understand?"

Tim shook his head.

"I've always tried hard, Tim, always worried a lot, and I just today figured out why. I've had to try hard, because I'm like an actor on a stage. I've been trying to fake it."

"Fake what?"

"I've been trying to fake being a human being, Tim. I've been trying to fake being a father to you and a husband to your mother."

"I don't understand."

David sighed and closed his eyes for a moment. "You remember Miss Otis." Miss Otis had been Tim's fifth-grade teacher; in the single year she'd lasted at the school she'd made enemies not only of the kids but of the parents as well. "She was a fake, wasn't she?"

"Yes, I guess so."

"What was she trying to fake?"

It took a visible effort for Tim to shift his mind to this irrelevancy. "I don't know. I guess she was trying to fake . . . being better than everyone else. Smarter. But you're not like that."

"I know. I'm a different kind of fake, Tim."

"But you're not! You're . . . You're . . ." The words got choked off in his throat.

David swallowed painfully. "I know, Tim. I don't seem like a fake to you. That's because I've worked hard at it. I've tried real hard and fooled everybody, even myself."

"That's not true."

"It's true. And I'm sorry as hell about it."

"But, God, I don't want you to leave. I mean, I don't want you to *leave!*"

David wanted to take the boy in his arms, but he knew that would only increase the pain. "Tim, I'm going to tell you something you probably can't understand now. You'll understand it later. Will you listen to it?"

Tim shook his head, rejecting the lecture.

"I'll tell you anyway: Becoming a father doesn't make you perfect. It doesn't really change you at all. If you're a foolish man, you'll be a foolish father. If you're a selfish man, you'll be a selfish father. If you're a violent man, you'll be a violent father. If you're a childish man, you'll be a childish father. Do you see what I mean?"

Tim shrugged.

"But all children want their parents to be perfect: to be kind and generous and wise and good-natured and good-humored and considerate and all the rest. But in fact they just go on being whatever they were before they became parents."

Tim stared at him in blank incomprehension.

"What I'm trying to say, Tim, is that I'm sorry as hell that I can't be what you want me to be and I can't do what you want me to do. And I'm really, truly sorry to let you down this way."

"But I don't understand why you have to *leave*."

David sighed, suddenly drained of energy. "Tim, look. Would you understand if I said I couldn't be a movie star for your sake?"

"Yes, but—"

"I know. You don't want me to be a movie star. But would you understand?"

"Yes."

"Would you understand if I said I couldn't be a quarterback for the Chicago Bears for your sake?"

"Yes."

"What I'm telling you now is that I can't go on being *this* for your sake. I'm sorry as hell, but I just can't."

"But . . ." Tim's face twisted painfully as he tried to keep back his tears. "But . . . couldn't I go with you?"

Oh God, David thought and nearly gave it all up. He even pictured it briefly: Tim's relief, Ellen's joy, Bob's delight. Even he would have been relieved—briefly. But in a week or a month or a year, he'd just have to do it all over again. He said: "Tim, if there was anyone I could take with me, it would be you. That's for sure. But it's something I have to do alone."

Tim nodded, swallowed, and finally stopped fighting the tears.

David started the engine and pulled away, feeling on a level with the slimes.

When they were a few minutes from home, he said, "Just before I picked you up at school, I spent a couple hours at the library writing you a letter."

"A letter?" Tim was shocked, incredulous.

"Yes. There'll come a time when. . . . You're not going to remember this conversation forever, Tim. And I've told you things I haven't told anyone, not even your mother."

"Why?"

"Because she's not my son."

After thinking it over, Tim nodded.

"I don't know what she's going to tell you in the years to come. You understand? She's probably going to tell you I left because I didn't love you—didn't love you or her."

Tim said nothing.

"You're going to wonder what it was all about, and you're going to want to hear it from me. That's what the letter is for." He took it out of his jacket pocket and shoved it across the seat. Tim made no move to pick it up.

"You can show it to your mother if you want to, but I'd rather you didn't. It's just from me to you."

"I don't want a *letter*," Tim snapped, staring out of the window.

It was still on the seat when they got out of the car at home. David retrieved it and put it back in his jacket.

Ellen, seeing them drive up, was waiting in the doorway. Tim tossed his book bag on a hallway table, said he was going out, and left.

David, awkwardly confronting his wife in the hallway, tried to find the strength he'd need to get through the next ordeal.

"I called your mother," Ellen said.

"Why on earth did you do that?"

"Don't you think she has a right to know what you're planning to do to her grandson?"

"To her grandson? Yes, I suppose she does."

"She wants you to call her."

"Yes," he said again. "I suppose she does."

They were still standing just inside the front door, as though he were about to leave that minute.

"She thinks we should at least talk to a marriage counselor."

"I'll bet she does."

"So do I."

David sighed. "There's nothing wrong with our *marriage*, Ellen."

"Gee, that's terrific news, David. You're leaving me flat, but there's nothing wrong with our marriage. I'm really glad to hear that."

He left her to go into the kitchen for a drink. A roast was in the oven—a pathetic touch of hopefulness. Ellen followed him and said, "She thinks you ought to see a psychiatrist, David."

"She's a thinker, Mother is."

"What's that supposed to mean?"

"Nothing much." It wasn't worth explaining.

"Will you talk to a psychiatrist—to someone? For my sake?"

"No."

"Why not?"

"Because I'm no more in need of psychiatric help today than I was yesterday."

"You weren't destroying all our lives yesterday."

It was a point he couldn't argue with. He took his drink into the living room.

"Will you, David?"

"It would be pointless, Ellen. I haven't lost my mind. I'm not confused. I'm just doing something you don't like."

"Jesus! Something I don't like? Do you realize what you're doing to Tim?"

He said nothing.

"Would you agree to see a psychiatrist if you'd picked up a knife and stabbed him?"

"Yes."

"What you're doing is a hell of a lot worse than that, David, and you know it."

He spent a while standing at the window, worrying a lot, trying hard to be fair. Finally he said, "I can't argue with you, Ellen, because for the first time in my life I'm on the wrong side of every argument. What I'm doing is indefensible—so obviously I can't defend it. I'm being completely selfish and completely unfair. I know that. To explain to a psychiatrist *why* I'm being completely selfish and completely unfair wouldn't change anything. It would just take today's agony and spread it out over the next six months."

"You can't know that, David. You might find some way of getting what you want without blowing our lives to pieces. You could at least look for a way, for Christ's sake. Don't you owe us that much?"

With that question, she'd offered him a shabby way out, and he took it without hesitation. "I owe you that and much more, Ellen, but I'm tapped out."

He left to go upstairs and start packing. As he shoveled clothes into a suitcase, he heard Ellen shrieking hysterically to someone on the telephone, but he blocked out the words and kept at it.

On his way downstairs David stopped in Tim's room and left the letter on his desk. Then, thinking better of it, he put it under some papers in a drawer.

Ellen was waiting at the bottom of the stairs, her face ablaze. "You're not leaving this fucking *minute*, are you?"

"I left the checkbook and the bankbook upstairs," he told her levelly. "I figured it would be fair to take a third of it."

"You bastard!"

He moved around her toward the door.

"I hope there's a God—just this once in my life—and I hope he creates hell just for you."

He put his suitcase down by the door and turned back.

"Don't get revenge by making Tim hate me, Ellen. That's not for my sake, that's for his."

"You've got nothing to say about it once you walk out that door."

"I know. I'm just telling you. Making Tim a hater isn't the answer."

"You know the answer, do you?"

He picked up his bag.

"You care a fucking lot, do you?"

He left.

He pitched his bag into the car, slid into the driver's seat, and backed out of the drive wildly, in a panic now that Tim might return before he got away. He turned into the street wondering what he'd do if he passed him. Wave lamely? Stop the car and grovel before him? No, he'd shrink down into the seat and drive on, staring straight ahead.

But he was lucky. He got away unseen—or so he thought.

CHAPTER 16

David's nervous departure was observed by Tim from a vantage point he hadn't visited for years: the platform of a treehouse across the street, begun in a previous generation and never completed. He hadn't gone there specifically to watch his father leave. He'd gone there to fulfill a need he wouldn't have been able to put into words: a need to find a position outside and above his house—a need for perspective.

In the hour since he'd climbed the tree he'd looked down at the house with an empty watchfulness, not knowing what to expect. Anything seemed possible. His mother and father might burst out of the house arm in arm, laughing at the joke they'd played on him. The house might explode or collapse in on itself. Or nothing might happen. Perhaps night would fall, the lights would go on, and he would go home to find that he'd imagined the whole thing, that Ellen was humming in the kitchen, that David was scowling at a manuscript in his study. Perhaps he'd wake up in his bed and realize he'd dreamed it all.

But he knew none of those things would actually happen. His father would soon leave the house, put a bag in the car, and drive away. He saw it happening again and again, already fixed in the sequence of his life, like a scene from one of those movies in which everything is destroyed because the hero makes one terrible choice, one fatal mistake. You know the scene is coming, know it has to come, because that's what the movie's about. Yet, when it comes, you say, "But *why*? Why do this thing when it's bound to lead to disaster?" Everyone in the audience can see it's a ghastly mistake, but the hero makes it anyway.

Finally it happened just the way it had to. His father walked stiffly out of the house, slung a bag into the car, and drove off, wheels chirping as he pulled out at the bottom of the driveway, as if another minute in that place was intolerable. Tim watched it happen and felt a vast hollowness open up inside of him. He didn't want to move, didn't want to get up and resume his life. He wanted to sit there forever, waiting. It was possible his father would get to the edge of town, pull over, cross his arms over the steering wheel, and bury his face in them, thinking, reconsidering. It was possible he would realize that he really couldn't do this horrible thing to his wife and son. It was possible he would turn around and come home.

It couldn't happen in a movie. But it could happen in a life.

When it hadn't happened by dusk, Tim climbed down from the tree and walked across the street, sick with dread.

Ellen was glad Tim hadn't been there during her last hysterical scene with David. She was even more glad that he'd given her a couple of hours to get herself together again.

After David walked out and her body had stopped pumping adrenalin, she had a drink: one. God knows, it was a day worthy of a booze-up, but Tim was going to have enough to bear without a drunken mother.

Now that it had definitely happened, she wasn't sure what she felt. She'd gone through a lot of emotions in the past eight hours: confusion, panic, despair, self-pity, fury. Sitting on the sofa with her drink, she tasted them all again and found their flavors exhausted. Oddly enough, the one emotion she'd expected to overwhelm her at this point was entirely absent: She felt no fear at all. In a way, David had done that for her, though she wouldn't thank him for it. David, pausing in his treachery to lecture her on how to raise the son he was abandoning, had given her a new emotion to build on. She smiled as she put a name to it: *defiance.*

She was going to show that cold-hearted, supercilious son of a bitch. She and Tim would manage without him. Would manage and live well. That would be their revenge—and it would be all the revenge they'd need. She couldn't be bothered to teach Tim to hate his father—he wasn't worth it. Tim could decide for himself what he thought of David.

She was just beginning to feel a little nervous about Tim's absence when she heard the front door close. She called out to him that she was in the living room. When he appeared in the doorway, she studied his face and told him not to look so goddamned glum.

Tim conjured up a feeble smile for her.

"Come sit down, kiddo." She patted the seat beside her. "We've got things to talk about." He sat down in a chair across from her, and she nodded, one corner of her mouth drawn down into a sour smile. "Like that, huh? Mad at the world."

"Yeah," Tim said.

"Me too, kiddo. We've been screwed." Seeing his startled look, she added, "That's the word for it, isn't it?"

"I guess so."

She got up and went into the kitchen. When she returned, she handed Tim a glass of whiskey and touched it with her own, now refilled.

"You ever tasted this stuff?"

He shook his head.

"You deserve a slug tonight. Go ahead, try it."

He took a sip, held it in his mouth appraisingly for a few seconds, and then swallowed it, poker-faced.

"Nasty, huh?"

He nodded.

"You know what, Tim?" she said, sitting down again. "You know what I wish I'd done before he left? I wish I'd slugged him."

Tim laughed.

"It wouldn't have changed anything, but I wish I'd thought of it. I'd be feeling a whole lot better."

"I know," the boy said.

Ellen studied his worried face for a moment. "One thing you've got to know, Tim. It's not the end of the world. I'm going to see to that, I promise you."

"Okay."

"But you're going to have to help me."

"How?"

"By not *making* it the end of the world. We're going to keep going, Tim. There's no reason why we shouldn't. We're not in bad shape. There are no debts, except for the mortgage on the house, and we can handle that. The car's paid for, and there's no reason why I can't get a job. We may not live as high on the hog as we used to, but we're certainly not going to be destitute. I promise you that."

"Okay. But isn't Dad going to . . . send us something?"

"I don't have any idea what your father's going to do, Tim. It looks to me like he's gone off the deep end—right off the edge of the cliff."

The boy frowned over this for a while. "Are you saying you think he's crazy?"

She shrugged. "What do you call it when a man you've been happily married to for fourteen years walks downstairs one morning and calmly announces he's abandoning you?"

"I don't know."

"I don't know either. What I do know is that it doesn't make much sense to count on him for anything at this point."

"True."

"So, kiddo. Getting hungry?" He shook his head. "No end of the world stuff, Tim. Check your stomach."

He grinned up at her. "I'm starving."

"Good. That roast has been ready for half an hour."

That was a Wednesday. On the following Monday they were setting up the pieces for a game of Parcheesi after dinner when the phone rang. Ellen made a face and Tim asked if he should get it.

"No. It's probably David's mother."

She walked over to the phone, picked up the receiver, and uttered an unfriendly hello.

"Ellen?"

The distant, strangely fragile voice raised the hairs on the back of her neck.

"Ellen?"

"David? Is that you?"

"Oh God . . ."

"David, what is it?"

"I don't know."

"What's wrong?"

"I don't know. I've been wandering around. . . ."

"Where are you?"

"Oh," he said, as if this should be obvious. "I'm in Chicago. I don't know what's going on."

"What do you mean, David? What's wrong?"

A long pause.

"David?"

"Yes?"

"Tell me what's wrong."

"I don't know. I'm . . . confused."

"Do you want me to come get you?"

Another pause.

"David, where are you?"

"Oh. A hotel."

"What hotel?"

"Wait." Ellen heard him turn away from the phone and talk to someone nearby. "It's the Edgewater Beach Hotel."

"Where's that?"

Another muffled conversation.

"He says it's on the lake just north of Bryn Mawr."

"Do you want me to come get you?"

"I can't remember where I left the car," David replied vaguely.

"David, *do you want me to come get you?*" She heard the phone being clumsily hung up.

"Stay there!" she screamed into the dead receiver. "*Stay there!*"

CHAPTER 17

Ten miles from the Illinois border, Ellen whispered "Damn, damn, damn," and put the accelerator pedal to the floor to make up for her blunder: she should have left Tim home in case David called again.

Very quietly, Tim asked her what was wrong.

"Nothing," she said, knowing it was too late to turn back.

These were the first words they'd exchanged since leaving the house. Ellen was gripping the wheel as if they were traversing a city under bombardment, and Tim was afraid to break her concentration with questions. Even under normal circumstances, she was a nervous driver. Now, plunging into the maelstrom of Chicago's traffic—in the dark—she was on the edge of panic.

The city's expressway system was like a vast river in flood, sweeping cars off to Joliet and Peoria and Elmhurst and Des Plaines—northward and westward away from Lake Michigan. With an almost physical effort, she fought her way eastward across the roiling currents and finally drifted out into the relatively calm stream of northbound Lake Shore Drive. After that it was easy.

A few minutes later she turned off the drive onto Bryn Mawr and headed north on Sheridan Road. She'd heard of the Edgewater Beach Hotel and had the impression it was a big one, but she told Tim to watch for it anyway. A dozen blocks later she turned back. "Just north of Bryn Mawr" couldn't possibly be past Devon.

A taxi was pulling out of a motel turnaround ahead of her, and she slammed on the brakes to block it. The driver honked and stuck his head out of the window to yell at her, but she was already running over to talk to him.

"I'm looking for the Edgewater Beach Hotel," she said breathlessly.

"What?"

"I'm trying to find the Edgewater Beach Hotel."

He frowned at her and then laughed. "You're twelve, fifteen years too late, lady."

"What do you mean?"

"They tore it down. Long time ago."

"That can't be."

He shrugged and rolled his eyes at the stupidity of some people.

"Look, I'll pay you to take me there."

"Take you where?"

"To the Edgewater Beach Hotel."

"Lady, I told you. It's gone. It ain't there."

"Take me to where it used to be."

"Where it used to be is just an apartment building."

"That's all right. Show me where it is. I'll pay five dollars."

"Okay. But if you're going to follow me, I need the money up front."

She went back for her purse and paid him.

The doorman listened to Ellen's story with lips pressed together and eyes full of distrust. He assured her that the owners of the new building were not responsible for anything that might have happened to— or at—the Edgewater Beach Hotel. She repeated it more slowly, and he assured her that no one answering David's description had entered the building or used the telephone in the lobby or the office. He gave some thought to her request to examine the directory of tenants and couldn't find any reasonable grounds for denying it, but kept an eye on her while she did it.

She found no names she recognized.

"Is there an Edgewater Beach *Motel?*"

"Not that I know of," he said.

"Do you have a telephone directory I could look at?" Seeing that she'd reached the limit of his patience, she handed him a five dollar bill.

There was no Edgewater Beach Motel, Restaurant, Lounge, or Bar.

Back in the car, she sank into her seat, lit a cigarette, and told Tim what had happened.

"He's got to be around here somewhere," Tim insisted.

"Maybe. But what good does that do us? He could be a block away and we wouldn't know it."

"He said the Edgewater Beach Hotel."

"I know, Tim, but there is no Edgewater Beach Hotel."

His shoulders sagged wearily. "Gonna go home and leave him here?"

"Tim, what else can we do? He can't reach us sitting here in the car. We've got to go back and wait by the phone."

Tim set his jaw stubbornly and glared out of the window. "I'll stay here."

"For God's sake, Tim, please don't be ridiculous. The only place we can be of any use is at home, and we've got to be there together."

"Okay," he growled, and climbed into the back seat.

Five minutes later he slid into an exhausted sleep.

It was nearly ten when Ellen noticed that the fuel needle was bobbing on empty, and she thought bitterly that running out of gas in the middle of nowhere would make a fitting end to the evening. She found a self-serve station outside Valparaiso—and just as she pulled in, its lights winked out. She ran over to the office and pounded on the door, and the teen-aged attendant looked up and said, "Closed."

"Please," she said, "I'm running on vapor." He slammed a drawer shut and unlocked the door. "You'll have to have the right change. I just put all the money in the safe."

She looked through her purse and found two twenties and a one. "All I've got is a twenty."

"Then you can buy twenty dollars worth of gas."

"It won't take twenty dollars worth."

He bared yellow teeth at her in a silent snarl. "Lady, it don't mean shit to me."

She shoved a twenty at him and went out to pump gas in the dark. The attendant watched her through the door and switched off the pump the moment the gas level rose high enough to turn off the nozzle.

"Thanks a lot!" she shouted.

"Screw you!" he shouted back.

She got into the car, slammed into gear, and roared back onto the highway.

Forty minutes later she pulled into the driveway of their house, turned off the motor, and sank back against the seat, letting her tension ebb away.

"We're home," she said.

She turned to give Tim a shake, and her stomach shriveled into an icy ball.

The back seat was empty.

CHAPTER 18

Lulled by the steady rolling of the car, Tim had slept heavily until they stopped at the gas station outside Valparaiso. With the cessation of movement, he stirred and realized groggily that his stomach was in the midst of an upheaval. He lurched out of the car, took in his surroundings dimly, and made for the men's room. Its door was locked.

The contents of his stomach were geysering up into his throat as he stumbled back into the weeds behind the station. He bent over and a column of fiery liquid gushed from his mouth. He staggered away from this first mess and knelt in the weeds, waiting for the rest to come. It surged up and he gagged, forcing it back. Again it rose and again he choked it back, leaving a searing trail in his throat.

He remembered a scene from many years back, when he'd had the flu: his father kneeling beside the toilet bowl and holding him in his arms.

"Let it go, Tim," he'd said. "Give it all up. Don't hold it back."

The next time it rose, he let it go. He crawled away and, head hanging, tried to gather enough saliva to clear his mouth of the foulness. He gulped a few times, spit, wiped the sweat off his face, and got to his feet unsteadily. At a drinking fountain by the rest rooms he rinsed his mouth out, took a long drink, and splashed some water over his face.

Turning to go back to the car, he stared stupidly at the dark, empty bays of the service station, and thought, "This can't be happening." Knowing the car couldn't possibly be hidden there, he nevertheless walked around to the front of the pumps looking for it. He actually gazed down at the grease-stained concrete, as if it might have opened up and swallowed the car. He looked up and down the highway; there were no taillights to be seen in either direction.

Dazed, he walked over to peer at the contents of the deserted office: a U-Haul calendar on the wall, a coffee maker on a shelf, stacks of motor oil, a pay phone. The Rolodex file on the desk fascinated him like an artifact from an alien spaceship. Finally he shuffled away to sit on the edge of one of the concrete pumping islands while he tried to puzzle out the meaning of this almost preternatural event.

Why had his mother stopped at a closed filling station? The obvious answer was that he'd told her he was going to be sick. He didn't remember doing so, but why else would she have stopped?

But then, if she'd stopped because he was sick, why didn't she wait for him?

He was certain that the lights over the pumps had been dark when he got out of the car. But it seemed to him that the office had been lighted when he stumbled past. Half asleep and his stomach boiling, he might have imagined that.

But suppose he hadn't imagined it. Suppose there had been a light—and someone inside the office.

Perhaps someone at the filling station had flagged Ellen down—someone with information about David. But how could anyone just standing on the highway recognize their car rushing by in the dark? No, it couldn't have been that way.

It had to have been a planned meeting.

Suddenly, in imagination, he saw his mother slip into the office and heard her say to the faceless person inside: "It's all right—Tim's sound asleep. We can talk now." Perhaps they talked about his father.

A thrill of terror chased itself up his spine.

Perhaps the man she talked to *was* his father. After the strangeness of this day and this week, nothing at all seemed farfetched. The obvious, commonplace solution to the puzzle didn't even come to mind for consideration.

For the next twenty minutes he watched cars flashing by in both directions. Then, as he stared dumbfounded, his father's green Volvo turned into the station from the east and slowed to a stop beside him. The stranger inside rolled down the window and said:

"You got a water hose?"

Paralyzed, his mouth hanging open, Tim gawked at him.

"Hey!" the man said again.

"Wh-what?"

"You got a water hose?"

"I don't know what you're talking about."

"Don't you work here?"

"No."

"Shit." The man frowned. "I got a hole in my radiator or something, and the thing's gonna blow if I don't get some water."

"Where did you get my father's car?"

The stranger turned his frown on Tim. "Are you stoned or something?"

"No."

"Well, if this is your father's car, it's news to me. I been paying on it for five years."

"Oh."

The man opened the door, got out, and looked around. Then, spotting a hose beside the office, got back in and pulled the car over to it. Watching him, Tim was struck by his resemblance to his father, of middle height, slender but broad-shouldered, dark-haired. Although completely unalike in manner, the two men had the same neat, economical style of movement.

After raising the hood, he gave the radiator cap a cautious half turn and leaped back as if expecting an explosion of steam. When nothing happened, he lifted off the cap, peered inside, and grunted.

He turned to Tim and said, "I think I better let it cool off for a while." He blinked at the boy curiously, as if seeing him for the first time. "What the hell are you doing out here, anyway?"

"I'm not sure myself," Tim said, then added: "It's a long story."

The man propped his backside on the fender of his car and folded his arms. "I got time to kill."

Again sitting on the edge of one of the pumping islands, Tim put his forearms across his legs and stared down at the cement between his feet, wondering if he should begin at the beginning. He decided he'd better.

When he was finished, the man said, "That's a hell of a thing."

"Yeah."

"You tried calling her?"

"She wouldn't be home yet. And the phone's in the office."

The man scratched the side of his jaw thoughtfully, as if debating with himself about something. "You know," he said at last, "I think I know where your dad was calling from."

"You do?"

He nodded. "Yeah. Maybe."

"Where?"

"Well, there's this place," he said vaguely. "A bar, cocktail lounge called the Yacht Club. . . . You're too young to remember, but the Edgewater Beach Hotel was pretty hot stuff back in the thirties and forties. I mean real fancy. There was this one restaurant that was decked out like the lounge of a luxury liner—all teak and brass, life-savers, portholes, that kind of stuff. It had surf sound effects, bells, foghorns, everything. You had to cross a sort of bridge to get to it, like you were boarding a ship, see? It was called the Yacht Club. Anyway, when they were going to tear the place down, some guys got together and bought the fittings and set it all up in a spot on Bryn Mawr, just like it was in the hotel."

"You mean *on* Bryn Mawr?"

"That's right."

"They told Dad it was a few blocks north of Bryn Mawr."

He nodded. "Yeah, that's the whole idea. See? The Edgewater Beach Hotel was a few blocks north of Bryn Mawr."

"I don't get it."

"Well, look. The idea is, this is still the Edgewater Beach Hotel. See? When they answer the phone, they say, 'Yacht Club, Edgewater Beach Hotel.' They use the same matchbook covers, the same ashtrays, everything. Everybody's supposed to pretend it's still part of the hotel, see?"

"That's really weird."

"Well, it's a sort of joke. A nostalgia thing."

Tim shrugged bleakly.

"Anyhow, I have to go practically right by it to get home if you want to check it out."

"You mean you'd take me there?"

"Sure, why not? It just means getting off at Bryn Mawr instead of Hollywood. No big deal." Seeing the boy's hesitation, he added, "We could leave a note for your mom in case she comes back."

Tim looked around uncertainly. "Where would we put it?"

The man snorted. "You want to be a success in life, kid? Remember this: for every problem there's a solution."

Three minutes later they were on their way.

The man introduced himself as Frank Orsini and said he was a printing salesman. But, as Tim found out, he was a missionary as well. As he warmed to his subject, he outlined the fabulous future Tim could expect to have in sales, detailed the course of studies he should pursue, described the sort of companies to ally himself with, laid down some basic principles he'd discovered for himself, and advised him about commission plans and stock option deals. Staring numbly out at the black flatlands sweeping by the window, Tim let the talk wash over him, grateful that he didn't have to listen to his own thoughts and that Frank Orsini was content with his role as monologist.

It was nearly midnight when they parked a few doors away from the entrance to the Yacht Club, marked by a red neon sign so discreet it was almost invisible. Inside, after passing an unattended cloak-room, they crossed a gangway over a simulated beach to two dark, portholed doors that opened onto a deck three or four steps above the main room. Along the left wall stood a long, dimly-lit bar, now nearly deserted. Portholes in the right wall overlooked a roman-tically moonlit Lake Michigan, whose sighs could be heard behind the Andrews Sisters and "The Boogie-Woogie Bugle Boy."

As they crossed the room, the balding, red-jacketed bartender watched with stony disapproval and greeted them with an unfriendly "Can I help you?"

"Yeah, maybe," Orsini said. "This boy's father's turned up a little missing, and he may have been here earlier tonight." He turned to Tim. "Tell him what he looks like, kid."

The bartender listened to Tim's description and shrugged indif-ferently.

"He made a call from here around seven thirty," Tim said.

"Not from here he didn't."

Orsini asked if there was a pay phone.

"By the front door, but it's out of order."

"There's gotta be another phone, right?"

"Behind the bar, yeah. But nobody's used it tonight, I can tell you that."

Orsini frowned and drummed his fingers on the bar impatiently. "No others?"

"One in the office out front, but that's been locked up since six."

He gave the bartender a baleful glare and then transferred it in-tact to Tim, as if the two of them had conspired to make a fool of him.

"Well, I guess that's it then," he said bitterly and turned to leave.

As they walked out of the bar, a slowly cruising police car came to a stop across the street. When its door opened, Orsini said, "Oh, shit! Get in the car."

"What?"

"Get in the goddamned car. And look—if he asks you, tell him I'm your father."

Tim started to ask him what was going on, but Orsini had already turned to meet the patrolman in the middle of the street. They talked for a minute, then walked over to the passenger side of the Volvo.

The policeman bent down to scan the interior of the car, then turned solemnly to the boy. "This man is your father?"

"Yes, sir."

He looked unconvinced. "How long were you in that bar?"

"A couple minutes."

"You sure of that?"

"Yes, sir. Absolutely."

He studied Tim's face skeptically. "This man is your father?"

"Yes, sir." He decided it was time to move a bit off the defensive. "What's wrong, anyway?"

Ignoring the question, the policeman straightened up, had a few more words with Orsini, and then went back to his cruiser.

"What was that all about?" Tim asked when Orsini slid into the seat beside him and started the engine.

"Asshole thought I was contributing to the delinquency of a minor." He pulled away from the curb, turned right on Sheridan Road, drove north a few blocks, and was stopped by a red light. He sat drumming thoughtfully on the steering wheel with his fists until the light changed, then turned left and went around the block. Coming back to Sheridan, he turned right and headed back the way they'd come.

Tim gave him a curious glance but said nothing.

A few minutes later the man said, "I got another idea, kid."

"Okay."

He pulled up at a bus stop. "I want you to wait for me here. I can't take you with me this time, where I got to go, see?"

Tim looked out blankly at the bench. "You want me to wait here?"

"Right."

"How long will it take?"

He shrugged. "Fifteen, twenty minutes."

"Okay."

Tim got out of the car, sat down on the bench, and watched the Volvo make a U-turn and disappear northward.

He was still there more than an hour later when a bus stopped in front of him and a huge man with a battered face stepped out, peered down at him with a puzzled look, and said, "Are you waiting for this bus?"

As Howard was putting this query to Tim, Tim's mother was walking into a police station less than two miles away. She was faintly surprised to find herself doing this; it was as if the decision had been made by her legs, and she was simply being carried along as an unwilling, semi-conscious passenger.

A man at a desk—she noticed nothing about him except that he was a man—spoke to her, and evidently some part of her understood what he said, because she answered him.

She sat down in a hard chair. Words flowed out of her, and evidently they made some sort of sense, because the man nodded and wrote things down on a pad in front of him. Finally she handed him the stiff, pale-green sheet of cover stock that she'd found wedged in the door of the gas station. The message written on it with a heavy red marker read:

Mom—
I've found someone who knows where Dad was calling from.
I'll call you from Chicago.

                                                    Tim

The man at the police station asked many questions about Tim and about David, and, though she couldn't remember what they were afterward, she answered them. Then he gave her some soothing half-truths to see her through the next few hours and told her to go home.

She shook her head.

He asked if she had a cell phone or if there was an answering machine at home. When she shook her head again, he explained to her that she really had to go back, in case Tim tried to reach her. She nodded but went on sitting in the hard chair, her eyes vacant, her body slack with fatigue, and he realized she was virtually unconscious. He called a nearby motel to tell them to expect another guest for the night, gave her detailed directions, made her repeat them, and handed her a card with two names written on it, one of them his.

When she didn't move, he told her to put the card in her purse, and she did.

With a sigh, he helped her to her feet and took her to her car.

Sitting on the bench at the bus stop, Howard listened to the boy's story and told him it was pointless to go on waiting for Frank Orsini. "It looks like you've been ditched three times in one week—twice in one day," he said. "That's got to be a world record."

Tim smiled wearily.

"My place is just a couple blocks away. We'll make some phone calls and bed you down for the night. Okay?"

"Yeah. Okay."

Howard's first call was to Tim's home; naturally that went unanswered. His second was to the Indiana State Police.

"Within the past two or three, four hours," Howard said, "you've probably gotten a call from Ellen Kennesey of Runnell, Indiana, about a missing son. They got separated by accident at a gas station outside Valparaiso."

"Hold on."

Tim, sitting with a Coke in his hands, watched expectantly as Howard waited through five minutes.

"Sorry. We've had no such call."

"Huh. She must be out there looking for him herself, since she's not home answering her phone."

"I see. May I have your name, please?" He gave her his name and phone number and told her he was a private investigator in Chicago. "Did Mrs. Kennesey hire you to find her son?"

"No, no. The boy hitched into Chicago, and I just happened to find him stranded here. The point is, if she calls, give her my number and tell her Tim's fine."

She chewed this over for half a minute. "You really need to turn the boy over to the authorities there."

"Yeah, I know, but it'd be no kindness, believe me. The kid's exhausted. He's already asleep on the sofa." He tipped Tim a wink.

"Well, I guess it's your lookout."

"Everything'll work out fine, officer. We'll have it all straightened out as soon as we get in touch with each other."

It was an appropriate ending for the day. Howard had called the Indiana police (instead of the Chicago police) because Tim had forgotten to mention the note he'd left behind for Ellen at the gas station. And Tim, taking it for granted that Howard was talking to the Chicago police, didn't think to mention it now.

CHAPTER 19

At ten Ellen fought her way up out of a drowning dream and spent a panic-stricken moment trying to remember where she was and what she was doing there. She went into the bathroom and faced herself in the mirror. She looked a wreck, her hair an unruly tangle, but there was little she could do about it. She washed her face and, while delving in her purse for makeup, found the card she'd been given at the police station the night before.

She dialed the number and asked for either Sergeant Wiley or Sergeant Horlach. After a couple of minutes she was connected with Sergeant Wiley, who told her there had been a development of sorts. A patrolman coming off night duty had seen a notice about her missing son and reported that he'd spotted such a boy coming out of a bar with a man he identified as his father.

"His description of the man tallies with your description of your husband," Wiley said. "And he was driving a green Volvo, 1988 or thereabouts. According to the report Sergeant Horlach left me, your husband told you he was calling from the Edgewater Beach Hotel. Is that right?"

"Yes. That's what he was told, anyway."

"That's very interesting," Wiley said and went on to explain the Yacht Club's association with the hotel. "It seems pretty well connected up, Mrs. Kennesey. It looks like whoever picked up Tim knew about the Yacht Club and got him together with his father there."

"You mean . . . he's actually with David?"

"That's the way it looks."

"But where were they going?"

"Well, you have to understand that the officer didn't know either one of them was missing. He only stopped them because he thought it was a little strange for a boy of Tim's age to be coming out of a bar at midnight."

"What did he say?"

"What did who say?"

"My husband."

"He said he'd just gone into the bar to find a friend who wasn't there, so he left."

Ellen shook her head. "That doesn't make any sense."

"Yes, well, not on the face of it. But you've got to realize that, if it was your husband, he probably wouldn't be in a mood to share his life story with some nosy cop. Like most people, his first idea would be to come up with a plausible tale that would make him go away. That's why the officer talked to the boy separately."

"And what did he say?"

Wiley hesitated. "Mrs. Kennesey, I'm not going to pretend that a great piece of police work was done here. In these circumstances, I might have been more curious than this particular officer was, but then again I might not have been. All he was trying to find out was whether some kind of funny business was going on there. He asked the boy how long they'd been in the bar, and he confirmed that it had just been a couple of minutes. He asked if the man was his father and he said he was. According to the officer, he was very definite about it."

"But you're not sure it was Tim."

"No, ma'am. But the man, the boy, and the car all fit the descriptions you gave us, and they were outside a bar that was once part of the Edgewater Beach Hotel. Frankly, I'd be amazed to find out it *wasn't* them."

Ellen spent a few moments trying to digest this. "So what would you do if you were me?"

"Have you called home this morning?"

"No."

"Then that's what I'd do."

"And if they're not there?"

"Then I'd go home and wait for them."

"And then? What if they don't come home?"

Sergeant Wiley stifled a sigh. "Look, Mrs. Kennesey, we've got to take this one step at a time. Go home, see what happens, and we'll carry on from there. All right?"

"Yes, I guess so. All right." She hung up, dialed the number at home, and let it ring for a full minute before hanging up. Her hand still resting on the phone, she gazed dully into the seascape on the wall, with its storm-tossed sailing ship, and tried to decide what to do next. She checked her watch: ten-thirty. She dressed, had breakfast at the motel coffee shop, and drove to Bryn Mawr. By then it was eleven thirty, but the Yacht Club wasn't open.

She drove back to Runnell and was mildly surprised to find the house still standing, still looking prim and safe and ordinary. She put the dinner dishes in the dishwasher, dug out some snapshots of David and Tim, packed a bag (to be on the safe side), and left a prominent note on the refrigerator:

Tim / David—

I hope to hell one of you (or preferably both of you) are here to read this note. If you are, for God's sake, *stay here*. I should be back by eight or nine tonight. Notice that I don't say where I'm going. If I did, sure as hell, you'd come looking for me and the whole thing would start all over again.

STAY HERE!!!

Ellen

Then she went to the bank and withdrew a thousand dollars. While she was pulling out of the parking lot to return to Chicago, Tim and Howard were entering the house she'd left just minutes before. As they walked into the kitchen, the dishwasher completed its final rinse cycle and clicked off. They stared at it incredulously and shook their heads at how narrowly they'd missed her.

"We might be able to catch her before she gets out of town," Tim suggested.

Howard shook his head firmly. "No, your mother's right. This comedy of errors has got to stop. No more chasing around after each other. You stay right here. Don't even poke your nose out the door."

"Okay."

"Do you want me to stick around till she gets back?"

"No, I'll be all right."

Howard dug a card out of his jacket pocket and handed it to him. "You give me a call when she gets here, okay?"

"Yeah, okay."

He turned to leave and then paused, frowning. "Tim, I want you to make me a promise. A solemn promise."

The boy shrugged. "Okay."

"Under no circumstances—no matter who calls or what happens —are you to leave this house without calling me first. Understand?"

"I understand."

"Promise?"

"I promise."

"To do what?"

"Not to leave the house without calling you first."

Howard nodded and went out to his rented car.

CHAPTER 20

As Ellen approached the entrance to the Yacht Club, a car door opened beside her and a man stepped out onto the sidewalk.

"Mrs. Kennesey?"

She turned and stared at him curiously. He was dressed in grubby house-painter's coveralls and had a ferret's face that was surmounted by a thatch of coarse red hair.

"Yes?"

"Detective Wolf, ma'am. Chicago Police."

She looked at him and at the car, a battered sedan from the 1970s. "I don't believe it," she said.

His thin smile was unpleasantly like a sneer. "You can't always go by appearances, Mrs. K. This is my partner, Detective Goodman." The door on the driver's side opened and a bulky, putty-faced man with close-cropped gray hair got out and nodded across the roof of the car. He too was dressed in coveralls.

"What do you want?" Ellen asked him.

"To talk to you, Mrs. Kennesey," the putty-faced man said. "Obviously." He had a voice like gravel flowing down a tin chute.

"About what?"

"About your husband and your son, what else?"

She looked from one to the other and said, "I'd like to see some identification."

Wolf laughed: a harsh gust of air through his nose.

"Lady, working undercover, we don't carry identification."

"I don't understand. What do my husband and my son have to do with your undercover work?"

"Not a goddamn thing, Mrs. K," Wolf said. "Look, we're just here to give you a message. If you don't want it, we'll be on our way."

"A message?"

He nodded.

"From whom?"

"From the sergeant. Something came in this morning he thought you might be interested in."

"Go on."

"How 'bout we talk in the car, Mrs. K? Much more comfortable."

She looked at the car again and shook her head.

"Okay, lady, suit yourself." He leaned back against it and folded his arms. "Around eleven this morning, one of the maids out at the O'Hare Holiday Inn goes into a room and finds a note under a pillow that reads, 'Please call my mother.' She turns the note in to her supervisor, who turns it in to her supervisor, and finally it gets to the day manager, who looks up the records for the room and calls us, just to keep his ass protected. The room was taken last night about one A.M., for one night only, by a Mr. David Kennedy, who is some kind of a joker. He lists his home address as Backhome, Indiana. He drives a Volvo, but the license number don't match your husband's. He pays for the room in advance, in cash, and asks the room clerk to make a reservation for tomorrow—that'd be today—at the Inn in Omaha."

Wolf smirked at her, one eye half closed.

"Did you say *Kennedy*?"

"Yup."

Ellen paused, blinking down at the sidewalk. "And you think this was my husband?"

"Nope."

She looked up, astonished. "You don't?"

"We're just messenger boys here, Mrs. K. The sergeant says, keep an eye on the Yacht Club and if the lady shows up, pass this on. He don't tell us to think."

"I see." She looked uneasily from one to the other. "I'm sorry. I guess I've been pretty rude."

"Gotta be rude to *somebody*," he observed cryptically.

"The note said, 'Please call my mother'? Nothing else?"

"Nope."

"Can I see it?"

"Sure. Why not?"

She looked at them expectantly. They stared back at her with vacant eyes. "Well? Where is it?"

"Out at the Holiday Inn, I suppose. If they kept it."

"You didn't tell them to keep it?" Wolf treated her to another snorting laugh. "Lady, I didn't tell nobody nothin'. I'm just passin' on a message."

Ellen sighed in frustration. "Look, I seem to have gotten off on the wrong foot with you. Let's start over, okay?"

He shrugged indifferently. "What's on your mind?"

"I'd like you to help me with this."

"Go on."

"What did this David Kennedy look like?"

"Jesus, lady." He shook his head in disgust. "Somebody finds a note that says 'Please call my mother,' do you think we mobilize the National Guard to look into it? Ordinarily the dispatcher just says, 'Yeah, that's swell, thanks for calling,' and forgets about it. It was just a fluke that the sergeant heard about it at all."

"You mean nobody *cares*?"

"Cares about what, for Christ's sake? The note don't say 'I'm being held prisoner.' The note don't say 'I'm being kidnaped.' It says 'Call my mom,' for Christ's sake. What are we supposed to do about that? Seal off the city? Declare a national emergency?"

Ellen looked helplessly at the other detective, who folded his arms across the car roof, rested his chin on them, and gazed at her without expression. She pressed her eyes shut for a long moment.

"Mr. Wolf, you're a difficult man."

"You want to report me? You want my badge number?"

"No, I don't want your badge number. I just want you to help me a little bit. I'm in trouble and I need some help."

Wolf's pinched features worked for a moment as if he were trying to transform his habitual sneer into something like a smile. When he was finished, he said, "Okay, lady. Shoot."

"You're a detective."

"Right."

"Well, I'm not. I need your advice. Should I go out to the Holiday Inn?"

"Sure. That's what I'd do. Probably there's nothing to it, probably it'll be a waste of time. But that's what I'd do. I'd ask around, see if anybody remembers this guy, see if anybody saw the kid."

"Thank you."

Wolf grinned. "Hey, Artie, you hear that? The lady said thank you!"

"I heard," the other grunted without lifting his head.

Ellen shook her head bleakly and turned to the entrance of the Yacht Club.

"Mrs. Kennesey." She turned back. "We already checked in there. Different bartender on duty tonight."

"Oh. Well . . . thank you again."

The two detectives laughed.

CHAPTER 21

Her eyes carefully alert and polite, the woman at the desk at the Holiday Inn listened to Ellen's story and said she hadn't been informed of the note found under the pillow. "That doesn't mean anything, of course," she added. "I'm sure lots of things happen on the day shift that we don't hear about."

Ellen asked if the note might have been kept.

"If it was, it should be in the lost and found locker." But it wasn't.

Working at her computer, she confirmed that a David Kennedy had checked in at 12:50 and had asked for a reservation at the Inn in Omaha.

"I booked it myself," she said, looking up.

"That means you saw him?"

"Yes, it means I saw him, but I'm afraid that's all it means."

Ellen showed her the snapshots she'd brought from home, and she shrugged. "It could be him, but I wouldn't swear to it. By the end of the day it's all just a blur." She gave Ellen a wistful little smile, as if apologizing for the fact that Ellen, too, would soon be just a blur.

"Is there anything to indicate he had a child with him?"

After a glance down at the computer screen, she said, "He booked a single, but that doesn't prove anything."

"You mean he *might* have had a child with him."

"That's right."

Ellen sighed wearily. "Do you have any suggestions?"

"Well, I suppose you could try the cocktail lounge. That's the only place open at that time of night."

The bartender, a hawk-faced Arab, listened to Ellen's story with an air of disdain, as if the suggestion that he might remember a customer at this place was a slur on his professionalism. "Where I work before, I know all the faces, all the names. Here," he said bitterly, "I just pour liquor and make money, no more."

"Please," she said, holding out the photo. "It's very important."

He snatched it from her hand and took it to a lamp beside the cash register. "No," he muttered angrily, "no." He tossed the picture on the bar. "I serve maybe ten, twenty men a night with face like that. All alike. Connie," he snapped at a passing cocktail waitress. "You look at this face. You see this face last night?"

"It would have been around one o'clock," Ellen said.

Connie shook her head over the photo. "If he was seven feet tall or wore a patch over one eye, I might remember him. Otherwise, if he just sat here and drank. . . ." She shrugged and handed it back. "Sorry."

"Thanks anyway."

The bartender leered at her triumphantly.

She ordered a scotch on the rocks and slumped back into the tall chair. When the drink arrived, she looked up and found a pleasant-looking elderly gentleman standing behind the next stool, waiting patiently for her attention. A couple inches shorter than Ellen, slender except for a neat little tummy, he reminded her of an amiable old sheep. He seemed vaguely out of place, as though until that moment he'd been in the parlor in his slippers, reading the newspaper with his feet up; he was wearing a shabby old cardigan sweater over a shirt and tie.

"Pardon me for eavesdropping," he said with a diffident smile, "but may I have a look at your picture?"

"Certainly. Please sit down."

He set his drink on the bar, climbed up onto the stool, and sat nodding over the photo. "Yes, yes, I think so. He didn't look so carefree as this, but I believe he and I shared a drink or two last night."

"Here?"

"Of course."

"You talked to him?"

The old man returned the picture and smiled gently. "Actually, he did most of the talking."

"What did he say?"

"Ah," he said, stroking his chin. "He is . . . ?"

"My husband."

"Ah. Ah. Then I suppose it's all right." He shrugged, absolving himself of the duties of a confidant. "I fear he was a trifle . . . tipsy. Not at first. At first he seemed quite sober. But after a bit he became, um, expansive."

"Go on. Please."

"He talked about a road."

"A road?"

"He said, 'There is a certain road.'"

"I don't understand."

He waggled his head apologetically. "I didn't either, of course. He said it several times, as if it were a discovery he could hardly bring himself to believe. 'There is a road, a certain road. . . .' But he didn't explain what he meant."

"That's all?"

"Oh no. That was at the end, when he was, ah, fairly well sloshed. Before that, he said . . . Oh, it was quite a little poem. I couldn't pretend to be able to repeat it. He said his life had been poured into a mold and that he'd given the mold a twist and the contents had spilled out, all smashed. He said . . ." The old man paused, gazing mistily into the distance. "I'm not sure of his words, but the image was of a set of molds, a nest of molds, his at the center. By destroying the mold of his own life, he'd destroyed all the others as well."

Ellen nodded, her throat tight. "Did he mention . . . our son?"

"Oh, indeed he did, Mrs. . . ."

"Kennesey. Ellen Kennesey."

"How do you do. My name is John Dee. Yes, he mentioned your son—with great emotion, I might add. He said he'd renounced his son along with the rest of his life, but that fate had ruled otherwise. He said that fate had, um, miraculously reunited the two of them. He didn't elaborate on that, I'm afraid. He took this to mean that, in some mysterious way, their lives were destined to be shaped in a single mold."

"Shit," Ellen said. "He's stolen him."

John Dee raised his brows curiously. "He's stolen your son?"

"Yes."

"I'm sorry. These things can be so . . . ugly."

She shakily lit a cigarette and, after a moment's consideration, realized there really wasn't any doubt about her next move. "Will you wait for me right here, Mr. Dee? I have to go make a plane reservation."

"Certainly."

She took a gulp of scotch and told him to order another round. At a phone in the lobby, she learned she could catch a seven-thirty flight if she left that instant, but that there was another at a quarter to nine; she reserved a seat on the later flight. Returning to her place at the bar, she asked the old man how David had seemed, besides being slightly drunk.

He peered thoughtfully into his drink. "Excited. Perhaps a bit giddy, like a boy just out of school for the summer."

Ellen winced. "Did he seem . . . I can't ask you if he seemed like himself, since you didn't know him before. But did he seem quite . . . sane?"

"Oh no," he answered with a small chuckle. "Not *quite* sane."

"What do you mean?"

He turned in his chair and studied her gravely. "Have you ever done an insane thing, Mrs. Kennesey?"

"No, not really."

"Then you don't know. For some men—perhaps all men—it's almost a necessity to do insane things from time to time: to confront the wild boar alone, spear in hand, to see the world from the top of an unscalable mountain, to risk one's entire fortune on the turn of a card. I think it's true of all men, personally, though nowadays most try to get along on risks taken by deputies—deputies in the boxing ring and on the football field."

"You mean . . . they have to test their manhood."

"Oh, it's not as simple as that, Mrs. Kennesey. When a man sets out to do something like this, he's not testing his manhood. He's testing the universe itself—he's testing the gods, if you will. He's finding out where he stands in the order of things. To best the rabbit or the deer means nothing, tells him nothing. But while he stalks the boar, he puts his fate to the test: he lives in the hands of the gods."

"And if the boar wins?"

"Ah, that's the whole point, Mrs. Kennesey. If the boar wins, then he dies in the hands of the gods."

"I don't understand."

"To die falling off a ladder or being run over by a drunk means nothing. But, for the man who lives and dies at risk, who puts his fate in the hands of the gods, death is never meaningless."

Ellen gave the ice in her drink a shake and took a sip of it. "You're quite a philosopher, aren't you?"

John Dee acknowledged her irony with an ironical little bow of his own. "Once long ago I was a physician, Mrs. Kennesey," he said. "Since then I've been many things, including a philosopher."

As the plane circled on its approach to Eppley Field, Ellen was surprised to see that Omaha, by its lights, seemed a vast metropolis. She closed her eyes uneasily. She preferred flying by night, when nothing but reflected faces could be seen in the windows. The lights of the city reminded her that only a fragile skin of metal separated her from the gulf below. She smiled, remembering how safe her life had seemed just a few days ago—and how fragile the skin separating her from catastrophe had been. A single seam had weakened and split, and the whole flimsy structure of her life had burst apart.

David had always maintained that, despite her veneer of liberal enlightenment, she secretly believed that all misfortune was fundamentally racial or ethnic—that three-fifths of the world wouldn't be in economic or political turmoil if it had had the good sense to be born white and Anglo-Saxon. She saw now that there was more than a little justice to the charge; if all this were happening to one of her African-American acquaintances, she would be horrified—but not really surprised.

At last she felt the reassuring kiss of wheels on runway, opened her eyes, and sighed. She'd put off till now thinking about the confrontation to come. Ordinarily she worked out all possible lines of attack and defense well in advance of an encounter expected to be hostile or contentious. But now, as she made her way through the airport toward the cab that would take her to the Holiday Inn, she realized that nothing could be worked out in advance—nothing. David might embrace her in hysterical relief, might gape at her in astonishment, might knock her down in fury.

What was it the officer at the police station had told her—good God—just this morning? *We've got to take this one step at a time.*

A protocol for a life in upheaval.

Room 262, the young man at the front desk told her, and gave her directions.

As she approached the door on slightly wobbly legs, she felt a spring being wound up in her stomach; it was like a coil of sharpened bamboo that, when released, could slash her to pieces.

She knocked and heard a muffled exchange of voices inside. Her second knock a few moments later seemed to provoke a low snicker. Looking down at the door handle, she realized that the door wasn't actually closed. She pushed it open.

The breath went out of her as though she'd been punched in the stomach. Her knees gave way.

Grinning up at her from the bed was the ferret-faced man who'd called himself Detective Wolf.

Consciousness dissolved around her like a bubble bursting in slow motion.

CHAPTER 22

When Tim phoned from Runnell at eleven that night to say that Ellen hadn't returned, Howard told him to sit tight and call again in the morning.

"Should I go to school?" Tim asked.

"Good God, no. You stay by that phone."

After making the boy renew his promise not to leave the house without calling him, Howard got ready for bed.

Unlike Ada, who could be dead to the world ten seconds after saying good night, he needed help falling asleep; over the years this help had taken the unvarying form of a large whiskey and a book, which he read till he was virtually comatose. Tonight he opened the book but didn't read. He was contemplating the only genuine mystery that had ever come his way: the mystery of the disappearing parents. It was as though David and Ellen Kennesey had simultaneously—or nearly simultaneously—gone crazy. The French had a name for it: *folie à deux.* Insanity for two; an infection of madness.

Tim said he'd wondered if his parents hadn't met secretly at the gas station where he'd been left behind. A lunatic idea, of course . . . unless they really were lunatics. Was it thinkable that they'd actually conspired to orphan their own son?

When David Kennesey phoned them in Runnel, Tim had heard

only his mother's side of the conversation. Had she reported the other side honestly?

How would she have reacted if what David had actually said was: *Ellen, I've had some time to think now, and I see what's wrong. I just can't cope with the responsibility of it all—wife, child, mortgage, job. I've just got to shed the burden. But I don't want to shed you. Let's run away, chuck it all, start over again someplace new.*

Would a normal woman go for a pitch like that?

You didn't ordinarily think of nice, conventional, middle-class folks reasoning that way; but then you didn't ordinarily think of nice, conventional, middle-class folks keeping tidy records of the number of Jews gassed in camp today either.

Strange things could happen to people.

Or maybe it really was an infection of madness. David takes off, thinking, well, this is a shitty thing to do to Tim, but, what the hell, Ellen will look after him. But then, after a few days of looking after Tim—of thinking of the long years of lonely responsibility ahead—Ellen says, hey, why me? I've got a life to lead too, you know. If it's all right for David to walk away from it all, why not me? Who says I have to bite the bullet here just because David doesn't want to bite it?

It was conceivable. As he drifted off on the tide of whiskey, something stirred in memory, and he thrust it back, for the sake of sleep.

Folie à deux.
The folly of duels.
A duel of swords.
A deuce of swords.
Adieux swords.
Adieux wards.
An orphan.
A boy.
Sleep.

The next morning a ringing telephone dragged him up from the bottom of an ocean of sleep, and he was only half awake when he stumbled across the room and picked up the receiver. Before he could get out a hello, the phone rang again. He took the receiver from his ear and gazed at it stupidly until he realized that there was *another* phone ringing somewhere. He turned around and stood facing the south wall of the apartment.

It was crazy: the ringing seemed to be coming from Ada's massive old sideboard.

He frowned and shook his head; his brain felt heavy and sodden, as if it had spent the night soaking in sludge. He was sure there was some sense to be made of this, but it was just out of reach. Thinking about it, he vaguely recalled that, at one time, he'd had a second phone.

The ringing went on tirelessly.

He was trudging over to the sideboard to open its glass-paned doors when he remembered: there had been two phones in the apartment they'd had before Ada died. One in the living room and one in the kitchen. The one in the kitchen had been wall-mounted, blue.

Suddenly it all flooded back: Ada. . . .

In a panic now that he'd be too late, he shouldered the sideboard aside, threw open the ancient door, flung himself across the kitchen, snatched the phone off the hook, and barked out an urgent hello.

"Well, well, sleepyhead," Ada cackled dryly. "It sure takes a lot to get you outta the sack nowadays."

"Ada," Howard croaked. "Where are you?"

"Where *am* I? You doped up or something, Howard? I'm at my sister's, of course."

"Your sister's?"

"Geez, honey, wake up. My sister who's having the baby, remember?"

"Oh," Howard muttered, an ancient memory stirring sluggishly. "Yes. I remember now."

"Look, honey, I called 'cause I gotta bawl you out about something."

"About what?"

"About that boy."

"Boy?"

"You know—Tim."

To Howard, standing in this kitchen and talking to Ada, the name belonged to another time and another world, and it was a moment before he realized who she was talking about.

"I don't understand, Ada. What am I supposed to do about Tim?"

"You're supposed to look after him, Howard."

"I *am* looking after him!" he protested.

"I know that, honey. I'm not bawling you out about what you been doing. I'm bawling you out about what you're *gonna* do."

"And what am I gonna do, for God's sake?"

"You're gonna turn the kid down."

"I don't know what the hell you're talking about, Ada."

After a pause, she said, "You listen to me now."

"I'm listening."

"You got some traveling to do, old man."

"Ada, what are you talking about?"

"I don't want to hear any excuses, any arguments. I don't want any crap from you. You take the boy where he needs to go."

"All right, Ada," he said with a sigh. He still didn't understand, but this acquiescence made him feel strangely serene.

"You take care of him. You hear?"

"I hear."

"Good. Now go answer the phone."

Howard frowned, confused. "What?"

"The other phone, Howard."

He turned his head to the door to his apartment. "It's not ringing, Ada."

"Howard, *go answer the goddamn phone!*" she shouted and slammed the phone down with an ear-jolting crash. Shaking his head, he went back to his apartment, shoved the sideboard back into place, and turned to the phone.

As he gazed down at it, it blasted into shrill life.

Grabbing the receiver, he snapped, "Yes?"

"Howard?" It was Tim, sounding startled by Howard's abrupt greeting. He was calling because he'd received something odd in the mail from his father—a check for a huge amount of money. Not exactly from his father, from a hotel in Las Vegas. But it had to be from his father, didn't it? Howard, feeling unaccountably jarred, couldn't understand why the boy was calling, couldn't grasp what he was saying. It seemed impossibly complex, completely muddled with some weird dream he'd been having when the call woke him up.

"Tim," he said, interrupting the boy in mid-sentence, "I'll call you back in a few minutes. I want to think this thing over. Okay?"

"Sure," Tim said, puzzled.

It was a lie. Howard didn't want to think anything over. He wanted to go back to sleep. He felt as if he'd left half his brain back in the bed, as if this abrupt awakening had shattered him. Half an hour's sleep seemed to reassemble him only partially, and he took a long shower to calm down. He realized that he now knew the meaning of that cliché about jangled nerves: the nerves in his spine and at the back of his neck were clanging like wind-chimes in a thunderstorm.

Getting dressed, he stewed over what Tim had told him. *So he got a check in the mail from his father—or from someone in a hotel in Las Vegas. What's that got to do with me? Am I some kind of welfare agency suddenly? I mean, enough is enough. I got problems of my own. I can't go running clear across the goddamn continent just because Tim got a check in the mail. He's a smart boy. He'll be able to understand that.* Having settled the matter in his own mind, he breathed a sigh of relief, reached for the phone, and started to dial the number in Runnell. Midway through the sequence he paused and replaced the receiver. After staring thoughtfully into space for a few moments, he reached for the telephone directory, looked up the number of the Greyhound depot, and called to get some information on bus connections between Runnell and Chicago.

Then he redialed Tim's number.

He asked him if he knew where to catch the bus in Runnell; he did. Howard told him to pack a bag and, after a bit of pondering, dictated a detailed note to be left behind in case Ellen showed up while Tim was gone.

Having repeated his instructions, he hung up, went back into the bathroom, and shaved. Then, after breakfast, he got his suitcase from the closet and packed. On his way out the door, he decided to be safe: he went back to the closet and dragged out his shabby old raincoat.

He met the boy at the Chicago bus station at one, and an hour and a half later they were on board a jet headed west.

Three hours later, if they'd known just where to look on the highway below, they could have seen the westbound car in which Ellen rode as an unconscious passenger.

PART III

There is a road . . .

CHAPTER 23

Driving at seventy miles an hour, it had taken David twenty minutes
to outdistance Runnell, to escape the uncanny feeling that the town
might still reach out and snatch him back. Then he turned onto southbound 31 and, knowing he was safe at last, eased his speed down to
the limit.

After a few minutes he felt a thrill building on the back of his neck
and shook his head to kill it.

No feelings, he told himself. *Not tonight. No remorse, no guilt. No relief, no exultation. Nothing till tomorrow.*

And so he drove like a robot, watching familiar landmarks slide
by and thinking, "I'll never see that again. . . ." The glow of the sunset melted away as he swept around Indianapolis and left the last of
the landmarks behind. From this moment on, it would all be new.

Not yet, he reminded himself. *No feelings yet.*

He turned on the radio and let the country singers whine at him
about their heartaches for a while, then, realizing he was punishing
himself, turned it off.

He had dinner at a steak house in Terre Haute, then went on to
Vandalia, where he found a motel with a cocktail lounge. He checked
in, dumped his suitcase in the room, washed his face, and went to the
bar. A few salesmen were trading jokes and lies at the tables. A few
local cowboys were guffawing at one end of the bar. David sat down

at the other end, ordered a double bourbon, and listened to a juke-boxful of Willie Nelson's sorrows, feeling nothing.

That night he dreamed of Soshal—short for Antisocial—a big, fat gray cat they'd had for many years and lost to a careless driver the summer before. A haughty creature, she'd felt degraded by her human associations and hated to be held by anyone. In the dream, set in the bedroom at home, David had perversely picked her up, plunked her down on the bed on her back, and started jumbling the fur of her belly—an activity that particularly infuriated her. She struggled to get out from under his hand, but he held her down, pretending she was really enjoying herself. Finally she got away, scrambled off the bed, and stood up on her hind legs, trembling with rage over her confinement. Then David saw that it wasn't really Soshal at all; it was a fur-covered boy. The boy picked up something from the floor and, glaring furiously, flung it at David's head. The boy was not a figure of Tim but of David—of the wild side of himself that he had held imprisoned for so long.

When he awoke, he found he'd willed himself another day without feelings. He wasn't free yet; the band that held him to Runnell hadn't been stretched far enough to break. He thought another five hundred miles might do it. Meanwhile he no longer had to keep reminding himself: he was so completely numb that he wondered if emotion would ever return. Sitting in the motel dining room, he felt insubstantial, ghostly, and was mildly surprised when the waitress acknowledged his existence by bringing him a breakfast menu.

It was like that the rest of the day, as he shot westward across Missouri and two-thirds of Kansas to Hays, where he repeated the previous night's routine exactly. Dulled by a couple of drinks, he wondered if Ellen had remembered the appointment he'd made to have the tires on her car rotated. Good tires, those were; a little over their budget, but they'd gotten a good price on them. He'd have to remember to remind her about it when he—

He smiled, having caught himself preparing for his routine away-from-home phone call.

Hi! How was your day?

Did you remember to get the tires rotated?

How's Tim? Still campaigning to spend the summer at that wilderness-survival camp in the Catskills?

Of course he would be. The brochure he'd written away for made it look genuinely testing, even a bit dangerous, and this worried Ellen, though she didn't like to admit it. She preferred to argue that it was in some mysterious way "out of character" for Tim to be scaling rocks and camping out, and therefore not to be considered. So far, David had stayed out of the controversy, giving the subtle impression he agreed with her. But eventually Tim would back her into a corner and she'd pass the buck to David, expecting him to play the heavy. She'd smolder for a while when he pulled the rug out from under her and said . . .

He was like a reformed smoker reaching for a package of cigarettes that wasn't there.

Before he went to bed he opened the windows wide, and at four in the morning a gale roaring down off the continental divide plucked him up out of sleep. Standing at the window with the wind gusting in his face, he felt the prison doors rumbling open, and the hair rose off the back of his neck. Without turning on the lights, he gathered up his things, threw them in the car, and climbed behind the wheel. At a touch, the headlights pierced the darkness like a probe into a hidden universe.

For the next twenty minutes he blundered through the streets of Hays like a fly at the window. With the power of two hundred horses waiting to be released beneath his foot, he couldn't find the way out—or the way out he was looking for. He could have gotten back on the expressway, but this wasn't a night to be spent in a herd of flatulent sixteen-wheelers. Finally, after passing it half a dozen times, he found it: a county road heading west.

He burst out of the city, thinking nothing now. Only feeling.

He was on a journey into the past and was drunk on an infusion of remembered youth, freedom, and mystery.

CHAPTER 24

On a night very like this one, twenty years earlier, he and Gil Binga-man had been cruising the countryside outside Columbus, Ohio, in the car David's parents had given him for his seventeenth birthday—his first set of wheels. They were going nowhere in particular, look-ing for nothing in particular. The car, the evening, the freedom of the road were like money found in the street, and they were spending it.

As the headlights probed the darkness ahead, David was silently reciting:

Ανδρα μοι ἔννεπε, μοῦσα, πολύτροπον, ὃσ μάλα πολλὰ πλάγχθη...

Tell me, Muse, about that wily man who wandered ...

His junior year in high school had been dominated by a voyage taken around the Mediterranean more than two thousand years ago. Almost every morning for nine months he had set out on the wine-dark sea beside the adventure-hungry Odysseus—had heard the Sirens' song, had surrendered to the charms of Nausicaa, had driven a smoking stake into the eye of Polyphemus, and had returned to Ithaca to slaughter a houseful of freeloading suitors.

This tempest-ridden journey, made at a speed of thirty or forty lines a day through Homer's dawn-fresh Greek, was the high point of his educational career, leaving him only vaguely aware that a real-life tempest was blowing up in a teapot called Viet Nam. Not being a newspaper reader or a watcher of televised news, he had no reason to suppose it would occupy any more of his attention than the War of Jenkins' Ear—and had no way of knowing that the idyllic summer of 1966 would be the last of its kind for him.

Although he wouldn't have thought of it that way, he was ready for an idyll. Summer, for him, wasn't just a welcome break from the prep-school grind; it was R & R, an escape from a battlefield where victories were as punishing as defeats. David was one of those un-lucky boys—ten years ahead of his peers in sophistication but inca-pable of winning anything but hatred for it because he was ten years behind them in savvy. He couldn't understand that, by sniggering over every occurrence of Homer's "rosy-fingered dawn," the boys were showing each other that their minds were in the gutter, where the minds of all real men should be. David sighed and rolled his eyes at their childishness—and marked himself a prig and a pansy. They liked to see him raise his hand in class. If he was right, they sneered; if he was wrong, they jeered.

Gil Bingaman found his classmates' determined loutishness as wearisome as David but had the sense to leave it alone. Although he slumped to minimize it, Gil at six feet two inches towered over most of his classmates—especially David, who still had two inches to go to reach his full height. His size alone (though he lacked the weight to go with it) had always guaranteed him a certain respect from his peers; they thought he was a loner when in fact he was just mortally shy—a condition brought on by gazing too long at his beaky, chinless face in the mirror.

Gil was the less assertive of the two but had the knack of leading from behind and generally managed to distract David from his more self-destructive impulses. It was a sort of mission for him. Until David, he'd never met anyone his own age who talked about things seri-ously, who felt strongly about things other than cars, sex, booze, and sports. He had the rather romantic notion that there was something special about David, that he was going to be important to the world—provided he managed to survive into adulthood. In spite of this, his manner toward David was far from deferential, and during the summer they could be counted on to have several bitter, never-speak-to-you-again battles, usually over some microscopic slight to David's feelings. It was an unspoken but inflexible rule (David's) that they had to take turns making overtures of peace afterwards, David calling one time to apologize for being too sensitive, Gil calling the next to apologize for not being sensitive enough.

This summer, so far, the car had a soothing effect on David's temper. It had been a characteristic choice for him: not one of Detroit's current crop of power monsters (which would have won him a measure of grudging admiration from his classmates), but a frugal little Honda, hardly bigger than a bathtub (which won him nothing but snickers). In just these few weeks, he'd grown dependent on it, not for transportation but for something he wouldn't have been able to name—something more than relaxation and less than enchantment. It fulfilled a need in him that others might meet poring over a stamp collection or walking in the woods or letting their hands wander aimlessly over a piano keyboard. Doing nothing was abhorrent to David's puritanical sensibilities, and he was too high-strung for idleness anyway. But driving, even just for the sake of driving, wasn't doing nothing; fuel was being consumed, carburetor, spark plugs, and pistons were laboring away, and the odometer was busily accumulating miles, even though they were miles to nowhere.

It was on this night, sitting beside Gil in a relaxed silence and driving nowhere, that he first realized how deeply satisfying it would be to stay on this road forever, to never turn back—to renounce achievement and the self-imposed pressure to achieve, to abandon the thrust to get somewhere. To purify himself of the very concept of *destination*.

No, not exactly that. To seek an uncommon destination: A road. A certain road. A road that doesn't lead to just another road, just another town, just another house, just another shop, just another factory.

A road that leads nowhere.

Having conceived it, David euphorically embraced it. Something as desirable as this couldn't exist only in the mind; it had to exist in fact. He wanted it to exist in fact, and, without his consciously willing it, his foot bore down on the accelerator.

Gil looked at him curiously.

Encapsulated in darkness, they were traveling south on Western Road, the glow of the city at their backs, the lesser glow of Rickenbacker Air Force Base at their left. At the junction of 762, David turned right, toward Commercial Point and Orient. Without taking his eyes from the road unfolding beneath the headlights, he said: "There is a road that leads nowhere."

Gil looked around doubtfully. "You mean out here?"

"Somewhere," David answered darkly.

Gil frowned. "All roads lead *somewhere.*"

"Not this one."

"Unless. . . . You mean an unfinished road? A road that never got to where it was going?"

David shook his head. "This one gets to where it's going, which is nowhere."

Gil grappled with this in silence for a while. "You mean someone *deliberately* built a road that goes nowhere?"

"Oh, don't be so goddamned prosaic," David snapped.

"Ah," Gil sighed, and slumped back in his seat. He knew where he was now. David was in one of his I-wandered-lonely-as-a-cloud moods. All the same . . . *a road that leads nowhere.* . . . . "Sounds sort of neat," he observed. "A road that goes on forever, getting nowhere."

David grunted and turned right into a gravel road.

"I'll bet this is private."

"It isn't," David said definitely.

A few minutes later, the gravel dead-ended at another paved road, and Gil carefully suppressed the comment that came to mind.

David turned right.

"This just leads to Shadeville, I'd say."

"Shadeville's further north." As if defying him, the highway curved northward, and David grimly followed it. "You notice no one lives out here," he said after a couple of miles.

"Come on, David."

Nevertheless, except for the glow of the city on the horizon, now ahead of them, the landscape was surprisingly devoid of life and lights.

Suddenly David jammed on the brakes. "What the hell was *that*?"

"What the hell was what?"

Turning around in his seat to look through the rear window, David backed the car up a hundred yards to the opening of another road off to the right.

"Shee-it," Gil crowed gleefully. "It's the road to Oz!"

David nodded. "Except that the bricks aren't yellow." He pulled the wheel over and turned in.

"I've never seen a brick road anywhere around here," Gil said. "Have you?"

"No. It must be old."

"Old, old, old."

David soon discovered that, although the road seemed to be in good shape, any speed above twenty miles an hour produced a bone-rattling vibration inside the car. As they crept along, a full moon rose at their left to illuminate the bleak flatland around them. It was like an unthinkably vast, abandoned airfield.

"This must have *belonged* to someone," Gil said.

"What do you mean?"

"I mean . . . someone must have had a *plan* for all this. A factory that was supposed to be built, a mine—*something*. It's obviously not being farmed or anything."

"So?"

"I mean, somebody must have bought all this a long time ago, built this road, and . . ."

"And?"

"I don't know. Died. Lost interest. Ran out of money."

David shrugged, wishing Gil would shut up, wishing he were alone. The road curved eastward and the land soon began to swell into low hills.

"Must be getting close to the Scioto," Gil observed. David nodded.

When it happened, a few minutes later, it was like a silent explosion: too many events compressed into too short a time.

They both saw her at the same moment: a woman standing motionless on the crest of a bank to their left. Silhouetted black against the moon, she might have been a statue except for her shoulder-length hair and her dress, stirring in the breeze. Hands at her sides, she stood looking out over the road as if waiting for a visitor to appear on the distant horizon.

David braked the car, turned off the engine, and opened the door.

"Where the fuck are *you* going?" Gil demanded.

David climbed out of the car and looked up. The woman turned away and leisurely began to descend the far side of the bank. As David crossed the road, Gil leaned across the seat and said, "David, for Christ's sake!" When this didn't stop him, he scrambled out and grabbed his arm.

"Get away," David told him.

"Stop it, David. For Christ's sake." David pulled his arm free and started across the shoulder to the bank. "Come on, David. *Knock it off!*"

The embankment was steeper than it looked from the road, and David had to attack it on hands and knees, grabbing bunches of weeds to hoist himself up. He was near the crest when Gil managed to get a hand on his ankle to drag him back. He twisted around and gave a kick that sent Gil crashing down into the weeds. Then he pulled himself to the top and stood up, expecting . . . something—a vision, a portent, a prodigy.

The ground fell away, ridge after ridge, to a distant line of trees that marked the river. In the valley at his feet, all chilly silver and black, nothing moved. Then, as he watched, a shadow stirred in the darkness at the base of the next ridge and slowly ascended to the crest to stand once again silhouetted against the moon. For half a minute she stood motionless. He was sure she hadn't turned around to face him; if she had, he'd have noticed the shift in outline. She just stood there, looking ahead at the moon, waiting. Then she started forward again and gradually disappeared behind the hill, as if sinking into the ground.

It was the last sight he had of her.

An hour later David slid back down the embankment to the car, where Gil sat in the driver's seat, tapping the horn every minute or so. He walked to the passenger side and got in without a word.

Gil studied his face for a moment. "Do you want me to drive?"

When David nodded, he started the engine and put the car into gear; he'd already turned it around, hoping at the very least to avoid an argument about where they were going. He ran the speedometer up to twenty-five and, when their teeth started rattling, slacked off to twenty.

"Well?" he said at last.

"Well what?"

"Did you . . . see her?"

"Yes. Once."

"Well, then what?"

David shrugged and looked out of his window.

"Come on, David. What the fuck happened?"

"Nothing happened. I saw her. I followed her for a mile or so. And then . . . that's all. I lost her."

Gil drove in silence for a while, fighting the urge to bear down on the accelerator. "You know that was a fucking stupid thing to do, don't you?"

David asked why, genuinely in the dark.

"Jesus, you are so goddamned naive! Tracking down a lone

woman in the country after dark? What did you think you were
going to do if you caught up with her?"

"I don't know."

"Shit. What would *she* have done if you'd caught up with her? She
could have blown your fucking head off and nobody would have said
boo to her."

"True. But she wasn't going to blow my head off."

"No? What was she going to do then? Take you home and feed
you cookies and milk, for Christ's sake?"

"I don't know."

"Shit. And you know you fucking *kicked* me?"

"I know. I'm sorry."

"You could've broken my goddamned *collarbone*."

"I said I'm sorry."

David's tone made it clear that this was as much as Gil was going
to get, so he let it go at that.

For the rest of the summer and during the next school year—the
last they were to spend together—neither of them ever mentioned
the night they'd spent foolishly looking for a road they both knew
didn't exist. Two or three times David went out alone to retrace their
route, but the sequence of turns he'd taken that night must have become muddled in his memory, because he never managed to find the
entrance to the brick road again.

In the years ahead he had things to think about that were far
more pressing, and in the end he came to half-believe that he'd
dreamed or imagined the whole uncanny episode.

CHAPTER 25

As he drove in the predawn darkness, turning at random into the winter-scarred gravel roads of Ellis County, Kansas, deliberately getting lost, David mused about that night and that road that leads nowhere. On the surface, it was of course a childish and romantic fancy. Bob Gaines or Ellen—maybe even Tim—would laugh at it. But he knew what he meant by it, and they didn't: *Human experience can never be definitively mapped. There is no map that shows all the roads.*

The schools, of course, teach otherwise. Not only have all the roads been mapped, they know where all roads lead: to the marketplace. The marketplace is the hub, the heartland of human experience; working, getting ahead, accumulating wealth and power is all there is, is what life is all about. They teach this because they exist to teach it; they've become dedicated tools of the marketplace, their function to supply ready workers—workers conditioned to believe that there are no roads to explore except the ones shown on the schools' map, conditioned to believe that any road that doesn't lead to the marketplace is by definition *a road that leads nowhere.*

But they're wrong. What happened to him that night outside Columbus wasn't on their map—wasn't on any map. And it didn't happen because he'd been driving on an old abandoned brick road. It happened because—for an hour or two—he'd *thrown away the map.*

The road that leads nowhere isn't a road of asphalt or gravel or brick. It's an interior road, and he was on it again, at last.

At the café in Gove, where he stopped for breakfast, they looked at him as if he'd stepped off a spaceship. He nodded amiably, because in a sense he had. Having wolfed down a plate of eggs, sausage, and hash browns, he ordered another, which raised his waitress's eyebrows. He thought of telling her he'd just escaped from prison, but decided this might be expecting a bit too much of the rural sense of humor. An old man in spotless coveralls—evidently the local daredevil—nodded to the car outside and asked if it was a Mercedes. David told him it was a Volvo, and the old man chuckled gamely, to show he knew his leg was being pulled.

Forty miles west of Gove the gravel road became a paved road for ten miles, turned back into a gravel road, and then after another ten miles merged with U.S. 40. He turned onto it with relief, glad to have a break from fighting the dust, ruts, and potholes.

Cranking down the window and resting an elbow across it, he was at ease, if not exactly at peace. He could feel the waters of guilt and remorse rocking massively behind the thin membrane of self-control he'd thrown up to contain them, but there was no point in tasting them now. They would drain away if he left them alone, and in a year or two he could take the membrane down and see how bitter the residue was.

For now, he would simply drive.

He was in sight of Mount Sunflower, and the road was rising toward the Colorado border when two figures stood up hopefully in the dust at the side of the road. Without turning his head (and admitting he'd seen them), he took in a scrawny Hispanic man and boy, both dressed in shabby jeans and work shirts. He shrugged and pulled off onto the shoulder. Watching in the rearview mirror, he saw them strolling forward in no hurry at all, and he mentally cursed them for wasting his time. He smiled grimly and shook his head at the stubbornness of old habits. He had no deadlines to meet now.

The two of them shuffled up, nodded at him incuriously, and without a word settled themselves in the front seat, the boy in the middle.

"Don't you even want to know where I'm going?" David asked humorously.

"Goin' west, unh?" the man said. The bones under his leathery skin looked as sharp as knives, but his eyes were dull, as if he found little in life to interest him. It was an ageless, alien face, and David wasn't sure whether he was the boy's father or grandfather.

"Going west," David agreed, and pulled back onto the highway. He glanced down at the boy beside him. Although he was three or four years younger than Tim, there was nothing boyish about him; his round, smooth face belonged to someone who had seen the world and wasn't impressed. He was staring ahead with bored eyes, his hands folded bonelessly in his lap.

Suddenly David was annoyed with himself. He remembered now that half the reason he hated picking up hitchhikers was that he always felt vaguely and irrationally obliged to entertain them, and these two were sitting there like lumps.

"Where are you headed?" he asked, hoping to hear that they'd be getting off at the next town up the road.

"Las Vegas," the man said tonelessly.

David stared at him, astounded. Las Vegas! What on earth was this grubby pair going to do in Las Vegas? Then he remembered that there's more than one Las Vegas.

"You mean in New Mexico?"

The man turned to him with a dark, wounded look. "I mean Las Vegas in Nevada."

"Ah," David said.

A few minutes later, still looking out of his window, the man said, "You should come too."

"Me?" David laughed. "Why should I go to Las Vegas?"

Man and boy exchanged an amused look. "Toney says so."

David blinked from one to the other; since entering the car, the boy hadn't uttered a single word.

"Why does he say that?"

"'Cause you got the nine . . . strokes. I guess that'd be the word in English: *strokes*."

"I don't understand."

"You got the nine strokes of luck."

"And what's that mean?"

The man laughed softly. "It means . . . for nine times you can't miss, can't lose."

"I see," David said, smiling. "And Toney told you this?"

He nodded.

"And how does he know?"

The two grinned at each other as if sharing a private joke. Then, still grinning, the man looked up and said, "You married, unh?"

Warily, David said he was.

"Your wife . . . she ever complain about a certain little thing?"

"I don't know what you're talking about," David replied stiffly.

The man lifted a slender brown hand and tapped the side of his nose meaningly.

David flushed.

"Sure. You got a certain smell, unh? Even I noticed it a little when we got in the car."

"You can get out and walk if it bothers you."

The man laughed delightedly. "Hey, don' get mad, man. This a very special smell. It comes out of the nine openings in your body. You can't help it."

In childhood, David had gotten used to taking two baths a day. If he didn't, his mother complained that he smelled like a wet sheep-dog. A minor crisis had occurred on the second day of his honeymoon when Ellen, mortified, had asked him if he wouldn't mind taking a shower before they made love. He'd subsequently asked a few doctors about it, but none had found the problem interesting enough to pursue.

"That's okay," the man went on. "It'll go 'way when you use up the nine strokes."

David made a face and went on driving.

"Don' believe me, unh?" He elbowed the boy in the ribs. "Hey, Toney, he don' believe me."

The boy looked up at David with a sort of shy leer. "Juan's right. When the luck's gone, the smell'll be gone."

His jaw clenched angrily, David said nothing. He was wondering how he was going to get rid of these two, and wishing that he had the nerve to just pull over and put them out. As if sensing his hostility, the man called Juan turned his attention to the increasingly barren landscape outside, and the boy stared without interest at the road ahead.

David's anger drained away, and he began to relax as the silence continued through Cheyenne Wells, First View, Kit Carson, and Wild Horse. At Aroya he stopped for gas. Inside the station he saw a refrigerator stocked with plastic-wrapped ready-made sandwiches, and, unappetizing as they looked, his mouth was awash with saliva. He bought two and then—cursing himself as a fool—four more, which he shoved at the old man without a word. Juan turned them around in his hand as if unable to make out what they were, then looked up with an amazed grin.

"Hey, man, that's nice."

David grunted, knowing there was nothing nice about it. He could abandon his wife and son but was just too goddamned squeamish to eat a sandwich in front of a pair of strangers who hadn't the slightest claim on his generosity.

Three quarters of an hour later they joined Interstate 70, and Juan pointed out slyly that this was the fastest way to Las Vegas.

"I'm not going to Las Vegas."

"Unh. Where you goin' then?"

"I don't know. Maybe up into the mountains."

The old man guffawed incredulously. "You wanna go up into the mountains?"

"Why is that so funny?"

"Still winter up there, man. Freeze your ass."

David shrugged, and his teeth chattered as he tried to stifle a sudden, overwhelming yawn. The man glanced at him and asked if he was getting tired.

"I'm all right."

"I can drive for a while if you want. I'm a good driver."

"I'm all right," David repeated grimly, but his eyelids felt like leaden shutters that were going to slide down millimeter by millimeter no matter how much resistance he offered. Thinking about it, he realized that, except for two brief breaks, he'd been at the wheel for nine hours straight—after only three or four hours of sleep. The idea of a nap on the back seat was almost irresistibly tempting.

He yawned again and, when his jaw snapped shut, saw a laminated card being thrust under his nose.

"Look. I got a driver's license an' everything."

David hesitated, knowing it was insane to turn the car over to this complete stranger. He glanced down at the boy to see what he thought of it. As if on cue, Toney said, "He's a good driver, mister. Really." He spoke with such authority that David wondered groggily if he'd underestimated his age.

Gratefully acknowledging defeat, he pulled over, crawled into the back seat, and was asleep so quickly that he didn't even feel the car turn back onto the highway.

CHAPTER 26

He emerged from unconsciousness by slow degrees, like a body drifting up from the bottom of a deep pool. Feeling immensely heavy and lethargic, he groped for the end of his dream—a weight that would pull him back into the depths where he wanted to be—but it slipped away. As he stretched out with a groan, his feet met an obstacle, and it took him a moment to identify it: the backseat door, of course. Suddenly alarmed, realizing that the car was motionless, he sat up and looked around.

And wondered if he wasn't still dreaming after all.

The car was sitting in a hollow between three rocky hills dotted with low pines, clumps of brown weeds, and shadowed pockets of decaying snow. Looking through the rear window, he saw no sign of a road—or even a trail; the weeds the car had been driven over had sprung up again behind it.

You wanna go up into the mountains?

His hitchhiking pals had driven him up into the mountains and abandoned him there.

Panicked, he reached for his billfold and found it was in place and still stuffed with bills. The car keys dangled from the ignition; he retrieved them and went out to check the trunk. His suitcase hadn't been touched. Evidently the old man was only a humorist, not a thief.

But why? Revenge?

Revenge for what?

For buying them food, maybe. Perhaps it seemed a patronizing gesture: *Here, eat, since you obviously can't afford to feed yourselves.* Yes, it had to be that, though the punishment seemed excessive for the crime.

Shrugging this away, David checked his watch. Five-thirty—four-thirty mountain time—time enough to get back on the road to civilization before nightfall. He assumed he couldn't be more than half a mile from that road—*some* road. Perhaps even less than that. After all, what price vengeance? The farther in they took him, the farther they'd have to walk out.

The car faced the westering sun; he turned it around and, in second gear, began to feel his way back—searching for the path of least resistance among the boulders and bushes. The ground rose slightly as it approached the saddle between two hills. At the crest of the saddle he paused, frowning. The descent on the other side was too steep—not too steep to be negotiated, too steep to be the right way. He'd be able to get the car down it, but no one would have been able to get the car up it in the first place—not a two-wheel-drive Volvo.

He backed to his original position and thought about it. Clearly his humorous friends hadn't just driven the car in and switched the engine off; they'd turned it around to mask the direction they'd brought it from. He couldn't have foreseen such subtlety, but he should have checked for tracks before doing his own turning around; they'd be hopelessly muddled now—if he could read them at all.

He got out and made a circuit of the area at a radius of twenty yards from the car. To the trained eye, he was sure, the back-trail would stand out like a scorch mark on a white sheet. To his own eye, however, it was invisible. There was no conveniently placed patch of smooth clay or sand to catch a tread mark, and if the tough-looking vegetation had been crushed by a car's passage, it had quickly sprung back to stand shoulder to shoulder with the rest.

He assessed the sun and the three hills around him. By the time he'd scaled the hill to the east, the land below might well be in shadow; but if he scaled the hill to the west, the land below would still be in sunlight. Nevertheless, his inclination was toward the eastern slope, maybe because it looked toward home and security.

He changed into jeans, tennis shoes, and wind-breaker and headed west. It was a dusty climb but not an arduous one, though he took it cautiously, not eager to complicate matters with a twisted ankle. The sun was just touching a distant mountain on the horizon when he reached the top. There was nothing in the intervening space to encourage him—no lights, no roads, no houses, no fences—just range after range of barren hills. Behind any one of them could be hidden a superhighway, a village—even a whole city. But from this vantage point it might as well have been a vista on Mars.

Looking to his right, he saw that he was standing on a ridge that led, after what appeared to be a shallow dip, to the crest of the northern hill, perhaps half a mile away. Although the sun would be gone by the time he got there, he judged it would be light enough to make out a road. But ten minutes later he discovered that his eye had been deceived. Hidden in the shallow dip was not an unbroken ridge to the northern crest but the root of still another hill jutting westward and then up to the summit he wanted to reach. He scowled down at the car sitting obscenely useless in the valley below and then up at the hill to his left. Except for perhaps the last two hundred yards, he'd have the car in sight the whole time. He glanced at his watch, set it back an hour to mountain time, knowing as he did it that, whatever the hands said, there was less than an hour of daylight left. Even so, there was no reason why he couldn't make the ascent and return to this spot in forty minutes.

Still, he looked back wistfully at the Volvo, wishing he'd had the good sense to turn on the hazard lights as a guide.

Staying on the high ground, he reached the northern crest twenty minutes later and found nothing encouraging in the view; empty hills extended to the horizon like a rough cloth carelessly folded. Some fifteen miles away a single light flickered on a hilltop like a dim star, hopelessly beyond reach. Turning around, he was mildly surprised to find that the valley in which the car rested was not so much in front of him as to his left, which meant that retracing his steps would be to take the long way round. He studied the descent thoughtfully. What had appeared from below to be a single hill was in fact two hills; he was looking at his car over the shoulder of the lower hill. He would descend the first and go around the second to the left to reach the valley floor.

By the time he'd completed the first leg of the journey it was fully dark, and he paused, trying to remember when the moon had risen the night before. He seemed to recall seeing it well up on his arrival in Hays. Or had that been on leaving Hays?

Then, looking down, he realized the question was irrelevant. Against expectation, he could dimly make out the shape of the car below him, a glossy roundness against the surrounding rubble. It dropped from sight a few minutes later, however, when he descended into a watercourse cutting through the valley floor. The far side of the arroyo was only some eight feet high, but it was a sheer wall of rock, and, bearing right, he was a few minutes finding a safe way up. The car, he calculated, would be to his left, and it was.

Except that it wasn't a car; it was a shelf of rock angled up out of the weeds. Looking around bleakly, he understood what every traveler lost in the mountains learns: in the dark, all hills look alike.

Still winter up there, man. Freeze your ass off.

Already shivering, he sat down on the rock to assess his chances of surviving the night. He carried no matches, no cigarette lighter, and dismissed his prospects of redeveloping some ancient fire-making technique from scratch, in the dark. He'd seen nothing like a cave he could block up to conserve body heat. What he had plenty of was weeds. He could trample vast quantities in the hours ahead and use the duff to pack inside his clothes. It wouldn't be as effective as down (and would be hellishly uncomfortable), but it would probably save his life. He could find a crevice and fill it with weeds that he could crawl under to spend the night. He did this first, figuring that he'd be virtually immobile once he'd stuffed his clothes with insulation.

All these chores were vastly easier to imagine than to accomplish, and it was midnight by the time he squirmed into his nest, completely exhausted. Ten minutes later he squirmed back out, choking on pollen and dust. He tore off another strip of shirt-tail (he'd already used two to tie off his pant legs), found a patch of snow, and froze his hands melting enough to moisten it. Then he crawled back inside and, with the icy mask over his mouth and nose, began to feel a sickening premonition of defeat.

Curiously, he found the situation more humiliating than terrifying. Lying there encased in weeds, every square inch of flesh burning either with irritation or with cold, he felt like a booby, unable to get through even three days outside his petty routine without bungling his life away.

There was a rock burrowing into the right side of his back, just below the kidney.

Naturally there would be. It was moving in on him, making a place for itself as a new organ, alongside spleen and liver—an organ of cold, designed to process heat away. Of course it wasn't really moving in on him; he was moving in on it—forcing himself on it. But that wasn't exactly right either. Something about equal and opposite forces there. He was pushing on the rock and the rock was pushing back—had to be or it'd be sinking into the ground. On the other hand . . . *there is no force, however great* . . .

What the devil was that?

There is no force, however great . . .

Poetry? Something.

Could he really lie there *(there is no force)* absorbing that rock *(however great)* into his body for the next seven hours without going insane? It didn't seem possible. Seven hours: four hundred minutes, twenty-four thousand seconds. If he could count slowly to twenty-four thousand, the night would be over.

One, two, three, four. . .

There is no force, however great . . .

Then the solution to the puzzle came to him, and he smiled blearily. Poor William Whewell of Trinity College—a fellow bungler. He'd wanted to be remembered as a poet but had achieved only derisory fame for a piece of inadvertent doggerel that had slipped into his *Elementary Treatise on Mechanics*. After hearing it recited for the amusement of his fellow dons in an after-dinner speech, he frantically revised it for later editions but never managed to expunge it from the literature of ineptitude.

> *There is no force, however great,*
> *Can stretch a cord, however fine,*
> *Into a horizontal line,*
> *Which is accurately straight.*

This anecdote was absolutely true, David knew. If he were at home, in the spare bedroom that had served as his office, he could have gone directly to the bookcase and the volume in which it could be found.

Although he couldn't sense it, his thoughts were moving with glacial slowness. William Whewell's unfortunate rhymes hadn't been recollected (as he imagined) in a minute or two; they'd floated together over a period of three quarters of an hour, like particles suspended in a heavy liquid.

He was interested to discover that he no longer felt unbearably cold. It occurred to him that the loss of any sense of discomfort is a classic symptom of hypothermia, but he discounted that; it was simply that his precautions, after all, were proving more effective than he'd hoped. Of course it was early yet. The real test would come, if it came, in the bitter hour before dawn, when

> *There is no force, however great,*
> *Can keep a man, however warm,*
> *From abandoning his mortal form*
> *To the comfort of a wooden crate.*

His greatest worry had been for his feet, poorly protected in their tennis shoes. But that had been taken care of at some dimly remembered point when he detached them and tucked them up into the hollow between buttocks and thighs, one to each side. He could feel them there quite distinctly. But now something was nagging at him for attention, which seemed unfair just when he was finally becoming comfortably settled at last.

A smell. The smell of the sea.

Absurd.

It was the bells that had put him in mind of the sea.

Six bells and all's well, cap'n.

Having found the right sense to focus on, he listened. Not bells. A piano. An old rinky-tink piano, playing some ghastly Victorian ditty.

I'm only a bird in a gilded cage.

Now that he'd identified the sound, others began to collect around it like moths around a light: people talking, someone laughing, the stir of feet on a wooden floor.

What the hell?

David sat up, throwing aside his cocoon of weeds, and realized that he wasn't dreaming it. Somewhere off to the right, not far away, there was a party going on. He kicked away the rest of the weeds with dead feet and spent the next few minutes massaging them back to agonizing life, terrified that at any moment the sounds would terminate with the suddenness of a tape-end flashing past the play-back head. Then he shook the debris out of his clothes and started toward them.

At the brow of the next hill he paused, dumbfounded, having to check his senses once again to confirm that he really was awake. In the valley below stood what looked like a segment of a Western movie set. A segment: thirty yards of street and square-front buildings, chopped off at either end as if by a giant chainsaw. Livery stables, alley with horse and wagon, saloon, hotel—*half a hotel*, sliced off from top to bottom at mid-room. All of it completely dark, except for a lantern hanging in the alley beside the wagon and the yellow lights streaming from the saloon.

As David stumbled down the hill, a tenor joined the pianist in *Silver Threads Amongst the Gold*, and a woman called out, "Drat you anyway, Jimmy Joe!" provoking a roar of masculine laughter.

When he pushed through the swinging doors, the noise stopped as if a plug had been pulled, and a dozen faces turned to him, blank with astonishment. They were all there:

The rouged tart in red velvet and net stockings.

The mustachioed piano player in bowler and sleeve-garters.

The dandified card-sharp—deck frozen in mid-shuffle under his hands.

The crooked, frock-coated banker, surrounded by his henchmen.

The cowpokes in for their booze-up from a long, dirty cattle drive.

The beefy bartender, gravely studying David for trouble, his hand on a sawed-off under the bar.

All gazing at him like switched-off clockwork figures—except for one, the only one not in period costume, a slight, elderly gentleman with the face of a benign old sheep, dressed in a cardigan sweater, shirt, and tie. Leaning casually against the bar, he was shaking his head at David with a look midway between disappointment and kindly amusement.

This old gentleman flapped an impatient hand at the others, and they resumed their roles with obvious reluctance, whispering over their drinks as the pianist groped for his place in the melody.

"I'm afraid," he said, taking David's arm, "that you really don't belong here."

"But . . . I'm lost."

The old man smiled tolerantly. "Well, of course you are. And of course I know that you are. But you really must go back."

"Back?" David stared at him open-mouthed and for the first time in many years felt a tingling behind his eyes that signaled the approach of tears. "You don't understand. I *can't* go back."

"Of course you can, my boy," the other said, nodding sympathetically. "It will all be arranged."

"Arranged?"

"Certainly. Just let me think a bit." After blinking into a space above David's head for a few moments, he turned and said, "Ted, Hilly, will you give me a hand?"

Two of the cowpokes exchanged a glance and stood up.

"Come along then," the old man said, steering David outside and into the alley, where the horse and wagon stood waiting. The horse, a massive old gray, turned a baleful eye to them, and David saw that the wagon was loaded with a long wooden crate.

"Ted, Hilly." The old man nodded at the two cowpokes as if identifying them for David's sake. "It seems we're going to need Mike's box."

Ted, a neckless troll with a torso like a barrel, glared at David reproachfully, but said nothing. Hilly, a tall, rangy man with impossibly wide shoulders, muttered, "Shit."

"Come on now, it's no big deal."

The two men shrugged, climbed up onto the wagon, and started to shift the box off the end, but the old man said, "No, no, leave it where it is."

"Aw, Christ." Hilly looked around the bed of the wagon, picked up a pry bar, and attacked the lid, which came up with nails shrieking. "Come on, Ted, Goddammit, grab it."

Ted pulled the lid off and carefully set it aside.

Then, as David watched in horror, they wrestled a nude male body out of the box and pitched it face down into the dirt at his feet. A red neck-rag tied around one wrist made its nakedness doubly obscene.

The old man tilted his head confidentially toward David and said, "We were having a wake, you see."

CHAPTER 27

"Jesus God," David whispered, unable to tear his eyes away from the corpse, obscenely hairless, its backside empurpled with settled blood.

Ted and Hilly had climbed down from the wagon and were leaning against it casually, bored. The old man looked at them with disapproval and snapped, "Well, get him up."

Ted rolled his eyes, shuffled over to the corpse, and gave it an unenthusiastic kick.

"Come on," the old man said impatiently. "It's cold out here."

The barrel-shaped cowpoke growled, hunched his shoulders, and leaped into a kick that stove in the ribcage with a sickening crunch.

"Jesus," David breathed, sagging at the knees.

"For Christ's sake, get him up!"

Ted shrugged helplessly. Hilly shook his head in disgust and said, "Grab his arms."

"Fuck it, *you* grab his arms."

"Oh, shit."

Together they managed to grapple the body into an upright position, with Ted holding him in a bear hug from behind.

"Come on," Hilly said, "hold him up."

"I *am* holding him up, asshole."

"I mean *higher*."

"Goddammit, I can't *go* higher."

"Oh fuck, give him to me."

The old man sighed as the two wrestled with the body again until Hilly had taken Ted's place, holding it from behind.

"Okay," Ted said, massaging his fist. "Ready?"

"Hold on." Hilly switched his grip on the body so that he was holding it on his hip. "Okay."

Ted twitched his shoulders up and down a few times to loosen them, then reared back and delivered a blow to the corpse's belly that would have felled a gorilla. In spite of Hilly's grip, the body folded up over Ted's fist, and a torrent of foul liquid erupted from its mouth to soak his shoulder.

"Oh, shit!" he screamed hysterically, trying to dance away from the drenched shoulder. "The fucker *puked* on me!"

Laughing, Hilly released the body, which dropped to hands and knees barking hoarsely, like a dog trying to bring up a bone.

"Go change your shirt, Ted," the old man told him calmly and walked over to hunker down beside the still-quaking corpse. He studied it for a few moments, then said, with great intensity: "*Mike.*"

Hilly, leaning against the wagon, his arms folded, chuckled as Mike went on retching convulsively.

"Mike, come on." The old man rapped him sharply on the head with his knuckles. As if electrified by this trivial blow, Mike stiffened to a catatonic rigidity.

"Mike. *See!*"

When he didn't move, the old man rapped his skull again.

"*See*, you idiot!"

Mike raised his head, his mouth hanging completely open.

"Come on." The old man knelt down beside him, took Mike's head in his hands, and turned it around to point up at David.

"*See!*" Mike gazed up, his eyes pools of staring blackness, and David shrank back, shuddering uncontrollably.

Still holding his head, the old man leaned forward to look first into Mike's face then up into David's, as if checking the angle. "Did you see?"

"Ungh," Mike groaned, his mouth still hanging open.

"Good, good," the old man said, releasing him to collapse into the dust. He stood up, brushed off his knees, and went over to confer with Hilly. As the two of them talked in low tones, David and Mike stared at each other. Both seemed equally horrified by what they saw.

"Well, that's all settled then," the old man said, taking David's arm. "There'll be time for a drink now."

"Time?" David croaked.

The old man chuckled. "I dare say you can use one."

Numbly, David allowed himself to be led inside and deposited at a table. The music and hilarity around him failed to penetrate his overloaded senses, and he gazed about in a stupor, feeling insubstantial, only superficially present, like an image projected on the wall. He wasn't thinking about what had happened in the alley. In a sense, he *couldn't* think about it; his mind simply rejected what his eyes had taken in.

When the old man arrived with glasses and a bottle of whiskey, David looked up and asked, "What *is* this place?"

The old man looked around doubtfully. "Why, I believe you could say that it's the Dead Man Saloon."

"I mean, what town?"

He smiled. "Oh, it's not a town, of course. You can see that."

"But where *are* we?"

"My dear fellow, I don't know what to tell you. Not every place on the earth has a name. If it's any help to you, we're in the mountains about a hundred miles west of Denver."

"I see." David took a sip of the whiskey and savored its fiery tingle as a confirmation of his reality. "Can someone help me get out of here?"

"All being taken care of, my boy."

David took another, larger sip and looked around cautiously. "Who *are* these people?"

"I'm afraid I don't understand your question."

"What are these people *doing* here?"

The old man frowned, puzzled. "I'd say they're . . . enjoying themselves."

His confidence returning, David poured himself another drink. "You seem to be deliberately misunderstanding me."

"Am I?" The old man pursed his lips in an innocent smile. "Perhaps you and I simply have different perceptions of the duties of hospitality."

"You'll have to explain that, I'm afraid."

"Really? How would you react to a stranger blundering into one of your own haunts and demanding to know who your companions were and what they were doing there?"

David paused. "Yes, but. . ."

"Yes? Go on."

"I mean . . . this is the middle of nowhere."

"Is it indeed? An amusing concept, that. And if it is?"

"Well . . . naturally I'm curious."

"You mean your curiosity is aroused by all this activity taking place in what you call the middle of nowhere."

"Yes, that's right."

The old man's aura of kindliness seemed to dissolve as he fixed David with a chilly stare. After sitting through two minutes of it, David asked what was wrong.

"Merely an attack of revulsion for those of your kind, I'm afraid."

"My kind?"

The old man cocked an eyebrow at him sardonically. "Surely you know what *kind* you are."

"Well, no, I guess I don't."

He gave him a bleak smile. "Perhaps that is the reason for my revulsion."

David shook his head, bewildered. "I'm sorry. I just don't understand."

The old man turned in his chair to survey the room, pausing when he spotted an enormous blanketed Indian sitting by himself in a corner.

"Horse Killer!" he called out. "Would you come here for a moment?"

The Indian glanced up without moving his broad, massive head. Then he rose, approached their table, and stood looking down at them in silence, his smallpox-ravaged face unreadable.

"Horse Killer, tell me: Do you know what kind I am?"

The Indian eyed him somberly for a moment. "I know."

"And do you know what kind you are?"

"Yes."

He flicked a finger in David's direction. "This one doesn't. He doesn't know what kind he is."

The Indian studied David gravely, his saturnine eyes filled with distaste, as if he were inspecting a not very promising hunting dog.

"Do you think you'd be able to enlighten him on this point?"

"Maybe. Probably not."

"Why not?"

He shrugged heavily and pushed his lips out in disdain. "Too old. Too ignorant."

The old man transferred his gaze to David and nodded. "Yes, I'm afraid you're right. Thank you."

As Horse Killer lumbered back to his own table, David frowned down into his drink, feeling bitter over this unjustified attack and wondering how he could defend himself against a charge so ill-defined. Before he could find a place to begin, the old man pushed back his chair and stood up.

"I believe they're ready for us now."

David looked around doubtfully and turned to the swinging doors. After a moment Hilly's knobby red face appeared above them and nodded once in their direction.

Walking out into the frigid air, David felt a tense expectancy around him, as if he were an actor making his entrance in a critical scene. The wagon had been drawn up in front of the saloon, and the steaming gray turned to look at him reproachfully. Ted watched from the driver's station, his face shadowed by a heavily stained cowboy hat. Hilly was propped up against the back of the wagon, his arms folded, a toothpick working in his mouth, but his eyes belied the non-chalance of the pose. Although he seemed to be completely en-grossed in studying the horse, the old man was obviously waiting for someone to begin the action, to deliver the anticipated line.

David, not knowing what else to do, started to climb up into the seat beside Ted but stopped when he felt the old man's hand on his arm.

"You'll be more comfortable in the back," he said quietly.

David looked into the wagon and saw that the wooden crate was still in place. Then his eyes grew wide as he looked again. The crate was filled to the top with *weeds*. He felt the breath leave his lungs as if he'd been punched in the stomach.

"No," he said in a choked whisper.

Hilly climbed up into the wagon, lifted off the top layer of weeds invitingly.

"No," he said again, edging away.

"But you must go back," the old man insisted.

"No."

The three of them watched with intense interest as David contin-ued to back away. When he reached the mouth of the alley, the old man spoke a single word.

"*Mike*."

As David turned, Mike was already gathering his feet under him, his black gaze fixed on David as if he were an apparition of horror.

"Mike," the old man repeated. "*Bring him.*"

David turned and ran.

At the crest above the town that wasn't a town, he stopped, pant-ing, and looked back. The resurrected corpse—almost luminescent in its paleness—was easily visible two hundred yards away, shambling toward him, lurching grotesquely with each stride to compensate for its crushed ribcage. Ted, Hilly, and the old man lounged around the wagon, watching casually, like spectators at an egg-and-spoon race.

While catching his breath, David tried to formulate a strategy.

Judging from Mike's progress, he felt he could stay ahead of him indefinitely, just by walking at a brisk pace, but the image of the two of them traversing the endless hills ahead, forever two hundred yards apart, was not an appealing one. He couldn't risk making it into a simple test of endurance.

Coming up the hill, he'd seen the moon ahead of him, presumably setting. As long as he kept marching toward it, he was in no danger of walking in circles, and this gave him an edge. Once out of visual contact with David, Mike wouldn't know what direction he'd taken and would soon be wandering through the hills at random, completely lost. David figured a ten minute jog would be enough to shake Mike off his trail.

It was also enough to do him in, and at the end of it he sank down into the dirt, panting, his throat as raw as if he'd swallowed a red-hot poker. As he waited for his heart to stop hammering and for his breath to return to normal, he wondered if it was necessary to move on at all. Checking his watch, he was astounded to see that it was only three o'clock—plenty of time to freeze to death if he didn't keep moving. He sighed and closed his eyes, deciding a ten-minute rest would be safe enough.

When he woke up twenty minutes later, it was because a pair of icy hands had closed around his ankles. David screamed and gave a convulsive kick that sent Mike spinning into the dirt. Then, once again, he was up and running.

After five minutes he stumbled over his own leaden feet, pitched headlong down the last twenty feet of an embankment, and lay there panting helplessly.

A man can walk down a deer.

His father, not a hunter but a tireless collector of unrelated bits of information, had told him this when he was a child. In his father's mind, it was proof of something or other—of the superiority of brains over speed, perhaps; of man's superiority over the rest of creation.

A man can walk down a deer. Was that what the old man was thinking?

Surely you know what kind you are.

Do you know what kind I am?

Is there a kind that can walk a *man* down?

David pulled himself up onto an elbow and looked around. Nothing moved; the air was as still and silent as if life had never been born on this planet. As far as he could tell, he'd left his pursuer far behind. But of course that's what the deer thinks too; spotting the hunter, it sprints ahead and imagines itself safe—until the hunter, moving at his own tireless pace, reappears and sends it into flight again—and again and again, until its energy is entirely spent.

He sank back into the dirt and gazed up at the remote, uncaring universe overhead, wondering if there was any stimulus at all that could get him back on his feet and running again. He was still wondering when he heard Mike scrabbling in the rocks above him.

He turned around so that he was on his knees, and sought out the black pits of Mike's eyes. *Do you know what kind you are? Do you know what kind I am?*

The creature that had once been a man named Mike and that now was of some other kind stared back in slack-jawed despair, appalled, as if confronting the vilest horror of hell.

And he kept coming without a pause.

Groaning, David pushed himself up and stumbled away. He was running, but he knew it was only a ghastly caricature of a run—the sort they must have done at Dachau for the amusement of the guards.

Pick 'em up and put 'em down.

Pick 'em up and put 'em down.

Come on folks, do *The Dead Man's Shuffle!*

He was only half aware that he was running with his eyes closed, but he became fully and painfully aware of it when he blundered into something waist-high that sent him sprawling through the air. The wind knocked out of him, he lay face down gasping for a minute. Then he turned over to see what he'd run into and began laughing breathlessly. He'd run into the loveliest thing he'd ever seen.

A dusty, dark green 1988 Volvo sedan.

He got in, turned the key still in place, and listened with ecstatic disbelief to the crash of ignition, the symphonic thrum of life itself. After opening the windows a crack for ventilation, he turned on the heater, climbed into the back, locked the doors, and curled up on the seat, stroking the velour with heartfelt affection.

If you can get me now, Mike, you're welcome to me.

He was asleep within seconds.

CHAPTER 28

In the thin mountain air, the sun turned the car into an oven by noon, and David stirred, moaning freely as his aching legs reminded him of the previous night's adventures. He sat up and made a methodical survey of the valley and surrounding hills before getting out and limping off to find a handful of snow to quench his thirst. His eyes moving constantly, he ate it hunkering in the shadow of a low pine while he made careful plans for the day.

Back at the car he emptied a plastic bottle of windshield-washing fluid, scoured it with dirt, and spent the next two hours melting enough snow to rinse it and fill it—another of those tasks easier to conceive than to perform. Then he wrapped it in a shirt, along with a bundle of spare clothes, to ride in the small of his back. Finally he detached from the rearview mirror a hitherto useless compass that Tim had given him a couple Christmases before.

While making these preparations, he'd considered the question of direction. West was out; he'd spend the rest of the day walking into the face of the sun. East was out; he was half convinced that the events of the previous night had been one long delusion induced by unwittingly immersing himself in hallucinogenic weeds—but only half; if the Dead Man Saloon was really out there, it was to the east. Between north and south he had nothing to go on but intuition, and intuition pulled him south.

So he headed south.

He estimated he could travel at least twenty miles before nightfall. In twenty miles there had to be something—a town, a ranch, a road, a power line. By four o'clock the landscape had changed somewhat. He'd descended perhaps a thousand feet, and the hills were gentler and farther apart. He was only vaguely aware of the difference. His legs were getting wobbly, and he was finding it harder and harder to shake off the recurring notion that it was time to stop and have something to eat. In fact, he was so preoccupied with fantasies of food that he was ten paces beyond them when he realized he'd just crossed a pair of tire tracks. He shook his head and went back, and there they were, crisp and fresh in the dust.

A long look in either direction gave him no sign of the vehicle that had made them, and he got down on hands and knees to see if there was anything in the tracks themselves that would tell him which way they were heading. There wasn't. Since it didn't seem to matter whether he followed them to their origin or their destination, he set out to the east to avoid being blinded by the declining sun. He decided his luck had returned at last when, half an hour later, he came over a rise and spotted the Jeep parked a quarter mile away. He started to run for it, then, seeing that it was empty, slowed to a walk.

He was about twenty yards away from it when a handful of the track ahead exploded into dust, and he heard the crack of a rifle. He stopped, stunned, not quite able to take in the fact that he'd been shot at.

"Just hold it right there, mister," someone called from his left.

Looking up, he thought for a moment that it was Hilly standing on the rise about fifty yards away. The shape was the same—tall and rangy—but the resemblance ended there. David laughed mirthlessly at the thought that popped into his head: *At least this one's human.*

He came on warily, the rifle at his side but pointed so that David had a clear view down the barrel. When he was close enough, he traded the rifle for a massive black pistol. He was accompanied by an equally massive black dog that looked like something shaped in a wind tunnel.

"Watch him, Beast." The dog lumbered forward, planted himself in front of David, and gave him a look at a set of strong white teeth.

"Take off that bundle, whatever it is."

David untied the shirt sleeves around his waist, and the bundle fell to the ground.

"Put your hands on your head."

"Look," David said.

"Shut up."

David put his hands on his head and waited through a careful search for weapons that weren't there. He winced when he felt the billfold leave his back pocket but didn't see any point in wasting words on it. He heard the other going through the cardfold, then felt it being returned to the pocket, which he took to be a good sign.

"You can put your hands down. Get in the car, back seat, right side."

David followed orders.

"Watch him, Beast."

Beast hopped in at the left and sat down facing him. The gunman got in, started the engine, and headed east.

"Get any sudden bright ideas," he pointed out, "and he'll turn you into hamburger."

"I believe it," David said. "What is he—what breed?"

"Pit bull."

Since he knew he wasn't going to have any sudden bright ideas, David didn't feel particularly menaced and could look at the blockish black head and massive chest with genuine admiration. He was a solid, well-designed fighting machine, like a Roman gladiator. David reached cautiously for his billfold, and the dog watched, interested but not alarmed. As far as he could tell from a quick inspection, nothing had been taken.

Now that he was no longer pointing a weapon at him, the driver didn't seem particularly menacing either. He was smoking, driving one handed, completely relaxed. Under the crumpled, sweat-stained cowboy hat, his leathery face was well-shaped, his expression serene and self-confident. Cleaned up, he would look like a young John Wayne in a sullen mood. Even with a gun in his hand, he'd seemed businesslike and disinterested rather than hostile, and David thought it would be well to establish this as the appropriate tone for their relationship.

"Believe it or not," he said, "I'm happy as hell to run into you."

"Oh yeah?" The response was distantly polite, as if David had announced he was a Dallas Cowboys fan.

"I've been wandering around out here lost for two days."

"Not a smart place to be wandering around, that's a fact."

David chewed on this ambiguous observation in silence for a few minutes, then asked where they were going. The driver ignored the question, and David decided that others like it would be ignored as well.

He had the feeling he should be more worried than he was, but he just couldn't seem to manage it after what he'd been through in the past twenty-four hours. After all, if the idea had been to kill him, he'd already be dead. He'd been trespassing, obviously—but also innocently. Once he had a chance to explain what had happened, he was sure there'd be no problem.

Ten minutes later they angled up a steep track to a mobile home perched on a butte with a panoramic view of the surrounding countryside. The hills were still empty as far as he could see, but at least there was a roughly-graded road leading up to the butte on the other side. With its feminine lines and pastel blue paint, the mobile home looked a bit like a girl stranded in the desert in a fifties party dress; it was up on cement blocks, unskirted, and there were no power lines in sight. A recent-model pickup truck and a 500 gallon propane tank were parked beside it.

The driver pulled up, got out, unholstered his pistol, and said, "Let's go."

"You don't need that," David protested, but the other just waved him on impatiently and followed him up a set of cement-block stairs to the living room.

Inside, an old man was lying on a couch, reading. He lowered the book and raised his head to peer curiously at David over his glasses.

"What have we here, Robbie?"

Robbie holstered his gun. "Found him wandering around over by the shed."

"I didn't see any shed," David put in quickly.

"Ah," the old man said, swinging his feet off the couch and sitting up. He pulled off his glasses and studied David with interest. His eyes, set in a long, horsey British face, were red-rimmed and heavily pouched. Though slim, he seemed as broad as a door and, when standing, would tower over David by three inches. His dusty-white hair was uncut and limp, giving him a look of dissipation.

"Want a beer?" Robbie asked, opening the refrigerator.

David said, "Are you asking *me*?"

"Sure."

"Yes, thanks."

The furniture was all from Goodwill: the old man's battered sofa, covered in a dingy flower print, two mismatched chairs, and a heavily stained and cigarette-burned coffee table. In a rather pathetic effort at hominess, someone had taken the trouble to hang curtains at the windows: cheap, sun-faded cotton with nursery-rhyme motifs.

Jack and Jill went up the hill.

The place smelled of sweat, dust, and cigarette smoke. Robbie tossed David a can of Coors and opened one for himself.

"I'm Harvey," the old man said, making it *Hahvey*, "and, in case he hasn't introduced himself, this is Robbie. There's no reason for us to be uncivilized, after all."

"My name is David Kennesey."

"How do you do? Sit down while we decide what's to be done with you."

"Why does anything have to be done with me?" David asked, sitting down across from him. "I just got lost in the mountains. All I want to do is get back to civilization."

"Ah, to be sure. What do you think, Robbie?"

"Yeah, that's probably right. Nobody who knew anything would be traveling the way he was."

"So," Harvey said, turning back to David. "You are innocent of any wicked intent, meant no harm at all. On the other hand, you're not young enough to think that innocence is an invincible shield against misfortune."

"No, I know it isn't."

"So, Robbie, what would you do?"

He shrugged. "Plant him."

The old man's faced crinkled into a delighted grin.

"There, you see? For this evening at least, I am your shield against misfortune."

"What do you mean?"

"Robbie is by instinct a barbarian, one who thinks all problems can be solved by giving someone the chop. Luckily for you, our lord and master, the all-seeing Charles, thinks otherwise. And so I am here."

"I'm sorry, I still don't understand."

"For a bottle of booze a day, a roof over my head, and a monthly pittance, I am Robbie's master, just as Robbie is the Beast's master. I am seventy-nine years old, an alcoholic, my eyes are gone, my legs are nearly gone, but Charles trusts me, because my mind is as good as ever."

Robbie sighed. "Chuck will tell us to plant him."

The old man peered at him disapprovingly over the top of his glasses. "Then we will plant him. Meanwhile, I shall indulge myself in conversation that consists of something other than grunts." He turned back to David. "You strike me as an educated man."

"Most people would say so, yes."

"Ah, and modest as well. You might not think of it to look at me now, the associate of riff-raff and losers, but I worked on the Manhattan Project."

David raised his brows politely.

"Oh, you needn't humor me, my boy. It's perfectly true. I wasn't one of the fairest of the fair-haired boys—I was too much a rebel for that—but you'll find me in a footnote, and I still receive a pension for my contribution."

Robbie groaned in disgust, got another beer, and said he was going outside.

Harvey laughed huskily. "He's as bored with me as I am with him. I can't really blame him."

"Would you mind explaining what makes me such a nuisance? As far as I'm concerned, I just want to get out of here."

"I take it you're not from these parts. If you were, you'd know it's not a healthy area for the casual explorer. A great many unmarked graves will open up out here on Judgment Day."

David frowned. "Marijuana?"

"Do you really want to know?"

"No. That's the whole point. I don't know anything and I don't *want* to know anything. And in fact I haven't seen anything."

"Ah, but I'm afraid you have. You've seen two men, one of them armed, and a mobile home tucked away up in the hills. Very valuable information to a great variety of people, some of them completely ruthless. Very dangerous information for you—and for us. You only have to think it through, my boy."

David spent a few minutes thinking it through and said, "Look, there's no reason for me to say anything about any of this to anybody. It's none of my business. All I want to do is get out of here. Once I do that, I'll be five hundred miles away by tomorrow night."

Harvey nodded approvingly. "Yes, personally, I believe you. I have a very trusting nature. I love everyone."

"Won't this Charles take your word for it?"

"Ah, Charles . . . . No, he won't take my word for it, because he knows I have a trusting nature. However, all is not lost. Charles is a gambler. If he likes you and is in an optimistic mood, then he'll stuff a hundred dollar bill in your shirt pocket and send you on your way."

"And if he's not in an optimistic mood?"

Harvey shrugged. "We must hope for the best."

David looked around the barren room. "How do you get in touch with him?"

"We don't. We're completely cut off here. But he'll be driving up in the morning. Would you like another beer?"

"No, but I could use some food. I haven't eaten in a day and a half."

Harvey chuckled. "I haven't eaten in a week myself—rarely do when I'm on the booze—but help yourself."

David was rummaging in the kitchen when Robbie stalked in and asked him what the hell he was doing.

"Looking for something to eat."

"Get out of there. I'll fix something." He opened a cupboard and started taking down cans.

"Did you think I was looking for a knife?"

"No. If you'd found one, I'd've taken it away from you," Robbie said. "I just don't like cleaning up other people's messes in the kitchen."

"Sorry."

Robbie snorted with grim humor, a man used to dealing with idiots and incompetents.

"Particle acceleration, I told them," Harvey said, sitting with a glassful of bourbon at the table while David and Robbie ate. "Of course, it's all the rage now, but I was telling them in 1944 that there's no future in fission. Very unpopular it made me then, I can tell you. Now, of course, they're beating their brains out trying to find a way to drive a proton into the nucleus of a hydrogen atom. Quite hopeless."

"Why is it hopeless?" David asked.

"Well, you see, they've fastened on the hydrogen atom because it's the simplest—only one proton. But, relatively speaking, its electron is as far away as the earth from the sun."

"You mean they're working on the wrong atom?"

"Definitely."

"Which one should they be using?"

"Ah," Harvey said. "I would say cobalt. Twenty-seven protons, and with the electrons much closer to the nucleus, you see. Much more compact, much more manageable."

Robbie wiped his mouth with a paper napkin, set it down beside his plate, and said, in a completely amiable tone, "You know, Harvey, you really are fulla shit."

"Ah, the Neanderthal awakens! And what is your choice, Robbie? Carbon, perhaps?"

"When was the last time you were in a laboratory?"

"Oh, it's been well over thirty years now."

"Then you don't know shit about it."

Harvey chuckled agreeably. "Robbie thinks the wizards of Los Alamos may have revised the subatomic structure of the universe in the past three decades without letting anyone know about it."

Robbie folded his arms and tilted his chair back. "Where do we stand right now, Harvey? We're even, aren't we?"

"No, you owe me." Harvey turned to David to explain. "He bet me ten thousand dollars that John Steinbeck wrote *The Good Earth*."

"Okay. I'll bet you another ten thousand that fusion is achieved with the hydrogen atom."

"You mean first, rather than with any other atom."

"That's right."

Harvey shrugged. "I won't live long enough to collect, but very well. You can pay it to my estate."

"Would you rather arm wrestle for it?"

"Why? Are you feeling stronger than usual tonight?"

"You want to arm wrestle or not?"

"By all means," Harvey said, rolling up his sleeve to expose a pale, flabby arm. He flashed David a raffish smile. "Someday I'm going to buy him a tee-shirt that reads, 'Born to lose.'"

The two men locked hands and glared at each other across the table. After a minute, their eyes were popping and their arms were trembling, muscles bunched. Harvey's face split in a foolish grin. "No cheating," he gasped.

"I don't need to cheat."

"Argh," Harvey grunted, forcing Robbie's hand down to within an inch of the table top. It hovered there for a few seconds and then began to rise.

"What now, Harvey?" Robbie taunted.

"Down!" the old man commanded.

Robbie's knuckles thumped on the table, and the two men dissolved in boyish giggles.

"I have *tremendously* powerful arms," Harvey confided, his redrimmed eyes sparkling with delight.

As he stood up to clear the table, Robbie gave David a sardonic wink.

David shook his head in wonderment.

"Oh, I drove them crazy! Wouldn't stay put, wouldn't keep my nose to the grindstone. But they couldn't just fire me—couldn't fire any of us, you see—because they were afraid we'd take what we knew to the Germans or the Russians.

"In order to study the effects of an atomic explosion in detail, they had to develop an ultra-highspeed motion picture camera. A thousand frames a second. The Mitchell Movie Camera was the fastest there was at that time—a quarter of a million dollars—but it would only do four hundred and fifty frames a second. The problem was the shutter. At the speed they wanted, the friction it generated simply ignited the nitrate on the film—literally blew it up. One day I was lying on the beach in Fort Lauderdale, Florida—completely AWOL, you understand—when the solution came to me. I went into a telephone booth and called my boss at Los Alamos. Jim McMahon—James Aloysius Xavier McMahon. Forget the shutter, I told him. Use a prism. Mounted on a spindle—a thousand frames a second, ten thousand frames a second, whatever you like. And that was it. That was how they solved the problem, and that was what got me my pension."

Harvey, drinking steadily, had finished off the last half of a quart bottle of bourbon, with a little help from David. Robbie, listening morosely to stories he'd already heard a dozen times, stuck to beer.

"Jim said, 'Harvey, what are we going to do with you? You know we can't go on this way.' 'Give me a pension,' I told him, and I'll get out of your hair.' And he said, 'What are you talking about, Harvey? I can't give you a pension.' And I said, 'Certainly you can, dear fellow. You know you can.' And he did."

He shuffled off to the kitchen and returned with a fresh bottle.

"Of course the devils didn't tie it to any cost-of-living index." He wiggled his toes. "I use it to buy a pair of handmade shoes every year. That's all it's good for now. Got addicted to them in Hong Kong. Was a gun-runner in China for more than a decade before the war, you know. Made a fortune in guns. It cost me my citizenship, of course, because—needless to say—they were being used against the British."

Robbie rolled his eyes, said he had things to do, and disappeared down the central hallway.

"Harvey," David said before he could get going on his next cycle of tales.

"Yes, dear boy?"

"You could let me walk out of here, couldn't you?"

The old man frowned thoughtfully. "It would do no good, I fear. Robbie and the dog would run you to earth in minutes."

"What about the Jeep or the pickup?"

He shook his head. "I don't have the keys, and I don't believe I could in good conscience let you have them if I did. Old-fashioned as it sounds, one must play the game, you know."

"But it's not my game, Harvey."

"No, no, certainly not. You're perfectly right to want to escape. For you, that is indeed playing the game. But I'm afraid asking me to collaborate with you is out of bounds. Puts me in an awkward position, you see. Morally speaking."

"My own position is pretty awkward, don't you think?"

"Not to worry, my boy. You seem a good lad to me, and I'll do my best for you. Charles respects my judgment."

David was tempted to point out that he'd said just the opposite a couple hours before but decided it would be impolitic to risk alienating him.

"I once spent a month in a jail in Singapore," Harvey said, discovering a way after all to segue into his China memoirs.

David sighed, poured himself another drink, and listened respectfully, like a good lad, until Robbie reappeared half an hour later to announce it was bedtime.

"Bedtime!" Harvey exploded. "Don't be absurd."

"Not for you, old man. For him. You can stay up till dawn if you want to, but I have to be up early."

"So go to bed and leave us in peace."

Robbie sighed grimly. "Harvey, you stick to the plasma physics and the bookkeeping, and I'll stick to security, okay? He has to go to bed so *I* can go to bed."

"Oh, very well," Harvey said in a huff, "take him away."

"I intend to. Come on," he told David.

David got up and preceded him down the hall.

"Last door on the right," Robbie said.

David opened the door and entered a small bedroom furnished with a single bed.

Robbie stayed in the doorway. "Just so you'll know, I'll be roping the knob of this door to the one across the hall. It wouldn't keep you in very long if you wanted to get out, but I'd be there in plenty of time to blow you away. Understand?"

"Yes."

"You can also get out through the window, of course, if you're ready to take on the dog. He'll be there all night, and he knows what to do."

David nodded.

"We're really not set up for keeping prisoners," Robbie added, as if apologizing for a defect in hospitality. Then he closed the door, and David heard him working at the doorknob. After a minute the door opened again as Robbie checked to see how much slack there was; evidently there was too much. He went back to work, checked a second time, and said, "Shit."

David listened as he walked back toward the living room and kitchen. He returned with two pots tied together at the handles, which he looped over the rope. He shoved David's door open, producing a satisfactory clamor, and closed it again.

As he walked away, David called out, "Have a nice day," and was answered by a dry chuckle.

David went over to examine the hinges on the door. As he'd hoped, the pins weren't completely seated. Working on the one at the top, he managed to get the edge of a quarter in between the head of the pin and the shoulder of the hinge, but he didn't have enough leverage to force it up. It was a useless idea anyway; if he managed to get the pins out, there'd be no way to take the door off without setting those pots a-clonking.

He sat down on the bed and considered the rest of the room. The side wall would probably be flimsy enough to cut through with a penknife—if he had a penknife; any other way would be too noisy. The ceiling and floor were even more hopeless, and the heating vent might have offered an escape route for a badger on a diet. He got up, turned off the light, and went over to the window. The Beast, comfortably curled up on the ground below, raised his head to give him a friendly grin, all good cheer until it was time to tear him to pieces.

David looked over at the bed. Throw a blanket over the dog and immobilize it? *Oh sure. Go to it, 007.*

With a sigh, he considered the window itself, which consisted of two sliding panes. He turned the lights back on, went to the bed, stripped off a blanket, folded it in half twice, and put it on the floor at one side of the room. Then he lifted one of the window panes out of its track and slipped it inside the blanket. After studying this arrangement for a moment, he got the other blanket, folded it, and put it on top. He contemplated adding the mattress, but decided it was too risky; one suspicious thump or scrape of bed-frame would put him out of business.

Taking a deep breath, he stepped into the middle of the blankets. The crunch of breaking glass was barely audible, even to him. He carried the top blanket back to the bed, unfolded the second, and smiled down at enough lethal weapons to arm a platoon. He'd correctly guessed that most of the shards would be dagger-shaped, and trusted to luck that at least one would come with a reasonable haft.

One did, and he wrapped it in a sock and tied it off with a shoelace. It made a formidable-looking weapon.

As he pulled off his shoes and got into bed, he wondered what the hell he was going to do with it.

It was the sound of running footsteps in the hallway that woke him up four hours later—running footsteps, hoarse cries, sounds of a struggle, something crashing to the floor. And then a mushy explosion that rocked the mobile home on its blocks. Sitting up, paralyzed but quiveringly alert, David listened, mouth dry, eyes straining in the darkness. Something slithered to the floor in the living room with a plop like a wet sack. There was a slow, heavy dripping.

He groped gingerly for the knife on the floor beside the bed and went to the door to listen. After a few moments the floor in the hallway creaked, and he backed up. The creaking continued until it was level with his room. Whoever was standing there seemed to be contemplating the meaning of the rope strung between doorknobs.

The pots clonked softly.

David retreated to the bed and, suffocating with terror, watched as the knob turned and the door opened a crack, straining against the rope.

An outdoor scent swept in through the crack, drawn by the open window.

The scent of crushed weeds.

The rope squealed thinly against the metal as the pressure increased.

Something inside David's head seemed to part with a twang.

CHAPTER 29

In his dream, he belonged to a strange sort of literary club, and its officers were accompanying him on a tour of its library, housed in a barn-like metal building. He stood with them before a revolving carrel that displayed an assortment of newspapers, and someone read out a headline: *Local man found behind wall.*

David looked for the headline but couldn't find it. They kept repeating it insistently, but, as far as David could see, it just wasn't there.

"Haven't you *read* this story?" someone asked indignantly, and he admitted he hadn't. The others received this news with shocked disapproval.

"Surely you can't expect people to read everything," he protested, but evidently they did. Each member was supposed to be familiar with the collection in complete detail.

"You'll have to wait down there while we decide what to do about this," he was told. David stepped down into a pit about three feet below floor level, and they proceeded to discuss his case as though he wasn't there.

As they talked, it became clear that they considered his omission a very serious offence indeed, one that couldn't be overlooked or excused. Even expulsion from the club wasn't a sufficient remedy. Finally David realized they were talking themselves around to a point where they had no choice but to kill him. As they calmly discussed the details of his execution, David backed away and discovered that the building was indeed a barn—it was part of a prison farm. It was cold, and behind him he could hear the clanking of cow bells.

He found a way out—a massive locked stone that sat like a plug in the wall. Knowing he only had moments in which to escape, he inserted his member's key in the lock and tried to turn it, but it was frozen from disuse, and the key bent like tin in his fingers.

David turned over in the bed and woke up to find the room flooded with early morning light. In the icy draft from the window, the door was tugging gently against the rope. Except for the restless murmur of the two pots, still in place, the house was ominously still. He pulled on his shoes and picked up the knife, which had miraculously fallen to the floor without shattering. After listening at the door for thirty seconds, he quietly called out Harvey's name and then Robbie's.

Getting no response, he used his foot to force the door open while he sawed through the rope. After the pots clattered to the floor, he waited for a reaction through a full minute. Then he stepped into the hallway, turned toward the living room, and saw that it had been transformed into a slaughterhouse. Blood blossomed and drooled on the walls like gouts of paint in an abstract expressionist painting. Furniture and floor were awash in a stew of burst organs, intestines, feces, and urine, from which protruded almost unidentifiable limbs, shattered bones, huge shapeless hunks of meat.

David hadn't taken it all in. With his first glance and the first wave of the stench, he was on his knees, giving up the thin remains of the previous night's dinner. When there was no more to give up, he crawled back into his room and sat down with his back to the door, his stomach and his mind heaving as he tried to swallow down and obliterate what he'd seen and smelled.

After a few minutes he stood up on rubbery legs and walked over to the window. The dog seemed to have abandoned its post, but he had to be sure before climbing out. Gnawing on his lower lip, he considered the pros and cons of calling it. He had to know if the dog was nearby, but he was reluctant to break the silence that enclosed the house like a dome—was reluctant to see what else besides a dog might be summoned by a call. The choice was to leave by way of the hall, and he knew he was never going to open that door again.

He leaned out of the window and whispered the dog's name, knowing he couldn't be heard—and terrified of being heard.

"Beast!" he croaked, his throat scorched raw by what he'd brought up.

When nothing moved and nothing answered, he climbed over the sill, slid to the ground, and stood leaning shakily against the house.

Robbie's gun would be in the living room, and David wanted it. He'd never wanted anything more in his life.

Thinking about it, he was certain the front door was open. He hadn't seen it, but the hall had been frigid and breezy. He wondered if he could go to the door and look into that charnel house, commanding his eyes to see nothing but a chunk of black metal. He decided he was going to have to try.

He circled to the front of the house, closed his eyes for a moment, and swallowed. As he started up the steps, his stomach lurched, and he had to stop, shut his eyes again, and remind himself that there was a treasure buried in that three or four hundred pounds of offal—a lovely, lethal treasure in matte black steel. Then he went in.

He was in luck. The gun was just inside the door and only partly buried under an unidentifiable mass of flesh and clothing. He kicked it away, and it skittered across the floor. Bending over it, he found he couldn't bring himself to pick it up, glistening with slime. He tore a curtain from a window, wadded it up, grabbed the gun, and got out of there, his stomach in an upheaval that wasn't going to be suppressed this time. He made it to the side of the house before he was down in the dirt retching again.

It was a while before he was aware of anything outside of his own body, shivering and icy with sweat, so he didn't hear the car thumping its way up the road. But he raised his head groggily when he heard the car door slam. He rubbed the gun down with the curtain, got to his feet, and stumbled around the corner of the house.

A stranger stood frozen halfway up the front steps, gulping and staring white-faced into the living room.

"Hold it," David gasped, holding the gun up in both hands.

The man turned and staggered as if the command had been a shot. Goggling at David in abject terror, he crossed his arms protectively across his chest, and it was obvious he thought David was responsible for the carnage inside.

"Charles," David hissed. "You motherfucker."

With the gun aimed at Charles's chest, he squeezed on the trigger. He squeezed until his hands shook—for the moment completely insane. Then he looked down at the gun, puzzled until he figured out what was wrong, and thumbed the safety catch off.

"Hey, man," Charles whimpered, "I don't even *know* you."

"You know me," David said. "You were going to kill me."

"I wasn't! I swear to God!"

Staring at him, David gradually calmed down. "You're Charles?" he asked doubtfully.

"Yes, but I swear to God I don't know you."

Looking at him, David found it hard to believe that this man was to have decided his fate. With his slight build and his smooth, characterless face, thick glasses, and receding chin, he might have been an assistant manager of a supermarket. He looked like a nineteen-year-old wearing the clothes of an older, more sophisticated brother—fawn-colored suede sport coat, tan silk shirt, and jeans.

"You're Charles?" David asked again.

The boy gazed at him in blank terror, his lower lip trembling.

Still holding him under the gun, David looked around and saw a brilliantly polished red Corvette parked nearby.

"Get in the car," he said. Charles moved tentatively away. "In the car," David repeated.

Charles, his hands raised, circled around him toward the Corvette.

"Get in the passenger side and crawl over the gear box to the driver side."

David followed him into the car and told him to start driving.

"To where?"

"To wherever you came from."

The young man started the car, turned around, and headed down the track.

"Where are we?" David asked after a few minutes.

"Where are we? We're about ten miles north of Winslow."

"That doesn't mean anything to me. Where's the interstate?"

"You mean I-70? It's another ten miles past Winslow."

"Okay." David sighed, thinking of the expressway: another world entirely, a broad swathe of civilization, with clear paths leading to motels, restaurants, department stores, theaters. "You grow marijuana up there?"

Charles blinked for a moment, thinking. "Yes."

"A lot of money?"

"A lot of money," he agreed. "A fortune."

"Harvey and Robbie were going to kill me if you said the word."

Charles ran his tongue over his lips but said nothing.

"I'm going to take your car. All right?"

"All right."

"You can buy another one, can't you?"

"Yes."

"I won't say anything to anyone about your operation up here."

"Okay."

"You understand? You can forget all about me."

"Okay."

David thought for a moment. "How far have we come?"

"You mean from the . . . house? About five miles, maybe."

"That's enough. You can get out here."

The young man looked at him in alarm.

"Just stop the car and get out. I'm not going to hurt you."

Eyes glazed, Charles took the car out of gear and lifted his foot off the gas pedal but seemed reluctant to bring it to a halt.

"Now," David said.

Suddenly he jammed on the brakes, flung himself out of the car, and started running back up the road.

The car began to roll forward, and David squirmed into the driver's seat, put it back in gear, and, unaccustomed to its power, took off with wheels kicking up dirt.

CHAPTER 30

Stopping for gas in Glenwood Springs, David visited the men's room. In the mirror, he saw why the attendant had been visibly impressed by his appearance; he looked like he'd just walked away from a plane crash. He washed his face and went back out to ask where he could buy some clothes.

"Not much open here on a Sunday," he was told. "Might find something in Grand Junction, though."

Before leaving, he bought a map.

At a men's store in Grand Junction, he explained he'd been in an accident and needed a bit of everything from underwear on out. An extra fifty dollars produced someone willing to do alterations on two pairs of jeans, two pairs of slacks, and a sport coat. He proceeded from there to a small department store where he picked up everything else he needed to fill a new suitcase.

Finally, looking fairly presentable but not smelling quite right, he checked into a motel and spent an hour in a hot bath. Then he shaved, got back into the tub for a shower, and washed his hair three times. Feeling clean at last, he pulled the spread off the bed, lay down naked, and stared up at the ceiling, luxuriating in the feel of cool, smooth sheets against his back.

He wondered if he'd feel any different if the safety catch on Robbie's pistol had been off—if the harmless-looking, weak-chinned

Charles were now lying up in the mountains with a big, bloody hole
in his chest and flies congregating in his astonished eyes. He decided
he wouldn't.

When he began to get hungry, he dressed, checked out, and went
looking for a drink and a steak.

Then he was on his way again—to Las Vegas after all.

The Corvette seemed to want to cruise at eighty, and David, feeling
reckless, let it have its way, so it was only a little after nine when he
turned onto the Las Vegas Expressway to go downtown. He knew
the city somewhat, from a convention reluctantly attended, and he
despised the pretentious posh of the Strip hotels. The gaudy carnival
of Fremont Street was at least honestly vulgar.

He checked into the El Moreno, one of the smaller hotels, had a
typical Las Vegas meal—tasteless and cheap—and went into the
cocktail lounge, where he drank until the trio started in on its second
round of *Satin Doll*. Then he took himself blearily off to his room upstairs, fell into bed, and slept like a hunk of granite until four A.M.,
when a slaughterhouse dream jerked him awake, sweating and wanting to be among people—lots of people. He splashed some water on
his face, got dressed, and hurried downstairs. After wading through a
tasteless breakfast in an empty dining room, he wandered into the
casino.

Finding a stool at an empty blackjack table, he sat down to watch
the action, which seemed at once more subdued and more intense
than at midnight. Under the sea of smoke that hung inverted from
the ceiling, the players looked like corpses, blinking down at their
choices with dull, indifferent eyes.

David reflected that the gambler's idea of heaven is a scene
straight from hell at five in the morning, when, without the midnight
crowds to hide it, the truth lies exposed. The players aren't there to
play; they're there to work. Under the watchful eyes of their
warders—the dealers and the bosses—the players shuffle hopelessly
from table to table, condemned to an eternity of grinding out the

club's percentage, of systematically leaving behind just a little more than they pick up.

Finding this a more agreeable nightmare than the one he'd left behind in his room, David slid off his stool, stretched, and went over to the roulette wheel to study the betting layout. The red-jacketed dealer, arms folded and idle without any players, nodded pleasantly and watched him with very bright, very dark eyes set in a good-humored, intelligent face. Unlike the players, he seemed fresh and alert. David handed him a hundred dollar bill and was given twenty casino chips. Seeing nothing more attractive to do with them, he put them all on the number one, and the dealer set the wheel in motion and flicked the plastic ball along the rim.

After sizzling along for a while, it drifted down from the rim, clicked off a few buffers, and settled in a pocket. The dealer saw which it was before David did and calmly announced it: "One."

For nine times you can't miss.

Faster than David could follow it, the dealer picked up two stacks of chips, slid five off of one of them, and added them to the original twenty.

"How much is that?" David asked.

"Thirty-six hundred, sir—with your original bet."

"I'll let it ride on one."

The dealer smiled indulgently. "You bet the limit, sir."

"I beg your pardon?"

"The limit on a straight-up bet is one hundred dollars."

David frowned. "Only one hundred?"

"It used to be fifty, but we have the *en prison* rule now."

Leaving the hundred behind, David scooped off the thirty-five hundred he'd won and asked what the *en prison* rule was. After listening to the explanation without comprehension, he asked about even/odd and red/black. He bet the limit on odd and red—one thousand on each.

The ball was sent spinning in its slot and after a few moments clattered into a pocket. With studied indifference, the dealer blinked and said, "One."

A quick tally told David he'd won fifty-five hundred dollars. He asked about the odds and limits on the other bets, and the dealer explained about the columns, the dozens, and high/low. David bet the limit on everything on the board, and the ball was set in motion. When it hopped out of the double zero to rest in the neighboring slot for the third time in a row, the dealer's composure wavered: he gawked for a moment before beginning the payoff.

When David looked up from clearing off his winnings, he found the dealer conferring with the pit boss. A slender, dark-suited man with bitter eyes, the pit boss nodded, shot David a wary look, and took the dealer's place at the wheel.

"You're having a lucky night," he said with a grim smile.

"So it would seem."

The pit boss glanced at the layout. "You're playing one again?"

"That's right."

He nodded as if his worst suspicions had been confirmed and slotted the ball into orbit with a professional flick. As it wound its way around the domed wheel, a player from another table drifted over to see what the excitement was. He scanned the bets, moistened his lips with the tip of his tongue, and transferred his gaze to the wheel. His eyes popped and David felt an electric charge run through him when the ball dropped into the pocket.

"Jesus," he whispered reverently as the dealer began sliding chips out onto the layout.

The pit boss gave David a sour smile. "Would you object to moving to another table, sir? A closed table?"

"A closed table?"

"Just for you, that is."

The player at David's right said, "You can't do that."

"If the gentleman prefers it," the pit boss said levelly. David thought for a moment. "I think I'd prefer not to have a riot."

"Meaning?"

"A closed table."

The pit boss nodded and the dealer pulled the cover off the wheel at a nearby table. As David looked down uncertainly at the mass of chips in front of him, the pit boss swept them expertly onto a tray.

David was setting out his bets at the next table when a cocktail waitress appeared to ask him if he'd like a drink, and he said a Bloody Mary would be nice. By the time the wheel was spinning, another five players, sensing action, had arrived to watch. The ball went spinning into its slot, tripped over a few buffers, bounded off the partition between nineteen and eight, and curved up into a graceful arc that ended in the one pocket. The spectators ah'ed in appreciation, as if David had made a basket from mid-court.

At a whispered command from the pit boss, the dealer disappeared. By the time he returned with the shift boss, David had made his seventh win and all other games in the casino had come to a halt as news of the miracle spread.

The shift boss was a rotund man in his fifties, dressed in a shapeless blue suit, bald except for a puff of grey at each temple, with thick glasses and blue jowls. After surveying the scene from the pit with a look of amused disbelief, he made his way around to David and gravely took his hand.

"Jack Golding," he said, "one of the owners here."

David introduced himself.

"They say you're having quite a run."

"Yes, I guess so."

The fat man looked around vaguely. "Got everything you need? A drink?"

"I have one, thanks."

He lifted his head and bawled, "Jacqui!"

"I'm here, Mr. Golding," the cocktail waitress called, blocked outside by the circle of watchers.

"Get Mr. Kennesey another drink, for God's sake!"

"Right away, Mr. Golding!"

The shift boss turned and studied the layout.

"I hear you got a thing for the number one."

"Well . . . you know what the prophets say: God is One."

Jack Golding chuckled massively. "That's good. That's very good.

My rabbi'll get a kick out of that. Got a sense of humor, God bless him. You don't mind me interrupting like this, I hope?"

"No, not at all."

"See, in five minutes every degenerate gambler on Fremont Street is gonna be in our joint."

"That's good?"

"That's good." He nodded at David's chips. "It ain't as good as this is bad, but it's something, you understand?"

"Yes, I guess so."

Golding looked up at the pit boss and growled, "Let Angie handle it," and the dealer resumed his place behind the wheel; he paused uncertainly, as if waiting for instructions.

"So?" the fat man asked. "You expecting trumpets? Do it, for God's sake. But give us a twenty this time, huh?"

The dealer slotted the ball and sent it on its way. Then he stepped back a pace and folded his arms, disassociating himself from the disaster. When the ball finished its hectic journey, it was circling comfortably in the slot numbered one. The crowd sighed in awe, and an ancient crone at David's left stroked his arm, muttering reverently.

"Jacqui!" the shift boss bellowed.

"Coming, boss!" the cocktail waitress shouted back, fighting her way through the crowd.

Jack Golding nodded in approval as she served David his Bloody Mary.

"And you can bring me a double strychnine on the rocks," he added.

"With bitters?" Jacqui asked blandly.

"With lotsa bitters, honey."

"Coming right up."

The shift boss looked up at David and shook his head. "What've you got against the El Moreno anyway? Why ain't you gambling at Caesar's Palace?"

"I'm staying here," David answered simply.

"Ah. We got all the luck." He shrugged expressively, studying

David's bets. "You got any idea what the odds are against the same number coming up nine times in a row on a roulette wheel? Trillions to one. *Trillions!*"

David shrugged back. "I feel lucky."

"Lucky!" he chuckled bleakly. "I like that. That's good." He gave the dealer a nod, and the ball went whizzing into its track.

Except at its edge, where newcomers were being filled in on the prodigy, the crowd fell silent.

Losing speed, the ball hissed down the side of the bowl, leaped from one buffer to another, flirted with the nine and the thirty-one, and floated into the one as if drawn by a magnet. The old woman at David's side buried her fingers in his arm possessively, and the silence dissolved into gasps, shrieks, sighs, reverent curses, and cheers.

The fat shift boss turned gray and shrank into his shapeless blue suit, shaking his head in disbelief. "Too much," he whispered. "Too much."

David cleared the board of his winnings and all bets except the original stack of twenty five-dollar chips. He left that sitting on the one, and nodded to the dealer.

"Luck run out?" Golding asked.

"All run out," David replied, starting to move his chips onto the tray.

He was still at it when the ball clattered to a halt and the dealer sang out, "Twenty-four!" A groan sprang from the crowd, but it had a distinct timbre of relief and amused vindication.

"You're not *quitting*, are you?" the shift boss asked.

"When the luck runs out, you quit," David said.

The old woman dragged him down to whisper something in his ear: "Don't forget to tip the dealer, honey!"

David counted out five hundred dollars in chips and pushed them across the table. The dealer glanced uneasily at his bosses and picked them up.

"Well, at least *somebody* made out here," Golding observed dryly.

A dozen players wanted to shake David's hand, and the old

woman demanded a kiss, but the crowd quickly returned to the tables, leaving a few behind to see if there was any residual luck in the wheel that had paid off nine times running.

Golding led David to the cashier's window and hurried off, saying he'd be right back. The cashier started counting the chips, and David realized with annoyance that the little old woman had followed him from the table and was supervising the count with a distinctly proprietary air. Now that she was no longer clinging to his arm, he could see what a disreputable creature she really was, with her stringy, dishwater-colored hair and cheap cotton house dress.

He pointedly turned his back on her.

The cashier finished the count, announced the total as $67,500, and asked David how he wanted it.

"Can you give me a check?"

"Sure."

The old woman punched him on the arm. "You send some of that to your family, you hear!"

"Now look—" David began and was interrupted by another punch.

"Don't you now-look me, sonny! You got a kid, don't you?"

"Yes, but—"

"You send some of that to your kid or you're a rat. A rat forever!"

Looking down into her thin, wrinkled face, contorted with earnest fury, David decided she was right. He turned back to the cashier and told him to make out two checks, one to Tim for twenty thousand and one to himself for the balance.

"Satisfied?" David asked.

The old crone gave him a raffish, snaggle-toothed grin and scuttled away.

"A local character?" David asked the cashier.

He shrugged indifferently. "Never saw her before."

David was slipping the checks into the breast pocket of his jacket when the shift boss returned and led him to the dining room.

"You had breakfast?"

"Yes."

"Want another drink?"

"Just coffee, thanks."

Golding beckoned a waitress over and ordered two coffees. Then he slid a room key across the table.

"What's this?" David asked.

"The key to the Presidential Suite—not that we get a whole lotta presidents. On the house, for as long as you want."

David raised his eyebrows. "Are you kidding?"

"Somebody's already up there moving your stuff."

David laughed. "I wasn't planning to stay."

"You stay, kid. It's all comped—room, meals, drinks, the works. Just sign for whatever you want. You need a car?"

"I've got a car. What *is* all this?"

Golding blinked at this unexpected naivete and faltered for a moment over what lie to tell him.

"God, kid, in the gambling world you're gonna be like Charles Lindbergh. John Glenn. In the history of the whole goddamned planet, nobody ever sat down and beat the wheel nine times in a row. Nobody. We'll put a bronze plaque on that wheel—hell, we'll bronze the whole fucking *table!* You understand?"

"No, I don't think so."

"Look, when the news gets around—and in this town it'll be front-page news—our handle's gonna double for at least a week, maybe more."

"Your what?"

"Our handle—what moves across the tables. Not what we win, the total of what's bet, you understand? That's not gonna make up for what you beat us out of, but it's gonna help."

"You mean players are going to come here just because *I* won?"

"You better believe it. Gamblers are believers, son, and this place is gonna become a shrine, like Lourdes or something."

"And you want me to stick around so people can point at me and say, 'There he is now!' Is that it?"

"You got it," Golding said, grinning but privately amazed that such an intelligent person could be so dumb.

And David, not wanting to disappoint the man by announcing that he'd probably be checking out the following day, merely shrugged.

CHAPTER 31

After finding the way to his new quarters on the top floor, David explored the Presidential Suite with amusement: two bedrooms (one with a circular bed), a vast living room with sultry leather furniture and a wet bar, all extravagantly carpeted, all with theatrical track-lighting and panoramic views of the Fremont Street light show. He smiled on finding his crisp new jeans hanging like waifs in a closet designed to accommodate a starlet's wardrobe.

On his way out at nine o'clock, he paused to puzzle over something sitting on the ornate "Mediterranean-style" cabinet in the entry hallway. He hadn't noticed it on his way in: a tray stacked with five hundred dollars in casino chips. He shook his head in bewilderment, still not getting the point.

After getting directions at the front desk, he went to the post office, where he mailed Tim's check, and to the El Moreno's bank, where he cashed his own, keeping out five thousand and opening an account with the rest. Then he went shopping, and discovered that it's not just the lights of Las Vegas that are flashy. In the third men's store he visited, he asked where the city's funeral directors buy their clothes, and, after a grave consultation with the manager, the clerk directed him to a shopping center near the university. His hopes sagged when he saw it was on the same street as the Liberace Museum, but he managed to pick up a few things that were okay.

Driving back downtown, he took his purchases up to his room, walked to the Four Queens for lunch, then back to the hotel. As he entered the dim, postage-stamp-sized lobby, two grinning figures rose from a sofa, and David stared at them in disbelief. It was the Hispanic hitchhiker and his son.

"Hey, man! You came after all! We heard about your luck!"

David felt his face flush with anger. "You bastard!" he shouted.

"Hunh?" Juan's grin faded into blankness.

"Why did you strand me in the mountains?"

"Hunh?"

"*Why did you strand me in the goddamned mountains?*"

"Hey, man, we din't strand you in no mountains."

"You stranded me in the goddamned mountains!"

The man shook his head, baffled. "You said you wanted to go up to the mountains! We just pulled off the road a little bit and walked back!"

David found himself shaking with fury. If it had been a less public place, he would've knocked him down. "You're a fucking liar. There was no road there."

Juan gaped at him, thunderstruck. "Hey, man, it was right off the road. You couldn' miss it!" He looked down at the boy for confirmation. "Ain' that right, Toney?"

The boy gazed up at David and nodded guilelessly. "You could see the road from where we left you. Honest."

David sighed in defeat and asked them what they wanted.

"Hey, man, we don' want nothin'. We just heard about your luck and came to congratulate you, unh?"

"Okay," David said wearily. "Thanks."

Juan elbowed the boy and leered. "He smells good now, unh, Toney?"

David started to walk away, but the man caught him by the arm. "You all done here now, unh?"

"What?"

"Now you go back, unh?"

"What the hell are you talking about?"

"Hey, man, it's nice up in the mountains now. Warm spell. No more snow."

David shook his hand off gruffly. "I'm not going up to the mountains."

The Hispanic gave him a stricken look. "Hey, man, you wanna go up there! You tol' me!" David turned away. "You go tonight, unh?" he called after him. "Really!"

David got into the elevator and pounded on the top floor button until the doors closed.

The message light on his phone was lit, and, calling down to the switchboard, he learned that a reporter from the Las Vegas *Review-Journal* had been trying to reach him.

"Oh shit," he muttered. "Can you keep him off? I'm going to take a nap."

"Sure, Mr. Kennesey. I'll tell him you're out."

"Thanks." David hung up, went over to the bar, and poured himself a drink, wondering why he felt in need of one. The visit of the old man and his son had left him shaken and angry. Why? For some reason, it seemed important to know. It wasn't because they'd denied stranding him in the mountains. He expected people like that to lie.

Interesting: *People like that.* What did he mean by that? Lower-class people? Hispanics? People with accents? No, he decided. He meant *people who would strand you in the mountains in the first place.* Okay, so he wasn't angry because they'd lied to him.

Then what was it?

He winced as it came to him. He was angry because what the old man had so offensively urged him to do was exactly what he *wanted* to do. Examining his feelings, it was very obvious. In spite of everything that had happened there, he wanted to go back to the mountains.

When he'd set out from Runnell, he hadn't had any specific destination in mind, but now it was plain that he'd overshot it. He certainly didn't want to go to Los Angeles or San Francisco; there was nothing for him there. And, God knows, there was nothing for him here. Whatever it was he was after was back there somewhere. With that settled, his good humor returned. He finished his drink and unpacked the clothes he'd bought. Then he drew the drapes against the white blaze of the sun, got undressed, and took himself off for a nap.

Not in the circular bed.

CHAPTER 32

He woke at six, took a long shower, pulled on a white velour robe, and opened the drapes to contemplate the sunset over a glass of Wild Turkey. With some amusement, he realized he was feeling more than relaxed. He was feeling smug—inordinately and irrationally pleased with himself. It was something new for him, and, even though he recognized it as essentially childish, he rather liked it. In the past three days, he'd escaped death in several forms, held a man at gunpoint (and very nearly killed him), stolen a car, become a legend in gambling history, and won enough money to keep him very nicely for a year or so. Not bad, for a stodgy, young-old man whose previous experience of excitement had been discovering a nifty way of introducing fourth-graders to division of fractions.

There was a knock on the door. He made a face and then shrugged his displeasure away; whatever it was, he wasn't going to let it disrupt this rare feeling of well-being.

What it was made him blink.

She was tall—in heels, an inch taller than David—built like a showgirl, with wide shoulders, narrow waist, and delectable breasts, sleekly packaged in a white silk evening gown designed for display and easy access. Professionally made up and softly glowing, her heart-shaped face was framed in a complex arrangement of glossy black hair. A playful smile tugged at her lips, and, when she blinked back at him, David expected to feel a draft from her eyelashes.

A bit breathlessly he said: "Yes?"

The smile twitched. She said in a low, velvety voice: "*Room service!*"

Feeling like an idiot, David said, "I didn't order anything."

She raised her brows, and her eyes became very wide and serious. "You could order something *now.*"

"Did you bring a menu?" he asked, deciding it was time to win a few points in this match.

She giggled. "Oh, I'm sure I did." She snaked a hand into the waist-deep cut of her neckline and seductively explored the area under her left breast. "It's here somewhere. Could you help me look for it?"

Mouth suddenly dry, David gave up and gawked. She laughed and swept past him into the living room. "Oh, this is nice! The El Moreno is so crummy I never would've guessed it." She turned and gave David a solemn look. "I've never been here before."

"No? I suppose it would be silly to ask why you're here now."

"It certainly would." She held out her arms and did a sensuous pirouette. "All yours. On the house."

"Wow. All the comforts of home."

"Oh," she said, slipping an arm through the side of her dress and shrugging aside the silk to expose one breast, "I'll bet home was never like *this.*"

And in the hour that followed, David would have had to admit it wasn't.

"I know your type," Michelle said, lying on her stomach beside David, her chin propped on crossed arms.

"You do?" David was watching the lights from the street winking across her broad back like sequins.

"You're the type who desperately wants to ask me what a nice girl like me is doing in a place like this but is afraid of sounding like a hick."

"I expect you're right."

She pulled herself up on an elbow. "You probably won't believe it, but I'm a published poet."

"Oh?"

"Yes, and not in those rinky-dink journals that pay you in copies printed in purple ink. I mean *The New Yorker, Atlantic, Partisan Review.*"

"I'm impressed."

"You should be. But of course there's no money in poetry. What I make on poetry wouldn't keep me in pantyhose."

"Always supposing that you want to be kept in pantyhose."

"Ha ha. Anyway, now you know."

"What a nice girl like you is doing in a place like this. There's a lot more money in it than poetry."

"You bet."

"Good. I'm glad I didn't ask. Is there any place for dinner in this town that isn't just for tourists?"

"What do you mean?"

"A place where they don't bring Keno cards to your table. A place where lovers go to stare yearningly into each other's eyes and the tab is over a hundred dollars."

Michelle snorted. "Are we going to stare yearningly into each other's eyes?"

"Sure, why not?"

"There's the gourmet dump at Caesar's Palace. I can guarantee the tab will be over a hundred dollars."

"It's not so much the tab as the atmosphere for staring yearningly. Soft lights, soft music, plush banquettes. No slot machines."

"You're dreaming, honey. This is Las Vegas. The only place they don't have slot machines is in the operating room at the hospital. But I think I know a place you might like. *I* like it anyway. It's in a new joint on the Strip."

"Lead on, then."

David laughed when he saw the Hotel Casablanca, but he liked it as well. It had started out to be a tribute to the Bogart film, but the decorators had evidently had too much money for such a drab concept, so they ended up doing it in the sinisterly lavish art deco style of the Dr. Phibes movies. Nevertheless the restaurant (predictably called Rick's) was beautifully lit and offered acres of plush banquettes in subtle brown and black stripes. The maitre d' showed them to a table, took their drink orders, and presented them with a menu that, except for its vast size, sleek design, and higher prices, was virtually identical to the one at the El Moreno.

"The idea," Michelle explained when he commented on it, "is to bore you to death with the food, so that you'll sit here and stare yearningly out at the slots."

"I suspected as much," David commented dryly. And then, after tasting his drink: "Do many men fall in love with you?"

She shrugged. "They fall in love, but not with me."

"Meaning?"

"They fall in love with a fantasy. That's what I'm here to provide. Not sex—fantasy. And that's why I'm tops in the business, because I know it."

David nodded, smiling. "Interesting: Knowing it doesn't change it. I mean, for me."

"Why should it? Men always fall in love with something in their heads, and I'm just something in your head."

"You're a solipsist," he remarked in mock disapproval.

"Sure. I'm the solipsist sex-queen of Sin City West." She gave him a snooty, lidded look. "See? You're not the only one around here who can talk dirty."

The dishes had been cleared from their table and coffee poured when the hum of conversation around them suddenly died away. Looking up, David saw the maitre d' leading a man dressed in black to a table nearby. The man, who looked to be about David's age, seemed regally unaware of the attention he was getting, though he would have been worthy of attention in any crowd whatever. Although not particularly tall or noticeably muscular, he radiated a kind of animal power; it was something in the way he moved—a restraint he exercised to avoid sending people bouncing off the walls. The impression was heightened by his clothes; they looked like they'd been chosen for their clerical severity, but the simple act of putting them on that body endowed them with an almost flamboyant elegance.

He sat down, spoke a few words to the maitre d', and nodded, and one realized that his face was as extraordinary as his bearing. Far from finding him classically handsome, one looked for a likeness in the animal kingdom—and thought of the bull. His complexion was dark, nearly swarthy, and his eyebrows met across the thick arch of his nose; his heavy black hair grew so far forward on his temples that it almost met his eyebrows. Yet there was nothing really coarse in any of his features. His mouth was wide but delicately shaped and good humored. His eyes were dark, swampy pools—warm and glinting with light but alive with daunting possibilities; when he casually sent them around the room, conversations were resumed as if a command had been issued.

"A local celebrity?" David asked.

"No, I'd know him if he were—a man like that," Michelle said. "But he will be if he sticks around."

David felt a twinge of jealousy but recognized that even he found the man's magnetism fascinating. Over after-dinner drinks, they considered film roles they would cast him in, and the conversation gradually became a literary contest as they passed through Macbeth, Faust, Ahab, and Dmitri to the Steppenwolf, K, and Wozzeck.

Finally Michelle said, "Definitely Joseph in *Little Drummer Girl*, instead of that doe-eyed wimp they used."

The waiter appeared at their table and set another round of drinks before them, and David looked up, puzzled.

"Compliments of the gentleman over there," he said, nodding toward the object of their discussion.

"Oh," David said, disconcerted. He and Michelle exchanged a bemused glance. "Would you ask him if he'd care to join us?"

"Certainly, sir."

There was another momentary lull in conversation as the man rose and approached their table. He looked down at them gravely, almost apologetically, and asked in a surprisingly pleasant baritone if they were sure he wasn't intruding.

"You're most welcome," David said formally. "Please join us."

He slid gracefully into a chair opposite them, and the waiter appeared to deposit his drink at his side.

"I am Pablo." Although he said it without emphasis, it was subtly clear there could only be one.

David nodded and introduced himself and Michelle.

Pablo gazed at Michelle for a moment and blinked, plainly dismissing her as an object of small interest. He turned and gave David a conspiratorial smile. "You must tell me if my intuition is correct."

"Yes?"

"As I entered the room, I felt that something remarkable had happened to someone here." He shrugged. "I'm that way, sometimes— very rarely. A touch of my mother. I sat for a few minutes before my attention was drawn to this table and to you."

"And?"

"And then I considered: Has something remarkable happened in Las Vegas recently? Yes, it's the sensation of the day. An extraordinary win at a downtown casino—a quite impossible win. Was it yours?"

David nodded.

"Ah," he sighed, with evident pleasure. "Is it true? The same number came up nine times running on two different tables?"

"Yes, it's true."

"Remarkable indeed. A staggering phenomenon. And they say that, after the ninth win, you withdrew all your bets except one, as if you knew the run was over."

"Also true."

"You knew it was over?"

David laughed uncomfortably. "Well, yes."

"How? If I may ask."

David glanced uneasily at Michelle. She was looking around the room with an air of injured boredom.

"I'm afraid it'll sound like a very silly story."

"No, no. I'm sure it isn't."

"Well . . . have you ever heard of the nine strokes?"

Pablo frowned. "The nine strokes?"

When David finished, Pablo fell back in his chair, astounded, and Michelle muttered, "Pushkin, *The Queen of Spades*," as if mildly disgusted.

Still sprawling gracefully, Pablo shook his head. "Even on such short acquaintance, I can only believe that it happened exactly as you say. But this story moves your win out of the realm of the extraordinary into the realm of the marvelous—into the realm of magic."

"Oh, I hardly think so," David said, feeling embarrassed.

Pablo raised his massive brows incredulously. "You think the prediction and its fulfillment may be unconnected?"

"I have to think so, honestly. I think that winning nine times is just what it seems—an incredible freak of luck. I mean, the ball was due to fall in the one slot nine times in a row whether I bet on it or not. And if I hadn't had the stupid prediction in the back of my mind, I would have moved my bets around just like any other player and ended up losing."

Pablo gave him an amused frown, as if David were trying to deceive him with a fairy tale.

David was sorry now that he'd allowed himself to be drawn into telling the story.

"And what do you think, Petal?" Pablo asked the girl.

She returned his smile coldly. "Why do you call me Petal?"

"Ah, because you are so very beautifully *white*, my dear." His tone was chillingly venomous. "I refer of course to your lovely gown," he added.

"I think it's all bullshit," she said, answering his question in a bored tone.

"Ah. A charming and most illuminating opinion, to be sure." He turned to David and raised a brow. "In contrast to Petal, I must say that I believe the man of the nine strokes should be prepared to meet an unusual destiny."

"Meaning what?"

He shrugged elegantly. "That it may be as foolish to pass off the mysterious as ordinary as it is to pass off the ordinary as mysterious."

"To tell you the truth," David observed dryly, "you make all this sound a bit . . . menacing."

"Menacing!" Pablo seemed genuinely startled. "Just the opposite! You yourself said that you wouldn't have made your fabulous win if you hadn't had the boy's prediction in mind. Isn't that so?"

"Yes."

"Then why belittle it now? Why turn your back on it? I can only think that the gods have something special in mind for you, David. But how can you discover what it is if you shrug it away in advance?"

David laughed and shook his head in embarrassment.

A sudden flush mottled Pablo's face, and for a moment a scroll-work of paler lines stood out on his features like the normally hidden scars of some old operation; then he smiled and waved away David's recalcitrance.

"Ah, there's no greater bore than one who becomes importunate over a gift. Isn't that so?" He neatly finished his drink and arose. "It has been a pleasure making your acquaintance, David. And yours, of course, Mademoiselle Petal." Without waiting for a reply, he nodded once and strode out of the room.

"Wow," David said.

"A con man," Michelle stated.

"Why do you say that?"

"He has the style. 'A touch of my mother' indeed. He knew who you were when he came in. He was here looking for you."

"You really think so? I don't see that he got anything out of it."

Michelle shook her head slowly, in amazed disgust. "I didn't say he was a pickpocket, for God's sake. Meeting you is just step one."

"Ah well. They say you can't cheat an honest man."

"Huh. And they say love makes the world go 'round."

The phone at the bedside was ringing insistently, and David fought his way up to consciousness to silence it. He took the receiver off the hook and glanced at his watch. It was four-thirty, and he'd been asleep for less than two hours.

"Hello," he groaned.

"This is Pablo. Is the girl there with you?"

"What?"

"Is the girl there with you?"

David looked across the bed, where Michelle was sleeping heavily. "Yes, she's with me."

"Then go to the phone in the living room. We must talk, and there's no need to disturb her."

David frowned. "Talk about what?"

"Please, David. It's important."

"Okay. Hold on." David rubbed the sleep out of his eyes and went into the living room, closing the bedroom door behind him and picking up the phone. "All right," he said.

"How much did you lose?"

"What?"

"How much did you lose at the tables before you went to bed?"

David blinked groggily. On returning to the hotel, Michelle had wanted to play blackjack, and he had gallantly bought her a hundred dollars worth of chips. After a few hands, she complained that it made her nervous to have him just sitting there to watch, so he bought a stack for himself and listened dutifully as she explained the rudiments of play.

The cocktail waitress kept them supplied with drinks as they worked their way through their chips. They spent a while at the crap table, but David couldn't make head or tail of the betting and refused to take the dice himself. After that, she tried to drag him back to the roulette tables, but, with other plans in mind, he balked.

"Indulge me," she said with a coaxing smile. "And I'll indulge you."

They spent perhaps an hour at it, David becoming a little drunk but sticking doggedly to the even-money bets while Michelle played the corners.

"Not much," David said in answer to Pablo's question.

"Five thousand?"

"No, not that much."

"Two thousand?"

"Well . . . maybe."

"David, David. Don't you understand yet what they're doing to you?"

"What are you talking about?"

"They mean to keep you there until you give them back their money."

"Give them back their money?"

"Across the tables, of course. Naturally they want it. That's why they've installed you in their finest suite. That's why they've given you the lovely Petal. To keep you there until you've returned their money."

David paused, thinking. "I can't believe it's that important."

"Oh, it's important, David. It's not just the money, though that's the greatest part of it. It's a matter of prestige—almost of honor. They've suffered a humiliating loss—and if you take your winnings away, it will be doubly humiliating. But if you give it back, then they will be made well. Don't you see? You just weren't drunk enough tonight. Petal will be vastly more persuasive tomorrow. In addition to her usual fee, she's down for fifteen percent of what they recover; she originally demanded a third, but of course that was just a ploy. If they have to, they'll literally prop you up at a table until you've disgorged what you've taken. Then Petal will kiss you goodbye, and you'll be informed that someone else requires your suite."

David sighed bitterly. "Yes, I see. I've been incredibly stupid."

"Just a bit naive."

"I appreciate the warning, Pablo."

"Don't just be warned. Leave. Leave now. I believe there's an exit directly to the parking lot. If you use that, you won't have to go through the lobby."

"Are you saying I'm in some danger?"

"No, no. I suggest that only to avoid a scene. If they let it be known—or even rumored—that winning at the El Moreno is an invitation to mayhem, they'd be ruined. The danger is one of seduction only, not violence."

"Yes, I see. I feel like a complete idiot."

"Don't lose heart, David. There are indeed times when one should trust blindly, just as there are times when one should not. Wisdom consists in being able to tell the one from the other."

"Yes. Thanks again, Pablo."

"It's nothing, David. Fare well."

Michelle never stirred as David dressed and packed. Before he left, he paused at the bedside and gazed down at her regretfully. Then he smiled, remembering that, in her own way, she'd warned him about her.

I'm just something in your mind.

Fremont Street south led him out of Las Vegas, becoming highway 93, which he followed to Boulder City, across Hoover Dam, and down to Kingman, Arizona, where he met the dawn and Interstate 40 East.

CHAPTER 33

Taos was a disappointment. He'd vaguely (and absurdly, he saw now) expected to find crumbling adobe houses, donkeys, men in sombreros, women shaping tortillas beside open fires, and a tavern patronized by a few seedy-looking Anglo artists and writers waiting for D.H. Lawrence to join them for sherry. Whatever fascination the place had held for Lawrence had been long ago swallowed up in curio shops, sleek adobe shopping centers, fast food joints, and used car lots. He'd also imagined it as a village clinging to the side of a mountain; instead, it was a small city pooled at the bottom of a bowl within the Rocky Mountains.

Driving up from Santa Fe past the wineries, roadside fruit stands, and taxidermy shops, he'd been surprised to learn that the lively turquoise-colored stream occasionally in view of the highway was the Rio Grande. He'd been tempted to get out and pay it a closer visit, but discarded the idea; after a disagreeable experience with the law in Gallup, he felt exposed and vulnerable, and wanted to get off the highway as soon as possible.

After exploring the old-town section for an hour alongside the tourists, he headed back the way he'd come and checked into a resort hotel just south of town; with the skiers gone for the season, he had it to himself. Although his room was spartan compared to the El Moreno Presidential Suite, its view of Wheeler Peak, still mantled in snow, made a refreshing change from the tawdry carnival of Fremont Street.

Feeling at loose ends, he changed into jeans and went back into town, where he bought some casual shirts and a couple of light-weight sweaters, some elegant boots, and a hand-woven poncho. The ensemble pleased him—and would have astounded his associates in Runnell, Indiana. Then he stopped in for a drink at the pleasantly dim old bar of La Dona de Taos. He wasn't exactly killing time; he was trying to take his mind off the almost unbearable tingle of excitement that was building in his stomach.

Then, though it was only five-thirty, he went back to his hotel and had dinner. Finally it was dusk, and he had to restrain himself from breaking into a run as he headed for the Corvette. As he drove south toward a promising-looking road he'd spotted on the way in, he reflected that he was becoming addicted to the scary exhilaration of being lost in the mountains.

After an hour he was certainly lost. The road had begun as quite a civilized affair, winding through an area of widely separated cabins, A-frames, and mobile homes. But, after following a couple of branches that tended upward, he seemed to leave the habited world behind; only an occasional rough track leading to the right or left indicated that the road served any purpose at all.

The moon rose at eleven; it was only a day or two off full, and shed enough light on the countryside to read by. Coming over a crest, he saw a car pulled to the side of the road below. Dark green or black, with the sleek, sinister lines of a Ferrari, it looked bizarre on this road, where speeds above thirty rattled your teeth. Slowing down beside it, he decided it was black—made even blacker by black glass windows all round. Behind the one on the driver's side there was a movement of white, and he pulled up and got out. For a few moments he thought he must have been mistaken, since there was no reaction to his arrival from within the car, but then the window came down and he was face to face with a Turkish princess.

He didn't know what made him think of a Turkish princess (since he'd never seen one); in fact, he rather doubted that Turks had skin as white as hers. Perhaps it was the long, aquiline nose, the aggressive cheekbones, the dark brown hair with fierce copper highlights. Or perhaps it was the bored, almost disdainful way she was looking at him, a cigarette dangling casually from one hand. She apparently didn't feel the encounter merited any comment from her.

"I wondered," David said, "if you needed some help."

"*Some*, yes," she drawled, making David feel unaccountably foolish. "This car is so damned delicate, I'd be better off with a Honda. I think it's something in the fuel line. I was driving along and it just started gasping and died."

"I'd offer to look under the hood, but it would just be play-acting. Half the engine could be missing and I wouldn't know it. But I'll be happy to give you a lift."

"That would be nice," she said without interest. She stubbed out her cigarette, rolled up the window, and slid out of the low seat with a practiced grace, giving David a view of a figure not quite as flashy as Michelle's but one that would leave no Turkish prince in any doubt that he'd found a woman in a million. He estimated that she was in her early thirties, an inch shorter than he, and so used to service and affluence that she took them for granted. She was formally dressed—for New Mexico—in a loosely-belted cream-colored dress that looked like raw silk.

She settled into the Corvette with a sigh and turned her face to the window.

"Straight ahead?" David inquired politely.

She looked at him as if he'd said something strange. "Yes. Straight ahead."

She didn't even give the Ferrari a backward glance as they pulled away.

"How far is it?"

"Oh, miles and miles," she said vaguely, turning back to the window.

She didn't speak again for half an hour, which David translated into almost fifteen miles. Then she gestured up to the right to an array of lights that looked like the windows of a greenhouse set into the hillside. "It's up there."

David wasn't surprised when, after twisting upward for half a mile, the road dead-ended in her driveway. From what he could see of it, the house was huge, complex, and ultramodern in design. The lighted windows he'd glimpsed from the road below angled off to the right; the rest of the house seemed to go on climbing to the crest of the hill. He was, however, a little surprised when the woman got out of the car and breezed into the house without a word of thanks or even a nod of acknowledgment. He was turning the car around to head back when she reappeared, stopped him with an angry glare, and said, "Where the hell do you think *you're* going?"

David laughed. "Well, I guess I thought I was going back to my hotel."

"Don't be ridiculous. Did you think I was going to send you away without even saying thanks? I'm not famous for my manners, but I'm not that bad."

"Well . . . I wasn't sure."

"Oh, turn off the stupid engine and come inside."

Without waiting for a reply, she marched back into the house and sang out, "Marianne! I'm back!"

When he walked in, David at first took the entry hall to be the living room—in fact he would have been delighted to have it as a living room. Entirely lit by recessed spotlights, its walls were jacketed in some dark brushed metal that dully reflected a jungle of plants. At one side, breaking through the wild tangle and looking entirely at home, was a large Chinese cabinet in lacquered red; David had the feeling that it and the Ming horse surmounting it would have been welcome in any museum collection. At the back, rising out of the welter and partly obscured by it, loomed a massive and rather menacing headless torso in wood and bronze.

The living room—or as he later learned to call it, the lower living room—staggered him, the vastness of its sophisticated barbarism reducing the entry hall to a mere closet. In the overall dimness, a single column of light compelled the eye to the centerpiece of the room, an enormous pre-Columbian stone head that David would have sworn couldn't possibly be found in any private collection; it stood in its own private jungle, eyes placidly closed, inexhaustibly radiating its ancient, mysterious power.

The rest of the room was in the same scale, with several groupings of long white sofas gathered around sleek low tables on which three or four couples could have danced comfortably. Above them, the air was peopled with giant human figures that seemed to be toppling, charging, swooping from the ceiling sixteen feet away. Some of them were swimming into or out of the metal-clad walls: a grotesque assemblage of emerging or departing limbs, torsos, heads. As if it were in danger of seeming cramped, the whole awesome space was visually doubled in a mirrored back wall. He wasn't searching for a name for the place, but one came unbidden to mind: *Troll House.*

While David struggled to take it all in, his passenger was going through her mail. She finished, tossed it carelessly onto a cabinet that was a twin of the one in the entry hall, and said, "I'm Andrea, by the way."

David introduced himself.

"Drinks, Marianne. Please," she said as a girl in jeans entered from behind the giant head. In her early twenties, she was a perfect contrast to Andrea—dark-complected, petite, boyishly slender, with long black hair tied back in a pony tail. She sent her eyes questioningly to David and, when he said bourbon, turned without a word and left.

"So," Andrea said, "who is David Kennesey?" He was considering his reply to this unanswerable question when she announced she was going to change her clothes and headed for a suspended stairway that soared up dramatically just in front of the mirrored back wall. As she began to ascend, she paused and looked at him impatiently.

"Well? You can't talk to me if you won't keep up with me."

David followed. One of the floating figures eerily turned to him as he drew alongside it, its hand outstretched as if begging for release from its airy limbo.

The second story appeared to be dedicated to bedrooms. The stairs continued to a third, but David followed Andrea to the end of a broad hallway and into a room that was nearly human in scale, being only about thirty feet square with a twelve-foot ceiling. Two-thirds of it was furnished as a living room, the other third being a sleeping area inside someone's fantasy of an Arab tent—countless layers of gauzy silk supported by slender, gaily-colored twisted columns, piles of goatskin rugs, mounds of fat pillows. The room ended in a wall of glass through which David could see a terrace built out onto the roof of the living room below and, beyond that, the distant lights of Taos.

"So," Andrea said again, "you were going to tell me about David Kennesey."

He turned from the windows just as Andrea pulled her dress up over her head. She tossed it into a closet and reached up behind her to undo her bra. As she shrugged out of it, she looked at him and said, "You're not one of those nontalkers, are you?"

"No," he said, but it came out a croak and he had to pause to clear his throat. "I'm a great one for talking. But the question is a little . . . unmanageable just at the moment. I'm in a state of . . . flux. Very much in a state of flux."

He knew he was gibbering but he didn't know why. There was nothing seductive about what Andrea was doing. She might as well have been undressing in front of a pet tortoise, but he was immensely relieved when she pulled on jeans and a sweater and Marianne simultaneously arrived with a tray laden with bottles, ice, and glasses.

"That goddamned car died on me again," Andrea told her. "Mr. Kennesey rescued me. David, meet Marianne." The girl shook his hand, gravely appraising him with round, dark eyes.

"Call those people in the morning—the ones who fixed it last time—and get somebody out to tow it into town."

"Okay. I'll need cash for the tow truck."

"Right." Andrea walked decisively toward an art deco lady's writing table David was leaning against, and he moved aside to let her open the single long drawer under the top. He goggled at its contents: neatly stacked and banded packets of new fifty dollar bills. She picked up one, slid a dozen or so bills out, and handed them to Marianne. Then, as she was returning the packet to the drawer, she looked up and, noticing David's interest, asked: "Would you like some of this? I've got plenty."

Startled, he backed away from the table. "No, no. No, thanks," he said quickly, as if she were offering him a collection of pornographic pictures.

She shrugged, shut the drawer, and told Marianne she'd see her in the morning. Then she led David over to a sofa and curled up at one end while David made their drinks.

"So," she said, "you're a man of mystery."

"Hardly that," he said with a laugh. "Just a simple runaway."

"Ah. And what are you running away from?"

Thinking about it, David was surprised to find how much there was to be run away from and had a sudden urge to catalog it all. "To begin with, a wife and son back in Indiana—not to mention a career. Yesterday I received a ninety-day jail sentence for illegal possession of a gun—but they suspended it, so I guess I'm not running away from that. There are some folks in Las Vegas who weren't too happy to see me leave with sixty-odd thousand dollars of their money. The Corvette is stolen, but I don't think the owner would like to see me back, because of some dead bodies and a marijuana operation. But then I wouldn't much care to *go* back."

"Why is that?"

He made a face. "Some people up there seem set on doing me in."

"Goodness," Andrea said, "you've been a busy fellow. Why are they set on doing you in?"

"I don't know."

A slow, incredulous smile crossed her face. "You don't *know?*"

"No, I don't."

She nodded soberly. "Some odd things go on out here."

"I believe it."

"And what are you running *to*?"

"Well, I guess that remains to be seen."

She gave him a long, direct look, then nodded again, as if a conjecture had been confirmed. "You lie very well, David—perhaps too well for your own good."

He blinked, taken aback. "Why do you say that?"

"Shouldn't I say that?" she asked innocently.

"Well . . ."

"You *were* lying weren't you? When I asked what you were running *to*?"

David stared down into his drink for a few moments. "Yes, I suppose I was, a little."

"And what's the truth?"

He laughed nervously. "The truth is that I'd feel foolish talking about it."

"That's much better, isn't it? The truth, I mean."

"Yes."

"No bones broken?"

"No."

"This is something I learned long ago, David. Lies are like sleeping pills. You should only use them when you absolutely have to. They spoil everything if you make a habit of them."

"True."

She shook her head in amused disgust. "You say 'true' as if you already knew it, and yet just one minute ago there you were, telling me a lie you didn't need to tell, simply as a matter of reflex." She gave him a knowing smile. "I'll bet you left your wife because you just couldn't stand lying to her anymore."

"Ouch. Are you a compulsive truth-teller then?"

"Oh no, far from it. I'm a very accomplished liar. But I never lie out of cowardice, and I don't care to be around people who do."

He frowned, digesting the implications of this.

"And now you're feeling affronted, aren't you?"

"No, I'm trying to *decide* what I'm feeling. Give me a little time and maybe I'll feel affronted."

Andrea laughed. "I'll bet you married young."

"What makes you think that?"

"Oh, men who marry young fall behind a bit. You have some catching up to do."

David shook his head helplessly.

"Say it, my dear. Be courageous."

"You're quite a handful."

She laughed again, and, in spite of himself, he liked the whole-hearted way she gave herself up to it.

"Well," he said, "I'd better be on my way."

"I won't hear of it," Andrea replied firmly. "You'd be sure to get lost and you wouldn't get back to town before dawn. Besides, I'd like you to stay. I get bored without people around."

"There's no one here but you and Marianne?"

"There's Dudley, of course, but he really *is* a nontalker. During the summer and the ski season the house is jammed with people."

"Who's Dudley?"

"Dudley Case. A post-graduate anthropology student. A very serious fellow."

"I see."

"I'm pretty sure the hook room is all made up."

"The hook room?"

Andrea laughed again. "I shouldn't call it that—it makes it sound sinister. Last fall we had a guest who was a chronic insomniac. She literally had to be rocked to sleep, and we suspended a sort of cradle from the ceiling for her. I haven't gotten around to having the hooks removed, so we've fallen into the habit of calling it the hook room. But it's not time to think of going to bed yet, is it?"

David agreed it wasn't and made them another drink.

She asked him about the career he'd abandoned and listened with more attention than David had thought her capable of. When he was finished, she said: "What you're saying is that you got out when you realized that the real function of the schools is to deceive."

"I don't know that I'd go as far as that. The real function of the schools is to produce workers—people who have no choice but to find someone who will give them money in exchange for labor."

"But they have to be *convinced* that they have no other choice, don't they?"

"That's certainly part of it."

"Then are they deceived or not?"

"I truthfully don't know. I'll have to think about it."

Andrea smiled. "Oh, you are truly an enchanted people."

"Enchanted?"

"I'm not a learned person—I wouldn't want you to think that. But there is one statement I came across in Plato's *Republic* that I thought was worth remembering: *Whatever deceives may be said to enchant*. You have been monstrously deceived—and are therefore monstrously enchanted."

"You speak as though you weren't one of us."

"Of course. Anyone who shakes off the deception shakes off the enchantment as well—and ceases to be one of you."

"And who is it who enchanted us?"

"Oh, you managed to do that for yourselves, long ago."

David shook his head. "I'm afraid we've reached a point where I don't have the slightest idea what we're talking about."

"Ask Dudley to explain it to you. He understands it very well— almost instinctively. His people have managed to resist the enchantment for three or four centuries now."

"His people?"

"He's a Navajo."

David made himself another drink and asked how she'd come by the pre-Columbian head downstairs. Without hesitation, she launched into a long, hair-raising tale that was a near relative to *Raiders of the*

Lost Ark. When she was done, he said, "I see why you call yourself an accomplished liar. And the truth?"

"Oh, the truth is rather boring. I picked it up before such things became fashionable." She answered his look of exaggerated skepticism with an arch smile and said: "I'm older than I look."

The hooks were definitely not what took the eye in the hook room. Though the furnishings were as elegant as elsewhere in the house, Andrea evidently understood that guests would need a relief from the flamboyance of her own personal style. Next to the ultramodern and the primitive, she seemed to like the work of the deco period, and this room was completely dedicated to it, with a platform bed, low, heavy sofas and armchairs, tables with glass tops and metal tubing legs, and a breathtaking cabinet running the entire length of one wall and filled with treasures of crystal, porcelain, bronze, ivory, coral, and silver. The other walls were given over to posters by Cassandre, Colin, Loupot, Gise, and Carlu. Incredibly, beside the crystal ashtrays and enameled silver cigarette cases, were set out 1930s matchbooks from the Providence Biltmore, the Gladstone, the Hotel Barnum, and the Zebra Room of the President Madison; David wondered whether anyone ever inadvertently used one of them.

The next morning, on coming out of the bathroom (opulent but strictly modern except for the Lalique light fixtures and an exquisite green and gold lacquer mirror), David discovered that someone had collected his luggage from the hotel. After hovering for a moment between being indignant and being flattered, he decided to be flattered.

It was eleven-thirty when he left his room to seek food and company. The hallway and the living room downstairs were empty. So was the immense dining room next to it and the kitchen (probably salvaged from the Titanic). A door from the kitchen led to the building he'd seen from the road the night before; it was what it had appeared to be, a greenhouse—uninhabited by either plants or people. He went back upstairs and knocked on Andrea's door: no response.

Beginning to feel a little neglected, he climbed the stairs to the third level of the house and found himself in another living room, as enormous as the one below, but more casually furnished and brightly lit by floor-to-ceiling windows at each end. It seemed to double as a game and music room, having a tournament-size pool table and a billiard table, a grand piano, and a stereo system with wall-mounted speakers the size of steamer trunks. This too was unoccupied, and he passed through it to a smaller dining room and finally into another kitchen, all stainless steel and butcher-block wood. Here at last he found a bit of human activity. A dark, barrel-shaped man in jeans and a plaid flannel shirt was stirring something on the stove.

He looked up, regarded David solemnly for a moment, and said, "I heard we had company. I'm Dudley Case."

David stared at him dumbly, and the man turned back to the stove.

"I'm just making some lunch," he said. "There's enough for two if you like Texas-style chili."

David, his mouth suddenly parched, still couldn't find his tongue. The last time he'd met this man his name was Horse Killer.

PART IV

*Three different readings
offer themselves . . .*

CHAPTER 34

While David was upstairs in Andrea's bedroom discussing deceit and enchantment the night before, other conversations had been taking place elsewhere. Howard and Tim, having arrived in Las Vegas in the early evening, were at the El Moreno talking to Jack Golding about the check Tim had received in the mail that morning. Ellen, having been transported to an isolated house outside Grand Junction, Colorado, was talking to her captors, the spurious Chicago detectives Artie Goodman and Nick Wolf.

Neither conversation proved very fruitful.

Jack Golding, comfortably ensconced in a booth in the dining room, was as affable as ever. His partners hadn't faulted him for his handling of David Kennesey nor blamed him for David's defection; they agreed that, short of shackling the man to a table, nothing more could have been done. It would mean a thin week for the casino, but the publicity had been welcome, room bookings were noticeably higher, and, as Golding had predicted, their handle was up. Though David had cost him some money and some prestige, Golding felt no personal animus toward him—or toward his son; after all, if he'd been in David's shoes, he knew *he* wouldn't have given back even so much as a nickel.

"But I don't know what more I can tell you," he said. "The man walked in, wiped us out like a bandit, and blew town. That's all there is."

"He could have just checked into another hotel, couldn't he?" Howard asked.

"Sure, but why? Here it was all comped—the best rooms in the joint, meals, drinks, everything. Besides, if he checked in anywhere else, I would've heard about it. You gotta understand, the man was a celebrity."

Howard nodded sourly and looked at Tim. Tim looked back, hands folded on the table in front of him, calmly waiting for Howard to pull a rabbit out of an empty hat.

"Do you know if Mr. Kennesey made any friends while he was here?" Howard asked. "Anyone he hung around with in the bar, for example?"

Golding shook his head with a clear conscience, knowing that Michelle was as much in the dark as he was. He nearly smiled, remembering the hooker's lethal fury at David's escape.

"When he left Indiana, he was driving a Volvo," Howard went on doggedly. "According to the register, he was driving a Corvette when he checked in here. I don't suppose he happened to mention to anyone how that came about."

"If he did, I don't know about it."

"And he didn't drop even a word about where he was going next? North, south, east, west?"

"Not a word that I know of." Golding scratched a blue jaw thoughtfully. "I tell you what I'd do if I were you, though. Vegas is a town of name-droppers if there ever was one—everybody wants to get next to somebody or make you think they're next to somebody. If I were you, I'd put out the word that you're looking for information about the guy who took the El Moreno for sixty-eight grand. If he did tell somebody where he was going, that might turn him up. What I mean is, he might just come around to see if you were somebody to get next to—somebody he could make a story out of."

Unable to think of any useful questions to ask beyond that, Howard thanked him and took Tim to another table to confer.

After ordering a cup of coffee, he closed his eyes. They felt scorched and achy, and he spent a few moments trying to knead away the pain.

It had been a weird day, and he felt disoriented, unbalanced, as if he'd gone to the circus and suddenly found himself in the center ring dressed in a clown suit. He couldn't completely take it in that he was in Las Vegas, asking foolish questions and making inept motions at being a detective. It didn't make sense. As a big-city dweller, he'd learned long ago not to let himself get sucked into other people's troubles—unless he was being paid to be sucked in, of course. There are just too many people with too many troubles for that. But he'd certainly slipped up this time—and what bothered him was that he didn't know *why*. Was he getting sentimental in his old age? Doing the Edmund Gwenn bit in *Miracle on 34th Street*? Whatever mad impulse had prompted him to undertake this foolishness, it was obviously clouding his judgment. In his right mind—if he'd been hired to find David Kennesey—he would never have gotten on a plane and flown to Las Vegas; it was disastrously wasteful, entirely unprofessional. Bringing Tim with him was even worse, the work of a lunatic. It was as though he'd forgotten all his years of experience. He was acting like an amateur, and it upset him.

And Tim upset him, with his unspoken and apparently limitless faith in him: Howard was now in charge of Tim's life and was going to make everything right again—was going to find his father, was going to find his mother, and was going to bring them all back together to live happily ever after in Runnell, Indiana. If Tim had been a client, Howard would have told him right at the outset, "Look, I'll do the best I can, but I can't promise miracles, okay?" But there was no question of saying that to Tim now. He wasn't a client, he was a ward, a responsibility, and Howard had nominated himself to be his fairy godfather. Making it all happen was something that simply had to be done, and if miracles were required, well, he'd just have to come up with them.

Tim, watching Howard rub his eyes, slumped over the table, knew that something was bothering him. On that first night he'd been affable, casual, solicitous. But in the hours they'd spent first on the plane and then waiting for Jack Golding to come on his shift, he'd become increasingly grouchy and tense. He'd seen this happen often enough with his parents not to worry about it and knew that the best thing he could do was to be as inconspicuous and undemanding as possible until it blew over. Which is what he thought he was doing now.

"Well," Howard grunted, straightening up at last, "what do you think?"

"What do *I* think?"

Howard made an elaborate show of looking around their table. "It looks like there's nobody here but us, Tim."

"God," Tim said. "You've had a lot more experience with this sort of thing than I have. I mean, this is what you do for a living, isn't it?"

Howard just barely managed to disguise his growl as a sigh. Then, thinking about it, he realized that Tim's question gave him an opportunity to clarify the situation and reduce the weight of his burden. "Look, Tim, I'm not exactly here in my professional capacity. If I were, I would have come by myself. I don't usually take my clients with me wherever I go."

Tim mulled this over for a moment. "What are you saying? That I'm not your client?"

"Something like that. In this thing, we're more like partners. Which is why I ask you what you think."

"I see," Tim said gravely. "Then I think we should follow Mr. Golding's suggestion and put out the word that we're looking for information. . . . Why are you laughing?"

Howard was indeed laughing, his whole body quaking, his head in his hands. He was laughing because it was obvious to him now that his brain was turning to mush over this thing. After one conversation, it was plain that they were at a dead end here, and he'd already decided that the only sensible thing to do was to turn around and fly home. But now, having named Tim a full partner in the investigation, he couldn't very well tell the boy that his opinion was worthless.

"I believe," he said, wiping his eyes, "that the expression is 'hoist with his own petard,' though I've never had the foggiest idea what a petard is or what it means to be hoist with one." Tim asked him what he was talking about, but Howard just shook his head.

"It doesn't matter. We'll start putting out the word tomorrow and see what happens."

"You've kidnaped my son," Ellen stated.

"No, lady," Wolf said, "we haven't kidnaped your son."

"Then you've kidnaped David."

The solid mass of red hair didn't stir as he shook his narrow head. "Lady, we haven't kidnaped anyone. Except you, of course."

This conversation was taking place in the living room of an old, shabbily furnished farmhouse that seemed to have retained the chill of winter in its bones. Artie Goodman was out trying to scare up enough wood for a fire in the stove. Ellen, sitting in the middle of an exhausted sofa, and Wolf, across the room in an oak rocker, might have been taken for a married couple worrying a subject they'd disputed a dozen times without resolution.

"Why?" Ellen demanded bitterly. "What do you *want?*"

Rocking, his hands folded in his lap, Wolf closed his eyes and shook his head.

"Do you want money, for God's sake? We don't have any money."

"We don't want your money, Mrs. K. Just take it easy. Think of it as a little vacation from Runnell. Relax. Imagine you're in Bermuda or something. It'll all be over in a couple days, and you probably won't even be needed."

"All what will be over?"

Wolf went on rocking.

"I probably won't be needed for *what?*"

Wolf hunched his shoulders in an expressive shrug.

CHAPTER 35

David would have had a hard time recognizing the old woman sitting with Howard and Tim at their breakfast table. Standing at the cashier's window pounding him on the shoulder, she'd been wearing a faded house dress and broken-backed slippers, and her hair had been a dingy, bedraggled gray. Now, in quite a smart little blue suit and high heels, wearing makeup that took a decade off her age, her hair rinsed with a discreet touch of life-giving color and swept up to make the most of what was there, she might have stood as a model for the president of the garden club.

She hadn't hesitated to take full credit for the fact that Tim had received a check for twenty thousand dollars.

"I stood there and looked him in the eye and told him a mother's curse would surely fall on his head if he didn't send some of that money home. And, believe me, he thought for just a second that he wasn't going to do it. I know that look; he had the fever, no two ways about it. But I looked him down, right down, till he came to his senses and did what a man should do."

She was no more hesitant when it came to advising them on their next move. "You just sit tight here for a couple of days," she told them. "He'll be back, that's for sure." She fixed Tim with a bright, accusing eye. "Your daddy's a school teacher, isn't he?"

"No. He's in educational publishing."

She nodded exactly as if he'd agreed with her. "I know the type, son—weak as bone soup. Seen 'em all my life. He'll be back. He's got the fever up."

But at that point, the waitress had arrived with a copy of the morning's *Review-Journal*, already turned back to a second page story that she displayed with an air of unconcealed triumph.

After scanning the story, which was headlined *Life In Fast Lane Too Fast For El Moreno Winner*, Howard read it aloud.

GALLUP, NM—David Kennesey, a recent Vegas visitor who made gambling history at the roulette wheel, was arrested Tuesday afternoon driving 50 mph in a 35 mph zone, according to city police officer Richard Valdez. Kennesey was detained and charged with illegal possession of a firearm when a search of his vehicle turned up a .357 magnum pistol for which he had no license.

With characteristic good luck, Kennesey slipped the toils of the law with a guilty plea, collecting a $500 fine and a suspended jail sentence.

Kennesey's legendary win, which observers claim exceeded $60,000, came when he backed the number 1 nine times running at two different tables at the casino of the Hotel El Moreno Monday morning.

"Well," Tim observed, "at least we know what direction he's heading in."

Howard nodded thoughtfully. Looking up, he saw that the old woman, apparently shaken by the story, had paled under her makeup.

"Do you think we should go to Gallup?" Tim asked.

Howard mentally consulted the map of the southwest he'd studied the night before; he was fairly sure Gallup lay on the interstate that ran through the center of New Mexico. "Looks like it," he admitted without much conviction. It seemed a very thin hope. David certainly wouldn't hang around Gallup after having a brush with the law there. But a direction of pursuit was clearly indicated now, and if they followed it, they'd have to pass through Gallup anyway.

"Yes," he repeated, "that looks like the way to go."

"Nonsense," the old woman spat out, her face contorted with disgust.

Howard looked at her curiously. "Nonsense?"

"Of course it's nonsense. Do you think he's still *there*? He's long gone."

"Of course he is. But he's only a day and a half gone from there. He's *two* and a half days gone from *here*."

"No," she stated flatly. "He'll be back. You just stay right here and be patient."

Howard shook his head and put some money down on their breakfast check. Then he counted out five twenties, handed them to Tim, and told him to pay their hotel bill while he went upstairs to pack.

"If you leave. . ." the old woman began as Howard stood up.

"Yes?"

"If you leave," she repeated, thinking furiously, "no one will know where to reach you." She nodded aggressively, as if this settled matters. "That's right. No one will know where to reach you."

"I really doubt that anyone will be *trying* to reach us."

Scowling, she licked her lips. "You're wrong. Someone . . ." She hesitated, obviously torn by indecision. "Someone's bound to know where that boy's gone. I'm sure of it."

Howard shrugged, thanked her politely, and left her plucking angrily at the table cloth.

A few minutes later Wolf answered the phone in the living room of the farmhouse outside Glenwood Springs. He listened, frowning, noted a number on the cover of an ancient telephone book, hung up, and turned to Artie Goodman, who was sprawled on the sofa, staring up at the ceiling.

"Get her," he said.

Artie pulled himself up, disappeared down a hallway, and returned a minute later with Ellen.

"What is it?" she asked in a frightened voice.

"You're going to be needed after all, Mrs. K," Wolf said, giving her a crooked grin. He held up a hand to forestall her questions. "In a minute I'm going to dial a number and ask for your son. You're going to talk to him. Okay?"

"I'm going to talk to Tim?"

"That's right. Will you do that?"

"Yes."

"I'm not looking for anything difficult. I just want you to tell him to stay where he is."

"To stay where he is? Where is he?"

"That doesn't matter. Tell him to stay where he is. Tell him. . ." Wolf paused and closed his eyes for a moment. "Tell him everything's being taken care of. Tell him you know where his father's going. Tell him to stay put till he hears differently. Understand?"

Ellen glanced uncertainly from one to the other. "Won't he want to know where *I* am?"

Wolf gnawed on a lip. "Tell him. . ."

"Tell him you're on your way to meet David," Artie said.

Ellen blinked. "Am I?"

The two men exchanged a look.

"Yes," Artie said.

She examined their faces and said, "I don't believe it."

Wolf folded his arms and stared out of the window for a few moments. "We'll leave in the morning. I swear it."

"To go to my husband?"

"Yes."

Ellen wavered, her lips set in a grim line. "All right."

Wolf turned to the phone, dialed, and, after rolling his eyes through a brief wait, asked to speak to either Howard Scheim or Tim Kennesey. Then, with a bitter sigh, he hung up.

"Just missed them," he said, shooting Ellen a venomous glance.

"They walked out the door one minute ago, while you were bab-bling."

She shrank back as if he'd dealt her a blow. "Does this mean . . . ? Will you still keep your promise?"

He gave her a sour, twisted smile. "Oh yes, Mrs. K. I guarantee it. We'll be gone by ten or eleven. There's nothing keeping us here now."

Driving down Fremont Street in their rented Ford, Howard caught himself enjoying a small sense of gratification because they were now traveling in David Kennesey's own tracks: fifty or sixty hours ago he had driven down this very street on his way southward out of town. It distressed him that he should feel gratified by something so idiotic, and he began to wonder seriously whether his normal professional instincts might have deserted him forever. It seemed entirely possible.

He slowed down as a stoplight ahead of him turned red, and watched curiously as a shabbily-dressed Hispanic man and boy rushed off the curb and began searching the cars ahead, ducking down to peer into the windows and then quickly moving on. The light turned green just as they reached the Ford. The man put his pinched brown face against the window beside Howard, did a double-take, and yelled, "Hey, man, we need a ride!" The boy on Tim's side echoed him: "Hey, give us a ride!"

Howard put the car in gear, and they started pounding on the windows and shouting. "Hey, come on, man! You got lotsa room!" As Howard moved off, they ran alongside, pleading and thumping windows and fenders until they were left behind.

"What was that?" Tim asked.

Howard shrugged. "Different cultures, different customs."

CHAPTER 36

Over a shared lunch of Texas-style chili at a table in the kitchen, David's bewilderment dissipated, and he began to question whether Dudley Case really was Horse Killer. He'd had no doubt at first sight that he was standing before the same man, but there'd certainly been no answering recognition in Case's eyes. It was true that Case was reticent and something less than friendly, but Horse Killer had been downright hostile. At one point, while still in shock, David had been tempted to ask him point blank if he had another identity but wisely restrained himself.

David asked him about his studies, and Case gave him a perfunctory reply that made it clear that, in his opinion, David would neither understand nor want to listen to anything beyond that. He complimented Case on the chili, quite sincerely, and was rewarded with a solemn nod.

They were just finishing up when Marianne appeared out of nowhere to tell Case he was wanted on the telephone in the living room. David was relieved to see him go. Belonging to two different generations, two different races, two different cultures, they seemed unlikely to ever get much beyond polite inquiries, polite replies.

Watching Marianne clear the table, wash the dishes, and scrub the counters, he analyzed his mood and realized that, for the first time since leaving Runnell, he didn't feel restless, wasn't itching to get back on the road and go someplace. He *was* someplace.

During his sophomore year at college he'd had a brief flirtation with Roman Catholicism and had made a retreat at an old Trappist monastery in Iowa. It was an unforgettable place, radiating security, harmony, mystery, completeness. Troll House, oddly enough, had much the same aura. It felt like a retreat house designed for a different sort of quest—more worldly, to be sure, but in its own way perhaps no less spiritual.

David smiled to himself, realizing that he was being completely fanciful.

Marianne turned from finishing her work and asked if there was anything she could get him. There was something waiflike and vulnerable about the girl, with her narrow, fragile-looking shoulders and undeveloped breasts. She wasn't even close to being pretty, but there was a lot sexy in the way she fell short of it. Her too-wide mouth demanded brutal exploration; her acne-scarred cheeks invited a sympathetic caress. Her wide set, luminous eyes promised more than her small, unalluring body, perhaps.

David told her he didn't need anything and asked where Andrea was.

She blinked. "Santa Fe, I think. Left early."

"Not in the Ferrari," David observed with a smile.

"The Mercedes."

He nodded. "Did you get the Ferrari taken care of, then?"

"Yes."

David felt mildly frustrated. She was standing there dutifully answering his questions like a schoolgirl summoned to the headmaster's office, making him feel old and beyond interest.

"And what are you doing here, Marianne?" As soon as it was out of his mouth he regretted it, remembering Michelle's description of him as the type who asks what a nice girl like you is doing in a place like this. But it was too late to be recalled.

She frowned over it for a moment and said, simply, "I live here."

David nodded wordlessly, not trusting himself to be able to take his foot out of his mouth any more gracefully than he'd put it in.

As she walked out of the kitchen, he glanced at her narrow,

denim-clad buttocks and was astonished at the thought that crossed his mind: *Next time, my dear, it will be the birch rod for you.*

A little exploring confirmed that he'd seen most of the house. He spent an hour in his room, examining the treasures in the cabinet. In a museum, untouchable, owned by the state or some faceless foundation, they would have held no interest for him. These were personal possessions and, by invitation, briefly his own.

He'd forgotten how entranced the artists of the deco period had been with the slender female form then in vogue and wondered whether the artwork had created the vogue or the other way round. She was there everywhere, the twenties girl, in dozens of postures—graceful, saucy, swooning, kittenish—only innocently alluring even in the nude, which she mostly was. He was particularly taken by a Lalique mermaid who drifted languorously in a swirl of bubbles within a glass plate—and equally by a bronze and ivory gamine, shrugging in her high heels, her hands plunged into the pockets of her clinging trousers, a cigarette dangling from her pouting lips. Not sleek enough for serious work, the male figure appeared only in caricature, as in a collection of rubbery black jazz men in glass.

He was tempted to take a look inside the other bedrooms to see if they were furnished with the same incredible extravagance as his own, but the doors were closed, and he didn't want to be caught snooping. Instead, he went down to the lower living room and spent a while just sitting, soaking up its dark, earthy presence.

Finally, bored, he went outside. Crossing the windowless front of the living room and the attached three-car garage, he went around the side of the house and began to ascend the hill against which it was built. It was a steep climb and apparently one rarely made, since there were no steps (though David reflected that an escalator would have been more Andrea's style). At the top he came to the wide patio outside the upper living room. He paused there and decided the patio was the only thing about the entire house he'd change; it was carpeted with redwood chips; he'd have decked it.

The view from this point was vast, with jagged mountains on every horizon. The bowl containing Taos lay to his right. West of Taos rambled a canyon that he supposed had been carved by the Rio Grande. A series of low hills lay in front of him, and, since he felt like walking, he decided to explore them. As he descended the first, he remembered doing much the same thing one afternoon at the Trappist monastery—wandering in a contemplative mood while pondering the Meaning of Life. Perhaps Andrea was right. Nearly twenty years of living hadn't profoundly changed him—not in the depths of his mind and heart. Though he hated to admit it, he was very little different from that boy briefly in love with sanctity, incense, and the echo of men's voices raised in hushed, yearning Gregorian tribute to the Virgin. He was a bit behind and had some catching up to do. Perhaps, in the end, that's what he'd really left Runnell to do—some catching up.

He was so wrapped up in his thoughts that, passing around a room-sized rock at the peak of the next hill, he almost walked into Dudley Case, sitting cross-legged in the dust. Startled, he backed up and very nearly went down stumbling over a rock. Case watched him with a puzzled frown, as if David were rehearsing a pathetic burlesque routine.

"You startled me," David said lamely.

"If I hadn't heard you coming, you would have startled *me*," Case replied.

David saw some papers in the Indian's lap and a pen in his hand. "Working?"

Case glanced at the papers and capped the pen. "Writing a letter."

"I'm sorry I interrupted you."

"That's all right, it's finished." He picked up the top sheet, gave it a brief glance, and skimmed it into the air in front of him. It traveled for about five yards and sank to the ground.

David stared at it for a moment and said, "You decided not to send it?"

The Indian gave his lips a sardonic twist and waved a hand at the letter. "It's sent." As if in response to his wave, the sheet of paper was lifted by a breeze and sent tumbling down the hill for another ten yards.

"Well," David observed brightly, "it saves on postage."

Case gave him a dark look. "I can't address it. I don't know where he is."

"Who?"

"My brother. Just got out of jail in Shiprock."

"Ah," David said, as if he now understood.

"Gets windy as hell out here in the spring." As though illustrating the point, a gust swam up from behind them and sent Case's letter bounding downhill a few more feet. "Good time for sending letters."

"I'll bet."

The conversation seemed to have come to an end, and David was considering his choice of exit lines when Case looked up and told him to sit down.

David thought about this, gazing out at the mountains, his hands in his pockets. He didn't feel much like sitting down, and it wasn't exactly an invitation—more like a command—and David was tempted to ignore it as presumptuous. On the other hand, it was an overture of sorts, even if rather gruffly tendered.

As he started to sit down, Case stopped him: "Not there. Across from me."

David sighed and moved to the indicated position.

After a moment Case said, "Andrea says you have a son."

"Yes, that's right," he replied, not entirely pleased that Andrea felt at liberty to share his confidences with anyone she pleased. A minute passed in silence, and he began to wonder if Case had made him sit down just to affirm that he had a son. Then the Indian said:

"You could send him a letter."

David decided to conform to the Navajo's conversational pace and make him wait for a reply, even though he already knew what it would be.

"Yes, I suppose I could," he said at last, adding, "if I thought it was a good time to do that."

Ignoring this clear invitation to mind his own business, Case offered him the pen and paper. David glared at them, his annoyance mounting, then thought, *Oh, what the hell difference does it make?* and snatched them from his hands.

The touch alone told him the paper was Andrea's personal stationery. Fifty percent rag bond isn't something you can pick up at a K-Mart; even quality printers rarely stock it. The letterhead design—and of course the name—confirmed it. Having bought hundreds of thousands of dollars worth of design in the course of his career, he recognized it as first-class work. Enclosed in a double circle at the top was an evocative scene in miniature: beyond a series of light-brown, piñon-dotted hills, a red sun was emerging from the sea. Above and to the right, a pale morning star hung in the brilliant indigo sky. Above sun and star hovered a glowing fetish: a bone-carved deer and a stone arrowhead bound together with a thong. Below the picture, sandwiched between two hairline rules, was her name in widely letter-spaced Baskerville: ANDREA DE LA MARE. Below that was an address, simply Morningstar Path, Taos, and a phone number.

He smiled; it seemed a little too romantic for Andrea.

Looking up, he found Case studying him solemnly. David shook his head, uncapped the pen, and poised it uncertainly. Then, after a moment, he began to write:

Dear Tim:

    How are you? I am fine.

    Now is the time for all good men to come to the aid of their party.

    The quick brown fox jumps over a lazy dog.

    Quick wafting zephyrs vex bold Jim.

                        Sincerely,

                        David

After signing it, he looked up and said, "Now what? I just toss it into the air?" To his consternation, Case held out his hand for the letter.

"Oh," David said, glancing down at it uneasily. "It's, uh, private."
The hand didn't waver.

David sighed, handed it over, and closed his eyes, feeling doomed and foolish. When he opened them a few moments later, Case was glaring at him with hatred.

"Well," David began awkwardly.

With a snap of his wrist, the Indian flicked the letter across the space between them, and the edge of it sliced into David's right cheek like a knife. Stunned, David put his fingertips to the wound and brought them away covered with bright blood. He stared at it dully, feeling shattered and profoundly confused.

"I'm sorry," he muttered, not really meaning anything, just filling up the space with words.

The Indian gravely held out another sheet of stationery, his eyes inky and unreadable, and David nodded in sudden comprehension. How could he have been so innocent, so blind? Of course this was Horse Killer.

He accepted the sheet of paper, and a drop of blood fell into his lap, just barely missing it. He wiped his cheek with the side of his hand and shakily uncapped the pen again. It was some moments before he was steady enough to begin. After a few sentences, his eyes clouded with tears and he had to brush them away before he could go on.

Dear Tim—

It's a strange world out here. Strange things go on. Maybe it's better to live without knowing. Maybe you wouldn't have made as many mistakes as I have. I think you were right—I should have brought you with me. I wish I had you with me now, Tim.

If you come out here, you should be careful. But being careful may not be the answer. There's a lot I'm not sure of anymore. Anyway, take care of yourself, and I love you.

David

When he was done, he sat for several minutes staring down at it. Then he looked up and for the first time met the Navajo's eyes directly; he wasn't sure what he saw there. Not anger. Pity, tinged with something else; perhaps disgust. Pity is always tinged with disgust.

At last Case jerked his head upward and pantomimed a toss into the air.

David nodded, glanced at the letter again, and sailed it into the air over Case's head. The wind coming up over the hill caught it and blew it back. He turned and watched it fall to earth a few yards down the hill behind him. It tumbled once and lodged under a small cholla cactus.

He started to get up to release it, but Case said: "Leave it."

To David's surprise, the Navajo was shaking his head, his face softened in a smile of gentle exasperation: a reward for the sadly earnest effort of a retardate.

"Go back to the house now," he told him.

But David was in no mood for the house; he needed time to recover himself, and so he turned and headed down the hill.

Case, still smiling, shook his head again.

CHAPTER 37

It was three hours before David began to feel like himself again. Even though nothing but a sheet of paper had touched him, he'd been more unnerved by the Navajo's act of violence than by being shot at by Robbie—perhaps because it had been directed at him in a such an intensely personal way. He'd felt stripped and helpless, undone by his own everlasting cleverness.

Tell me, Muse, of that clever man . . . oh, yes.

As he stumbled through the hills, he thought about the cringing "letter" he'd written to Tim. Thankfully, he didn't remember it all, but what he remembered mortified him. "I should have brought you with me, Tim"—*so you could console me now.* "I wish I had you with me, Tim"—*so I'd have someone to hide behind.*

He was grateful Tim would never actually see it.

Strange things go on out here.

What the hell did that mean?

It seemed to mean: *If you go wandering around like a fool, you're going to get trampled on.*

Wasn't that, in the end, the sum of what he'd learned in the course of this great voyage of discovery? Sighing, he touched his cheek and examined his fingers. Except at the very center, the wound seemed to have closed. He began to pick off the blood that had clotted down the side of his face and wondered what the hell he was doing here.

What was Dudley Case, anyway? Not a student of anthropology—a student of aggression, intimidation, domination. Getting even with the white man by bending David to his will and making a fool of him.

And what was Andrea de la Mare? That wasn't so easily answered. An immensely self-confident person, certainly. And who wouldn't be, within the impregnable fortress of her wealth? Wise in the ways of the world: perhaps. Beyond *asserting* her superior wisdom, what had she done or said that was wise? But she laid claim to much more than mere wisdom. According to her, she was uniquely enlightened: well qualified to dismiss the bulk of humanity as pitifully deluded.

Again he wondered what the hell he was doing here.

What he seemed to be doing was proving to himself that there were people in the world who could lord it over him, with or without justification.

He shook his head. Just three or four hours ago he'd been thinking of Troll House as an idyllic retreat set in these hills for the sole purpose of receiving him. Now, because he'd had an upsetting half-hour, he seemed to be talking himself into running away from it. Maybe he was taking things a little too seriously, especially Dudley Case. That had always been one of his flaws. He'd let the Navajo get under his skin (which had undoubtedly been the idea), but now that he knew what to be on guard against, he didn't have to let it happen again.

With that resolution, his confidence returned and he made his way back to the house. Back in his room, he pulled off his ruined shirt and gently washed the blood off his cheek in front of the green and gold enameled mirror. The cut was closed but far from invisible. Swollen and red-rimmed, it sat just under his cheek bone, obscenely like a new mouth ready to open in speech. He hoped Andrea wouldn't ask him about it.

He made a face at himself.

He hoped Case wouldn't tell her about it.

To hell with it, he told himself. *You held a man at gunpoint and would have killed him if the safety hadn't been on. Stop being so god-damned sensitive.*

He took a shower, got dressed, and went downstairs. The giant room was untenanted, except by the ancient god brooding in its jungle and the huge figures cavorting madly overhead in eerie silence.

Andrea, Dudley Case, and an oddly-dressed stranger in a wheelchair were at the far end of the upper living room, and they looked up from their conversation when David arrived. She rose and came to meet him, and her eyes fastened at once on his cheek. With her hands on his arms, she frowned over it for a long moment, then looked up into his eyes.

"You mustn't go off into the hills by yourself for hours at a time," she told him gravely.

David smiled. "Why not, Andrea? Are they haunted?" Still holding him, she sighed. "David, David. You must try to stop being a fool."

He flushed angrily, and she shook him. "Stop it!"

His anger drained away to be replaced by bewilderment, and he stared at her blankly.

"What you're looking for isn't there," she said.

"I don't know what you're talking about."

She closed her eyes in bleak disappointment and released his arms. Then, as if putting all this behind her, she smiled. "Come see what I found in Santa Fe this afternoon."

He followed her obediently and soon saw that the man in the wheelchair wasn't a man at all. It was a grotesque mannequin in Edwardian evening dress, which had been rolled up beside Dudley Case's chair and now sat there staring at some distant horizon, solemnly bored, as if waiting for the conversation to resume.

David exchanged a neutral glance with Case and looked down at the mannequin.

"Go on, look at it," Andrea commanded, her hand resting possessively on its shoulder.

David hunkered down beside the wheelchair and studied the figure's face, which had been painted as if for the stage, with bright red lips, rouged cheeks, and eyelids accented with black. Though clearly artificial and inhuman in its perfection, it was a striking face, artfully framed by a mane of slicked-back black hair, with a long, aristocratic nose, elegant cheek bones, and delicate, almost feminine mouth. Its unmoving glass eyes were the least convincing feature; they should have been haughty but were merely empty.

David jerked back as the eyes swivelled in their sockets to meet his.

"Jesus," he said.

Andrea laughed. "There's a button on the shoulder that does that." She pressed another button and the eyes returned to the front. Then the whole head turned to David with a distinct creak. "There's a floor pedal for that. There are controls all over the thing." As if in affirmation, the head nodded twice and turned again to the front.

David stood up. "What was it for?"

"Ah," Andrea replied. "Tell David what you're for, Samson." There was a wheeze, a clank, and a long crackling hiss, like a needle on a scratchy record, and a hollow, squawky voice emerged from the thing's chest:

"I am Samson. My eyes are blind, as you see, but my vision is clear. Ask, and I will answer. Samson sees all, tells all. Ask and you shall know."

"Goodness," David said. "A fortune-telling automaton? But how did it work? They can't have recorded all the answers."

"Watch this."

Squeaking plaintively, the figure's right arm jerked up, turned to the side, and dropped. After a moment its fingers closed with a snap. Then the forearm swivelled up into a vertical position. With another wheeze, clank, and hiss, the tinny voice resumed: "Don't keep everyone waiting, Delilah. Read the answer." David nodded, thinking it out. "So there was a box or something, and the answers were fed through on cards by a confederate below the stage."

"So it would seem. Isn't he lovely?"

Samson's head turned eerily, as if to hear David's reply.

"Lovely indeed," David said. "Where did it come from?"

"Apparently he was all nicely packed away in a crate that's been sitting in a warehouse since the thirties. A lucky find."

"May I ask what an object like that sells for?"

"Oh, not all that much. If it had been one of the famous French or German automata of the eighteenth or nineteenth centuries, it would be worth a fortune."

"But how much?"

She shrugged indifferently. "Twelve thousand." He understood her shrug. It would have meant no more to him if she'd said four thousand or forty thousand. Looking down, he saw that the Navajo was regarding him with somber amusement.

"Marianne!" Andrea called out. "Bring David a drink!" She moved around the automaton, picked up a delicate tulip glass of white wine from the table, and sat down on a long white sofa.

David sat down on a matching sofa at right angles to hers just as Marianne came in with his drink on a tray. She was wearing a simple white jersey shift that clingingly emphasized the skimpiness of the features under it. He gave her a nod and a smile as she approached, but she gazed back at him blandly, as if he were a cast iron doorstop.

As she bent over the table, he thought: *We'll have that skirt up now, my girl. A touch of the birch will warm you.*

He crossed his legs over what was suddenly swelling between them and mentally shook his head. He didn't know why the girl inspired him with such bizarre and uncharacteristic fantasies.

Case was saying something to Andrea, and after listening for a moment in confusion David realized it was in a foreign tongue—not one he recognized. Andrea pondered briefly and replied, presumably in the same language.

"You speak Navajo?" David asked in amazement.

Andrea smiled. "I speak many languages."

"I don't suppose I should ask what you were talking about."

"Why not?" she asked, still smiling. "Dudley just thought of something wonderfully ingenious to do with those silly hooks in your room."

"Such as what?"

She laughed. "It's a project. You'll like it."

David looked at Case with a vague frown of suspicion. The Navajo nodded back benevolently, then stood up and stretched, his hands clasped over his head. "I think I'll take a shower before dinner," he said.

He and Andrea had another brief exchange in Navajo, and he left.

Andrea leaned over the table, drew one of her long cigarettes from a case, and lit it. Realizing he had nothing to say, David half wished he was a smoker so he could light one himself.

After a moment she gave him a sidelong look and said, "Dudley likes you, you know. He simply doesn't have a friendly manner."

David made a face. "I have to doubt that. I mean, about his liking me."

"He does, really, and he could teach you a lot. If you'd ask him."

"He doesn't invite asking."

Andrea shook her head, frowning and smiling at the same time. "You're a strange man, David. You turn everything the wrong way round. You tremble at the easy things and sneer at the hard ones. I don't know what to do with you."

"Do you need to do something with me?"

"'David asked with a sneer.'"

He blinked. "Was I sneering?"

"You were careful not to let it show."

"Perhaps. What are the easy things and the hard things?"

"Keep watch on yourself and you'll find out. Take note of the things you tremble at and the things you sneer at, and you'll see."

He felt his face stiffening under Andrea's humorless character analysis. He turned with a smile to the mannequin in the wheelchair. "Does Samson know?"

Samson stared back at him glassily.

With a sigh, she got up to see about dinner.

David picked up his drink and went over to inspect Andrea's library, which occupied most of one wall. Not surprisingly, it consisted entirely of outsize volumes on the arts, architecture, crafts, antiques, collectibles. There was not a single work of literature, history, philosophy, or science. He was leafing through *The Art of Maurice Sendak* when Dudley Case returned, his hair wet and slicked back, rather like Samson's. They exchanged a nod, and David resumed his perusal of the macabre fantasy drawn to Mozart's *Quartet No. 19 in C.*

It was after nine when they started dinner. The three of them served themselves, and David asked where Marianne was. Andrea said she was occupied elsewhere. Evidently Andrea's bizarre and exquisite tastes didn't extend to the culinary arts. The roast beef was rare and delicious but plainly served with potatoes, carrots, tossed salad, and French bread.

For the most part, it was a silent meal. Andrea seemed preoccupied and disinterested in her food. Case consumed his as if he were alone, looking up from his plate only to stare into a distance far beyond the walls.

David decided to ask Andrea to have dinner with him alone in Taos or Santa Fe tomorrow. Within her own environment she was too complacent, too much inclined to lecture and advise.

She visibly brightened once the meal was over and the dishes had been deposited in the kitchen. Returning to the living room, she linked her arm with David's and asked if any of his youth had been misspent in pool halls.

"I played a little in college. There was a table in the dorm."

"Then we must have a game." A chuckle rumbled in Case's throat and David glanced at him to see what was funny.

"Don't let her talk you into playing for money," the Navajo said. "She's a shark."

"Of course we'll play for money," Andrea said gaily. "It's no fun otherwise. A hundred dollars a game is nothing."

David asked Case if he played.

"Very, very badly. I can move the balls around, that's all." He grinned. "I'll rack for you."

As a matter of fact, David had a natural talent for the game. In the first few months he'd played, he'd fought an impulse to get down, sight quickly, and shoot; instead, he'd examined the angles mathematically, picked the exact spot to hit on the target ball to send it where he wanted—and did poorly. Then one night, so far behind against a good player that it didn't matter, he let his instincts take over and just started shooting—and cleared the table.

He wasn't up to that standard in his first game against Andrea. From long disuse, his instincts were sluggish, and she beat him easily. She won the second as well, by a narrower margin, and he left only a single ball behind at the end of the third. Finally relaxing completely, David took the next two.

"Ah," Andrea said, studying the balls she'd left behind, "Minnesota Fats begins to sweat. He needs the stimulant of an incentive." She looked up and gave David an arch smile. "Five hundred a game?"

David nodded agreeably.

"Now we'll see what's what," she said, getting down to break.

Andrea's play picked up noticeably, but David won the next two games anyway.

"Hmm," she said, shaking her head thoughtfully. "Let's see how good your nerve is, Fast Eddie. A thousand?"

David laughed. "Carry on."

The next game was a close one, but he won it. The one after that was Andrea's. Easily.

"Now I'm finding my stride," she said. "Let's make this a real test. Five thousand."

Smiling, David shook his head and laid his cue on the table.

"I tell you what," Andrea said, "I'll take Dudley as a partner. You against me and Dudley for five thousand."

David gave the grinning Navajo a speculative glance. Even if Dudley was as good as Andrea, he wouldn't be ready to play at their level in a single game.

"All right. Provided he shoots second."

"Agreed."

Rolling his eyes comically, Case went to pick out a cue from the rack.

David broke, sinking the eleven ball. He followed that with the nine, then missed on the ten. Andrea looked over the table, chalking her cue. Then she got down and pocketed the two ball, the seven, the four, and the three. The six wobbled against the sides of a corner pocket and drifted away.

David dispatched the fourteen, but left himself blocked behind a cluster of solids. He managed a shot on the thirteen but couldn't do anything with it.

Case came to the table with a straight shot on the six ball, worried over it through a full minute, and miscued, hitting nothing.

"I told you I was lousy," he said, straightening up. Andrea spotted the four ball.

David now had a clean shot at the thirteen, and he sank it. Then he turned to his last two balls. The fifteen was going to be a problem, lying dead against the cushion and blocked by the eight and the six. With one of his best shots of the evening, he simultaneously put away the ten and sent the cue ball backtracking to clear away the block on the fifteen.

Andrea applauded ironically.

The fifteen, however, was still dead against the cushion. The angle made a bank shot unpromising and he decided to nudge it gently into the corner along the cushion. Unfortunately, his nudge was too gentle and the ball rolled to a halt at the very lip of the pocket.

"Too bad," Andrea said, hefting her cue.

The need for pretense gone, she approached the table decisively and, moving from shot to shot without hesitation, sent the balls scurrying into pockets like a bunch of terrified mice. It was all over in under two minutes.

On her last shot, the cue ball, after downing the eight, drifted down the length of the table and insolently tapped David's fifteen into its pocket.

"I told you, man."

David nodded, stunned. "Very educational. And if I'd won I would've been properly hooked."

The Navajo chuckled.

Andrea was racking her cue. "I don't know about you two, but I'm ready for bed."

"At least you're a good winner," David observed.

Andrea smiled. "Only second-raters gloat. See you in the morning."

Case said good night and followed her downstairs.

David, his adrenalin still flowing, went back to the bookshelves looking for something to read himself to sleep with. After a few minutes he decided to stick with the Sendak.

Opening the door to his room, he paused, blinking.

A flickering circle of candles had been arranged on the floor, but this wasn't what drew his gaze.

In the center of the circle stood a slender, life-size female figure in profile, in a typical art deco nude pose: arms outstretched to the sky, head thrown back in ecstasy, back arched gracefully, toes just touching the ground. Then with a jolt he realized what he was seeing and the heavy book fell to the floor, forgotten.

It wasn't a statue, it was Marianne. And she wasn't standing, she was *hanging*—unconscious, her wrists roped together and strung up to one of the ceiling hooks.

"Jesus God," David whispered, every muscle in his body jumping almost beyond control. She'd been hanging here in the candlelight since before dinner:

Something wonderfully ingenious.

He approached on rubbery legs, horrified and almost unbearably aroused, and stood before her trying to subdue the storm of emotions that had burst within him, trying to bring his wildly shaking hands under control. He swallowed, his eyes fixed on her tiny breasts, made even slighter by being stretched taut, her nipples pink and pathetically vulnerable.

It's a project. You'll like it.

With an effort, he tore his eyes away and began to work clumsily on the knot at her wrists but soon saw that he'd never get it untied with her dead weight pulling it tight. But if she were awake. . .

"Marianne," he whispered. But he knew he didn't want to rouse her—didn't want to meet her eyes.

He cast his mind around the room, frantically looking for knives, razors. Then he hurried over to the curio cabinet and pulled out the exquisite Lalique mermaid dreaming in her cloud of crystal bubbles.

Andrea de la Mare: Andrea of the Sea.

Holding the edge of the plate in two hands to keep that much of it intact, he smashed it against the floor and hurried back to the hanging girl. Even with her weight holding it taut, he had to use one hand to hold the rope steady while he sawed with the other, so that, when it finally parted, she slumped to the floor before he could catch her. She lay face down in a twisted sprawl, her bound hands drawn up protectively under her chin, her boyish rump against his shoe.

We'll have that skirt up now, my girl.

Without hearing himself, he groaned.

He turned her over gingerly, scooped her up, and carried her to the bed, conscious of the fragile ribs pressing into his hand and of her lolling head. Holding her hands up, he covered her with the edge of the bedspread and sat down beside her to work on the knot. It was just beginning to loosen when Marianne moaned and her eyes fluttered open. She blinked at David groggily as if unable to bring him into focus. Then memory and awareness returned, and she scrambled to push herself away from him, whimpering and struggling helplessly against the rope. Her back against the headboard, her hands drawn up in fists to cover her breasts, she gazed at him with bruised, hopeless eyes, like an animal in a trap.

"Marianne," he whispered, nearly whimpering himself, "I'm not going to hurt you."

Her expression didn't change.

"It's all right," he said gently. "I'm not a rapist, Marianne."

Liar!

He saw that he may as well not have spoken. Her senses were clogged by pain and shock. He moved forward on the bed to take her hands, and she cringed.

"Marianne! Give me your hands and I'll untie them. I'm not going to hurt you, I swear."

She blinked over his words for a long moment, then hesitantly held her hands out to him.

He found, after a bit of fumbling, that he had to press her hands down onto her legs so he could steady his own. His fingers seemed to belong to someone else; they moved feebly over the knot like pale, drunken spiders.

"I'll have it in a minute," he said.

Then, in a triumph of concentration, he forced thumb and forefinger to close usefully over a loop of rope at the center of the knot, and he tugged it free. After that it was easy. In a few seconds he had it off and was unwinding a silk scarf that had been wrapped around her wrists to protect them from the rope. When he was finished, she drew her hands back and began rubbing her wrists, never taking her eyes off of him.

"I'll get you something to wear," he said and went into the bathroom for his white velour robe.

She followed him with her dark, unreadable eyes as he returned and lay the robe across her legs.

"I'm sorry, Marianne. This wasn't my idea."

Not exactly.

He walked away and began gathering up the pieces of the shattered Lalique plate. In a few moments he heard the door open and close.

When he turned back to the bed, he saw that she'd left the robe; he tore off his clothes and threw himself down to find release from his tormenting arousal.

CHAPTER 38

When Ellen got up and went into the living room the next morning, she felt an odd blend of bitterness and relief on discovering that Wolf had spoken the literal truth the day before. He'd said, "We'll leave in the morning. We'll be gone by ten or eleven."

He just hadn't specified who comprised that *we*. Except for her, the house was empty. She checked over her purse and suitcase, which they'd let her keep in the bedroom, and found everything intact. She tried the telephone and found it dead.

On her way out, she saw that they'd left something behind for her: a story clipped from a newspaper and tacked to the front door.

MYSTERY CAR FOUND IN MOUNTAINS

WOLCOTT—Twelve-year-old Felipe Martinez, while exploring a few miles north of his home last Tuesday, made an unexpected discovery: a 1988 Volvo sedan parked in the hills miles from any road. After overcoming some initial skepticism, Felipe led officer Dale Hoskins of the sheriff's substation to the site on Wednesday, and the find was confirmed.

"How the vehicle got there is anybody's guess," Hoskins said. "I wouldn't know how to drive it out, so I can't imagine how anyone drove it in, but it sure is there." He went on to say that the Volvo is in an undamaged condition and estimated it has been at the site "no more than a few days or weeks. Certainly not months or years."

Papers found inside the car indicate its owner is an Indiana resident, but further details are being withheld until authorities there can be contacted.

Hoskins said no search of the area is planned at present. "As yet," he pointed out, "no one has been reported missing."

Ellen put the clipping in her purse and went outside to walk the quarter mile to the road. She'd noticed that the sparse traffic on it was generally northbound in the morning and southbound in the afternoon and evening, and so assumed there was a population center to the north, though she hoped she wouldn't have to get there on foot. She was lucky. A young man in a pickup stopped for her after fifteen minutes and deposited her half an hour later at a car rental agency in Glenwood Springs—with some relief. A woman who has to ask which of the United States she's in is a woman in some kind of trouble (though she hadn't elaborated on it and he hadn't asked her about it).

At the police station they shrugged without interest over her clipping and referred her to the sheriff's substation at Wolcott.

Officer Dale Hoskins, a large, leathery man who looked shabby and disgruntled in the battered mobile home that served as the substation, wasn't much more helpful. After Ellen told him as much of the story as she thought he needed to know, he confirmed that the name on the Volvo's registration was her husband's, but stubbornly resisted the idea that the situation called for some action on his part. David Kennesey was not, to the best of his knowledge, missing; Ellen herself hadn't reported him as such. The fact that David Kennesey had abandoned a car in an inaccessible place was newsworthy, but not criminal. In the eyes of Eagle County it made him no different from someone who abandons a car in a church parking lot.

She asked if he would take her to the car, and he referred her to Felipe Martinez, the boy who had found it in the first place.

"Even if I took you there," he said, "we'd have to have him along anyway. On my own, I couldn't find the thing again in thirty years."

Following his tortuous directions, which relied heavily on such things as abandoned vehicles, "a big pile of dirt," and unfinished buildings for landmarks, Ellen found her way through a labyrinth of dirt roads to a ramshackle aggregate of adobe, wooden shed, and trailer that comprised the Martinez residence. A girl of seven or eight listened to her story at the screen door and went to get her mother, an enormous, cheerful woman who agreed enthusiastically that Felipe would be delighted to take Ellen to the car for five dollars. However, Felipe was "out somewhere" just at the moment but would probably return in an hour or two. She recommended that, since they wouldn't get far in Ellen's sedan anyway, she use the time to go back and rent a vehicle with four-wheel drive.

Ellen returned to Glenwood Springs, had a late breakfast, and changed into jeans in the ladies' room. Without any expectation of reaching anyone, she called home. Then she turned in her sedan for a Jeep and drove back to Wolcott. Felipe was waiting for her, hunkered down in the dust outside the Martinez house. A slender but well-developed boy, he stood up with an air of assurance, brushed off the seat of his jeans, and regarded her with dark, somber eyes. Except for his delicate, almost feminine features, he reminded her a bit of Tim.

"Hi," Ellen said from behind the wheel of the Jeep, "I'm Ellen. Are you Felipe?" When he nodded, she asked if his mother had told him what she wanted.

He nodded again and said—not pressing, just stating a fact—"I think it's worth ten dollars."

"So do I," Ellen agreed with a smile.

Felipe swung up into the passenger's seat with an easy grace and told her to turn right at the end of the driveway. "By the way," she said, "the reason I'm interested in the car is that it belongs to my husband."

"Not anymore," the boy said promptly.

"What do you mean?"

"Don't belong to anyone now. Unless you can bring it out with a helicopter or something."

"I see what you mean." She asked him how close the road would take them to it.

He thought about this for a bit. "It's about fifteen miles away, I guess. Four or five miles off the road, maybe."

"You get around," Ellen said, impressed.

He shrugged. "I like to walk."

"Will we be able to take the Jeep all the way in?"

He shook his head. "*Might* be a way to do it. Never looked for one—no reason to."

"How close can we get, then?"

"A mile or so."

Looking out at the bleak, rocky hills around them, Ellen wondered how she'd stand up to a mile hike. She was wearing the walking shoes she'd brought from Runnell, but they were designed for city streets, not mountains.

"How do you think the car got up there, anyway?"

The boy was looking out of the open window on his side of the car, and for a few moments Ellen thought he hadn't heard her question. Then, without turning, he said: "The witches put it there."

She looked at him with a smile, thinking it was a joke. He glanced back, took in the smile, and shook his head disgustedly.

"The Anglos think we're stupid," he said, politely refraining from *you Anglos*. "The Anglos think they know everything."

"I don't understand."

"There *are* witches out here. Always have been. *We* know it, but the Anglos know better, so they laugh."

"I'm sorry," Ellen said. "I didn't smile because I thought I knew better. I smiled because I'd never heard there were witches here."

"Well, there are," Felipe said.

Ellen thought it was a bit unfair of him to turn sullen after she'd already admitted her ignorance.

"What do they do?"

He made a face. "They do what witches do. Witches' business."

Ellen decided to leave it at that. She would have had to in any case, because the boy soon directed her to leave the road, and, for the next half hour, driving occupied her full attention. As they rattled across the rocky countryside, the wheel twisted and leaped under her hands like a machine gone berserk.

"You don't have to go so fast," Felipe said after a few minutes.

Ellen glanced at the speedometer and saw that she was doing five miles an hour. She eased up on the accelerator and found the wheel almost manageable at two.

"We could *walk* this fast," she said.

"You *think*," he replied scornfully.

This first part of the journey was a fairly steady climb in a straight northwesterly direction. At one point Ellen needed some coaxing to plunge into a dry stream bed that crossed their path, and Felipe had to get out to show her the tracks Hoskins had made, proving it could be done. At another point they came to a hill that, tracks notwithstanding, she refused to try, and Felipe guided her around it, the Jeep canted at a hair-raising angle. Other than that, it was a fairly straightforward trip.

They left the Jeep at the edge of a shelf overlooking a grim maze of hills that seemed to extend to the end of the world.

"The car's in there?" Ellen asked.

Smiling, Felipe nodded.

"God. You say a mile?"

"About that."

Ellen knew what a mile of city streets was. Tim's school was a mile from their house, and she'd walked it many times. Half an hour at a leisurely pace.

"It's not as bad as it looks," Felipe said, reading her mind. "Distance flattens the hills, makes 'em look straight up and down, but they're not. You can make it."

Ellen sighed and told him to lead on.

Two hours later, she saw him stop at the crest of a hill to let her catch up; the palms of her hands were scraped and one knee was bruised from a fall, but otherwise she thought she was doing pretty well. At the end of an hour she'd been ready to turn back, but then she'd gotten her second wind—something she'd always thought was purely imaginary. Coming up beside him, she wondered why he was smiling. Then, looking into the bowl at their feet, she understood— and felt a chilly tingle race up the back of her neck.

There was something incredibly eldritch about finding such a homely object as a green sedan sitting in this inhospitable wilderness. It didn't seem pathetic or forlorn, or even out of place. Rather, in some uncanny way, it made the *hills* seem out of place, as if they might dissolve at any moment to be replaced by a shopping mall full of cars.

Minutes later she was cautiously peering in through the Volvo's dusty windows, half afraid that previous examinations might have overlooked her husband's body lying on the back seat or the floor. Then she opened the door beside the driver's seat, and a wave of trapped warm air flooded out, smelling of baked plastic and metal. David's suitcase was lying on the back seat. Hoskins had told her, a bit defensively, that he'd left it, not wanting to be encumbered on the return trip. She was glad it was still there.

As she opened the back door to look at it, she became aware of Felipe, hunkered down a few yards away, watching her. She turned to him and said, "You don't have to hang around anymore, Felipe."

"What do you mean?"

"I mean, I can find my way back."

He blinked at her, astonished. "You kidding?"

She held out an arm and pointed unwaveringly to the southeast. "The Jeep is there. Right?"

"Right," he said, visibly impressed.

She smiled at him. "Other people have perfect pitch. I have a sense of direction that's just about infallible."

"Even so," he said doubtfully. "I don't mind sticking around."

"I know, but *I* mind. I just need a little time by myself. Do you understand, Felipe?"

"Yes, but . . . I could go away and come back."

"Just go home. I'll be all right."

He shook his head, perplexed by the decision Ellen was thrusting on him. If he'd been a few years older, a little more experienced, or a little more guileful by nature, he would simply have smiled and taken his leave—and then waited for her on the other side of the hill. But deviousness of this sort was beyond him as yet, and he saw no middle ground between flatly refusing to move (obviously impossible) and going home (obviously wrong). What decided him was wondering what he would do if it were his mother telling him to go home instead of this woman. There was no doubt about that; he would go, instantly and without argument. He had the feeling there were other aspects of the matter to be weighed and considered, but he knew that if he started looking at them, he'd never be finished. On the whole, Felipe preferred dealing with rattlesnakes and tarantulas, who follow a simple rule: *You leave me alone and I'll leave you alone.*

He stood up, accepted Ellen's ten dollar bill, and headed back, hoping his decision was the right one. In case it wasn't, he would keep his mouth shut when he got home.

He was guileful enough for that.

Ellen was immensely relieved to be rid of him. It was puzzling, but she'd definitely felt a huge, protective calm envelop her when she first approached the car. It was as if a powerful ghost of David's presence had stayed behind to welcome her and help her reassemble her shattered life. Eyes closed and head back against the cushion, she absorbed the dry heat the sun had stored there for her and let it bake out her anxieties and fretfulness.

Incredibly—and perhaps just for this moment—it seemed to her that the whole bewildering disaster hadn't been a disaster at all. She could see very clearly now that the life she and David had been living in Runnell was an emptiness—perhaps even more an emptiness for her than for him. What, in that life, had she been becoming but a cipher? A lovely, smooth oval, perfectly symmetrical on every axis, and hollow. Oh, it wasn't that she longed for achievement; she didn't envy David (or anyone) on that score. She was happy to leave glory to others. She hadn't been playing a role—perfect mother-and-wife—back there in Runnell. Someone playing a role has, by definition, another life hidden under the role. She'd been *becoming* a role. She'd been becoming a middle-aged Jane married to a middle-aged Dick—a person whose face is so bland and standardized that no caricaturist could find a feature to fasten on. Mouth, yes, pleasant. Eyes, two, twinkling. Nose, yes, noted vaguely between eyes and mouth.

That was what David had shattered: her future as a role, all spoiled now. That's why she'd been so furious with him—not because she loved him, not because she needed him, not even because of what he was doing to Tim. But because, by refusing to be Dick, he'd made it impossible for her to go on being Jane. He'd left her with no choice but to become a person. The hollow inside the oval now had to be filled in; the face couldn't go on being the automatic quick sketch the advertising artist gives the woman buying the refrigerator (the same one he gives the woman pushing the shopping cart) resolutely cheerful and vacuous.

Even this incredible business with Tim had been for the best. Until they'd been separated, Ellen had been clinging to the past, to her life as Jane. How would Jane have reacted if the unthinkable happened, and Dick abandoned her? Why, she would have Gone On— resolutely cheerful—and Made a Good Life for her children and Spot. Mustn't forget Spot.

Of course she still had to find Tim. But that would work out. After that, things would be different. No more Dick and Jane. They'd sell the house and move to an apartment in Chicago: right downtown, Michigan Avenue. She'd divorce David—to hell with him. Or, if he came to his senses, she'd have him back. If he could accept the fact that she wasn't the person he'd left.

It was all going to come right.

She opened her eyes and stretched blissfully. The sun was westering and, checking her watch, she saw it was time to get back. She too left the suitcase where it was. Before Felipe left, she'd intended to go through it—a sort of sentimental journey.

But it didn't matter now.

CHAPTER 39

At the same time that Ellen was talking to Officer Dale Hoskins at the sheriff's substation in Wolcott, Howard and Tim were talking to Officer Richard Valdez in a motel coffee shop in Gallup. Unlike Hoskins, Valdez was young, sleek, and willing to help. He was sleek in spite of being padded with thirty pounds he didn't need; he carried them with assurance, as he did a fine black mustache.

"See, this is what happened," he told them. "After I pulled him over and checked his driver's license, I called in the plate number. Just routine. Then they called back to say the number was flagged and I said, stolen? No, just please inquire. So they were inquiring. And finally the word comes back that the car belongs to a known drug dealer—a big one."

Valdez paused to enjoy their look of astonishment.

"Right. So here I am. You wouldn't know, but I-40 is a major artery of drug traffic in this country—probably millions crossing daily, and not much we can do about it, since we can't stop and search without probable cause. Well, a speeding violation is probable cause, so I get the guy out and put him up against the car and go over him, and he's saying 'What, what, what?'

"Then I put him in the back of the cruiser and go over the Corvette. No drugs—lucky for him—but right there in the glove compartment under some maps is this big hunk of iron, an S & W

.357 magnum. Not so lucky. I go back and ask if he's got a license for this firearm, and he says, 'No, officer, I don't, because it isn't mine. I didn't even know it was there.' And he explains that he just borrowed the car from a friend. I ask him, Charles Petronis?—that's the drug dealer—and he says, yes, that's right.

"So I say, 'Well, friend, you are busted. Well and truly busted for illegal possession of a firearm, not to mention speeding,' and he says, 'But officer, I swear to God I didn't know the gun was there,' which is beside the point, of course. Okay, so I'm taking the man in, and while I'm doing that I'm trying to remember where I know the name David Kennesey from. It seems to me I heard it just recently, so I ask the man where he's from, and he says Indiana. Then I ask where he's coming from, and he says Vegas, and then I've got it."

He leaned across the table, smiling confidentially. "See, I grew up in Vegas. Still spend time there, vacations and things, and the day before I pick up your man a friend calls and tells me about this guy Kennesey, who tore up this downtown club with nine straight spins, betting the max on everything. So I say, are you this guy? And he says yes, I'm that guy. Now I start thinking. I ask him how close he is to this Petronis, and he says, 'I only met him once, I needed a car and he lent me this Corvette.' And I tell him this is a known drug dealer, not a man to get close to, and he says, 'You're kidding. He seemed like a nice guy.' And I tell him drug dealers hug their kids too, just like everybody else.

"Anyhow, I pull over and bring him up into the front seat to talk. Look, I told him, I've got to take you in, because I already called in to tell them about the gun rap and to get a tow on the Corvette, you understand? But if we play it cool, you can be back on the road in an hour or two. And he says, okay, that's great. Then he sits there swallowing for a while, and I can see he's wondering if he's supposed to slip me a bribe. I laugh and tell him I just want to be able to say that the guy who broke the bank at the Four Queens or whatever it was is a friend of mine, and we shake hands. Well, to make a long story short, I hustled up a judge and told David to plead guilty to both charges, and he said, 'But I'm innocent,' the jerk. And I explained that he was definitely in possession illegally, no two ways about it, and not knowing the gun was there was just an extenuating circumstance, so cool it. I said, don't get in a sweat, the judge and I are drinking buddies, and if I vouch for you all will be well."

Valdez paused to chuckle over the memory.

"You should've seen his face when the judge sentenced him to ninety days. I thought he was going to have a coronary on the spot. But of course he suspended it right away, and David paid that fine so fast the money was smoking as it came out of his hands." Valdez shook his head and chuckled again. "Anyway, when it's all over David says, can I buy you a drink? And I say, sure, if I can buy you one. I want to be able to say I bought a drink for the man who broke the bank at the Four Queens." He shrugged, his smile fading as the golden moment slid into memory to await its next recall.

"That's all there was. We had a couple drinks and I sent him on his way."

"And he didn't say where he was going?" Howard asked.

Valdez shook his head. "We were talking about Vegas. He was heading east when I pulled him over, so I assume he went on heading east."

Howard glanced down at Tim. "This Charles Petronis. Where does he live?"

"In Colorado someplace. They told me. Let me think." He smoothed his carefully-tended mustache for a moment. "Some resort town."

"Aspen?" Howard suggested.

"Not Aspen."

Tim said: "Vail?"

"That's it. Vail. You think Petronis might know where he was heading?"

"Maybe. But mainly it's the Corvette. If he lent David a valuable automobile, he must expect to see him again sooner or later."

"Yeah, you got something there. I should've thought of that myself."

As they stood up to leave, Howard asked Valdez if he knew how the Las Vegas paper had happened to get the story of David's arrest in the first place.

"Sure do," Valdez said with a grin. "I phoned it in myself."

"You're a man who's going far," Howard said, smiling as he shook the hand that had shaken the hand of the man who'd broken the bank at the Four Queens. Back in the Ford, Tim asked Howard if he was going to call Petronis.

He shook his head. "If he's what they say he is, Petronis wouldn't give you his middle initial over the phone," he told him. "We'll drive up there."

He took out their map of the southwest, spent a while computing, and then sighed, having reckoned it a ten-hour drive.

CHAPTER 40

Felipe's ingenuous plan to say nothing of leaving the Anglo woman behind in the mountains failed for the simple reason that his mother (who missed little of what went on in the neighborhood of her home) saw him returning on foot while he was still a mile away. Since he seemed to be in no hurry, she wasn't alarmed. The woman had probably stranded the Jeep on a boulder or broken an axle, and as she went out to meet her son she began to formulate the steps that would have to be taken to rescue her and the vehicle.

When she confronted him, however, he immediately blurted out the truth, and she went insane with fury, dancing in the dusty road and shrilly lamenting the day she'd borne a child without the brain of a cockroach, who meant to bring ruin and disgrace on them all, who would land them all in prison for murder if any harm came to that woman, who was absolutely certain to lose her way and be devoured by coyotes.

Felipe listened to it all, his narrow shoulders trembling, and said he would go back and find her.

"If you don't find her, don't bother to come home!" she screamed at him. "Just find a rattlesnake hole and crawl inside!"

His head bowed in defeat and humiliation, the boy turned and headed back.

"Run, empty-head!"

He ran. Until he was sure he was out of sight.

Never again, he told himself. This settled it. He was going to become a hermit. One day he would simply disappear into the mountains. His hair would grow until it reached his ankles; his clothes would rot and fall off, and he'd dress in the skins of animals killed with his bare hands. He would find a cave and throw rocks at anyone who came near; he would shriek at them in a strange language he'd invent for himself, and they'd say he was crazy. That would be fine with him; he'd be the crazy man of the mountains, and no one would bother him. And one day, many years hence, someone would say, "Whatever became of the crazy man of the mountains?" And they'd go to the cave where he'd died all alone, scorned and feared by all, and find his bones, chewed on and scattered by the coyotes.

Until then—until he was ready to disappear—he would live as a mute. Not one word would anyone have from him, ever again. Let them think he was an idiot. When they said, "Do this," he'd just look at them blankly, as if he hadn't heard. He'd make them carry him from place to place; he'd make them spoon food into his mouth.

And then one morning he just wouldn't be there. They would look at his bed and say, "Where is the idiot Felipe? But what's this on his pillow? It's a note! And it's signed *Felipe!*"

Oh yes, he'd leave them a note all right. It would be short and wickedly cruel, and they'd writhe on the floor with grief and remorse. And they'd cry out, "Come back, Felipe! We understand now! We'll be good to you now!"

But it would be too late for them then.

The boy was still composing the note in his mind when he passed the Jeep, headed down into the chasm below, and began climbing the hill opposite. He was halfway to the top when he heard a clatter of rocks to his right, and he realized that the Anglo woman was descending one gully as he was ascending another beside it. He scrabbled up the rocky spine that separated them and saw that he was right. She was about a hundred yards away, slightly downhill from him.

Then a movement at the crest behind her caught his eye, and he began to run toward her, shouting.

CHAPTER 41

Had he been human, the dog would have been classified a traumatic schizophrenic. His world had been blasted to pieces six days before, and, having no equipment for reassembling it, he had been living an endless, compulsory nightmare ever since.

The nightmare was compulsory because he had failed.

Incomprehensibly and unforgivably.

God, in the person of Robbie Carmichael, was dead because of his failure.

In the ordinary course of things, a dog will long remember a person, a place, a scent, a route, any trained behavior. But canine memories of the events that make one day different from another dissipate almost as quickly as smoke. Not so, with these. The events of that night had worn a deep groove in his memory, and he was retracing them perpetually, like a needle caught in a flawed phonograph record.

This was what had driven him mad. Other dogs forget traumatic events and remain sane. The Beast couldn't forget.

It had all begun with the arrival of the stranger with the odd scent. The Beast had never encountered anyone with a scent like that, and it had worried him a little. He'd wanted to tell Robbie about it, but Robbie never tolerated whining. Then, later, Robbie had told him to guard the window of the stranger's room. That was easy.

That was all right.

But then the others had come.

Whenever he came to this part of the groove, his fury was so overwhelming that he lost control of his body. Writhing and twisting in a paroxysm of rage, he fell to the ground, snarling, whining, barking, snapping his jaws on the empty air.

Because they had cowed him. Made him whimper. Made him slink along the ground belly down.

Just by talking to him.

Just by talking to him, they'd driven him away from his post. And, groveling in the dirt under a bush, the Beast had broken faith with God; he'd heard Robbie's voice, had heard the terror in Robbie's voice, and had stayed where he was, trembling and whining until it was over.

At dawn, too late, he'd tried to return to the mobile home, but that area had been interdicted to him. It didn't matter. He knew by the stench and the silence that God was dead. He circled the area for a while, feeling lost and useless; then, already a little insane, he found an insane reason to exist: He began to backtrack, to seek the origin of this catastrophe.

He followed the tracks of Robbie's Jeep back to the point where they intersected the track of the stranger with the odd smell; even after a day, David's tracks were easy to follow, and he followed them northward all the way to the Volvo. He retraced the whole of David's journey there, bringing him back once again to the Volvo. Then, still intent on his insane purpose, he followed the tracks south and then east—back to the mobile home.

And the needle jumped in its groove for the first time.

Soon he was padding westward again to backtrack to the Volvo. A few hours later he returned.

And the needle jumped in its groove for a second time.

The pattern of his derangement had been fixed.

Day after day he made the journey, stopping to gobble down a rabbit or lizard or snake only when hunger became unbearable. On the second day he came across a new set of tracks at the Volvo; they didn't interest him. He recognized the scent as belonging to a boy who frequented the hills. On the third day he came across still another new set of tracks, but these didn't interest him either. The scent belonged to a man Robbie met with regularly, a uniformed man Robbie treated with contempt.

But on this sixth day, just at dusk, he found a third set that he received the way a saint might receive a vision. He was electrified. Quivering with excitement, nose hovering over the ground, he set off at a steady trot toward the southeast. The hills melted before him. He didn't notice them. The scent was pulling him forward inexhaustibly, reeling him in like a fish on a line.

He'd been tracking for less than half an hour when, coming to the crest of a hill, he saw a Jeep perched atop the next crest half a mile away. Then he saw the woman below him, picking her way cautiously down the slope.

Transfigured with new purpose, his muscles rippling with manic energy, he plummeted down the hill, devouring three yards with each stride.

Suddenly a boy appeared at his right, shouting and waving his arms, and the Beast faltered. The boy rushed into his path as if to block him, and the Beast's head plunged into his chest like a cannonball. The boy flew backward, tumbling fifteen yards in the scree. Then the dog was on top of him and away again without a break in stride.

Only a sharp-eyed observer could have seen that, with a single flick of his head, he'd torn out the boy's throat in passing.

The Beast galloped past the screaming woman without giving her a glance.

The needle had jumped into a new groove. The pattern was broken, and the Beast, though still insane, was free again.

CHAPTER 42

Waking up to the sight of a rope dangling from the ceiling, David had felt instantly and obscurely depressed. He twitched it down off its hook and stowed it out of sight in an Art Deco wastebasket that was trying hard to look like something more important. He wondered what to do with the candles and decided that they, with their holders, could go right along with the rope. When he was finished, he was tempted to put the wastebasket out in the hall but compromised by hiding it in a closet. Having normalized his environment, he went and took a long shower: washing off the past before contemplating the future. He studied his face in the mirror afterward and winced at his swollen, flushed cheek; he was usually a fast healer, but he'd obviously infected the paper cut while dabbing away at it the day before.

It was after ten by the time he was dressed in fresh clothes and sitting on the terrace outside his room, ready to consider his options. The first came to him readily enough, in the form of a moving picture: him with his luggage walking out the front door (head held resolutely high), going to his car, and driving away without so much as a goodbye or a backward glance. He didn't care much for it. It was a picture of outraged innocence, stuffy and childish. Perhaps even a bit hypocritical. Confront Andrea and demand to know what the hell she was playing at? It may have been Dudley Case's idea, but it was her house, her servant, her guest, and her responsibility. What would she say?

Why David, my dear, did I misread the signs?

And what would he say to that? He could hear her prompting him: *Be courageous, David. I never lie out of cowardice and don't care to be around those who do.*

He shook his head, rejecting confrontation.

Although there was at least one other, he decided his only option was simply to ignore the entire episode, to pretend it hadn't happened. Let Andrea make of that what she would.

Evidently Marianne had chosen this option as well. When he found her in the kitchen, she regarded him with the same opaque disinterest as the morning before and asked what he wanted for breakfast.

"Have the others already eaten?"

She nodded.

"Gone out?"

She nodded again.

"Look, Marianne, you really don't have to make breakfast just for me."

She lowered her eyes, and for a moment her mouth worked with something like disgust. Then she looked at him and said, "I do, you know. That's my job."

"All right. Two eggs, scrambled. No toast. Bacon or sausage."

"Which?"

David sighed. "Sausage."

After breakfast he went into the living room and paused as he was passing the still figure of the automaton in its wheel chair. Curious, he ran his fingers lightly over its shoulders, feeling a battery of buttons under the cloth of the black coat. He was bending over to look for the controls on the chair when a rattle of pans from the kitchen stopped him. He didn't want Marianne to catch him playing with Andrea's toy.

He drifted over to the pool table and racked up the balls for a game. Playing against himself—"himself" being the one who broke first—he'd won three games out of five by the time Marianne passed through to attend to the bedrooms on the floor below. He finished the sixth game, evening the score, racked his cue, and returned to the automaton.

Half an hour's experimentation discovered all the controls Andrea had displayed the afternoon before, plus a whole series she hadn't. There were six buttons that activated the thing's voice—presumably recorded on six separate cylinders. The first cylinder was the one Andrea had played in part yesterday, and the second was similar—containing general-purpose responses for what must have been a standard performance. The next three were much different, obviously intended for individual consultations. They were cleverly scripted. Samson's questions were worded so as to elicit predictable replies that laid the basis for his own prerecorded responses (which could be delayed for the long-winded at the touch of a pause button). As a safeguard against the client slipping in a question where only a reply was expected, his responses were routinely prefaced with a vague aphorism that would serve as an excuse for not answering it:

"Ah, soon perhaps all will be known."

"The universe is filled with mysteries hidden from my eyes, I fear."

"I know there must be many questions that trouble you."

After a while the ear accepted it as simply part of Samson's rather pompous conversational style.

The subjects covered on these three cylinders were so specific that there must at one time have been many others, if Samson pretended to any versatility as a fortune-teller. The three in place when he was packed away David mentally dubbed "Recently Bereaved Widow," "Young Woman Searching for a Husband," and "Difficult Decision (Investment)." The last in the series was entirely different, although David didn't know it when he punched the button and sat down beside Samson to listen. To enhance the conversational effect, he had turned the mannequin's head so that it seemed to be speaking to him.

After the usual clank, whir, and hiss, Samson gazed at him with his glassy eyes and said: "We must talk seriously now." The voice that issued from the automaton's chest was recognizably the same hollow squawk as on the other cylinders, but the speaker had abandoned his customary histrionic manner; his tone now was casual, intimate.

David smiled and said, "All right."

"You are very ill."

"Am I?"

"Yes. You must believe me in this."

"All right. I hope it's not *too* serious."

David blinked at Samson's reply: "It is serious indeed. If you don't attend to it, it will be fatal."

A question on the nature of this illness seemed in order at this point and David asked it.

"It's difficult to explain," Samson replied. "You understand that I am not a physician but rather a seer, and what I see would appear under no microscope, would in fact be laughed to scorn by any traditional medical practitioner."

Smiling, David asked what it was he saw. "A glass rod," Samson answered simply.

"A glass rod?"

"Yes, a glass rod. Cold, clear, and pure."

"I'm afraid I don't understand."

"It stands at the center of your being. I can say little more than that. Frankly, its mechanism puzzles me. I don't know why a glass rod should endanger your life, but it plainly does."

"Where did it come from?"

"I see nothing beyond what I've told you. It must be shattered if you're to live."

"How do I go about that?"

"I can only speak a moment more. You must shatter it. I don't see where you are, who is around you. Seek help. Accept help. Tell them about the glass rod."

Smiling, David shook his head. "A fat lot of help *you* are."

"Tell your friends about the glass rod. They may understand better than I what it is and what can be done to shatter it."

"Thanks a lot."

There was a hissing pause and David, wondering what conceivable occasion the interview had ever served, assumed it was over. But Samson had a final, almost pathetic, comment to make:

"I'm not entirely a charlatan, you know."

For an area consisting almost exclusively of rocks, it didn't produce many that were smooth, nicely rounded, and of a size to fit comfortably in the hand. After half an hour's search under the mid-afternoon sun, David had found just enough of them to cover the bottom of the woven basket Andrea had given him to fill. He went on, eyes to the ground, selecting and rejecting.

Looking fresh and crisp in town clothes, Andrea had made her first appearance of the day in the lower living room, where David had been napping under the benignly inscrutable gaze of the old Aztec god. Not in a chatty mood, she seemed preoccupied, troubled. She frowningly examined the cut on his cheek and laid a hand on his forehead to check for fever. Then she lit a cigarette and paced the room, wrapped in an air of abstraction. Apparently coming to a decision, she went upstairs and returned with a basket, which she asked David to fill with stones. She described the kind she wanted.

David had thought of asking if this was another "project," but decided to leave well enough alone.

When he returned, he saw that she'd changed into jeans and shirt. She was waiting on a sofa just in front of the stairway to the upper levels, about midway between the stone head and the mirrored back wall of the room. She looked up, smiled, and said *Ah*, as if David were bringing her a treasure.

Feeling slightly ridiculous, he set the basket down on the table in front of her, and she leaned over at once to examine its contents.

"Yes," she breathed. She picked up a rock, hefted it thoughtfully, and set it aside on the table. She tested a second and a third and discarded them. The fourth she cradled in her hands for half a minute. After nodding her acceptance of it, she got up, moved away from the sofa, and turned to face the back wall. She stood for a moment studying herself in that immense expanse of glass soaring up sixteen feet into the air.

Then she hurled the rock into the middle of it, and David involuntarily leaped six inches off the floor.

There was more than a shattering of glass; there was an explosion. In the exposed plaster wall behind the mirror was a smoking hole that looked like it had been made by an artillery shell. The lights in that half of the room blinked out; evidently Andrea's stone had smashed its way into the wiring.

She was gazing up at the damage, nodding with tranquil satisfaction.

"Jesus Christ," David whispered.

Marianne appeared on the staircase. Halfway down, she stopped and stared open-mouthed at the hole gaping in the wall. Then she looked around, took in Andrea, David, and the basket of stones, and came down the rest of the way.

Andrea calmly resumed her place on the sofa.

Marianne walked to the table and stood looking down at the stones, her face alive with interest.

"Where did these come from?" she asked.

"David found them."

Marianne gave him a look of astonished respect and began sorting through them just as Andrea had done. When she found one that satisfied her, she straightened up, and began to search the room for a target. Her eyes stopped at the stone head of the god, still glowing under its spotlight, and David said, "No!"

Ignoring him, she drew back her arm, and he lunged at her. They wrestled in grim silence for a moment, and then she shoved him away with surprising strength. As he staggered back, she set herself, took aim, and let fly.

The rock impacted the giant head like a contact grenade, completely shattering its left temple.

Dumbfounded, David turned to Andrea, expecting to see her leaping off the couch in outrage at this sacrilege, but she was still sitting there, nodding placidly, as if appraising the merits of the throw. After a moment both women turned and gazed up at him expectantly.

He looked from one to the other and said: "Are you *crazy*?"

They went on staring at him in hopeful silence.

"What's the matter with you, for God's sake?"

With an air of defeat, Andrea sighed, leaned back, and lit a cigarette. She gestured with it toward the stones on the table.

"You can take these away, Marianne." The girl nodded and began to return the rejected stones to the basket.

"And, while I think of it, ask John if he can do something about these lights when he comes in the morning."

Marianne nodded again.

Completely forgotten, David left to go up to his room. He felt a headache coming on.

David's headaches, mercifully rare, were devastating. He'd learned from experience that a handful of aspirin taken early could abort one. Ignored, it soon swelled up into a monster that couldn't be shaken off, its claws probing every crevice of his brain, shutting off every sense except pain; at that point there was nothing to do but crawl into bed and wait. The monster never survived a night's sleep.

After checking the medicine cabinet in his bathroom (which he already knew to be empty), he lay down on the bed and covered his eyes, hoping to find he was mistaken, that it was simply a momentary reaction to stress. He sent an exploratory tendril of sensory awareness up toward the crown of his head and knew it was no mistake. The monster was there, half an inch below the skull, still an infant but already restless and quickly learning how to coordinate its limbs for the attack.

As much as he hated the idea of asking either Andrea or Marianne for anything right now, he was going to have to get some aspirin. But perhaps he could find it on his own. He got up and went upstairs. There was a bathroom off the living room, but there was no aspirin in it. He went into the kitchen and began to go through the cabinets there. He was still at it ten minutes later when Marianne arrived and asked him what he was looking for. She went promptly to a closet filled with medical supplies and handed him a bottle. Then she drew a glass of water for him.

He swallowed a handful, knowing it was already too late. The monster was out of its cradle and on the move.

David explained about his headaches and told Marianne he wouldn't be at the dinner table.

"I'll bring you a tray," she told him.

"Thanks, but don't bother. I wouldn't be able to eat anything. Truly."

Then he went back to bed to begin the ordeal.

Around ten o'clock there was a knock on the door and David groaned an invitation. Andrea came to his bed, sat beside him, and laid a cool hand on his forehead. He squinted up at her, his face twisted with pain.

"This is all so unnecessary, David. You could be well."

He shook his head feebly. "Not now, Andrea. Please."

"All right."

She stroked his head until he was asleep.

CHAPTER 43

David slept till ten—and would have gone on sleeping if Marianne hadn't come in to wake him. He peered up at her blearily, feeling battered and weak, as if he'd spent the night being tumbled in a washing machine. But the headache, at least, was gone.

"What is it?" he asked her.

"John's going to try to fix the wiring downstairs."

David's answering laugh was tinged with hysteria. "I wish him well, Marianne. I really do. Give him my regards."

She stared at him, waiting, as if he hadn't spoken.

"Am I supposed to be there? Am I supposed to witness this startling event?"

She continued to stare at him indifferently.

"Oh, all right, all right. I'll be there. Fifteen minutes."

She turned and left.

Getting out of bed, David fell down. It puzzled him; his legs had just buckled under him, as if they hadn't gotten the message that he was going to be using them now. On his next try they paid attention, and he made his way to the bathroom feeling wobbly and strangely lightheaded. He couldn't recall ever being this way after a headache, but it didn't surprise him. He wouldn't have been surprised if his head had literally exploded during the night. He took a shower but didn't bother to shave; he didn't feel up to it, and being a witness to electrical work didn't seem to warrant it.

The scene downstairs was macabre—and slightly comical just because it was macabre. Andrea and Marianne stood on either side of a twelve-foot ladder, each directing a flashlight beam up into the hole blasted in the back wall. The man at the top of the ladder looked like a surgeon probing a giant, bloodless wound. Working with his own flashlight, his head actually inside the hole, he seemed in danger of being swallowed up in it.

"I'm afraid, my dears," he said after a while, his voice echoing from within the wall, "that this is far beyond my feeble skills in the electrical arts."

Nevertheless, he went on working for a few minutes before withdrawing his head and descending the ladder. The three of them turned off their flashlights and headed out into the brighter part of the room, where David was waiting beside the ruined stone head.

"Ah, David!" the man said, beaming with pleasure.

David's legs once again seemed to forget their business, buckling momentarily so that he nearly collapsed.

Pretending not to notice, the man held out his hand in greeting.

"I don't believe I introduced myself when we met at the Dead Man Saloon," he said. "I am John Dee."

Not knowing what else to do, David weakly shook his hand.

"Come and sit down, my boy," the old man said, leading him to a sofa.

When David was seated, Dee gently tilted his head up to examine the cut on his cheek. He shook his head over it and put a hand to David's forehead.

"You're running a fever."

David said, "I know," though he hadn't.

The old man sat down beside him. David looked around for Andrea and Marianne, but they were gone.

"Andrea tells me you've had many adventures since we met."

"Yes."

"And what do you make of it all?"

"I don't know," David said mechanically, feeling as empty as poor old Samson.

"You really must *try*, you know."

David suddenly felt a dark cloud of depression settle over him. It seemed to isolate him from Dee—from all living things. He felt frozen and very lonely.

"David always tries," he said. "David is a man who tries real hard and worries a lot."

The old man paused, puzzled by the oddness of this locution. Then, giving up on it, he said, "Perhaps you should stop worrying entirely and try something else."

"Something else?"

"Yes. Isn't that what you wanted?"

"Wanted?"

Dee sighed. "It's time now for you to think very, very seriously about what it is you want. You really must do that."

"All right."

The old man shook his head. "You're not listening, David. You haven't listened to any of us."

David's head turned woodenly from side to side in disagreement. "David listens well. David tries real hard and worries a lot."

Dee frowned for a long moment, then suddenly nodded in comprehension. "Yes, I see. I understand what you're telling me now." David looked at him blankly. "You don't understand?" David shook his head. "You're telling me you're like that pathetic mannequin upstairs. Your will can only respond to a set of messages you yourself recorded in your mind long ago. Isn't that it? You can no more *try* something different than Samson can *say* something different."

David nodded thoughtfully. He'd known, of course, that he'd been imitating Samson's style of speech, but he hadn't consciously meant anything by it.

"You mustn't accept that, my child. But now at least you understand what the problem is, don't you?"

"Yes, I guess so."

"Then you must use this understanding to break free. Now. At once. We'll help you."

"All right."

The old man breathed a sigh, his long sheep's face heavy with concern, and stood up to leave. Then he paused for a few moments, staring into the distance as if considering a fresh idea. "Remember this, David," he said at last. "You are ultimately not like Samson. Samson is only metal and wires and old recording cylinders."

David nodded absently.

"No. You're not listening to me. Samson is only metal and wires and old recording cylinders."

"I know that."

The old man shook his head impatiently. "Perhaps from the beginning you've *known* too much that you should have been trying to *learn*."

David was still trying to sort out this dark saying when Dee turned away to mount the stairs. After a few minutes he decided to follow him, at least to the second floor, where he intended to return to his room and his bed.

He was halfway up the stairs when he became aware that someone was descending in the semi-darkness overhead. He didn't know who it was, but he seemed to be making heavy work of it, clinging to the handrail, his legs splaying out awkwardly like those of a vaudeville drunk. But when he began to speak, with a whir and a clank and a crackling hiss, David knew.

"David!" Samson squawked, lurching down a step. "Look!"

His heart constricted as if in the grip of a powerful hand, David backed down a step.

"Look, David! I'm *walking*!" The familiar muffled voice trembled with joy and pride. The mannequin stumbled down another step and would have fallen if it hadn't been grappling the rail. David retreated in front of it.

"I never *walked!* Never!" It flung out a hand. "Here! Take my hand!"

David charged past it, knocking it off its feet and sending it tumbling down the stairs in a muddle of twisted limbs.

"David, wait!" it groaned. "Listen to me—"

But David was already halfway down the hall to his room. When he had the door closed behind him, he leaned on it, his breath raw in his throat, until he was sure no one was coming after him. Then he quickly struggled out of his clothes, climbed into bed, covered his head with a pillow, and let the roar of the fever drown out his thoughts.

When he awoke to find Marianne standing beside the bed, David had the nightmarish feeling he was going to relive the day. But her message was different this time: "Andrea would like you to rake the patio."

"What?" He was now feeling very lightheaded indeed and was sure he'd misheard her.

"Andrea would like you to rake the patio."

His laugh was half a whimper. "Rake the *patio?*"

"You know. The redwood chips. She said to tell you that she'd appreciate it."

Laughter welled up inside him like bubbles in champagne, and he lay shaking helplessly until it all frothed away.

"Well?" Marianne demanded.

"What time is it?"

She glanced at her wrist. "Four-thirty."

Exhausted, he pulled himself up onto an elbow. "Tell Andrea that I will be honored to rake the patio. Deeply honored."

Marianne gave him an expressionless nod and left him to stagger into his clothes.

By now he was definitely staggering.

He paused at the entrance to the upper living room and very nearly went back. Samson, motionless in his wheel chair, was sitting directly between him and the patio. After watching through several minutes, he risked stepping inside, and the mannequin remained silent and inert. Nevertheless, he approached it ready to flee and edged his way around it well out of reach. He was glad to be outside and able to close the sliding glass door on it.

The rake was standing beside the door—a heavy, old-fashioned garden rake, not a leaf rake. He picked it up and looked around with a sigh at the huge expanse of redwood chips dotted with groupings of outdoor furniture. He tried out the rake and soon found the work easy enough, though it seemed to have little effect except where there were obvious mounds and gouges. In fact, after a few minutes he began to find it rather soothing. With very little effort (throw out the head of the rake and draw it back), he was restoring order to what had become chaotic.

When this is all over, he thought muzzily, *perhaps I'll become a gardener.*

He wasn't pleased when Andrea, Dee, and Marianne walked out of the living room and sat down around an umbrella-shaded table, distracting him from his reverie.

As if responding to an afterthought, Andrea gave the patio a careful appraisal and said, "It looks very nice, David."

"I'm not finished," he replied gruffly.

"Don't do more than you feel up to," she said.

"I'm fine." And in fact, except for an annoyingly persistent whine in his ears, he felt better than he had all day. He went on throwing out the head of the rake and dragging it back.

After another ten minutes, however, Andrea said, "I really think you should stop now, David. Come and sit down."

Grudgingly, David straightened up and walked over to join them. He set the rake down by his chair, intending to finish the job when they left.

"Well?" he said.

Behind him he heard the rumble of the sliding glass door and, turning around, he saw Dudley Case manhandling a heavily laden wheelbarrow out onto the patio—spoiling, David noted, work he'd already done. He stopped after a few feet and upended the barrow to dump its contents with a crash. David blinked over them for a moment, trying to assemble the ungainly mass into a recognizable shape.

Then he had it: it was a naked human body. He nodded, dazed.

Of course: *Mike.* Naturally the old man would have brought Mike with him.

Having parked the barrow by the house, Case parked himself beside it, arms folded, waiting.

David looked at the faces around the table and saw Marianne give Andrea and Dee a questioning glance. They nodded encouragingly.

She stood up, went over to the sprawled body, and looked back in hesitation. "What do I do?"

"You have to get his attention, my dear," Dee said. "A sharp rap on the skull works well."

After tugging one of Mike's arms aside to get at it, she bent down and gave his head a blow. When nothing happened she gave it another.

"Dudley," Dee said, "get him up on his hands and knees. That should help."

The Navajo pushed himself away from the house and wrestled the body up into position. Mike's head hung down to his chest, and the old man told him to pull it up. Case put a hand under Mike's chin and lifted it.

"Now, my dear."

Marianne gave him a sharp rap on the temple and his eyes popped open. Case removed his hand and the head stayed up.

As Marianne bent forward to speak into Mike's ear, the old man interrupted her. "First you have to point him, Marianne. In this condition, he's worse than an idiot."

"Point him?"

"Take his head in your hands and point it right at what you want him to see."

She pointed Mike's head at David.

"Get down and make sure you've got it right."

She put her head down alongside Mike's and looked up into David's eyes.

David looked back numbly.

"Good. Now tell him to *see*."

"See," Marianne said.

"Very forcefully, my dear."

"*See!*"

Mike's eyes widened and he blinked once.

"Good. Now you may proceed."

Marianne moved her lips to Mike's ear and said: "*Tear him to pieces.*"

Mike lowered his head wearily for a moment, as if this were too much to ask of him. Then, as Marianne backed away, he lurched to his feet and fixed a bleary gaze on David, his head bobbing stupidly.

David looked around helplessly at Andrea and Dee. They nodded, smiling, but their eyes were grave, full of some earnest but unreadable message.

He picked up the rake and moved away from the table. Mike's eyes tracked the movement, and he took a wobbly step forward.

David swung the rake at Mike's head but was too far away. The cast-iron teeth whistled through the air inches in front of his nose. Taking no notice of it, not even blinking, Mike staggered a pace closer, and David swung again.

This time he was too close, and it was only the handle that met Mike's head; nevertheless, it was enough to crush the side of his face and sweep him off his feet. He crashed into the redwood chips and lay there blinking slowly for a minute, as if pondering this unexpected reverse. Then he began to gather his limbs under him in an effort to get back on his feet.

Before he managed it, David swung again. This time he had the range; the end of the rake-head buried itself in Mike's skull and he sprawled into the chips, jerking the rake out of David's hands. Grabbing the rake and working it back and forth to get it out of Mike's head, David tore away a slab of bone, exposing the mangled brain underneath. The wound didn't bleed.

Only one of Mike's eyes was blinking now, at long intervals.

After moving around so that he had Mike's head at his feet, David raised the rake like an axe and smashed it into his neck. Two more blows severed the head completely, and Mike stopped blinking.

For a full minute David stood there staring down at the body, waiting for it to move. Finally satisfied that it wasn't going to, he turned to the others.

Case and Marianne were standing by the house, watching him without expression. Andrea, her eyes down, was listlessly tapping a cigarette ash into a tray. John Dee was slumped back in his chair, looking profoundly discouraged.

Suddenly David began to shiver uncontrollably. The rake slipped from his hand, and he wrapped his arms around himself. His teeth were chattering as if driven by a motor.

"Take David in, would you, Dudley?" Dee said, looking up. "He should be in bed. And Marianne, you might find some extra blankets for him."

In a moment David felt the Navajo's hand on his arm, but his body was so occupied with shivering that he couldn't get it to move. His legs were locked in place.

"Come on, David," Case said gently. "You'll feel better in bed."

With a painful effort, David shuffled one foot forward a few inches.

"That's right. It'll be easier once you get moving." Little by little, Case guided him into the house, across the living room, and down the stairs to his room, where he helped him out of his clothes and into his bed.

"C-c-c-old," David said.

"You've got a chill."

"I sure d-d-d-do," he replied with a giggle.

Marianne arrived with an armful of blankets they piled on top of him. Case began tucking them in around him as Marianne left.

"Better?"

"Y-y-yes. Thanks."

The Navajo nodded, smiling, and turned to go.

"Wait," David said. He turned back. "What was I *s-s-s-supposed* to do?"

Case studied him solemnly. "Something."

"Like what?"

He shrugged. "Anything."

"Anything?"

"Anything but what David Kennesey of Runnell, Indiana, would do."

"I don't understand."

"I know. I'm sorry."

David sighed as the shivering ebbed away under the warmth of the blankets. "Andrea said . . ."

"Yes?"

"Andrea said you could . . . teach me."

"Yes."

"Would you do that?"

The Navajo paused. "Yes."

Smiling peacefully, David closed his eyes. "I'd like that."

Case waited for a few moments, then shook his head and walked out, closing the door quietly behind him.

In the middle of the night David was tormented by dreams of suffocation: a great weight was pressing him down into the mattress, and his lungs were fighting for air. He awoke drenched in sweat, and found Andrea, totally nude, sitting back on her haunches in the middle of his chest.

"Andrea," he gasped. "I can't breathe."

"You *can* breathe, David."

"Yes, barely. But why are you *sitting* on me?"

"I want you to see me."

"I can see you."

"I know."

David tried to laugh but could only manage a choked cough.

"Could you bring me some water?" he asked.

She smiled. "I knew you were thirsty."

David passed his tongue over his parched lips. "Well . . . could you bring me some?"

"I came to bring you water, David. But you mustn't reject it."

"I won't reject it."

"This water will wash away your fever and make you well. But you must accept it."

"I will, Andrea."

"Very well. Watch."

Andrea stretched out her arms, and for the first time David was really aware of her nakedness, of her strong shoulders and full breasts. As he watched, her body began to glow with a pale green phosphorescence and seemed to become gradually translucent. He blinked his eyes and shook his head to rid himself of the illusion, but it persisted and grew. Her translucency faded to transparency and the phosphorescence clarified into an emerald glow.

She had become a statue sculpted in sea water. She looked down at him, and all her features were there—lips, eyes, nose—but they were shaped in water now, not flesh. Behind them moved schools of tiny fish, mists of algae, trails of wavering bubbles, strands of floating vegetation.

She nodded silently at her arms, her legs, her torso—David understood that she had no breath with which to speak now—and he saw that the whole of her body teemed with busy life. She was heavy with it, composed of it. She slowly leaned forward until her face hovered above his, and he gazed with wonderment into her sightless eyes. Her lips moved, and the word he saw formed there was: *Breathe*. David took a deep breath and held it.

Then she put her lips to his and flowed into him and over him, and he was suddenly swept away and engulfed.

When he opened his eyes, he was floating in the depths of an endless sea. Still holding his breath, he spun around slowly, expecting to find Andrea floating beside him. But he was alone. Completely alone. Except for the lazily wandering fish and the green glow of the sea all around him.

He spun around again, and his stomach clenched in panic. A sea bass gazed at him incuriously and swam away. Looking up, David saw that the glow was brighter overhead. His arms thrashing, he began to swim upward toward what he hoped was the surface. After a few moments, he was sure he was right—but it seemed impossibly far away. He struggled on, his lungs trembling, straining toward the inevitable explosion.

A hundred yards, he thought. He could see the sun now, smiling down on a world of clouds and trees and birds—a world just moments beyond reach.

At thirty yards, when he was certain he wasn't going to make it, his limbs went berserk and began flailing the water uselessly.

At fifteen yards, his lungs burst, and, back arching in a final convulsion of agony, David gave himself up to death.

CHAPTER 44

After plunging into unconsciousness during Andrea's visit, David slept fitfully, tormented by feverish, incomprehensible dreams that seemed to drag on for days. In all of them he was in pain and desperately thirsty. Around nine o'clock the aches and thirst of his dreams imperceptibly became the aches and thirst of consciousness as he wallowed in his sweat-sodden bedclothes; the sheets were silk, but under his painfully sensitive hands they were as rough as burlap. With a tremendous effort, he pulled himself upright, feeling as if his head were about to topple from his shoulders.

"Like some water?"

The voice came to him as an echo from every surface in the room, and David had to look around to find its source.

John Dee, smiling gently, was sitting in a chair at his side.

"Yes," David whispered hoarsely. "Water."

While he drank, two rivulets of water coursing down his chin on either side of the glass, Dee plumped up the pillows behind him. He sank back into them, and the glass rolled from his hand.

"I'm sick," he said, sounding surprised.

The old man nodded gravely. "Yes, I'm afraid you're very sick indeed. It's been a long, long time since I practiced medicine, but the symptoms are unmistakable. Septicemia—blood poisoning."

"You're a doctor?"

"Long ago."

"Am I going to die?"

"Yes, I'm afraid so."

David thought about this for a few moments. "I don't want to die."

Doctor Dee gave him a kindly smile. "Oh, I think you do."

"Why do you think that?"

"Because, in a very real sense, you're dying by your own hand." He touched his cheek on the spot corresponding to David's wound.

"I don't understand."

The old man shrugged. "I suppose we may as well talk. We have some hours to pass."

"Go on."

"I don't know that I can satisfy you, David. I think that, no matter how many questions I answer, you'll find fresh questions to ask. However, I'll do the best I can." He sighed and spent a few moments gathering his thoughts. "Twenty years ago you went venturing into the hills beside the Scioto River in Ohio. Do you remember?"

"I remember. How did you know about it?"

"You were following someone."

David gave him a puzzled look.

"Don't you understand who it was?"

Frowning, he spent a while thinking about this. "It was Andrea?"

The old man nodded.

"Ah," David sighed. After a few moments he shook his head regretfully. "Yes, I see."

"She waited for you that night, David. She felt the hunger that drove you, and, if you'd pressed on, you would have been accepted. But you succumbed to your fear of seeming ridiculous and turned back."

"Yes."

"Twenty years later you went looking again, but those twenty years had hardened in you tendencies that made you unfit for the company you sought: the tendency to reject anything outside your compass as unreal or unworthy of attention, the tendency to fortify yourself within a shrine of self-regard, the tendency to scale everyone against yourself. All these things defeated you.

"From the outset, you were like someone who avidly sets out to explore a foreign country but stays only at the Hilton and associates only with other tourists. You happily gave yourself up to be duped by those of your own kind but were rigidly on guard against those who were trying to guide you into the company you set out to find. You refused every invitation, failed every test, resisted every effort to jolt you from the ruts of your old life. You wanted to shatter the walls that imprison you, but you wanted more to crouch behind them and protect them from assault."

"I didn't understand what was going on," David protested feebly.

"My dear child! You ventured forth to discover uncharted lands of experience and then fled in terror when they proved to be truly uncharted. You wanted to probe beneath the surface of the piddling life your culture gives you to lead—but you wouldn't tolerate being disconcerted. Oh my, no. You wanted your adventure to be all nicely under your control; in fact, you wanted it to be indistinguishable from the life you'd abandoned."

"True."

"Of all of us, only Dudley came close to smashing through to rescue you from your prison. By humiliating you and forcing you to do something you thought absurd, he shattered your fortifications."

"Yes."

"And having done this, he told you to go back to the house. Do you remember?"

"Yes."

"Why did he want you to go back to the house?"

"I don't know."

"Because Andrea was waiting for you. In that moment you were free—vulnerable in a way you hadn't been since childhood—and she would have made you hers."

David nodded bleakly.

"But you wouldn't listen to him. You desperately wanted to go off and rebuild the fortifications around your little shrine of self-regard."

"Yes." David spent a few minutes absorbing this into his system, wishing the truth didn't taste so much like poison. Finally he asked: "Then why did you bother with me at all?"

"Ah. Andrea hadn't forgotten you. She still wanted you, though there seemed little real hope of breaking you out of your prison at this late date."

David shook his head groggily. "If that's an answer, I don't understand it."

"No, I don't suppose so," the old man said with something like embarrassment. "It was necessary either to win you or to put you to use."

"I still don't understand."

"I'm being evasive to spare your feelings, David. You would have been valued in yourself, but through your own choices you put yourself beyond reach. Still, you have served your purpose as a tool."

"A tool for what?"

The old man shook his head. "That really doesn't concern you."

David closed his eyes and listened to the sound of his breathing for a few minutes, trying to make sense of it all. "Is that why you tried to kill me?" he asked at last.

Dee frowned, puzzled. "We never tried to kill you. We protected you."

"You protected me?"

"Certainly. You would have frozen to death that night in the hills if we hadn't woken you and herded you back to your car. And who did you think dispatched those two in the mobile home and drove off the dog?"

"Yes, but . . . Marianne told Mike to kill me."

The old man sighed. "From the very beginning you've stubbornly refused to understand anything."

"What do you mean?"

"A moment ago I said that you scale everyone against yourself.

Some you perceive as smaller than you, and those you treat with contempt; others you perceive as greater than you, and those you treat with mindless awe. This is principally what made it impossible for you to find a place among us. Dudley and Marianne are of your own kind, but you refused to take a place beside them, because you perceived Dudley to be smaller than you and Marianne to be greater than you. Do you see?"

"I don't think so."

"Dudley is a master of winds, but you treated him with contempt —and will pay for it with your life. Marianne is just a child, really, but you wouldn't dare to test your arm against hers when it came to throwing stones."

"But that doesn't explain about Mike."

"Poor Mike. To anyone but you it would have been obvious that he was no more than a dog—less than a dog, really, because a dog is faithful to its master. But Mike, as you saw, was faithful to no one; he obeyed anyone who commanded him. That was what Marianne was trying to show you—but you had already made up your mind that she was greater than you. If you had dared to see yourself as her peer, you would have told Mike to kill *her*—or merely to lie down and go to sleep."

"And he would have done it?"

"Certainly. He would have done it that first night in the mountains as well. But, having scaled everything to yourself, you felt you had no choice but to flee in panic. You simply would not test yourself. You would not risk finding out where you stood in relation to me or Marianne or Dudley—or to the universe itself. Ultimately you refused to risk *anything*."

"Yes, I see." David nodded mournfully, just beginning to see how much he had to grieve over. After a few minutes he drifted off to sleep again. On waking, he drank another glass of water and asked: "Who are you, anyway?"

The doctor smiled. "And who are *you*?"

"Who am I?"

"Who are *all* of you."

David blinked over this for a minute. "We're . . . people."

Dee raised his brows humorously. "And Andrea and I aren't people?"

"I mean . . . we're the people who *live* here."

"And where do you imagine we live, David?"

"I guess I mean that we belong here."

"And what special wisdom is it that enables you to determine who belongs here and who does not?"

"Well . . . We *grew up* here."

"As did we, child." He shook his head in amusement. "Did you think we were invaders from outer space? No, we've been here longer than you, though we haven't always taken this shape. Yet we know no better who we are than your people know who they are. Like you, we're simply *here*."

David sighed and closed his eyes.

"Oh, I know what you want, David. You want to know how we fit into your *scale*—into your kind's understanding of the universe. Isn't that so?"

"I guess."

"I can't really give you a definitive answer—because your kind has fitted us into so many *different* understandings of the universe. In our time, we've been called sprites and nymphs and sylphs and satyrs and dryads. We've been called the Fair and the Good Folk. We have been called trolls, goblins, kobolds, and gnomes. We have been called Robin Goodfellow. We've been called Hill Watchers—which is perhaps the closest to a name we might choose for ourselves. We've been called werewolves and vampires and shape-shifters. We've been called familiars, demons, fiends, witches, and devils." The old man paused to smile. "There's a young man in Chicago who calls us yoo-hoos. We've been called guardians. We've even been called angels. For that matter, we've even been called gods. We were known to every ancient people —and are known now to every people who still live, shall we say, in the open. Do you find enlightenment in any of that?"

"Some, yes."

"Good. I'm pleased."

"But what are you *doing* here?"

The old man chuckled. "You never learn, David. Do you know what *you're* doing here?"

David subsided into his pillows with a deep sigh. "I guess, once upon a time, I *thought* I knew."

"But now you're no longer sure."

"No."

"Then perhaps you've learned something after all."

David fell silent and in a few minutes drifted into sleep.

On waking an hour later, he began to talk about Ellen and Tim and about people John Dee had never heard of: Bob Gaines and Gil Bingaman and others. He was talking to himself, really, knitting together the various parts of his life, but the old man understood he had to be there as a silent, nodding audience. It was as if, curiosity satisfied and anxiety stilled, David had suddenly found time to revisit rooms within himself that had long ago been locked up and forgotten.

His naps soon became longer and longer, and in between them the thread of his thoughts became more and more frayed. He exacted incomprehensible promises, which the doctor had to repeat and solemnly swear to. He asked for forgiveness from everyone, and the old man assured him it was already given. At dusk he pulled himself up and took a long, strange look into Dee's eyes.

"You seem . . . benevolent," he whispered. "You all seem *benevolent.*"

The old man smiled, knowing that, although David was speaking from delirium, he desperately wanted a reply. "No, you mustn't think that. We're not benevolent. It's *your* kind that is benevolent. But neither are we exactly malevolent. Actually, we're no more all alike than you are—but none of us would be so mad as to pretend to *benevolence.*"

David listened to this with an intense stare of amazement.

"Ah!" he breathed and fell back into his pillows as if all his questions had been answered. "Ah," he said again and fell into a deep, exhausted sleep.

He awoke a few hours before dawn and was momentarily disoriented to find himself lying on the ground back in the hills, feeling wonderfully fit. Then he laughed gloriously as he recognized where he was and *when* he was: these were not the barren, rocky hills of New Mexico. He sprang up and the strength in his seventeen-year-old legs was so great that his feet left the ground, and he laughed again. He stretched out his arms till they were ready to part from his body and felt the power of life surge and tingle through the muscles of his back.

So it had all been a dream.

Poor Gil was sitting back there somewhere, fidgeting and fretting, chewing his fingernails to the elbow wondering where the hell David was.

Ellen (if there even *was* an Ellen) had just finished ninth grade in a suburb of Saint Louis; she would find someone—someone who would make her happier than David ever had done in his dream.

And Tim—Oh God, how rapturously wonderful!—Tim had not been born to feel the knife of David's betrayal! Tears of joy flooded his eyes as he realized what a stupendous reprieve he'd been given: a brand new life, whole and pristine.

He looked into the sky and saw it was no wonder he'd had to stop and take a nap; the moon was nearly set—he'd been wandering for hours out here. No matter; he felt more alert, more alive now than he'd ever felt in his life. It was as if he'd been plugged into a thousand-watt battery. He began to run, and the hills rose and fell under his feet like images on a screen—he could run forever if he had to. But there was no question of that. He knew where Andrea was now. Why on earth had it baffled him before? She was waiting for him at the Scioto, just a few miles ahead. He could feel her there, just as she felt him.

"I'm coming!" he shouted, but simply for joy—she already knew he was coming.

In a few minutes he saw her ahead on the crest of a hill overlooking the river. As before, she stood with her back to him, facing the eastern horizon, where a smudge of amber light heralded the approaching dawn. He slowed to a walk, feeling that to arrive on the run would hardly suit the solemnity—no, the majesty—of the moment.

Soon he was climbing the last knoll, and he could see the breeze off the water lifting her hair and rippling her gown. It wasn't until he stood at her side that she turned her head to look down at him. Looking up into her dark, smiling eyes, he felt profoundly, intimately *acknowledged*, as if all were known, all accepted between the two of them. Exploring those eyes, David wanted to plunge into them, to lose himself forever in their black depths. After a few moments she gave him a welcoming nod and turned back to the dawn.

Following her gaze, he gasped, electrified by what he saw.

The Scioto. . .

My God, the Scioto wasn't a river, it was an *ocean*, stretching out below them to the horizon and beyond—far beyond. And for all these years—like everyone else!—he'd seen nothing here but a muddy little river. How incredibly blind he'd been!

A great, almost suffocating, laughter swelled up inside him as he looked anew at the glowing hills around him, at the red rim of the sun hovering over the water, at the vast, heaving sea at his feet. Tears welled up in his eyes and tumbled down over his cheeks as, feeling joyously small and foolish, he finally *understood*.

CHAPTER 45

Any piece of paper taken by the wind, no matter what it is, must go somewhere. This one meandered northward up the San Luis valley, crossing and recrossing the Rio Grande, hissed across the sand dunes west of the Sangre de Cristos, fluttered through the Poncha Pass, then tumbled northward across the eastern slopes of the Sawatch range for nearly a hundred miles. During the still hour before dawn, it rested in the dry foliage of a chamisa bush. Then an easterly breeze plucked it away, carried it across Highway 24, and flattened it against the door of a motel room, where Tim found it when he and Howard were returning from breakfast.

By agreement, breakfast was to have been their last meal in Colorado. They'd driven up from Gallup on Friday, talked to Charles Petronis Saturday morning—learning nothing beyond the fact that he had, for some undiscussable reason, given David a thirty-thousand-dollar car—then spent the rest of the day (at Tim's fanatical insistence) simply waiting. Now, the plan was, they were going to turn in the car in Denver and fly back to Chicago.

Naturally, the arrival of David's letter changed all that. Howard, instinctively suspicious, spent an hour trying to find out who had put it there but finally had to admit that it didn't much matter; it was addressed to Tim, who certified the handwriting as his father's, and it was unarguably a lead that had to be followed. They discussed calling the phone number on the letterhead and agreed that, since they were going to Taos whatever they heard over the phone, they might as well just go.

So they went.

They arrived in Taos around six and spent an hour trying to find someone who could direct them to Morningstar Path. Not only could no one direct them to it, no one had even heard of it. But it seemed there was nothing unusual about that. If a millionaire wanted to buy herself a piece of wilderness, build a house, and grade a road in to it, she could name it whatever she pleased.

Finally they decided to check into a motel and, much as their inclinations were against it, to use the phone. It rang a dozen times and Howard was about to hang up when a young woman's voice answered.

"Yes," Howard said. "I'm wondering if you can help me. I got a letter today from someone staying there at your number or someone who may have been staying there a few days ago. David Kennesey?"

"There's no one here right now," the girl said. "Call back tomorrow."

"Wait. Can you give me directions to Morningstar Path?"

The girl paused. "You're in Taos?"

"Yes."

"Where are you?"

"Does that matter?"

"How can I give you directions if I don't know where you are?"

"True," he said, and named their motel.

She seemed to think for a moment. "There's no one here right now. Call back tomorrow."

"Hey, wait—" Howard began indignantly, but she'd already hung up. He immediately redialed the number but gave up after listening to it ring through a full three minutes.

He gave Tim a helpless shrug and they went downstairs to dinner. Over coffee, he asked the waitress if she'd ever heard of Morningstar Path.

She shook her head. "Not that that means much," she said. "There are lots of roads around here I don't know. I've only been in Taos a year." He asked where she was from and smiled when she told him Bloomington, Indiana—less than a hundred miles from Runnell.

A few minutes later a wiry man dressed like a thirties gangster sauntered over to their table. He had a smug, foxy face and a mop of brick-red hair that looked like you'd need a curry comb to get through it. He didn't introduce himself, but Ellen had known him as Nick Wolf.

Howard distrusted him on sight.

"Hey," he said breezily, "I heard you asking the girl about Morningstar Path."

"That's right," Howard said.

"Yeah, well, I know where it is."

"Do you?"

The skepticism in Howard's voice seemed to disconcert him, and he glanced at the two of them uneasily before answering. "Yeah, well, I do."

Howard gazed at him coldly, and Tim decided to take a hand. "Could you give us directions? Or draw us a map?"

"Yeah! Yeah!" the man said enthusiastically. "That's what I was gonna say! I could draw you a map! All right if I sit down?"

"Sit down," Tim told him, ignoring Howard's disapproving look.

He took out a ballpoint pen, turned over a place mat, and hesitated. "You're not thinking of going out there *tonight*, though, are you?"

"Why not?" Howard inquired aggressively.

The man chuckled. "'Cause you'd lose your ass out there in the dark, that's why."

"Could *you* find it in the dark?"

"Well . . . sure, man. I know the road."

Howard gave him an ingenuous smile. "Then maybe we don't need a map. Maybe you could show us the way."

The man stared at him, his face suddenly the color of old putty.

"Hey, man, you're being *unfriendly*." The idea seemed to inflame him, and he bared his teeth. "I don't *like* people being unfriendly around me."

Howard nodded, his curiosity satisfied. "I'm sorry. I didn't realize it would be such an imposition. We'd appreciate the map, though."

"Oh sure, sure," Wolf said, at once turning his attention to the place mat. "Okay. Here is where we are. This is Kit Carson Road. You gotta go back to the stoplight and turn left onto the Santa Fe Road. That'll take you right out of town. The tricky part starts about three miles later when you turn off the highway here." He went on to describe each branching of the road as he sketched it in. "When you get onto Morningstar—there ain't no sign or nothing—you can't miss, because the road ends right at the house," he finished up.

Howard's lips twitched with a smile, but he frowned it away. In all his experience, he'd never been offered a chance to play this hoary trick.

"What house?" he asked innocently. "I didn't say anything about a house."

The redhead's reaction came in three parts: blank incomprehension, alarm, and resentment. "What house?" he cried, thinking furiously. "What do you mean, what house?" Then he found the solution. "Hey, man, there ain't nothing on Morningstar *but* this house! So, anybody goes to Morningstar goes to this one house, see?" He grinned in triumph, his resentment forgotten.

"I see," Howard said.

"Well, I gotta go," Wolf said, rising hastily. "You two have a nice evening."

"We'll do our best," Howard replied to his retreating back. Tim gave him a curious look.

"Are we going out there?"

"I suspect it would be a waste of time, Tim, even if we found it."

"Why?"

"Because they obviously don't want us out there tonight. Tomorrow yes, but not tonight."

"I must have missed something," Tim said with a frown.

"The woman on the phone said she had to know where we were so she could give us directions, but as soon as I told her she hung up. Two hours later our red-headed friend strolls in and obligingly draws us a map, after making sure we won't use it tonight. Not a very subtle message."

"Detective work, huh?"

Howard chuckled. "Detective work, kindergarten level."

"But we could still go out there."

"People aren't obliged to answer the door, Tim."

"True."

It was a little too early to think of sleeping, so they took a tour of the closed shops along Kit Carson Road. Then Howard sent Tim off to bed and went into the bar, where he had a couple of sleep-inducers and a pleasant conversation with an elderly gentleman in a baggy old cardigan sweater.

CHAPTER 46

Following the map on the back of the place mat, they got lost only once, guessing wrong at one turning that had been omitted—insurance, Howard thought, in case they had ventured forth the night before in defiance of the redhead's warning. There was something about the house he didn't like when it came into view—something beyond its weird modernist lines—but he wasn't able to put his finger on it till later, when he was inside.

As they pulled up into the graveled area in front of the house, two men, one of them a Native American, came through the front door carrying a long wooden crate that they shoved into the back of a pickup truck. Howard parked so as not to block their access to the road.

They were met at the door by a striking-looking woman whose dark hair shone with copper lights. She was dressed in a simple dress of dark green jersey, belted loosely at the waist, but she wore it with a regal air.

After listening coolly to Howard's explanation of their presence there, she told them to come in and led the way through a vast, dark room that (if he were being polite) Howard would have described as grotesque; privately, he considered it creepy. It wasn't properly a room at all; it was a cavern, out of all human scale, and he felt diminished and insignificant in it. He didn't pause as they passed the ruined stone head, but he raised an eyebrow at it. As they mounted the stairs, he tried to take a peek inside the hole blasted in the mirrored wall, but it was too far away and too dark to see anything. He wondered what had gone on here to produce such devastation. The upper living room, designed for recognizably human activities, was more to his taste.

The woman, who had introduced herself as Andrea de la Mare, settled them on a sofa at the back of the room and called out:

"Marianne! Coffee! For three." The last had been half a question, which she directed at Tim with her eyes.

"I'm allowed," Tim said, smiling. "In moderation."

She smiled back and sat down opposite them across a low table.

"So," Howard said, getting down to business, "I take it David Kennesey was here when he wrote that letter, since it was on your stationery."

"Yes, that's right."

"But he's not here now?" She shook her head, smiling apologetically. "Did he leave last night, by any chance?"

"You're very astute, Mr. Scheim. But I'm not quite sure why I'm answering your questions. What is your interest in David?"

Howard frowned. "None, as a personal matter. I'm asking on his son's behalf."

"But his son's right here. I'm sure he can ask his own questions." Turning to the boy, she asked, "What is it you'd like to know, Tim?"

At this point Marianne arrived with a tray. When they'd all been served, Tim said: "What was my father doing here?"

"He was looking for something. When he left you and your mother, you understand it was because he was looking for something."

"I guess so. But what was he looking for?"

Andrea smiled. "He wasn't completely sure himself, Tim. That's why he isn't here to greet you. He would have been if he'd found what he wanted. As it happened, he had to leave, had to carry on the search elsewhere. Do you understand?"

"No, not really."

"What I'm telling you, Tim, is that it's time to let your father go. He's in the midst of his journey as you're in the midst of yours. He would have liked to have you with him, but he knew when he left that this was impossible. It was necessary for him to take a path different from yours, and now you must leave him to it."

"Excuse me," Howard said harshly, "but you seem to be taking a lot on yourself here. According to Mr. Kennesey's letter, he wanted Tim with him."

"What exactly did he say, Mr. Scheim?"

Howard dug the letter out of his jacket pocket. "He says, 'I should have brought you with me. I wish I had you with me now.'"

"'I wish'? It seems to me that 'I wish' falls far short of 'I want,' Mr. Scheim. If he had intended to have Tim with him, why didn't he wait for him here?"

"Miss de la Mare," Howard said, "I don't want to seem rude, but the fact is that we only have your word for any of this. For all we know . . ."

"Yes?"

"For all we know, David could be right here in the house."

"He isn't, but feel free to look anywhere you like."

"That's not exactly the point. The point is that we didn't come here to have you explain David's letter to us. We didn't come here to hear what you think Tim should do next. We came here to get some information, and when we have it, Tim and I will decide what to do next."

Andrea nodded, smiling. "You make it very plain, Mr. Scheim. But of course it's within my discretion to give you information or to send you away."

"I realize that. I'm not *demanding* information. I'm asking for it on behalf of a boy who lost both father and mother within a single week, whose whole life has been turned upside down."

"Very reasonably put." Andrea turned to the boy. "Tim, you haven't known me for very long, but will you trust me for a few minutes?"

Tim looked up, and for a long moment they gravely searched each other's eyes. "What do you want me to do?"

"Let me talk to Mr. Scheim alone for a bit. We have business that's just between the two of us."

The boy sent Howard a questioning look. It was answered with a nod; with Tim out of the way, Howard could deal a bit more forcefully with the situation.

Tim stood up and looked around doubtfully.

"Why don't you go out onto the patio?" Andrea suggested with a smile. "You might find someone you can talk to there."

Out on the patio Tim quickly spotted the man in the wheelchair, off to one side. He was sitting beside a table with his back to Tim and seemed to be gazing at the distant horizon. Tim looked back at the house, but Howard and Andrea were out of sight from this angle.

He was surprised and a little worried when the man didn't turn as he approached, his feet crunching in the redwood chips; if he was hard-of-hearing, Tim didn't much relish the idea of having a conversation with him. But after a few more paces he paused and a delighted frown crossed his face as he saw that the thing was a life-size dummy of some kind. He went around to the front of it and peered into its face. He jerked back, startled when its glass eyes shifted to meet his. After a clank, a whir, and the sound of a scratchy needle on a record, a squawky, muffled voice came from its chest:

"Hello, Tim. They told me you were coming."

Tim gawked at it wide-eyed. "They did?"

"Yes. I'm sorry I can't shake hands with you. My name is Samson."

Not quite understanding this, Tim asked him why he couldn't shake hands. The thing responded with a wheezing laugh that was rather ghastly to hear.

"My arm doesn't work that way, Tim. Do you want to see?"

"Yes."

"Go around to the back of the chair. On the crosspiece at the top, you'll find three levers. Do you see them?"

"Yes."

"Good. Pull over the top lever."

Samson's right hand jerked up from his lap and dropped over the side of the chair.

"I don't know exactly how it works. I suppose it's an arrangement of wires and pulleys. Now feel under my coat for a button at the point where my arm meets my back,.."

Samson's fingers snapped closed.

"Now pull over the middle lever."

His arm rose as if presenting Tim with something he'd picked up.

"Good. Now pull over the bottom lever."

His arm descended and his hand returned to his lap.

"That's my repertoire of arm movements, Tim."

"I see." Tim moved around in front of him and sat down.

"But yesterday I *walked*. No, it was the day before. I've never done that before. It was tremendously exciting."

"I'll bet. Why don't your lips move when you talk?"

"Oh, I think that would spoil the effect entirely. Don't you?"

"I don't know."

"I'd look like a ventriloquist's dummy."

"I suppose."

"Would you like to see how my head moves?"

When the glass door had rumbled shut behind Tim, Andrea gave Howard a grave smile and said, "I'm sorry you've settled on the idea that I'm your enemy. I'm not quite sure how that happened."

Howard shrugged. "It's my job to be wary."

"Of course it is. Nonetheless, I want you to know that you have no enemies here. We think of you as one of us."

"One of who?"

Andrea smiled and shook her head. "Tell me what you think has been going on here."

"Where is 'here'?"

She smiled again. "It's where you are. It's where Tim is, too, obviously. But I'll rephrase the question. What do you think all this has been about, Howard? Do you mind if I call you Howard?"

A heavy cloud of depression seemed to sink into his brain, dimming hope and comprehension. "I'm sorry to keep sounding like a parrot," he said huskily, "but what do you mean by *all this*?"

Andrea thought for a moment. "I don't know if the story will be familiar to you, but it's said that, before Jesus began his ministry, he was led away by the Spirit into the desert to be tempted by the devil. In one of these temptations, the devil took him to the top of a high mountain and showed him all the kingdoms of the world in their glory, saying, 'All this will be yours if you will but fall down and do me homage.' According to the story, Jesus replied, 'Begone, Satan!' But would you like to know what he really said? He said, 'What do you mean by *all this*?'"

Howard stared at her blankly, his mouth half open.

She went to a set of built-in drawers at the side of the room, and after a brief search returned with a familiar object: a set of the Rider Tarot cards. She took them out of the box, shuffled them three times, and handed them to Howard.

"Three times, please," she said.

"Don't be silly."

"Indulge me, Howard, please. You don't have a plane to catch."

He shuffled them three times and cut them. After this, he was directed to draw off the top card and turn it over between them.

"This is you," she said. "The King of Pentacles. The suit of pentacles is generally about work, craftsmanship, and fortune. Like this king, you're a dark man, and you came to me over a matter of business. Turn up the next card and cover the king with it."

When he had done so, she said, "This is what covers you, what's presently setting the tone of your life, what's influencing you and will continue to influence you in the near future. It's the Seven of Swords. As you see, it depicts a crafty fellow—a fellow just like you— sneaking away from an armed camp with five swords in his hands. But he seems to have overlooked two others lying on the ground behind him. You armed yourself for a battle but overestimated your own cleverness and underestimated the strength of your enemy. Please take the next card and lay it sideways across the Seven of Swords."

With a heavy, doomed sigh, he did so.

"This crosses you," Andrea went on. "This is what threatens you in your endeavor: the Two of Pentacles. It depicts a young man with a pentacle in each hand, and the pentacles are bound together in a figure eight on its side—the symbol for infinity. The pentacles there-fore represent grave extremes: the beginning and the end, life and death, the infinite past and the infinite future, good and evil, light and darkness."

She looked up at him with a smile.

"You might think this can't be you, because, after all, it's clearly a *young* man. But in your heart you know you're still a young man, don't you, Howard? Just like him, you too can *dance*—given the right setting and the right invitation. Isn't that so?"

She turned her attention to the card again. "Having grown young in heart, you're no longer afraid to take the weighing of these grave matters into your hands. You've seen that the light and darkness of conventional wisdom are not so far apart when mingled in the smoke and shadow of reality. . . . In the background, two ships on a storm-tossed sea are trying to reach shore, but, as you can see, the dancing man is unaware of them as yet. David Kennesey and his wife had already embarked on their separate journeys, but you didn't know anything about them at this point in the story."

Skimming a few cards from the top of the deck, Howard thumbed past the Eight of Cups, the Three of Wands, and the Five of Wands to produce the Page of Swords.

"Yes," Andrea said. "This is what lay before you: a youth striding through the countryside. Though he holds his sword aloft, he's unar-mored, defenseless, and he gazes back over his shoulder rather wist-fully, as if he rather regrets having left home."

"Tim," he said.

"Of course. Three different readings offered themselves," she added with a smile, "but only one was correct. A lost child, perhaps even an orphan, Tim would need your protection. But it was his sword you would follow, even when it led you into circumstances you couldn't begin to comprehend."

Howard threw the cards down on the outlay signaling that the reading was at an end.

"Will you listen to me now, Howard?"

He nodded.

"We're older than you, and in some ways more powerful, but this doesn't mean we can order everything to our ends. Not by any means. It was our intention to bring Tim and his father together here for a great purpose, but David . . . couldn't come this far. I'll tell you bluntly that if he'd made it, Tim's mother would be dead now. A killer had been dispatched to her, but at the last moment we gave him another target in order to spare her."

"Why?"

Andrea shook her head sadly. "We're not monsters, Howard, whatever you or others may think. It was never our intention to orphan Tim. We mean him no harm at all. Very far from it."

"Are you saying that you'll let me take Tim back to his mother?"

"Certainly. Did you think we'd keep him here by force?"

He was so stunned by this reply that he was momentarily speechless.

Eight hours later, with a little hustling and a lot of luck, Howard and the boy reached Albuquerque in time to board an eight o'clock flight to Chicago. Before leaving Taos, he had called Runnell in hopes that Ellen might actually be able to meet the plane, but the phone wasn't answered. In fact, at this point she was still in Colorado and wouldn't leave until after the funeral of Felipe Martinez, whose death had left her physically and emotionally shattered.

Tim was strangely silent, almost inert. Once they were in the air, Howard ordered a drink, but Tim wanted nothing. Eventually, as he knew he would—as he always did on long flights, from sheer boredom—Howard dozed off. When he woke after an hour, the seat beside him was empty, and he assumed the boy had gone to the toilet. After twenty minutes, he went to check and found all the rest rooms vacant. After surveying the passengers on the chance that Tim had, for some unfathomable reason, decided to sit with someone else, he asked a flight attendant if the boy seated next to him had been invited to visit the cockpit.

She looked at him blankly and said, "What boy?"

"The boy who got onto the plane with me. The boy who's been sitting beside me since we left Albuquerque."

The flight attendant, sensing that she might need some help on this one, called over a colleague, who agreed that the seat beside Howard had been empty throughout the flight.

"That's just not true," Howard said.

An officer summoned from the flight deck explained that FAA regulations required them to know exactly who was on board before takeoff, and they did. A seat had been reserved for Tim, but he was listed as a no-show.

"Mr. Scheim," the officer said, "you've got to realize that if this boy was on board when we pulled away from the gate, he'd be on board now, and he's not. That's definite. This isn't like a boat, where someone can fall overboard."

"I know," Howard said wearily. "I was asleep just now, and I guess I dreamed it."

They were more than happy to leave it at that.

CHAPTER 47

When Andrea came to join them on the patio, after seeing Howard off, Tim was still investigating the mannequin's controls.

"Where's Howard?" he asked.

She sat down at the table and patted the chair beside her. When he was seated, she said: "Howard and I talked things over, Tim, and he feels he has one more lead that's worth pursuing. While he does that, we thought you might like to stay here with me."

Tim blinked and looked around doubtfully. "Here?"

"Yes. I think you'd like it a lot. What do you think, Samson? Do you think Tim would like it?"

"Oh, yes! We'll have a lot of fun!"

Seeing that Tim was still doubtful, Andrea said, "Of course, you can go back to Runnell if you'd rather. Though I have to tell you that the house is as empty as when you left it."

"How do you know that?"

"Howard called. Still no answer. But if you'd rather not part with Howard, I'll certainly understand."

"Oh, it isn't that. I'd like to stay here, I think. But . . ."

"But what?"

Tim frowned down at the table. "Are you sure you want me to stay? You don't even know me."

Andrea laughed. "Don't worry about that at all. I'm a good judge of people, Tim. I wouldn't ask you if I wasn't sure."

"Well . . . all right. That sounds fine."

She stood up and held out her hand. "Let's take a walk together. There's someone else I want you to meet."

He looked back at the house. "Can I say goodbye to Howard first?"

"He's already on his way, Tim. It isn't as though he's leaving forever. I'm sure he'll be back as soon as he can be."

"Okay," Tim said thoughtfully.

"See you later, Tim," Samson squawked.

Hand in hand, they walked down into the low hills ranging to the west.

When they reached the crest of a hill about a mile from the house, Andrea released Tim's hand and said:

"You can go on by yourself from here."

Tim looked up at her doubtfully. "Go on by myself?"

Andrea nodded.

"To where?"

She smiled. "Just keep going."

He watched her turn away and head back down the hill. Then he shrugged and went on. Coming around a huge square block of rock, he nearly stumbled over a man sitting in the dust. He stepped back and blinked down at him.

The man was dressed in jeans and a casual shirt, but Tim's father would have had no difficulty in recognizing him as the man he'd known in Las Vegas as Pablo. Turning his dark bull-like face up to Tim, he gave him a solemn welcoming nod.

Tim spent a full minute exploring the man's eyes. As he'd seen once before, a universe of mysterious life seemed to move in their depths.

"What happened to your horns?"

The man smiled and tapped his temple. "They're in here. I only bring them out to frighten little boys."

"I wasn't frightened."

"I know, Tim. That's why you're here now."

Tim sat down beside him in the shadow of the rock, clasped his hands around his knees, and gazed out into the hills that rolled endlessly before them. After perhaps half an hour had passed, Tim asked:

"Was it you who . . . arranged all this?"

Pablo thought for a while before answering. "Tim, your father left you in order to find something he wanted. Something he wanted but wasn't strong enough to have. He became . . . lost. Your mother followed him and she too became lost."

"That's not exactly an answer. Is it?"

"Your father and mother followed their own promptings, Tim. I don't know what more to tell you."

His face expressionless, Tim continued to stare at the distant horizon.

"What is it you most deeply want, Tim? Do you want to go back home and school with the other boys? If that's what you want, I promise you shall have it. You mustn't stay here if your heart yearns for the small, humdrum world you left."

Tim said nothing.

"Think, Tim. Tell me what you want."

"I don't know what I want."

"Look here, Tim." Pablo opened his hand and in the shadow of the rock Tim saw a column of sunlight standing in his palm. In it a swarm of sparks gamboled in a swirling dance.

"Motes of dust," Tim whispered.

Pablo shook his head. "A world, Tim. You can visit it, if you like." He closed his hand and the column of light vanished. "That's only one world. There are many others I can open to you. If you want it."

His stomach tingling with apprehension and delight, Tim nodded to show that he understood.

As the sun mounted, the shadow in which they were sitting gradually shrank and disappeared.

"We must remember to find you a hat," Pablo said with a smile. He got to his feet and stood gazing off toward the western horizon.

Without turning, he said: "You know that the people you've grown up among say we're evil—Andrea and I, and others of our kind. Don't you, Tim?"

"I guess so."

"Do you understand *why* they say we're evil?"

"No."

"It's because they know we belong entirely to *this* world."

"You *belong* . . . ? I don't understand."

"You don't belong to this world, do you, Tim?"

"I don't know what you mean."

"This world of matter isn't your true home. Isn't that what they tell you, Tim? They say this world is just a way station on your journey —a testing ground. Your true home is elsewhere—in heaven—far, far from here, utterly beyond the soiling touch of matter. Isn't that what the people of your kind teach their children?"

"Yes, I guess so."

"They teach you that this world is trash: corrupt, vile, unwholesome, malign."

"True."

"Then you should be able to understand why they believe we're evil. Since we belong *entirely* to this world, it follows that we too are corrupt, vile, unwholesome, and malign."

"Yes, I see."

"The God worshiped by your kind is nothing like us, Tim. He's remote and sublime, unsullied by the world. He'd have you think of us as 'strange gods,' but it's He who is the stranger, sequestered beyond the farthest galaxy, beyond matter itself. A cosmic absence: silent, unresponsive, indifferent—but hungry for adoration. Do you understand?"

"I guess so."

He turned to the boy with a smile. "I must warn you, Tim: If you decide to stay, you will become as we are—unredeemably sullied by the world."

Tim returned the smile uncertainly, wondering if he was being teased.

"I won't press you for your choice, Tim. There's no hurry at all. Spend a few days getting your bearings. See how you feel about relinquishing the past—and all the dreams you once had for your life."

Pablo paused to look around. "Get to know this place."

"Is this a special place?"

"Every place is a special place, Tim." He stood for a moment, blinking down at the ground. "Let me show you something," he said, turning to descend the hill toward the west. After heading at a diagonal halfway up the next, he abruptly stopped and sat down in the dust. When Tim was seated beside him, he pointed at something a few feet away and said: "What do you think of that?"

The boy blinked at it. It was a slender, sickly-looking cholla cactus about ten inches high, listing to one side as if it were about to expire from sunstroke.

Tim looked at Pablo doubtfully. "Do you mean the cactus?"

Pablo shook his head. "It's not a cactus. Spend some time in its company. Get to know it well—so well that you forget its name. On the day you can look at it without thinking *This is a cactus*, it will speak to you. It will tell you a secret forgotten among most of your kind for thousands of years—a secret that will forever change the way you see the world."

PART V

Her house is the entrance to Sheol . . .

CHAPTER 48

When he finally got home, Howard slept like a dead man for twelve hours, then spent the rest of Tuesday in bed reading two old mysteries by Arthur Upfield, his favorite author after Rex Stout. It was firmly in his mind to go back to work the next day—whatever "work" might mean—but when the time came, he had not the slightest inclination to do so, refusing to spend even one second thinking about the disastrous adventure of the previous week. After checking his supplies, he had to go out for some groceries and booze, but that was it. Monday morning he'd start doing whatever had to be done about Tim and the others. Meanwhile, he had sixteen more Upfields to read.

He turned the last page of the last one at eleven-thirty on Sunday night.

By Wednesday afternoon, the house in Runnell, Indiana, had become haunted: by Ellen Kennesey. She seemed to float through it on a different plane and had to force herself to reach down into the world of matter. It felt like a betrayal to dress herself Thursday morning, to feed herself, to pick up the mail, to glance at a magazine, to watch television. Performing these actions seemed to say that there was nothing to be done except continue to live. Felipe was dead, David was gone, Tim was gone.

She had no right to live, no business being alive. And so she wandered the house like a ghost awaiting release, eating little, smoking endlessly, drinking much—she allowed herself that. Periodically her more sensible instincts told her it was time to turn her back on Felipe and David and Tim—time to put an end to this chapter of her life and start a fresh page, but so far she'd managed to throttle these impulses before they were fully born.

One thing she had done, unghostlike: The day after returning from that nightmare in Colorado she'd gone into a sporting-goods store and bought a pistol, a .25 caliber revolver. It was for protection (she now knew how badly she needed protection) but it was really for murder. She intended—cheerfully and without hesitation—to murder Nick Wolf and Artie Goodman if she ever had the opportunity. She was sure that this would release her from her spectral existence, would make her solid and whole again. She kept the pistol, loaded, on the table beside her bed, hoping they would someday come for her.

It didn't even cross her mind to file a missing-person complaint. Reporting Tim's disappearance to the police would have struck her as about as useful as reporting it to the weather bureau.

Friday night seemed special to her, and she drank a little more than usual, because this was the first week's anniversary of her encounter with Felipe—valiant little Felipe, who died so pointlessly, saving someone who had no business being alive at all.

On Monday Howard was mildly surprised to wake up feeling almost normal. He had no terrible misgivings about the future, no inclination to berate himself for the terrible mistakes he'd made in the past. Yet, after all he'd been through, it felt peculiar to feel so . . . unpeculiar —to shower, shave, eat breakfast, put on a suit, and go to his office as if were just another workday.

After going through the mail that had piled up during his absence and changing the message on the answering machine, he swivelled his chair around to stare out the window. Time at last to wonder what he was going to do next.

He decided to start with something simple: dialing Ellen Kennesey's number in Runnell. Sounding groggy, as if woken from a deep sleep, she answered on the fourth ring.

"Sorry," Howard mumbled, "wrong number," and hung up.

Well, at least he knew that much. Tim had someone to come home to. All Howard had to do now was figure out how to extricate him from that nightmarish house on Morningstar Lane. It seemed more like a job for Doc Savage than for Howard Scheim. He knew, of course, that he wasn't strictly obliged to do anything. In theory, he could tell Ellen where to find her son and let her handle it, but, having personally delivered the boy into Andrea's hands, this was unacceptable.

He needed to assemble a board of advisors.

Knowing that Richard Holloway, the expert on yoo-hoos and computers, would be the hardest to reach and the hardest to pry loose from a busy schedule, he started with him and got lucky.

"Hey, Howard, how are you doing? Shake that cold finally?"

"Yeah, days ago."

"Terrific. What's up?"

Howard outlined what he had in mind and was answered by a long silence.

"You there, Richard?"

"I'm here. I'm thinking. I hope you won't mind my asking, but . . . do I owe you something?"

"Not at all. If anything, I'm in your debt."

"I'm glad, Howard, because I don't want to hear about your adventures in Colorado or New Mexico. I hate to say it, but I'm not curious and I'm not interested and I don't want to be involved in any way."

"I'm sorry to hear it," Howard said, "but I guess I understand."

"I hope I'm not a huge disappointment to you."

"Absolutely not," Howard said, lying gallantly. "I wouldn't want to involve you if you didn't want to be."

Not a great beginning, but in truth Richard was the least essential member of the board.

He next called Aaron, who could have no possible grounds to back out, and asked if he was planning to be at the club tonight.

"No," the old man said. "Not tonight or tomorrow night. I have guests."

"Wednesday night?"

"Yes, I can be there then. You got something to report?"

"I've got lots to report. Can you reserve the conference room for seven-thirty? I'll be bringing two other people, and we'll need privacy."

"I'll take care of it."

He had to think about the best way to handle Denise Purcell. A personal visit would be more compelling, there was no doubt about that. But having him right there, she'd probably insist on knowing the whole story before agreeing to attend the meeting. He didn't want to spend an hour with Denise at this point, he wanted to spend two minutes, so he dialed her number.

When he had her on the line, he said, "Hi Denise. This is Howard Scheim, the King of Pentacles."

"Hello, Howard," she replied levelly. "How are you?"

"Bewitched, bothered, and bewildered, more or less the way you said I'd be." She didn't accept this invitation to inquire. "I'd like to have an opportunity to tell you what's been going on and to ask your advice."

"Advice about what?"

"You said I'd be following the sword of the Page of Swords. I don't know if you remember. . . ."

"I remember every reading I give."

"Well, you were right about that. I've been following this lad's sword, but we've become separated. You might say that he's . . . stranded. He's a very nice twelve-year-old named Tim Kennesey—you'd like him."

"Howard, don't try to con me with that 'you'd like him' bullshit. I don't want to get involved in this. I've got plenty of people to like already."

"I'm not asking you to get *involved*, Denise, believe me. I'm just asking you to listen."

"Howard, look. I don't even want to *hear* about it. Can't you get that through your head?"

"I understand that, but at least let me explain why I think you *should* hear about it, okay?"

"Okay," she said with a sigh.

"When I showed up at your place a few weeks ago and started asking a lot of foolish questions, you told me a cautionary tale about a young woman who made the mistake of getting involved with some things she should have left alone. You remember?"

"Go on."

"As it happened, the train of events I got involved in was already under way by the time I hopped aboard. Maybe that's irrelevant, but in any case this whole thing is not something I set in motion through my inquiries. It was *already* in motion. In your reading you said, in effect, that I was making myself available to be used, and I was used."

"What's this got to do with my cautionary tale?"

"I want to give you another one, involving not just a single individual but a dozen, ranging across half the United States."

"I don't *need* another cautionary tale, Howard. I'm fully cautioned."

Howard's heart sank as he realized he had only one card left to play, a card he'd hoped to bury forever.

"Six days ago, in a house in New Mexico," he began, "a woman took out a deck of Tarot cards, shuffled them three times and handed them to me. She never touched them after that. I shuffled them three times and cut them. The top ten cards were the same ten cards in your reading, in the same order. As I turned them over, she repeated your reading almost verbatim. At one point, you said, 'Three different readings offer themselves.' She told me which of the three was correct."

After a long, icy silence: "Howard, if you were standing in front of me and I had a gun in my hand, I'd have to restrain myself from putting a bullet through your brain."

"Okay, I understand that, but listen. Do you remember how I got in touch with you? You had talked to a friend of mine who works for the *Tribune*. You did that of your own free will. He talked to you because you were doing readings at a psychic fair—again something you were doing of your own free will. You can't go around shooting people just because you don't like the consequences of the choices you make in your own life. You of all people should know this."

"What do you *want*, Howard?" she snarled. "Tell me exactly."

He told her.

This left Ellen Kennesey, about whom he knew next to nothing. Mainly he didn't know how she'd react to the idea that Howard knew where Tim was but wasn't galloping off to rescue him. Thinking some more, he realized it was much worse than that. For all he knew, she might have reported Tim's disappearance as a kidnaping. In fact, a very plausible case could be made against *him* as a kidnaper. He couldn't just call her up and ask, because that's exactly what a kidnaper *would* ask.

He spent twenty minutes working on the problem, then realized there was another way to look at it. Would anyone *believe* it was a case of kidnaping? All any official would see from her story is that Tim slipped out of her car when she stopped at a gas station; from a cop's point of view, Tim was a runaway, not a kidnap victim by any stretch of the imagination.

That still left the original problem. Would Ellen sit still for two days waiting for a meeting to materialize? He decided he couldn't risk her taking some precipitate action like calling the cops or a lawyer, which would complicate everything disastrously. He would defer calling her until Wednesday.

Two hours later, as he was leaving the office to go to lunch, another thought popped into his head. *For God's sake, all you have to do is lie a little bit. How will you feel if you find out on Wednesday that Ellen Kennesey blew out her brains on Tuesday?*

With a groan, he went back to his desk and dialed the number. When she answered, again on the fourth ring, she still sounded like she'd been wakened from a deep sleep.

"Mrs. Kennesey," he said, with as much calm authority as he could muster, "you won't recognize my name, but it's Howard Scheim, and I'm a private investigator licensed in the state of Illinois."

"Yes?"

"Again, you won't know this, but I've been looking into the disappearance of your husband and son."

"The *hell* you have," she said, surprisingly.

"Well, yes . . . the hell I have."

"Do you think I'm going to believe anything *you people* tell me?"

He started to ask *what people?* then thought better of it. "I think I know the people you're talking about, Mrs. Kennesey. I think the two of us have been dealing with them almost nonstop for the past three weeks. I think you followed them to Colorado."

"No, I was *taken* to Colorado."

"So was I, Mrs. Kennesey, though not against my will. I think your husband was too."

"*Where is he?*"

"Believe me, I have no idea at this point."

"He's dead, isn't he."

"I have to admit that that's a definite possibility."

"And Tim? Where is Tim?"

"I can't swear to his exact location, Mrs. Kennesey, but I'm pretty confident that I know where to find him. That's what I want to talk to you about."

"What do you mean?"

"Two other people have been involved in this, and we're meeting on Wednesday evening to talk about what to do next."

"Two other people have been involved in this, and you're only contacting me *now?*"

"Take it easy, Mrs. Kennesey. I should have said that two other people have been involved with *me*. One of them has never heard of you, your husband, or your son—hasn't got the slightest idea that you exist. The other heard of you for the first time just this morning. I should also point out that you haven't been around to be contacted. I know, because I've tried, several times."

"Well, you've got me there," she said. "I'm sorry I jumped on you. But why do we have to wait till Wednesday?"

"Because one of the others, Aaron Fischer, can't make it till then, and he has some resources we may need."

"What kind of resources?"

"Mrs. Kennesey, we need all the resources we can get."

"You can say that again—and please call me Ellen."

CHAPTER 49

While Howard was dealing with Ellen Kennesey, Tim was walking the hills west of Andrea's house, head down, lost in thought. With part of his mind he was preparing for his next encounter with a sick-looking ten-inch cholla cactus. With a greater part, he was mulling over his life in this place, trying to sort out his feelings about it. It was, he thought, like finishing a terrific meal with the feeling that something wasn't sitting quite right in your stomach. How do you sort through the mess to find out which part was no good?

He liked everyone he'd met here—Andrea, Pablo, Dudley, Marianne.

No, that was wrong. He didn't *like* any of them. He was in awe of Andrea and Pablo. He was impressed by Dudley. Marianne? He didn't know what to make of her. The only one he actually *liked* was Samson, who was just . . . what? Andrea once called him her "creature." He was just a sort of toy.

All of them treated Tim as if he were somehow very important, and he wasn't sure how he felt about that. Or rather, he did know: it excited him, but it was also very wearing. He felt he couldn't relax, couldn't be himself, couldn't just open his mouth and let something come out. They were all so relentlessly intense.

This thing with the cactus, for example. *It will speak to you*, Pablo had said. *It will tell you a secret forgotten among most of your kind for thousands of years*. The trouble was, he couldn't just shrug that off; he knew Pablo wasn't kidding. But believing it laid an enormous burden of responsibility on him. Did he want such a secret? Well, who wouldn't, maybe? But did he? *A secret that will forever change the way you see the world.* Did he want to change the way he saw the world? And when he changed the way he saw the world, what then? This was obviously just a first step—but where did the path lead?

He had talked to Dudley about it. Or rather had tried to talk to Dudley about it. Did Dudley know what Pablo was talking about? Yes. Did he know the secret? Yes. Did the cactus tell it to him? *No; he'd learned it from his own people, who had never forgotten it.* Could he teach it to Tim? *Not as well as the cactus could.* Why was that? *You'll see.*

Tim told him he'd spent hours with the cactus and nothing had happened. *Might take years,* Dudley replied. What should he do? After a lot of thought: *Make yourself a stranger to it.* Pablo said just the opposite, to get to know it well. *To get to know it at all, you have to begin by meeting it as a stranger. You're still thinking, 'This is a cactus, just another cactus.' When you see it and don't know what in the world it is, then you can begin to know it.*

It seemed impossible; the more time he spent with the damned cactus, the more familiar it became—and the less he felt a stranger to it.

He'd mentioned the task to Samson, but it obviously meant nothing at all to him. Thinking about the mannequin, Tim remembered the unsettling conversation he'd had with him the day before. He'd come out onto the patio after breakfast and joined him at one of the tables. After exchanging good mornings, Samson—usually an irrepressible chatterbox—had been strangely silent. Tim asked him what was wrong.

"I'm thinking," Samson said.

"I guessed that," Tim observed wryly. "What about?"

"Things."

Tim laughed. "It's not like you to be inscrutable, Samson."

"I'm sorry." Then: "You know, Tim, I like you a lot."

He seemed to want a response, so Tim said, "I know."

"It's because I like you that I'm going to say this."

"Okay."

After a pause: "I think perhaps you should leave this place, Tim."

The boy's brows shot up. "Why?" Although Samson remained as immobile as ever, Tim had the impression he was feeling uncomfortable.

"I overheard the others talking about you last night—Andrea and Pablo and Dudley. I wasn't eavesdropping. I was just there, and they ignored me. You understand?"

Tim said he did.

"Have they told you . . . ? Have they discussed their plans with you?"

"Their plans for what?"

"For you."

Tim's stomach twinged with apprehension. "No. Not exactly." When Samson remained silent, Tim asked him to go on.

"I can't tell you what those plans are, Tim—they weren't making them last night, you understand. They were made long ago. They were talking about things taken entirely for granted among themselves."

"I don't understand."

"It seems you are destined to be someone of great importance in the scheme of things, Tim."

"Don't be silly, Samson."

The mannequin stared glassily into the hills through a full minute. Then he said: "Tell me: would you like to see the world very much changed?"

"Changed how?"

"Changed in the way people live in it."

"You mean . . . would I like to see people live a different way in the world?" Samson nodded. "Well, yes, I guess I would. That's not so strange. I think a lot of people would."

"Then perhaps you were well chosen."

Tim was startled at the sharpness of his tone.

Then Samson sighed, with a sound like wind in an empty oil drum. "Do you believe the world might be better ruled than by mankind?"

"Good lord, Samson. What are you talking about?"

"Tim—Andrea and Pablo spoke of *breaking humanity's hold on the world*. Do you understand that?"

Tim thought about it for a bit and then shrugged. "I *understand* it, Samson. That doesn't mean it's going to happen."

"You believe that breaking humanity's hold on the world is something they can't do?"

"That's right. I believe that breaking humanity's hold on the world is definitely something they can't do."

"Perhaps it's something *you* can do."

"Don't be ridiculous, Samson."

"I must tell you this, Tim. I believe this is what's in their minds: they mean to break humanity's hold on the world, and the instrument they mean to use is *you*."

"This is all bullshit," the boy snapped and stood up angrily. He hovered over the mannequin for a moment, willing him to retract it all, to say that he may have been mistaken or that he'd been joking. When Samson continued to stare ahead in silence, Tim stalked off into the hills, telling himself it was just a lie, a malicious lie or a jealous lie, but some kind of a lie.

But telling himself this didn't help much. A gray cloud of uneasiness had dimmed the rest of the day for him.

Tim sat cross-legged before the cactus.

It was a single stalk as yet, a cruel vegetable parody of a human phallus sheathed in a quiltwork of olive-green lumps and studded with long, viciously sharp, gray needles. A clump of limp, dusty-rose tendrils sprouted from its tip like an ejaculation of semen mixed with blood. It was not an impressive or attractive object, and it hadn't spoken a word to Tim.

Stiff after half an hour of sitting, Tim unwound his legs, stood up, and stretched. Then he lay stomach down in the dust and, crossing his wrists under his chin, looked up at the cactus just inches from his nose.

"You're not a cactus," he muttered. "That's what Pablo told me.

So what are you? If you don't mind my asking?"

A gust of wind pounded the side of the hill, but the cactus didn't even quiver. It stood there unmoved, impassive, as if absorbed in its own primitive thoughts. A movement at its base caught Tim's attention, and he lowered his eyes to watch a dusty black beetle picking its way fussily through the shattered rocks that covered the ground.

"And where are *you* going, sir?" Tim inquired. It looked just like a businessman in a dark suit hustling off to his office. "Hold on," he said, laying a finger in its way. "I want to talk to you for a second."

The beetle hesitated briefly, scuttled over the obstruction, and went on its way. Heaving a discouraged sigh, Tim closed his eyes. He'd been at this for how long? Four days, three or four hours a day? He wasn't any closer to success now than when he'd begun. The cactus was still a cactus. Whatever knack was required to look at the thing without recognizing it, he obviously didn't have it, and he didn't think he'd have it a year from now either. It seemed pointless to go on.

Pablo would be disappointed in him, but maybe that was just as well. Let him find out right at the beginning that Tim was, after all, just an ordinary kid. Then he wouldn't expect so much of him.

It seems you are destined to be someone of great importance in the scheme of things, Tim.

He wasn't at all sure he wanted to be someone of great importance. In fact, he was beginning to feel that what he really, deeply wanted right now was to get together with a bunch of guys and knock a baseball around till dusk, till it was too dark to see the fly balls. This had nothing to do with the game itself—or with sports, which mostly just bored him to death. This was a spring thing, a ritual to usher in the new year, because in fact spring was the beginning of the year, not January first.

It was the smell of the oiled glove, the feel of the fresh ball, the crack of the bat, the roar of the imaginary crowd. . . .

Under the shadow of a wide-brimmed straw hat, Tim dozed off, a rushing, oceanic sound in his ears very like the sound of a crowd.

As his vision cleared, he saw that there really was a crowd—a vast, holiday crowd that filled the streets of some city he'd seen only in movies. Rome? He thought he recognized a huge dome in the distance but couldn't remember the name of the church it belonged to.

He seemed to be floating just above the crowd, and everyone was looking up at him, pointing at him, waving at him, calling out frenzied greetings. Then he realized he wasn't floating; he was being carried through the massed streets on a sort of palanquin. This conveyance was made of wrist-thick boughs of wood, but somehow they were still alive; as he watched, leaves came into bud and opened on them. Over his head arched a canopy of vines; these too were alive and he could see fresh tendrils spreading out everywhere, gracefully intertwining in sinuous, lacy patterns.

Gradually the truth came to him: this enormous crowd—which he knew extended to the very limits of the city—had gathered for a single purpose: to greet him. He tentatively lifted a hand to wave—and the crowd roared back its delight.

There were two men sheltering in a doorway who didn't wave or shout a greeting. Dressed in long black cassocks, they stared at him with dark, hostile eyes. As Tim passed, one of them raised his hand—index and little finger extended—and jabbed it furtively in his direction. Clearly a gesture of contempt, it disturbed him; it was a jarring note in this vast symphony of adoration.

Someone nearby in the crowd said, quite calmly, "Don't worry about them, Tim. You can hardly expect *them* to love you!"

Tim looked around to find the speaker, wanting to ask what he meant, but no one in the frenzied crowd nodded to identify himself.

Suddenly the procession reached the edge of the city, where the mountains formed a vast natural amphitheater. The crowds swarmed upward, leaving Tim in the basin below. They weren't abandoning him; they were spreading blankets and sitting down, and soon fell silent as if in anticipation of a performance.

Tim wasn't sure what he was supposed to do. He was standing in the middle of a wheat field that filled the entire basin between the mountains. It was uncannily still. No insects buzzed, no birds sang, no breeze stirred the stalks of wheat around him. But, in spite of the silence, they could hardly be expecting him to make a speech; he was too far away to be heard. Thinking he might be able to address one group after another, he began to wade through the wheat toward the nearest of the hills.

After he'd taken a dozen steps, the crowd gasped.

Tim turned around and saw why: Where he'd walked, a wild tangle of weeds, flowers, vines, and young trees had sprung up. A spider was laying a misty web among the branches of a mulberry bush already beginning to bloom as Tim watched. A swarm of bees hummed over a clump of purple thistles. A squirrel darted down a tree trunk to retrieve a fallen nut. There was a clatter of wings and he looked up to see a pair of brilliantly-colored finches settle on a branch; after a moment one of them swooped down to pluck a bee out of the air.

Looking around, Tim saw that the wall of wheat around him was quickly receding. At first glance, he thought it was being devoured by the wilderness; then he saw that it was *engendering* the wilderness. It looked like a gray prison wall melting to release a riotous diversity of botanical forms that had been immured within it for centuries and were now springing forth to an exuberant new life in the sun.

Soon the growth around him was so tall and thick he could no longer see where this process was taking place—though he somehow knew it would go on until the entire valley basin had been transformed. Under the canopy of leaves, ten thousand voices spoke in a joyous babble of chirps, trills, tinkles, grunts, growls, howls, chatters, zings, hums, whoops, cackles, clicks, hisses, roars, and rumbles. The air was alive with birds and insects. Small, spotted wildcats stretched in the trees and ignored the shrill, teasing monkeys. The earth bubbled up black and teeming over wandering burrows. Dark eyes peered out of the grasses and from among the leaves.

Beams from a westering sun stood aslant the forest floor, misted here and there with slowly-passing clouds of gnats. In a pool of light at Tim's feet glowed the tawny face of a tiger lily, one of the dozen or so flowers he could name on sight, and his favorite. As he hunkered down to peer into it, a ladybug lumbered out of its velvety depths and shuffled its wings uncertainly, as if wondering if it still had the knack of flight. Then it shot up into the air—straight into Tim's face.

He jerked his head back—and was instantly, if groggily, awake.

He opened his eyes and found an alien creature towering over him—a visitor from the stars, bristling with silver spikes and armored in glossy green. In the tenth of a second during which Tim's mind struggled to reimpose order and sense on the world, he saw that the creature meant him no harm—accepted him as an equal, seemed to enfold him in its own aura of vibrant power and dignity, as if to say, "It's all right. I see that you too are alive. No more is required. We are comrades."

The surface of the creature's armor suddenly began to cloud, pearling with a liquid iridescence that moved across it like a melting rainbow—and involuntarily Tim sucked in a breath that was almost a sob: never, never had he witnessed anything so majestically lovely as this. It was vastly more than a visual experience of beauty; in an act of unimaginable generosity, the creature was revealing to him the very nature and substance of its life. The iridescence flowing across its surface wasn't a color, wasn't the mere reflection of light. It was a vibrant, sublime energy emanating from within, pulsing inexhaustibly from each atom—a conflagration almost beyond control, surging irresistibly outward, so that the tip of each of its spines was a glittering fountain of energy.

Tears were coursing down Tim's cheeks in a flood, and he made no effort to check them. Astounded, awed, and humbled, Tim was weeping for sheer joy, dragging each breath up from the depths of his bowels.

He had of course long ago realized that what was before him was the cactus he'd spent so many hours with. Recognizing it now made no difference, because now he was recognizing it for what it truly was: not "just a cactus"—indeed not a cactus at all—but rather a unique, unclassifiable individual whose moment in the thundering, never-ending drama of creation would never be repeated here or anywhere else in the universe.

Standing up to look around, Tim saw that the world was every-where ablaze with the same thrumming effulgence that shook the cactus. Each dry, gray chamisa, each stunted piñon, each blade of grass, each scruffy weed was crackling and trembling and all but ex-ploding with the awesome power that animated it. Hungry to see more, he climbed to the crest of the hill and looked down into the valley of the Rio Grande, already resplendently green. If it had been a sound instead of a sight, it would have been the jubilant roar of a million voices. Every leaf of every tree was radiant, lustrous—incan-descent with a power that was unmistakably divine.

A truck chugged uphill along the highway beside the river, a lump of dead matter—a black hole of lifelessness in a landscape scintillant and effervescent with glorious vitality—and Tim thought, "Oh, you poor things. If you could only *see*."

Half an hour later, the effervescence began to subside like cham-pagne going flat, and his vision gradually returned to normal. This is how he thought of it. He was like a blind man who had briefly been given the gift of sight simply to experience once in his life the blue of the sky. To such a man, it would be an ecstatic revelation; but he would know without the slightest doubt that—ecstasy notwithstand-ing—he was merely seeing what's always there to be seen. And when his blindness returned he would know unshakably that, though invis-ible to him, the sky is forever there and exquisitely, shatteringly blue. Tim, too, knew that what he'd experienced was no hallucination; briefly given the gift of sight, he'd merely seen what was there to be seen—what had always been there and would always be there.

He hadn't the slightest doubt that, though he could no longer see it, that joyous bonfire was still blazing all around him and would blaze for as long as there was life on this planet.

Pablo was waiting for him in his place under the rock. Although he looked up solemnly into Tim's tear-stained face, he offered no greeting. Tim sat down beside him and looked into the sun settling over the distant mountains.

After a few minutes Pablo said: "So. You saw."

Tim nodded. It was a while before he was sure he could speak. "Was that something you . . . arranged?"

"No, Tim. Such a gift is beyond even my power to give—though I sensed it had been given."

Tim nodded again.

"Would you rather not talk, Tim? I'll leave if you'd like to be alone."

"No. I don't feel like talking, but I'd like to hear you talk. I'd like you to tell me . . ."

"Yes?"

". . . what I saw."

Pablo smiled. "You saw the fire, Tim."

"Go on."

"You saw it, Tim."

"I know, but go on."

Pablo laughed softly and gestured to the world around them. "This is the smoke of that fire."

Tim nodded. "Yes. Yes, I see. Go on."

"Andrea and I are guardians of the fire."

"Go on."

Pablo laughed again. "You know whom we serve, Tim."

"What do you mean?"

"Look into my eyes."

An endless time passed as Tim gazed into his eyes. At last he said: "I don't know."

"Of course you know. What you saw today was a *manifestation*, Tim. A manifestation of what?"

Tim stared into the hills for a moment. "Of God."

"The real one, not the one that lives beyond the universe. The one who lives *here*."

CHAPTER 50

No one was late. By seven-thirty they were all seated around a table on the second floor of the Herman Litvak Chess Club: Howard, Denise, Ellen, and Aaron.

"I'm afraid we're in for a long night, but that can't be helped," Howard began, clearly addressing Denise and Aaron. "A great many things have happened to Ellen and me in the past three weeks—things you could have no inkling of, things whose meaning and purpose only became clear at the end of this period.

"When I called Ellen to invite her to this meeting two days ago, she didn't know me from Adam, and she said, 'Do you think I'm going to believe anything *you people* tell me?' And I had to convince her that I wasn't one of *those people*. Denise, you know who I mean by *those people*, don't you."

"I suspect I do, Howard," she replied dryly.

He turned to Aaron. "The last time we met here, you urged me to consider going to the Middle East, Jamaica, or Haiti to find out what I could about *those people* for you. As it turned out, I didn't have to go anywhere, because they *came to me*, and that's what you're going to hear about tonight. I know how improbable this sounds, and I can see the skepticism in your eyes, Aaron, but at this point you haven't heard anything.

"Let me start with a sort of overview that will put everyone in the picture. For reasons we may never know, those people wanted two of *our* people: Ellen's husband, David, and their twelve-year-old son, Tim. Three weeks ago, give or take a day, David abruptly decided to leave home. This much I know from Tim. There was no warning whatever—no marital discord, no strife, no problems of any kind that he was aware of. Bang, suddenly David felt an overwhelming urge to hit the road, and in a matter of hours he was gone, taking his own car, a green Volvo.

"Two days later they received a phone call from David, or someone impersonating him. Evidently in deep distress, this person said he was calling from the Edgewater Beach Hotel. Tim and Ellen leaped into her car and headed for Chicago. Of course the Chicagoans in this room will know they didn't find the Edgewater Beach Hotel, which was demolished long ago. On her way back to Runnell, Ellen pulled into a gas station. That's as much as I know of her story, because it's as much as Tim knew of her story. It's also as much as Ellen knows of Tim's story, because he wasn't in the car when she left the station to continue on to Runnell. I don't know what she thinks happened there, but Tim told me he was asleep in the backseat and woke up feeling violently ill. He headed for the weeds behind the filling station and spent the next few minutes emptying his stomach. When he returned, Ellen was gone and the filling station was locked up and empty.

"He stood around for a while not knowing what to do. Then a car that was a match for his father's pulled up. I strongly suspect that it was driven by one of *them*—or at least one of their minions. When he heard Tim's story, the man said he thought he knew where David had been calling from, a cocktail lounge called the Yacht Club, on Bryn Mawr, which apparently is fitted out to resemble the Yacht Club in the old Edgewater Beach Hotel. He took Tim there but found no indication that David had ever been there. As they were leaving, they were stopped by a policeman, who wondered what a boy of Tim's age was doing in a bar at that time of night. To throw off suspicion, the man claimed to be Tim's father and signaled Tim to back him up.

Tim and the man got back in the car and drove around aimlessly for a few minutes, then the man dropped Tim off at the corner of Sheridan and Ainslee, saying he had an idea to pursue and would be back in a few minutes. Of course he never returned. Instead, after half an hour or so, a bus stopped. A man stepped off and said to Tim, 'Are you waiting for this bus?' That man was me."

He looked at Aaron. "I was returning from the meeting I'd had with you here at which we discussed my going to Syria, Jamaica, or Haiti to find out what you wanted to know about *those people*. I took Tim up to my apartment, put in a call to Ellen, and got no answer. Doubtless she'll tell us where she was when it's her turn. To make a long story short, there was nothing to be done till morning, so we went to bed. In the morning, still getting no answer at Tim's house in Runnell, I rented a car, took him home, and told him to stay put. He stayed put, but Ellen didn't return. The next day Tim got something completely inexplicable in the mail from a Las Vegas hotel: a twenty-thousand-dollar check, made out to him. Assuming this to be a lead to his father, I took Tim to Las Vegas, where we learned that David had made a phenomenal win there and then disappeared. When I say it was a phenomenal win, I mean a win that almost defies belief."

With that, Howard invited Ellen to take up her story from the point where she unknowingly left Tim behind at the gas station outside Valparaiso. Her account took her from Runnell back to the gas station, then on to Chicago and her dealings with the police, her confrontation with "detectives" Wolf and Goodman, her abduction to the house outside Glenwood Springs, Colorado, her abandonment there, the trek to find David's car in the foothills of the Rocky Mountains, where nothing short of a helicopter could have deposited it, and the death of Felipe.

"After talking to you two days ago, Howard," she went on, "I remembered that Wolf had mentioned your name. Or rather he made a call to someone and asked to speak to either Howard Scheim or Tim Kennesey. He was told that you'd just left."

Howard gave that some thought and said, "If I have the timing right, he was probably calling our hotel in Las Vegas. In fact, come to think of it, there was a peculiar old lady there who was frantic to keep us from leaving. I mean, she almost physically restrained us. At the time I didn't think anything of it. Now, in light of what you've just told me, I have to assume she was one of *them*, and her task was to keep us there a bit longer. Possibly the call from Wolf was supposed to send us off on another wild-goose chase for a day or two."

Ellen had something else to add. "I felt it would be cowardly of me to rush home before Felipe's funeral. He would have been alive except for me, and of course I knew there was nothing to rush home for anyway, since Tim wasn't there. I talked to Felipe's mother a lot during that time, and she told me one thing that I now believe without any doubt, that the native peoples of that area know *those people* and their doings very well. They don't call them *those people*, they call them witches, but they're not talking about hags on broomsticks, and they don't talk about them the way we talk about ghosts or angels or UFOs. They're talking about people they personally know, people they have personal dealings with—when they can't avoid it. They told me about a place where witches gather that's not too far from where David's car was found, done up like a town in an old Western movie. I offered a lot of money to be taken there, but no one was even slightly tempted. I originally scoffed when Felipe told me witches had put David's car in a spot you can't even reach in a Jeep, but I'm not scoffing now."

"I should point out," Howard said, "that Ellen and I can only give you two strands of this story. The strand that connects these two strands is David's, which is pretty much a total mystery and likely to remain one. We can name a few places where we know he went, but we have no idea what drove him from one to the other. We don't know, for example, if he was in the Volvo when it was deposited in the mountains. We don't how he ended up driving a flashy red Corvette on loan from a drug dealer in Vail—but I should tell the story in order, from the time Tim and I got on a plane to go to Las Vegas."

When he was finished, he said, "About the only thing that's completely clear is that Andrea's house was meant to be David and Tim's final destination, where some 'great purpose' was going to be achieved. Andrea said David couldn't come that far, but she was obviously speaking metaphorically. David was there at one time, beyond all doubt, because he sent Tim a letter from there, the letter that brought us to Taos and to Morningstar Path."

"I've got a couple questions," Aaron said with the air of someone who has a lot more than just a couple questions. "I'm sitting here listening to all this—I don't know what to call it—this epic melodrama, about a whole lot of people I never heard of, and I'm trying to figure out why you think I should be listening to it. Don't interrupt, Howard. You know I'm not stupid. Tell me if I'm right. You got involved in this whole mess because of the thing I asked you to look into for me. Is that what you're saying?"

"I don't have any doubt of it, Aaron. Andrea knew all about the reading Denise did for me when I consulted her on your behalf. She knew all about the evening I spent at Joel Bailey's establishment with Verdelet and Délices on your behalf. It's inconceivable that mere coincidence planted Tim directly in my path minutes after you told me I should go anywhere in the world I might find the answers you wanted."

"I'm not arguing with you, Howard. But I've still got a question."

"Go ahead."

"If these people are who you think they are, then why the hell did they have to go through all this elaborate rigamarole to get David and Tim to where they wanted them to be? If they're the people you want me to think they are, they could've done it with a snap of the fingers, couldn't they?"

Momentarily stunned by the question, at once so obvious and so obtuse, it took Howard a full minute to think of an answer that would mean something to Aaron. "If God was really God, Aaron, why did he have to go through all that elaborate rigamarole to free his people from the Egyptians—the plagues, the locusts, the boils, the maggots, the hailstones, the killing of the first-born, the parting of the Red Sea, and so on? Why not just snap his fingers and make all the Egyptians vanish instantly? Or, even better, why not just snap his fingers and transport his people to the Promised Land instantly? Wouldn't that have been a more impressive display of his power?"

Aaron nodded, chuckling softly. "Yeah, you got me there, Howard. No argument."

"There's more to it than that," Denise said, "or maybe just another way of looking at it. God didn't just want his people to be *transported* to the Promised Land. He wanted them to reach the Promised Land transformed by their journey. The same is true of David and Tim." Drawing a set of Tarot cards from her purse, she made a brief search and laid a card face up in the center of the table.

"The Fool," she noted. "A blithe young traveler—unarmed and with all his meager belongings on his shoulder—gazes blissfully up into the heavens, unaware that his next step will take him over the edge of a mile-high cliff. This is the zero card," she continued, "the card before even the first card in the deck. It isn't the archetype of a dolt but of a person at the beginning of the hero's journey, setting out with utter trust in the benevolence of the universe and putting his fate entirely in the hands of the gods. In essence, it's where we all begin—*if* we begin. The end of the hero's journey is *this*." She turned over another card. "The Magician. Years older now, the Hero is the master of all the Tarot suits, which you see laid out on the table before him—wands, pentacles, cups, and swords. This means he's seen it all, come through it all—wealth, poverty, weakness, power, hardship, joy, sorrow, strife, deception, love, and danger—and now he stands alone, completely poised, completely balanced and at rest. No halo surmounts his head. Rather, it's the symbol of the infinite. *Magician*, with its suggestion of performance and conjuring, isn't quite the right cognomen for him. In some decks he's more correctly call the Magus. This was David's destination, to become one of *them*, but he fell short. As Andrea said, he just couldn't make it, and we'll probably never know why." She turned to Ellen. "You met a man in a bar at the Holiday Inn who said he'd talked to David."

"That's right. According to him, David kept saying, 'There is a road, a certain road.'"

"This suggests that he wasn't completely in the dark about what he was doing. He *knew* about that road. Perhaps he'd begun that journey once before but had abandoned the road. That last morning in Runnell, he seems to have awakened knowing that he had to get back on it, whatever the cost. Just like the fool in the picture, he didn't hesitate to step off the cliff and put his fate in the hands of the gods."

"And Tim?" Ellen asked.

"He's only at the beginning of his journey, of course. He couldn't be in a position to fall short as yet. He's hardly begun, after all. But I can tell you this. Whatever happens now or in the future, like his father, Tim will always know that there is a road, a certain road . . . that ordinary folk can't travel, that leads someplace ordinary folk can't go."

Ellen, looking befuddled, shook her head.

"I have to ask this question, Ellen," Howard said. "It may sound silly, but it does have to be asked. Do you want to get Tim out of there?"

"Of course I want to get him out of there! Why would you even ask such a question?"

Howard shrugged. "To get the ball rolling, Ellen. To find out if we *need* to get the ball rolling. If you thought Tim was where he belonged, there'd be nothing more to talk about. Since you don't, there is."

"How *do* we get him out of there?" Ellen wanted to know.

"To be honest with you, I don't have the foggiest idea," Howard said. "My first thought—again being honest—was to mount a commando-style rescue. Just foolishness, of course. Nothing like that could succeed."

The four of them sat there for a minute, thinking about it.

"One thing struck me," Aaron said. "People like this—*these people*—driving cars, using telephones, probably cooking with microwave ovens. . . ."

"Yes?" Howard asked.

"They have driving licenses. When they built that house, they had to have a survey, probably had to get a permit. To put in a septic system, there'd have to be some kind of drainage test. All that business."

"Yes? So?"

"They've got a front to maintain, Howard. It isn't like living in the cellar of an abandoned castle in Transylvania."

Howard nodded, beginning to see what he was getting at.

"There's no way to hurt them, obviously," Aaron went on. "But they've opened themselves up to being bothered, to having their front ruffled maybe a little bit."

"Like how?"

Aaron shrugged. "Could be done all sorts of ways. Suppose you arrived with a cop in tow, for example. There's nothing he could do to them, of course. That's not the point. Bringing the cop along just poses a question: How much do you value this nice, quiet setup you've got here?"

"Yeah, that makes sense."

Denise growled, and everyone's eyes swivelled to her.

"Sometimes I despair of the human future, with cowboys like you running around," she said. "Howard, I don't know the country out there, but it's my impression that, if she'd wanted to, Andrea had hundreds of square miles in which she could have made you disappear."

"Yes, that's absolutely true."

"And you told us something about a killer that had been sent to Ellen. I'm not sure I followed that."

"She said a killer had been dispatched to Ellen, but when David failed to make it—which I take to mean he died—the killer was given another target to spare her. At the time, of course, this didn't make any sense to me. If you want to call off a killer, you just call him off, you don't have to give him another target."

"But *you* know what she meant by this, don't you?" she asked Ellen.

"Yes. The dog was coming straight at me when Felipe stepped between us. It ripped out his throat and tore off past me as if I wasn't even there."

Denise leveled a disgusted look at Howard. "Aren't you capable of putting all this together?"

Howard nodded glumly. "Yeah, I guess I can. If David had made it, whatever that means, Ellen and I would be dead, and Tim would be theirs forever."

"But since David didn't make it, they spared Ellen and sent you home with a simulacrum, a phantasm. What does this indicate about their plans for Tim?"

"It indicates they wanted him for a while but know they can't keep him, not without his father."

"So what are they expecting next, Howard?"

He grimaced painfully. "That I'll come back and get him."

"Exactly. Sorry to deprive you of your big, Rambo-style rescue."

"I want to be there too," Ellen said flatly.

Howard shook his head. "I think we should keep it simple."

"He's right, Ellen," Denise said. "Don't give them ideas they don't already have. As things stand right now, they don't view you as a substitute for David, but if you offer yourself, who knows?"

"I'm not offering myself, I just want to *see* them."

"Of course you do, and that's exactly where it starts."

Howard lifted a hand to interrupt. "What would you think of my taking Aaron?"

"For what purpose?"

"Well, he gave me a commission to *find* these people. . . ."

Aaron's face twisted into a humorless smile. "I know you can't resist being a joker, Howard. You've earned your fee. I'll put a check in the mail tomorrow."

"You shouldn't have done that, Howard," Aaron said when Ellen and Denise were gone.

"Done what, Aaron?"

"Talk about taking me with you."

Howard saw, to his puzzlement, that the old man was seriously angry. "I'm still struggling to get my feet under me, Aaron, so maybe I slipped up, but I'm not sure how. Tell me what's bothering you."

"I didn't send you on a safari to find me a rhinoceros to shoot."

Howard nodded, still in the dark.

"I said I'd put a check in the mail, and I will, but you and I aren't finished. You still owe me something."

"I'm well aware of that, Aaron," Howard said, though in fact he didn't have the slightest idea what the old man was talking about. "I'll call you as soon as I get back."

Assuming, he added mentally, that I *do* get back.

CHAPTER 51

Andrea seemed genuinely pleased to see him when Marianne brought him up to the third floor of the house two days later.

"I was expecting you a bit sooner than this," she said brightly.

"It took me a while to figure it out."

Andrea smiled. "You want to take Tim back with you."

"That's the idea, of course."

"It'll be up to him, you understand. If he wants to stay, you'll have to respect that."

It wasn't a possibility he'd considered, but, having no other choice, he nodded.

"He's outside someplace. Marianne will find him. Meanwhile, make yourself at home. I'll be right back."

Howard looked around, reluctant to take a seat. He wandered over to inspect Andrea's library, which took up most of one wall. It seemed to consist almost entirely of coffee-table books. He pulled out a copy of *The Art of Maurice Sendak*, which seemed an odd thing to find in such a place. After browsing through it for a few minutes, he decided maybe it wasn't so odd after all.

Andrea returned with a couple of letter-sized envelopes in her hand and waved him over to the table where, eleven days before, they'd reviewed Denise's Tarot card reading.

Sitting back in her chair, she said, "You know David's dead, don't you?"

"Yeah, I figured as much."

She pushed an envelope across the table to him. "The money he was carrying at the time is in there. It's quite a lot. I'll leave it up to you to decide what to do with it. Give it to Ellen, put it in a trust for Tim, or whatever seems appropriate."

She slid the second envelope across. "That's a letter for Tim. I'd like you to hold it for him till he asks for it."

"How do you know he's going to ask for it?"

"Maybe he won't, Howard. If he doesn't, he doesn't."

He looked at the envelopes but made no move to pick them up. "I don't get it, Andrea. Why me? You don't need me to do these things."

"You're right, of course," she said with a smile. "But I like to have people do me favors."

"People of *my* kind."

"That's right. Especially people of your kind."

He sighed and shoved the envelopes inside his jacket.

"I like you, Howard. Did you know that? You're not the brightest man in the world—or the best or the bravest, but . . ."

"But I got lotsa character."

Andrea laughed.

At that moment the sliding glass door to the patio rumbled open, and Tim stepped in, blinking, sun-blind.

Rising, Andrea said, "Look who's here, Tim!"

Howard stood up, and the boy gazed at him as if he were an apparition.

"Howard brings good news, Tim. Your mother is alive and well back at your house in Runnell."

"Really?" Tim asked, looking from one to the other of them.

"Really," Howard said. "I'm here to take you home."

"If you want to go, of course," Andrea added.

Tim looked at her doubtfully.

"It's entirely up to you, Tim. Believe me, you won't hurt my feelings if you want to go back. I'm sure Pablo and Dudley will feel the same. I *know* they'll feel the same. We'd all love to have you stay, but not if you'd rather go home."

"Wow," Tim said. He looked a question of some sort at Howard, who nodded. "When? Now?"

"If we leave now, we can catch a flight that leaves Albuquerque at eight o'clock."

Tim glanced again at Andrea as if still not quite sure of her consent. "Then I'll go get my stuff."

When Tim was gone, Andrea led Howard out onto the patio and strolled toward a black-suited figure in a wheelchair some ten yards away.

"David failed a crucial test out here," she said. "I honestly think you might have done better."

Howard could think of nothing to say to that.

"This is Samson," Andrea announced, pausing before the mannequin. "Tim's going home," she said, and Howard looked at her curiously.

The mannequin moved not at all, but after a muffled clank, a sort of hissing, grinding moan issued from within: "I'll miss him, Andrea, but it's probably for the best. Please give him my regards."

"I'll do that, Samson."

She turned back toward the house. When they were inside, she said, "There's something I could do for you—nothing to do with the favors I've asked for. Not a reward."

"Go on."

"There's a door in your apartment that's not of the ordinary kind. Don't bother to pretend you don't know what I'm talking about."

"I'm not pretending anything."

"If you like, I can tell you how to open that door at will."

A terrible shiver raced up his spine. "Andrea, I'm glad you like me and think I've got lots of character, but you don't understand me as well as you think you do. That's my way of saying no thanks."

Andrea nodded. "I rather thought you'd say that. All the same—"

But Howard didn't get to hear the rest, because at that moment Tim returned, carrying his familiar suitcase.

"Is Mom really okay?" Tim asked once they were on their way.

"Completely okay. The way we left it was that, unless she heard otherwise, she'll be at the gate when we land at O'Hare."

Back on the highway after leaving Morningstar Path, they traveled for half an hour in a tense silence until Tim finally said, "I don't want to talk about it, okay?"

"I wasn't waiting for you to talk about it, Tim." Then he wondered if he *had* been waiting for him to talk about it.

Glancing over at him, he saw that Tim's face was blank. Whatever was going on behind it certainly wasn't ready for public display. He lifted his eyes to Howard's, searching for something. Understanding? Forgiveness? Howard couldn't be sure. One thing was certain: they weren't the eyes of the boy he'd met at the bus stop two weeks before; childhood was over for Tim. Howard gave him a slight nod, acknowledging . . . something. Something that existed just between the two of them. He wasn't sure what it was, really.

CHAPTER 52

In the hours following his return, Howard used every trick he knew to set up his meeting with Aaron at some place other than the old man's house but in the end managed only to excuse himself from the ordeal of another dining spectacular. When he arrived at seven-thirty, Ella gave him a friendly nod and led him back to the elegant English gentleman's study where it had all begun.

Aaron looked up from a volume open on his lap and waved him to a chair that embraced him like a returning son.

Aaron laid his book aside, gave him a long look, and said, "So."

"So," Howard replied, still completely in the dark about the purpose of the meeting.

"You got my check."

"Received, endorsed, and deposited, Aaron. Thank you very much. And cashier's checks are always appreciated."

Aaron waved that away.

Howard crossed his legs: something to do. When the old man showed no sign of starting (or of even thinking about where to start), he said, "The other night you told me I still owed you something."

Aaron nodded.

"What's your idea of what that is, Aaron?" As if he was reserving his own judgment about it.

Instead of answering, the old man began the lengthy ritual of lighting one of his giant cigars. When he finally had it going to his satisfaction he said, "My wife was a great reader of mystery novels, did I tell you that? And to make her happy I sampled a few—Chandler, Christie, Hammett. At the end of all these books, most of the time, the detective gets everybody together and puts the puzzle all together for them. You know what I mean?"

"Sure, Aaron."

"Lines up all the suspects, all the clues, and explains how he figured it all out."

"Right. But—if I understand where you're heading with this—what we have right here isn't a whodunit. I didn't solve any mystery, didn't unmask any culprit. You didn't hire me to do that."

"No, I didn't. But I also didn't hire you to track down Tim Kennesey's missing father."

"No, you didn't."

"But that's what you did."

"That's what I did, Aaron."

The old man nodded. "I guess my question to you is, how do you figure that doing something I didn't hire you to do ends up being what I hired you to do?"

"Wow, Aaron, how do *you* figure it? Sending me a check was your idea, not mine."

Aaron shook his head. "Sending the check was my move, Howard, like in a game of chess. Now it's your move. Explain to me how you earned your fee. That's what you owe me."

Howard sank back in his chair as if clubbed, his face blank, all thought driven from his brain.

"Excuse my bad manners," Aaron said quickly. "Can I offer you something? Brandy? Whiskey?"

"A scotch would be nice, Aaron."

"Soda? Water?"

"Just plain, thanks."

The old man used a house phone to ask Ella to bring brandy for him and scotch for Howard. Evidently she had some alternative brands to offer, and after listening for a moment and giving his guest a searching look, he said, "I think any of those will do, my dear."

Howard knew Aaron was allowing him this interval to collect his thoughts, but nothing came, except: *I've been in over my head in this goddamn mess from the beginning.*

When he had a heavy glass in his hand and a third of a triple scotch inside him, he said, "You hired me to do an impossible thing, Aaron."

"I know that. But I paid your fee without a word, and now I want you to tell me why."

Howard couldn't help it: he laughed. "Aaron, you are the craziest bastard I ever worked for."

Surprisingly, Aaron grinned. "Yeah, that's us, Howard, a pair of crazy old Jew bastards." Then he started chuckling. Howard joined him, and for thirty seconds the two of them guffawed madly, teetering on the edge of hysteria.

When they had their breath back, it was clear that the paralyzing tension between them had been broken, and Howard said, "Do you really not know why you sent that check, or is this just another one of your goofy tests?"

"I honest to God don't know, Howard."

Howard sighed, gave himself up to the embrace of his chair, and had another taste of scotch. "Aaron, you wanted to know what happened to the gods that for six hundred years the Israelites preferred over the one that led them out of Egypt—Baal, Ashtaroth, and so on. That's what you hired me to find out, isn't it?"

"Yes."

"Well, did I find out? Did I get you what you were looking for? Only you can answer that question, all I can do is ask it. That's my move. Your turn."

Aaron shook his head woozily. "I'll tell you, Howard, my brain is like mush over this thing."

"Believe me, I know what you mean."

"There was a time when it looked to me like you were on the

track. That last time we talked, when I said, look, you think there might be an answer in Haiti, go to Haiti. Then suddenly you disappear, you're all wrapped up in finding this kid's father."

Howard nodded. "So the answer wasn't in Haiti, Aaron, it was in Taos."

"But you didn't go there to get my answer, you went there to find David Kennesey. Make sense out of that. Your move."

"Christ, Aaron, this is like slogging through knee-deep mud."

"I know. It's because . . ."

"It's because I'm afraid to look at it."

"It's because we're *both* afraid to look at it. You think that because I hired you to do this thing . . ."

"Because you hired me to do this thing, Tim was separated from his mother and set down on a bench where I practically tripped over him getting off the bus. Because you hired me to do this thing, I was elected to bring him to Andrea's house. David was just the bait."

"What did they want with Tim?"

"I have no idea, Aaron."

"How did they get David there?"

"Again, I have no idea."

"I can't stand it, Howard."

"I know."

There was a soft knock on the door that startled both men as if it had been a hammer blow.

It was Ella, who announced that there was a gentleman at the door. "He says you're expecting him." She looked at Howard strangely. "Both of you."

"Who is he?" Aaron asked. "I mean, what's his name?"

Again she glanced at Howard. "He said, 'They wouldn't recognize the name, but it doesn't matter. They're expecting me.'"

After giving Howard a bewildered look, the old man told her to let him in.

As one, they got to their feet. Howard wasn't sure whether it was out of simple courtesy or so as to be ready for anything.

"Do you know anything about this?" Aaron asked.

"Not a thing, Aaron. No one knew I was coming here. Who would I tell?"

When the visitor was at last standing before them, an imposing block of a man with black hair, dark complexion, and immaculate black suit, Howard recognized him—not as a person but as the human embodiment of the bull-faced black dog that had haunted his dreams in the early weeks of the investigation.

"May I join you? I believe you've been looking for me," he said to Aaron. And to Howard: "Perhaps Andrea or Tim mentioned my name to you. I'm called Pablo."

CHAPTER 53

"What makes you think I've been looking for you?" Aaron demanded.

"Don't do that, Aaron," Howard told him. "This man . . . this person . . . has had us under his eye from the beginning."

"Not at all," Pablo said with an easy smile. "Your venture was just something in the wind—and we listen to the wind. . . . But may we not sit down and speak sensibly?"

Howard and Aaron looked at the chairs as if they'd never seen them before, but they sat down, and Pablo joined them.

"We can't hear people's thoughts or eavesdrop on every conversation that takes place in the world, like the God of your scriptures," Pablo went on, "but we're capable of paying very close attention to things that arouse our curiosity."

He nodded to Howard. "You busied yourself with certain inquiries, which led you to persons of ongoing interest to us. The tendency of these inquiries was clear enough: you were trying to make your way to us. This opened you to involvement in another enterprise, and so we folded you into our plans, killing two birds with one stone, so to speak."

"Howard," Aaron said, then evidently changed his mind and turned to Pablo. "What are you saying? Who are you?"

"I'm one of those you sent Mr. Scheim to find."

"Howard," Aaron said again, obviously agitated.

"What is it, Aaron?"

"Are you crazy?"

Pablo interrupted. "Mr. Fischer hasn't had your experience, Howard. Though he may have heard about it, he didn't live through it."

"And so?" Howard asked.

"And so he thinks I'm just one of your kind. In other words, he thinks you're being fooled. This is why he asks if you're crazy."

"Is that it, Aaron?"

Aaron looked from one to the other and said, "Yes, that's it."

Pablo smiled. "When Tim Kennesey was a small boy, five years old, I paid him a brief visit, but not in this guise—very far from it, in fact. Despite this, he recognized me when we met at Andrea's house in Taos a few weeks ago. Would you like to see what Tim saw when I visited him, Mr. Fischer?"

Aaron shrank into his chair and shook his head.

"Or I could tell Howard that, having seen you, I now understand the real motive behind this quest—perhaps unexamined even by you."

"No."

Pablo shrugged. "It's a matter of complete indifference to me what you believe. Having invited myself in, I'll be happy to invite myself out."

"No," Aaron said again.

"What then?"

"Tell me who you are."

"I've told you. I'm Pablo."

"Then *what* are you?"

"We're not *you*. That's really the best answer I can give you."

"But this doesn't tell me what you *are*."

Pablo shrugged. "Metaphysics doesn't interest us, Mr. Fischer, hard as that may be for one of your kind to believe. Like sharks and snapdragons, we're perfectly content merely to exist, without examining our nature or the cause of our being. We're just not curious about it."

"But how can you live this way if you're . . . How can you live this way?"

"What do you mean?"

"I mean, you've got money, cars, houses. . . . I don't know—maybe bank accounts, stocks."

"Certainly. All those things. Should we live in cloud-castles, ride in chariots?"

Aaron shot Howard a look of abject helplessness.

"Maybe I can cut to the heart of this," Howard said. "The Israelites were constantly attracted to the gods their neighbors worshiped—Baal, Ashtaroth, Moloch—I don't remember all their names. The Bible doesn't say these *weren't* gods. What the Bible says is that they were *false* gods. What Aaron asked me to find out is what happened to these false gods, and, now that he's got you here, what he wants to know is, to put it bluntly, are you one of them? Are you Baal?"

Pablo shook his head gently. "I'm not Baal. There was never one of us who was Baal. But this is the wrong place to begin the story—if you want to hear it."

Both men nodded.

"We've been your friends from the beginning—from the time before you were humans, before you were primates, before you were mammals, even before you were land animals. This is to say that, rather like dolphins at play in the ocean, we were creatures at play in the fire of life that has coursed through this planet for billions of years. We are certainly born of that fire in some way, the way that heat or light is, but we're not *of* that substance, as you are. This is simply to say that we're not biological entities. We have no function here, no destiny—at least none that we're aware of."

"Are you spirits?" Aaron asked abruptly.

"What is a spirit?"

"I don't know."

"Neither do I."

Oddly, Howard remembered having an almost identical exchange with Richard Holloway.

"When I say we were your friends from the beginning, I don't mean that this represented something new to us. We didn't say to ourselves, 'Aha! At last someone truly worthy of our attention and friendship!' The gradual emergence of human intelligence was no more a cause for special rejoicing among us than the gradual emergence of amphibians or reptiles. We regarded you with the same affection as beetles or bats. But at a certain point in your development, something entirely new happened: *you began to look back at us.*

"An awareness grew up among you that you were not alone here, that there were others *not of your kind* who shared the world with you. We don't keep track of millennia any more than you keep track of seconds, but the period I'm talking about was perhaps a hundred thousand years ago. The curious and venturesome in every generation sought us out to participate in our own lives, and we welcomed them. These you would call shamans, and from that time to the present they haven't gone away. We extended invitations to them, and we still do, though of course not all accept the invitations. Andrea extended an invitation to David Kennesey when he was a few years older than Tim is now. He never forgot it, but it took him some twenty years finally to accept it, to throw over his settled life and come looking for us. I extended an invitation to Tim when he was five."

Pablo smiled. "But you want to know about Baal and those other 'false gods.' With the emergence of your civilization, the shamanistic tradition died out among the people of your culture. Or you might say that it became formalized in state religions. Shamans were displaced by priests, and we were promoted to the status of deities—in the minds of the faithful. They put us on Mount Olympus and gave us names like Zeus, Apollo, and Hermes. They erected altars to us and called us Baal and Ashtaroth and Moloch. It meant nothing more to us than a new game that we were happy to play. We didn't know what a god is any more than we know what a spirit is."

"You didn't care?" Aaron asked. "You allowed them to worship you?"

Pablo frowned. "We're not your monitors, not your custodians, dedicated to leading you to some ultimate truth. We didn't invite these people to worship us, and it was no more flattering to us than the worship of rabbits would have been . . . I see that this shocks you. To say such a thing isn't *nice*. But we've never been *nice*, Mr. Fischer. We've never pretended to be holy or just or even moral, much less worthy of anyone's adoration."

He waited a moment to see if Aaron had anything more to say, then went on.

"I hardly need tell you what the Hebrews did. They wrapped us up into a unitary abstraction and banished us to the sky. But of course that was just something happening in one small corner of the Old World. Elsewhere in the Old World we continued quite happily to play the roles it pleased you to assign us."

"Are you saying that these people *saw* you?"

Pablo laughed. "What they wanted to see and expected to see, we gave them to see. We're nothing if not adaptable—and obliging. Did you imagine that these people were complete fools just because they lived long ago?"

Aaron gave Howard a guilty look, remembering that he'd once said much the same thing to him.

"Under Christianity, things changed again, of course. Under the Hebraic dispensation we were false gods, but under the Christian dispensation we were demons. To us, it matters not at all what people say we are. We remained what we'd always been, and those who sought us out found us. And elsewhere in the world—in Africa, Australia, the Americas—we continued to interact with people the same way we'd been doing from the beginning, for tens of thousands years."

"And now?" Aaron asked.

"And now," Pablo said with a grim smile, "for the first time in our long history, we have an enemy. This enemy is the vast machine the people of your culture have constructed to destroy the life of this planet. Every day hundreds of species we've known and loved from their birth are crushed out of existence by this machine. You built it unwittingly—we realize that—but now you seem unable or unwilling to disassemble it, even though in the end (not far off now, I'm afraid) it will crush you out of existence as well."

The two men were silent.

"Mr. Fischer, why not tell your friend the truth? It can't matter now."

"What truth?"

"Tell him what prompted you to embark on this quest."

"It wasn't that way. It wasn't 'this, so that.' I didn't see the connection at the time."

"Don't temporize. You see it now."

Aaron gave Howard a guilty glance, and his face twisted with pain. "It's cancer."

"Not treatable?"

"Oh, treatable, sure, Howard. There's always some quack who'll sell you a treatment. The point is, it's incurable. It's invaded the bone."

"I know what that means," Howard said. "I'm sorry."

"They say I have to be prepared to . . . It's the most agonizing end possible."

"I know. Why didn't you tell me?"

"I didn't want your pity."

"But what's it got to do with the wild goose chase you set me on?"

"I don't know, Howard. At the time I was thinking, what a great enterprise! And . . . something to be involved in, something other than just . . . waiting."

"I understand."

Howard gave Pablo a long look. "Why are you here, really?"

"Why do *you* think I'm here?"

"If I'd known in advance that you were coming, I might have thought it was to punish us."

Pablo shook his head. "We have nothing you would call morals,

Howard, and are capable of behavior that would seem to you completely ruthless, but we're not monsters, not vindictive fiends. I'm
here because I'm curious—and I have all the time in the world in
which to indulge my curiosity."

"Do you know a man named Joel Bailey?"

"I know of him."

"Many of the things he says sound like echoes of what you've
been saying here tonight."

Pablo made a face. "Bailey's of the same stripe as those who
turned us into gods. He names us Satan and calls us Lord. All the
same, not everything he says is nonsense. If those of our kind
indulged in metaphysical musings—which we don't—they might
sound very much like his, which is remarkable, considering that he
came to them entirely on his own."

The door to the study opened, and Ella stepped in, blinking.

"Someone . . . called," she stammered. "I thought I heard someone call."

"You're right," Pablo said. "I called. Your master is dead."

Wide-eyed, Howard looked to where Aaron was sitting and saw
that the man he knew was indeed gone, his chin resting on his chest,
his face—formerly shaped by intelligence and wry wit—now sagging, blank clay.

"He suffered a massive heart attack, and death was instanta-
neous," Pablo was telling the stunned Ella. "I suppose you must call
an ambulance, but tell them he's completely beyond recall."

When she was gone, Pablo turned to Howard and said, "I merely
did for him what his God would not."

CHAPTER 54

It's over, Howard told himself guiltily fifty times over the next two days—guiltily, because he thought he should be grieving over Aaron instead of thinking about himself and his own loss—of momentum and purpose. It was as if he'd become an addict for the action.

It's over. Howard Scheim's greatest case was over. He wondered if the depression he felt was anything like postpartum blues.

The worst of it was that it was a weekend. Pointless to go to the office. Nothing he could do with the money Andrea had given him for Tim. Nothing he could do with the letter she'd written, which he intended to give to his lawyer to hang on to.

He wanted badly to call Denise but knew she didn't want to talk about it any more than Tim did. Of course he thought of going to the club, but everyone there would be memorializing Aaron. So desperately did he want to talk to *someone* that he even considered calling Joel Bailey. He would have invited Délices to dinner at the Pump Room if he'd known how to reach her. And of course Hayes Peterson, legendary leg man, was always good for a few laughs over drinks and dinner, but Hayes would want to know what had come of Howard's meeting with Denise. He'd want the whole story—but would scoff if he heard it. And that would be intolerable.

Sunday afternoon he went to his office. There was nothing for him there—no message on his machine or note slipped under the door—nothing but one last, dreary chore. He had to rake through, annotate, and file all the trash he'd accumulated while running around the country for Aaron and Tim: receipts, ticket stubs, tape cassettes, maps, notes to himself, and . . . one item he'd have to return to Tim: the elegant, battered piece of stationery that had traveled hundreds of miles on the wind, carrying a message from David to his son.

Without giving himself a moment to think about it (because if he thought about it, he wouldn't do it), he picked up the phone and dialed the number on the letterhead, hoping someone would answer on the first ring.

No one did.

After the second ring, he told himself he'd give it one more and then hang up. After the sixth he started to relax, because obviously the house at the end of Morningstar Path was empty, perhaps even abandoned. He'd give it one more ring, exactly one, and then it would be over.

The phone at the other end was picked up: just picked up.

Howard's mouth was as dry as sandpaper.

"I'm still here, Howard," Andrea said at last.

He was sure he hadn't intended to speak at all, had only wanted . . . what? To hear a voice? Was that it?

He managed to squeeze out five words: "Don't know why I called."

She said, "Of course you do."

EPILOGUE

One voice spoke the

truth . . .

Tim caught the phone in the middle of the second ring and hoped it hadn't woken Ellen. It was eight o'clock, Sunday morning.

"Well, well, well. The wanderer returns." The voice on the phone was familiar: Frank Hawkins, a classmate. "And may one ask where the hell *you've* been? The truant officers are out in force, frothing at the mouth."

"It's a long story," Tim said, thinking he'd have to concoct one pretty soon.

"You better have something better than that, dude."

"I will."

"Huh. I didn't expect to find you there. I've been calling off and on for two weeks."

"Yeah, well . . ."

"Listen, some of the guys are gonna knock a ball around at the school yard. You want to come?"

"Uh . . . yeah, sure. When?"

"Any time. I'm leaving now."

"Okay. I'll be there in a while."

Tim's glove, molded around a ball, was wedged at the back of the closet in his room. He took it to the bed, sat down, worked his hand into it, tossed the ball into the pocket a couple of times: *plok, plok.* Then he walked over to the window. Drawing aside the curtain with his gloved hand, he stared out at the backyard, the houses, the featureless horizon under a gray sky.

You saw the fire of life, Tim.

He let the curtain fall back into place.

Tim, your father left to find something he wanted but wasn't strong enough to have. He became lost. Your mother followed him and she too became lost.

Lost. *Became* lost. Nothing to do with us. He wondered why he hadn't asked Pablo what *lost* meant. Probably because he had a pretty good idea what it meant—or was afraid to hear the truth.

Of course: *There is a lie to be told about everything.*

What would he have felt if Pablo had told the truth?

It was arranged that a dog would get your mother out of the way, Tim, but at the last minute we decided to give it another target.

No, the truth couldn't have been trusted to do the job: They would have lost him forever.

Wouldn't they?

What is it you most deeply want, Tim? Do you want to go back home and school with the other boys?

Why hadn't he said yes?

Suppose Pablo had said, "Do you want to go back home to your mother?"

He would have said yes to *that*.

Wouldn't he?

It seems you are to be someone of great importance in the scheme of things, Tim, Samson had said. *They mean to break humanity's hold on the world, and the instrument they mean to use is you.*

Tim shook his head. That had to be a lie. All of it. But they'd *hidden* it from him—as if it were the truth. As if it were a truth to be revealed only when he was ready to accept it.

He threw the ball into the pocket of his glove with all his might, stinging his palm. Then he went down to the kitchen and left a note for his mother on the refrigerator: "Going to play ball with some of the guys. Back in time for lunch."

One voice had spoken the truth, he was sure. He'd heard it as he left Andrea's house with Howard: Pablo's voice, firm, calm. True, he'd heard it only in his head, but that didn't matter. It was unmistakable; he hadn't imagined it. If he had, it would all be easier. So much easier.

At least one voice had spoken the truth.

Outside he reared back and threw the ball as far up into the air as he could and chased it across the yard. He caught it on the run and, feeling the sap rise in his body, just kept on running.

We'll wait for you, Tim. Not forever. But we'll wait.

Also by Daniel Quinn

Hardcover
$12.95 • 96 pages
1-58642-074-7

Tales of Adam

Adam, a hunter-gatherer standing at the threshold of human history, passes the gift of wisdom to his son Abel through seven profound but delightfully simple tales that illuminate the world in which humans *became* humans. This is the world seen through animist eyes: as friendly to human life as it was to the life of gazelles, lions, lizards, mosquitos, jellyfish, and seals — not a world in which humans lived like trespassers who must conquer and subdue an alien territory.

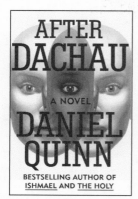

Paperback
$13.95 • 240 pages
1-58195-215-5

After Dachau

Imagine that the Allies surrendered. The Nazis continued to press their campaign to rid the world of "mongrel races" until the world was populated only by white faces. Two thousand years in the future people don't remember, or much care, about this distant past. The reality is that to be human is to be caucasian, and what came before is ancient history, until a crack appears in the cosmos, and a traumatic accident causes memories from a life lived centuries before to pour into the present.